# RIVER OF LIFE

# River of Life

# CAROL ASHBY

CERRILLO PRESS

RIVER OF LIFE
Copyright 2024 by Carol Ashby

All rights reserved. No portion of this book may be reproduced, stored in a re-trieval system, or transmitted in any form or by any means—electronic, mechan-ical, photocopy, recording, scanning, or other—except for brief quotations in critical reviews or articles, without the prior written permission of the publisher.

Publisher's Note: This novel is a work of fiction. Names, characters, places, and incidents are either products of the author's imagination or used fictitiously. All characters are fictional, and any similarity to people living or dead is purely coincidental.

Scripture quotations marked (ESV) are from the Holy Bible, English Standard Version, copyright © 2001, 2007, 2011, 2016 by Crossway Bibles, a division of Good News Publishers. Used by permission. All rights reserved.

Scripture quotations marked (CSB) have been taken from the Christian Standard Bible®, Copyright © 2017 by Holman Bible Publishers. Used by permission. Christian Standard Bible® and CSB® are federally registered trademarks of Hol-man Bible Publishers.

Cover and interior design by Roseanna White Designs
Cover images from Shutterstock.com

ISBN: 978-1-946139-39-9 (paperback)
       978-1-946139-40-5 (ebook)
       978-1-946139-41-2 (hardcover)

Cerrillo Press
Edgewood, NM

# Scripture

Jesus said, "Truly, I say to you, there is no one who has left house
or brothers or sisters or mother or father or children or lands,
for my sake and for the gospel,
who will not receive a hundredfold now in this time,
houses and brothers and sisters and mothers and children and lands,
with persecutions, and in the age to come eternal life.
Mark 10:29-30 (ESV)

But even if you should suffer for righteousness' sake,
you will be blessed. Have no fear of them, nor be troubled,
but in your hearts honor Christ the Lord as holy,
always being prepared to make a defense to anyone
who asks you for a reason for the hope that is in you;
yet do it with gentleness and respect.
1 Peter 3:14-15 (ESV)

And we know that for those who love God
all things work together for good,
for those who are called according to his purpose.
Romans 8:28 (ESV)

*To my children, Paul and Lydia,*
*for their love, support, and encouragement*
*and our granddaughter, Payton,*
*for the joy she brings to our lives.*
*And especially to my husband, Jim,*
*whose love and encouragement*
*brighten every day.*

*And most of all, to Jesus.*

*Soli Deo gloria.*

Sharing our faith. In a world where people can take offense at the slightest thing they don't already agree with, it can feel risky.

It can be risky. For many people around the world, telling someone they believe in Jesus and follow him as Lord can lead to rejection by family and friends, exclusion from work opportunities, physical persecution, and even death.

Even for those of us blessed to live in a country where freedom of religion is official policy and mostly respected by the government, it can cost us. Staying faithful to what God has revealed to us through His prophets and apostles can end friendships of many years. Not because we want it to, but we can't control what others think and do.

But eternity depends on what each person decides to believe about who Jesus is and what he did. If we truly care about someone, how can we not care about their decision about him? How will those we care about most know the truth about Jesus if we aren't willing to take the risk and share our faith?

We need a way that intrigues and attracts others. It should lead them to ask themselves the question Jesus once posed to his own disciples: "Who do *you* say that I am?" How can we share what we believe so others understand all that they need so they can say from their hearts, as Peter did, "You are the Christ, the Son of the living God?"

There is no single simple formula for it. Jesus's words to Andrew right after his baptism were "Come and see." At the beginning, our actions say more than our words. Caring relationships grow over time, and we listen more openly to words spoken by a proven friend than those of a stranger. In our daily actions, do others see the fruit of the Spirit? Love, joy, peace, patience, kindness, goodness, faithfulness, gentleness, self-control—their importance in our lives shows in the way we treat others, both our closest friend and the stranger we've barely met.

Forgiveness isn't listed as one of the fruits, but we need all of them to be able to forgive. It's hard to be patient or kind toward someone when harboring a grudge. Jesus told us we could forfeit the forgiveness he purchased for us if we refuse to forgive others. The commitment to forgive others isn't normal these days. It isn't even valued by many. But it is a powerful witness that our faith is real, that we try to obey God, even when what He tells us can be so hard to do in our own strength.

But actions are easy to misunderstand if we don't use words as well. There are many genuinely nice people who don't know Jesus. We need to ask the Holy Spirit to guide our words. He will show us the time to speak and the time to wait. He will give us wisdom in the words we chose.

It isn't only how long we've known someone that sets the time when we should share. In *River of Life*, Timon has tried for years to share his faith with his best friend Lusario. Neferu hasn't known Lusario and Caelus for even a week when God opens the door for her to share with them. God knows the who, when, and how for the good news of what Jesus did to reach anyone. We just need to be guided by Him in our actions and words so someone will listen to what we share and heed God's call to them.

May we always be eager and ready, as Peter wrote in 1 Peter 3:15, to explain to anyone who asks the reason for the hope that we have, and let's do it with gentleness and respect.

# Characters

People in Alexandria

Caelus Publilius Martinus (21): young Roman studying to be an architect/builder

Lusario (26): Caelus's Cyrenian manservant, studying with Caelus to be architect

Achilleus (23): wealthy student who is an Alexandrian citizen, a Christian

Timon (30): Lusario's Greek friend, manservant to Achilleus, a Christian

Dareios: pilot of Achilleus's riverboat, a Christian

Zenon: famous architect guiding Caelus's and Lusario's studies

M. Aemelius Regillus: relative of Caelus's father's friend

L. Aemelius Rectus: cousin of Regillus

G. Vibius Fundanus (21): good friend of Caelus and Lusario

T. Vibius Latro: Fundanus's uncle

Statia Tranquilla (early 40s): Fundanus's aunt

People near Arsinoe

Neferu (22): daughter of Kanefer, a Christian

Peduhor: Neferu's uncle

Sasobek: wab priest of Sobek's sanctuary,

Theodoros's people

Theodoros of Arsinoe: son of Stephanos, father of Jason

Corinna (22): wife of Theodoros, friend of Neferu and Phoebe

Jason (6): son of Corinna and Theodoros

Gaidaros: donkey wrangler for estate

Voskos: an old shepherd

Kosmos: Theodoros's estate steward

Menander: Jason's baby brother

Stephanos's people

Stephanos of Thmoinepsi: Jason's grandfather

Akhom: Stephanos's steward

Zenobia: Jason's aunt

Horion: Theodoros's older brother

Stephan (11): oldest son of Horion and Zenobia

Karpos (8): second son of Horion and Zenobia

Koshari: donkey wrangler at Stephanos's estate

Menmet (60+): Neferu's neighbor and healer for the estate

Setne: gardener who fills in for Koshari when he's gone

Nikaure: stableman at Stephanos's estate

PEOPLE FROM THE JOURNEY UP THE NILE

Temhotep, son of Siamun: pilot of the riverboat taking Lusario and Caelus upriver

Narmer: helmsman of the riverboat

Hermos: owner of inn in Naucratis

Inyotef, son of Hebny: donkey owner at the Great Pyramid near Babylon

PEOPLE IN CARTHAGO

Volero Publilius Martinus (40): Caelus's father, councilman of Carthago

Artoria Prisca (36): Volero's wife and Caelus's mother

Taurus (30): gladiator bodyguard for Volero

Graptus: steward of the Martinus town house

G. Acilius Glabrio (22): Roman tribune commanding the XIII Urban Cohort in Carthago, member of senatorial family, a secret Christian

Martina (20): Volero's niece, wife of Glabrio, Caelus's cousin, a secret Christian

G. Flavius Sartorus (26): former optio, now personal aide to Glabrio, a secret Christian

Platana (26): Martina's lady's maid and Sartorus's wife, a secret Christian

OTHERS

Heron: Hero of Alexandria, one of the most famous architects of his time

Joannes: Greek version of John

Lukas: Greek version of Luke

Markos: Greek version of Mark

Matthaios: Greek version of Matthew

EGYPTIAN GODS

Sobek: the crocodile-headed god with major sanctuary in Arsinoe

Horus: falcon-headed national god of Egypt, protector of the ruling pharaoh

Khnum (Greek Chnoúbis): ram-headed god who guarded the source of the Nile

Hapi: the baboon-headed god who controlled the Inundation (Flood), a god of underworld

Hathor: cow-headed national god, mother of Horus and symbolically the pharaohs.

# Locations

1 Alexandria: capital of Egypt since Alexander the Great

2 Arsinoe (Krokodilopolis): capital of Arsinoite Nome, home of major sanctuary of Sobek

3 Babylon: present-day Old Cairo

4 Hermopolis Mikra: town where canal from Lake Mareotis reaches Canopic Branch of the Nile

5 Heracleopolis Magna: nome capital on Tomis, the canal connecting Lake Moeris with the Nile

6 Memphis: Capital of Pharaonic Egypt until Ptolemies built Alexandria, near present-day Cairo

7 Naucratis: Greek town on Canopic branch of the Nile

8 Peme: town near the pyramids of the 12th dynasty pharaohs, near present day El Lisht

9 Terenuthis: town one day south of Naucratis; present-day Tarrana, Egypt

10 Thmoinepsi: Town across from where the canal from Heracelopolis connects to the Nile.

11 Troia: primary quarry for limestone in ancient Egypt, between Babylon and Memphis

Mare Nostrum: "our sea," what the Romans called the Mediterranean Sea

A  Faiyum: the area around Lake Moeris

B  Canopic Branch of the Nile

C  Lacus Mareotis: large lake on south side of Alexandria; connects to canals to Nile

D  Lacus Moeris: large lake in the Faiyum

E  Tomis: canal connecting the Nile with Lake Moeris north of Arsinoe in the Faiyum. Called Bahr Yussef (Canal of Joseph) today

F  Trajan's Canal: canal connecting the Nile to the Indian Ocean

G  Gulf of Suez: access to Indian Ocean

Not on Map

Carthago: Roman Carthage, near present-day Tunis, Tunisia

Cyrene: city in present-day Libya

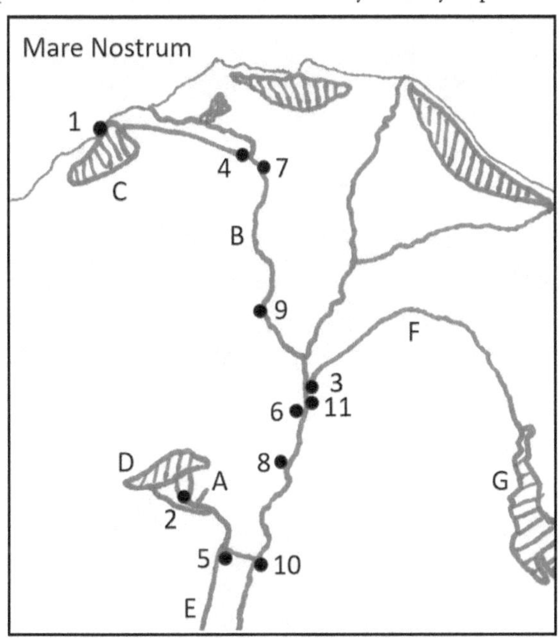

# Chapter 1

## Another Loss?

*Alexandria, Egypt, fall of AD 129, evening of Day 1*

Lusario hummed to himself as he strolled into the *peristyle* garden of the Latinus town house in the Greek quarter of Alexandria. With a bundle of clean clothes balanced on his shoulder, he bounded up the stairs and entered the large second-floor room he shared with Caelus Martinus, his current master who'd become a good friend.

When Lusario was used to settle his drunken Cyrenian master's gambling debt three years ago, he'd feared what awaited him. Being taken to Carthago, a city he'd never seen, by the lazy, lying son of a councilman who felt threatened by what Lusario knew about him—every scenario he'd imagined ended in pain and maybe death.

Who would have thought he'd end up back in Alexandria serving a young man who saw him as his intellectual equal and treated him like a friend? If Lusario believed in the Roman gods, he'd say Fortuna never smiled more broadly than when he changed owners in Carthago.

Caelus encouraged him to master everything about architecture and engineering that he was learning himself. He saw Lusario as essential to the success of his own ambitions. Caelus planned to become a sought-after designer and builder for the elite, and he wanted Lusario working at his side.

Lusario set the laundry on his bed in the far corner. "The fuller thought he could get the stain out of your toga. He put his best man working on it."

"He'd better finish quickly. I've been summoned back to Carthago." Dull resignation coated Caelus's usually cheerful voice.

Lusario walked around the screen that divided the sleeping and study areas. "What's happened?"

Caelus sat at his desk, elbows on the desktop, head in his hands. "I just received another letter from home, and I can't ignore this one. It's not Mother pestering me about when I'll be returning so she can show me off to prospective fathers-in-law. If it was, I just write back without giving her a date."

He waved a papyrus sheet at Lusario. "This is from Father. He's telling me to come home right away."

"For good?" Lusario's stomach knotted. He'd lost one future he'd wanted when he couldn't go back to Cyrene. Was he about to lose another, even better one?

"He says for a month or so. But I think he means longer. Listen to this." Caelus held the sheet in both hands, and a sigh drained his lungs before he read the first words. "'It has been over three years since your grandfather sent you to Alexandria, so I assume you have finished the studies needed to be an engineer.'"

His lips tightened. "Father has no idea how much an architect must know. Neither did I when I started, or I would have told them I'd need more time."

With another deep sigh, he stared at the paper. "If only Grandfather were still alive." He swept a hand toward the shelves holding their leather-bound sheets of lecture notes and the trunk of scrolls and codices. "He understood what I'm learning will let me do something important on my own. He wouldn't make me quit before I could start just because three years were up."

Lusario bit his lip and nodded. What could he say? The only time he'd heard Caelus talk with his grandfather was during the farewell at the pier. It was Caelus's father who'd bought him because he knew Alexandria. He'd ordered Lusario to keep Caelus from wandering into unsafe places with dangerous people.

What had been impossible with the gullible Cyrenian he'd served had been unnecessary with Caelus. His youthful master was discerning about the people he dealt with and always thought before he acted. Lusario had never seen a young man less likely to wander into danger.

He owed Volero Martinus for giving him a future. That purchase rescued him from the hatred of the liar and probably from death in the arena or mines. Then Master Volero sent him back to the city with the best library in the Roman world and the lecture halls where even a slave could listen. In Alexandria, Lusario felt like a man, not a slave.

But his wholehearted loyalty belonged to Caelus, who'd once risked dying to save him. Caelus valued his intelligence as much as his service. What Caelus studied, he studied as well. They'd learned so much, but had they mastered enough to make their dream of being architects come true? If they left now, would they even get a chance to find out?

Lusario's sigh was as deep as Caelus's.

Caelus cleared his throat and read on. "'There are some new developments in the family businesses since his death, and you need to become familiar with them. Sooner than you probably expect, you'll become *paterfamilias*. You will be needed in Carthago to take my place, as I did my father's. You'll have full responsibility for the *familia*. More importantly, you'll need to fulfill our family duty to serve Carthago as our ancestors have done for generations. You should know what's involved firsthand before that happens.'"

Caelus squeezed the back of his neck. "It's hard to argue against that. I'm the only surviving son."

He laid the papyrus on the desk and leaned on his forearms. "Here's the disturbing part. 'We'll discuss whether you'll be going back to Alexandria after your visit and for how long.'" He slumped in the chair and crossed his arms. "The rest is the formal closing. Nothing about what's going on with the rest of the family. He only wrote it to order me home."

Lusario fingered his lip. "That part about sooner than you expect…is he trying to tell you there's something wrong with him?"

One corner of Caelus's mouth lifted. "Father never had any problem telling me the truth as he saw it. He's Stoic to the bone. He'd tell me directly if he was sick or dying."

Caelus leaned one elbow on the desk and rubbed his forehead. "There's still so much for us to learn here. We also need to go up the Nile to see more of the ancient monuments and the newer temples the emperors have been building. But when a Roman father tells his son to do something, a Roman son does it. Until the day Father dies, he owns everything I treat as mine and can tell me what to do, as if I were a child."

Lusario massaged his temple. Caelus would do what his father said, and Lusario would do what Caelus decided. Neither of them was free to choose his own path.

"Should I find us passage on a ship to Carthago?"

"Father will be expecting me to come right away. But we don't want to miss that lecture on the first ever map of China by Marinus of Tyre. So, reserve us a private room in the cabin for some time after that. I can send a letter tomorrow telling Father which ship we'll be on and when it should arrive. That should satisfy him that I'm obeying his summons fast enough." Caelus rubbed his jaw. "But I'm going to pay ahead for this room for a few months. Father said it's a visit, so why wouldn't I assume we'll be returning?"

He slipped the letter into the desk drawer. "It won't feel like home with Grandfather gone. He believed I would succeed here, not Father. Mother can already brag that I studied in Alexandria. She'll be telling Father that I've been gone long enough and it's time that I marry the daughter of a rich city leader and stay in Carthago."

With eyes closed, he squeezed the back of his neck. Then he fixed a determined gaze on Lusario. "So, I need to convince Father that staying until I've learned all an architect must know is an investment, not an expense for my own pleasure."

He stood. "At least I'll try."

"Will he listen to reason?" Lusario offered an encouraging smile. "You win most of your debates."

Caelus was a skillful orator, but did logic even matter if a father's decision was already made?

"Maybe, but maybe not." Caelus shut the drawer, and his knuckles rapped the desktop three times. "I have no idea what will work…yet. But there must be a way to sway him toward my way of thinking. If I could convince him I'll be adding another money-making business to the family holdings…that would help."

The gong that summoned the household to meals sounded, and they headed downstairs. Caelus turned into the *triclinium* with the other elite lodgers, and Lusario headed to the tables off the kitchen where servants and slaves ate.

Lusario took his usual place, but while the others chatted as the bowls of stew were served, he remained silent. He'd already lost his family and the friends of his childhood in Cyrene. If Caelus couldn't convince his father to let them stay, he'd soon be losing these friends as well.

# Chapter 2

PASSING THE TEST

*Arsinoe (Krokodilopolis), capital of the Faiyum, Egypt, Day 2*

With a flourish, Neferu checked off the final entry on the papyrus sheet. Then she placed the last of the flasks into the crate and added straw to cushion it. As soon as she tied down the lid, the scented oils destined for the sanctuary of Sobek would be ready to go.

On each flask, her cousin had painted an image of the crocodile-headed god that was worshiped by so many in the Faiyum. Arsinoe drew worshippers from up and down the Nile to watch Sobek's priests taking deadly risks with the almost-tame crocodiles kept in a special pond near the temple. They fed the vicious beasts often enough that they seldom tried to eat the men who cared for them, but that wasn't the most foolish thing the priests did.

Giving their lives to the service of a god who was no more alive than the stone carvings in their temple instead of to the one true God who made the heavens, the earth, and every living thing—that was worse.

She'd believed in the gods of Egypt herself until she met Phoebe. With Phoebe as her guide, she learned about Jesus and embraced the truth. But her uncle sold scented oils, and his biggest customer was the nearest sanctuary of Sobek. So, neither Uncle Peduhor nor her two grown-up cousins valued truth enough to even listen to her. They would embrace the lie as long as it gave enough profit. But she hadn't given up on them yet.

The tinkle of a bell announced the opening of the shop's front door. Uncle was on the other side of the curtain that separated workroom from storefront, so he could deal with the new customer. She carried the sheet to the row of cubicles hanging on the wall. Her cousin had painted the crocodile god on the edge of the shelf that held the records of the sanctuary purchases. It held at least eight times as many sheets as any other.

"Sasobek, welcome." Her uncle's voice was as warm as she expected with their

5

best customer. "Your latest order is ready for delivery, but if you need something more, just ask."

Neferu crept to the doorway, staying to the side of the opening so her feet wouldn't be seen under the curtain. Sasobek was the *wab* priest whose job was to buy the oils for the lamps of both the sanctuary and the housing of the priests and temple workers. Every four months, it was his turn to serve in the temple for a month. He restocked their oil supply each time. An important job, or so he thought, and his condescension toward her uncle always irritated her.

But since his wife died a month ago, he'd become too friendly toward her when he saw her in the marketplace. With two small children and a baby at home, he was looking for a replacement. *Neferu* meant beauty, and with the way most men looked at her, no false pride was involved in admitting she fit her name.

If she still worshiped the gods of Egypt, her uncle would have encouraged him, even though he was closer to Uncle's age than her own. But Uncle knew the trouble that could cause. As a child of God, she'd never want a priest of Sobek. If Sasobek ever discovered what she was, he wouldn't want her.

"That order…" Arrogance dripped from the priest's voice. "There is a problem."

"A problem?" Unease coated Uncle's voice. "Was there something wrong with the oils in our last delivery?"

"The problem isn't the oil. It's the one preparing it. A faithful worshipper of Sobek came to ask whether we needed a different supplier of sacred oils, one who wouldn't disrupt the ma'at of the temple. He told me something about you that upset me greatly. I've come to see if it's true."

"I'm sure it can't be. I have always been honest in my dealings and faithful in my worship of the great gods Sobek and Horus. In fact, I honor all the gods of Egypt. I have tried to behave in accordance with ma'at all my life."

Sasobek's snort startled Neferu. "Where is your niece?"

"She might be in the workroom, but she had several errands to run."

Neferu crept toward the back door. Uncle knew she had no errands, and his words were a concealed command to get out of there before the wab priest could talk with her.

But the curtain rustled, and before she could escape—

"Stop right there, girl." Anger simmered behind the priest's words.

Neferu turned to face him and bowed slightly from the waist to show the respect he always expected from her. "How may I help you today, Sasobek?"

"What is your name?"

A strange question. He'd known her since Father died and she started helping Uncle with the oils.

"Neferu, daughter of Kanefer."

She raised her eyes long enough to see his sneer. "Why didn't you tell me you are Neferusobek? That's the name your father gave you at your naming ceremony."

Neferu fought the urge to swallow hard. What could she say that was both true and capable of more than one meaning to satisfy him? "The name no longer fits me."

"Why?" Crossed arms accompanied his scowl.

"I am no longer the Beauty of Sobek."

His eyes scanned her from head to foot and back, and they changed from angry to calculating. She shuddered when his gaze lingered on the places only a husband's eyes should.

He stepped close and drew his fingers along her jaw. She wanted to bat his hand away. It felt too much like a caress. But he bought more than three quarters of what her uncle sold each year, and Uncle could be in trouble if she did anything to anger this man.

"No longer a beauty? We've both seen how other men look at you. Don't pretend you don't know you're pleasing in any man's eyes."

Sasobek's thumb and fingers clamped onto her cheeks, and he tilted her head so he could stare into her eyes. She took a half step back before the wall stopped her.

"You are too old to still be unmarried. Why has no man taken you as his wife?"

What would be wise to say but still true? No man that she knew followed Jesus as she did. Any local man who might marry her would be furious when he found out he'd chosen a woman who would never worship his gods to preserve ma'at in his home.

Sasobek's arms shot out, and he rested his palms against the wall on each side of her. He stood too close, but trying to move would mean touching his shaved forearm.

His eyes were like a cat before the pounce that would kill a mouse. "Or are you rejecting Sobek's claim on you?"

No answer would be safe, so she said nothing.

"I have heard you've become one of the worshippers of Jesus." He spat out the name of her Lord. He leaned closer, and his warm breath made her turn her face away. The scented oils he wore almost gagged her. "Is it true?"

Her heart raced. Silence wasn't a safe choice either. *God, please protect me after I speak the truth.*

"Yes." In her mind, she spoke the word proudly, but it came out barely a whisper.

"Yet you dangle yourself before me and other men who faithfully worship the great god Sobek. Are you hoping to corrupt them, as you have been?" With one hand, he gripped her throat and squeezed. "Were you hoping to corrupt me?"

He stepped back, his nostrils flaring. "You will renounce that choice and worship Sobek again, as you were born to do. No worthy daughter of Egypt worships that foreign god."

She cleared her throat. "No." Her voice held steady. "I can't turn back from what I know is true."

"True? The ancient gods of Egypt are the true gods of this land. Not the god of the Jews. Not some Jew who claimed to be that god's son."

She raised her chin. "There's only one true God, and it's not Sobek."

The back of his hand hit her mouth, and she licked the blood from her split lip. She tensed, waiting for him to strike her again, but he merely brushed his hand across her chest to wipe off the blood.

He turned to her uncle, who stood, ashen faced, in the doorway. "This woman denies the truth. She is the enemy of ma'at. She disrupts the balance and harmony of all who live in this house, of everyone forced to work where she lives. Unless the ma'at is restored, I cannot allow any of your oils to be brought to the sanctuary of Sobek. The chaos she brings to everything around her could damage the ma'at of all those who come to worship."

He glanced over his shoulder at her and scrunched his nose. "The stench of her presence fills this room. She must reject this teaching and return to the worship of the gods of Egypt before I will allow anyone to use the oil she has touched."

Her uncle's eyes saucered, and Neferu's gut clenched. Without the sales to the temple, Uncle wouldn't have enough to feed his family. He couldn't pay his workers. He wouldn't even be able to sell his house and move somewhere else if this priest spread the word that its ma'at had been disturbed.

Neferu's gaze locked onto her uncle. His mouth opened, then closed. The eyes he turned on her pleaded with her to say no more, lest she pour more oil on the flames of Sasobek's anger. "I will convince her by tomorrow."

"You will convince her, or you will get rid of her. Don't send that cart to the temple until you can swear to me that you have done one or the other."

His mouth twisted into a triumphant sneer as he raked her again with his gaze. "You will yield and worship Sobek again, Neferusobek, to restore the ma'at." He drew his fingers up her throat to her chin, tipping her head back and forcing her gaze to meet his own. "I will examine you myself to be certain you have yielded both body and mind to serve the great Sobek as I think fitting."

He stepped back and clasped his hands at his waist. "And you will never question the power of the gods of Egypt again."

With stately elegance, he turned and strolled from the shop.

Uncle's blinks came too fast, and he breathed like a man who'd barely escaped a charging hippo. "I promised my brother I'd care for you like one of my own. I'm telling you now what I'd tell my own boys. You must renounce your god and do exactly what Sasobek said. If I lose the temple sales, this family will lose everything. We'll all starve."

She bit her lip. He was right. The hatred in Sasobek's eyes as he spoke Jesus's name—it was terrible to behold.

"I can't deny my Lord Jesus, but…" She drew a deep breath. Her next words would mark the end of any future she'd expected. "I won't stay here to bring ruin on you all. You can tell Sasobek I refused to obey so you ordered me to leave and not return until I worshiped Sobek once more. That should satisfy him that ma'at has been restored to your house."

First relief, then concern washed across Uncle's face. "But where will you go?"

"I'm not sure, but I shouldn't tell you even if I knew. Not while Sasobek is watching so closely. You have to tell him you made me leave to fend for myself, that restoring ma'at is most important to you. That I brought whatever happens next on myself and I'm dead to you."

*God, where can I go so that priest won't find me?*

She closed her eyes, and Corinna's smiling face filled her mind's eye. Her childhood friend had married the son of an elite Greek with a large farm nearby and an even larger estate on the main course of the Nile. Corinna lived not far from Arsinoe at the farm.

If she could convince Corinna to take her on as a servant, one who never went anywhere near the sanctuary of Sobek, that could solve her problem.

At least for now. What the future would hold, only God knew.

Uncle Peduhor went to the desk drawer and unlocked it. "At least let me give you some money in case you can't find somewhere to stay right away." He took out a handful of drachmas. When he held them out to her, she drew back.

"Put them on the counter, but don't watch me pick them up. Then if Sasobek asks, you can tell him you didn't give me anything before I left. If I take it without you seeing, that will be true."

While his back was turned, she took a small sack from the drawer and swept the coins into it. She added some smaller value coins to the sack before tightening the drawstring.

"I'll get a few things from my room, and then I'll slip out the back."

"You don't have to go, you know." He turned to face her, then squeezed the back of his neck. "You can simply renounce your god in front of Sasobek and display your return to the Egyptian gods with an offering at Sobek's temple."

"I know you want to protect me, Uncle, like you promised Father." She drew a deep breath. Uncle had never let her explain what she'd heard and seen, why she'd chosen to believe. How could she make him understand?

"Since my brother died, I've always done what I could for you, but only you can fix this. All you have to do is tell Sasobek you were led astray by that Greek friend of yours. Tell him what a foolish Greek woman thought was right is wrong for a good Egyptian to follow." A glimmer of hope lit his eyes. "You wouldn't have to mean it as long as you act like you do."

"I can't do that. God tells his people we can never worship anything except Him. But Sasobek won't be in charge of oil purchases forever. When he's gone, maybe I can return."

Uncle's shoulders drooped. Then he offered her a wavering smile. "I suppose your maybe is better than saying never."

"It won't be forever." She touched his hand where it rested on the counter. "My God will watch over me and guide me until then. And even after."

He rolled his eyes. "That god hasn't watched over you before. I have. But if you won't listen to my advice, I can't help you now." He withdrew his hand. "When you come to your senses and are ready to worship Sobek again, you can return." His eyes saddened. "I hope you live long enough."

The shop bell rang, and Uncle took a step toward the shop door, then turned. "When I finish helping whoever that is, you should be gone."

The curtain closed behind him, and she blinked hard to stop the tears. Phoebe had warned her what following Jesus might cost, but she'd never expected she'd pay the price. At least not this way.

*God, I'm afraid. What if Corinna can't take me in? Where will I go? What can I do?*

She closed her eyes. Remember that God can work anything for good for those who love Him, and give thanks in all things. Those had been Phoebe's last words before she boarded the boat and headed upriver with her husband to share about Jesus in another town.

No one knew what the next day or week or year might hold. But the sooner she left, the sooner she'd know how this dreadful day would end.

*God, please let me find something good in this.*

Clutching the sack of coins, she climbed the narrow steps to the living quarters above the workshop. Once inside her tiny bedchamber, her gaze swept the rope bed and the small trunk in the corner. She didn't have much, but she still couldn't take all of it. But what should she take?

*God, when I go to Corinna and ask to be her servant, please let her say yes. If she says no, I don't know where I could go.*

Her heart rate ramped up. If Corinna said no...

Several deep, slow breaths slowed her heartbeat. She had chosen to stay faithful. God would lead her where He wanted her to go. If Corinna's farm wasn't that place, He'd show her the way to get where He wanted her.

She took the light bedsheet and folded it to make a square. On it, she placed her spare tunics, her extra sandals, and the items every woman needed.

She reached under the straw mattress and pulled out the linen pouch that held her most precious possession—her copy of the gospel written by Markos. When Phoebe learned she was a scribe, she'd asked Neferu to make a spare copy in case something happened to the one she and her husband had brought from Alexandria. She'd made several and kept one for herself. Phoebe took the rest when they sailed upriver. Maybe someday she'd have the chance to make more copies for other believers…if she ever met any.

From the shelf above her bed, she took the small acacia-wood box. With three fingers, she caressed its river scene of a small boat centered between a stand of papyrus and an ibis. It wasn't a fine work of art. Father had carved it, and he was no artisan. He'd been a scribe who sat in the city market and wrote things for people who couldn't write themselves.

But a woodworker had paid him with carving tools, and he'd tried his hand at making a box for her tenth birthday. The papyrus plants were too short, and the ibis's head was too large, but nothing was more beautiful in her eyes when he gave it to her.

The box and her father's pens and styluses within it—they were all she had left of him. Would it be better to take it or leave it? Would Uncle set it aside and keep it safe until her return or try to sell it? He would rent out her room as soon as he could. Would he leave it for the renter to keep or toss out?

Father had taught her to read and write both Greek for legal documents and Demotic for ordinary Egyptians. Many wanted to send a message to family or friends that another scribe would read to them. He'd praised the beauty of her handwriting. Could she earn enough as a scribe to support herself?

She slipped off the brass filigree ring that had been Mother's and the cloisonne necklace that Father had given Mother when they wed. It was safer to look like a servant who had nothing of value. The cut in her lip that Sasobek had given her would help with that.

The jewelry went into the treasure box beside the pens, and she placed the sack of coins on top. After closing the lid, she shook it. Nothing jingled to reveal the coins within.

Around the box, she tied a sash to keep the lid closed. Her spare sandals lay on each side of it, putting the box at the center of the stack. Then she gathered the corners of the sheet and knotted them to make a bundle that she could balance on her head. It would look like she was taking laundry somewhere, not carrying all she owned in this world.

She left through the door to the outside stairway and threaded her way through the alleys to the edge of town. As she started down the road that led to Corinna's farm, she switched the arm that held her bundle in place. It would be an hour or two before she reached Corinna, and her neck and shoulders were already protesting against the load.

*God, thank You for the courage to pass this test of my faith. Please protect me now. Please guide me to a place where I can safely follow Jesus as my Lord.*

Leaving had saved Uncle and his family from losing everything to Sasobek's outrage. Serving in Corinna's house could provide a safe haven. But for how long?

# Chapter 3

## Preparing to Leave



*The Latinus town house, morning of Day 2*

The first light of dawn met Lusario's eyes when he opened his eyelids half-way. After hours of trying to sleep while tormented by visions of another lost future, he'd finally dozed off. But the scrape of chair legs on the other side of the curtain dividing their library from the sleeping area popped his eyes open.

A quick glance revealed Caelus wasn't in his bed, so Lusario rose as well. When he stepped around the curtain, he found Caelus, elbows on his desktop, hands clutching the top of his head.

"You're up early." Lusario moved to the edge of the desk to read the tablet Caelus was staring at.

"I couldn't sleep." Caelus scrunched his eyes and rubbed his forehead. "So, I figured I might as well work on the letter I want to send Father today. It might be the most important one I'll ever write."

He tapped the frame of the wax tablet with his stylus. "I have a first draft here, but I want you to tell me if I have the right "dutiful son" tone. After the lectures, you can book passage for us leaving in a week or so. Get a cabin room. After you add the name of the ship we'll be on and when the captain expects to reach Carthago, this can go to the courier service. It should reach Father in two weeks. He'll have someone waiting when our ship docks."

He glanced at the stack of chests in the corner of their room. "We'll take some of our recent building plans to show him our talent for design, maybe some of the scrolls that show how complex what we're learning is. But since I plan to pay the rent for this room for six more months, we don't have to take much. We'll crate the rest of the scrolls in case I can't convince Father, but they can stay here until we know. I want enough to make Father think I came home in good faith for a visit only, that I don't suspect he's planning to make me stay."

The cabinet of scrolls drew Lusario's gaze. "Perhaps Vitruvius's first scroll where he describes what we need to master?"

"Definitely that one." Caelus pushed the chair back from the desk. "With the reproductions of all the drawings, it is a thing of beauty. He'll be impressed that we saved so much by your friend Timon finding us a scribe to copy both words and drawings from the scrolls in the library."

Caelus rose. "Let's eat. Before the lectures, I want to see if Zenon knows of anyone who might be willing to give us a commission. It wouldn't have to be anything spectacular. Just something that we'd get paid for. Surely a referral from the most famous architect in Alexandria will count for something."

Lusario followed him down the stairs. When Caelus turned into the triclinium, he continued to the servants' dining area. If only he knew someone who might hire them. But except for Gaius Fundanus, Caelus's closest friend who considered him a friend as well, all of his own friends were slaves.

*Harbor area of Alexandria, afternoon of Day 2*

When the door of the courier service closed behind him, Lusario couldn't stop the frown. He'd added the name of the ship they'd be taking and the date it should arrive to Caelus's letter to his father. It would be on the first ship to Carthago in the morning. In a week, they would follow it. But would they ever board a ship to return to Alexandria?

For his visit to Eunostos Harbor where most of the commercial ships docked, he'd donned an old tunic that had been left behind when a rich student moved out. The young Roman had used his father's money for every indulgence, but he spent as little as he could on his manservant's needs. No wonder his valet had left it crumpled in the corner. Stained and mended, it was perfect for a man alone carrying something of value.

What he wore as Caelus's manservant looked too expensive in some parts of the city. The quality linen tunic with blue edging around neckline and armholes was better than what most free men had. When going away from the library district by himself, he often chose to dress as if he were poor. Looking like he had nothing meant no robber would give him a second glance. Certainly no one would suspect he carried enough for cabin passage for two to Carthago.

Before they sailed, he'd wear that tunic again for a final stroll through the poorer parts of the city to places that held special memories for him. Looking poor was as good as having a bodyguard for making robbers seek a different target.

At the end of the Heptastadion, he paused. The three-quarter-mile causeway divided the Eunostos from the Great Harbor that the warships of the Alexandrine

Fleet used. It connected the main city to Pharos Island. On the eastern end stood the lighthouse, over 350 feet tall with a square base, octagonal middle section, and cylindrical top. One of the great wonders of the world, people came from all over the empire to see it. Climbing it one more time to view the city he loved—he'd find time to do it, but not today. Caelus would want to do that as well, and something awe-inspiring is always better when shared with a friend who felt the same.

Sharing with a friend—nothing gave more satisfaction or could cause more pain. Lusario kicked a pebble aside and started walking.

Timon hadn't been at the lecture halls that morning. Or in the library. Had Achilleus taken him upriver to his grandfather's estate again? Would he return before they had to board the ship to Carthago?

Lusario's shoulders sagged. Timon was a rarity—a true friend. For more than four years, they had shared almost every interest except one. Timon insisted that Jesus of Nazareth was more than a man executed by Rome during the reign of Tiberius. The Senate in Rome had declared almost every emperor divine after their death, but Timon claimed Jesus was the son of the Jewish god before he was even born.

He'd reached the brassworks by the Great Harbor that belonged to Timon's Christian friends. It was only a few hundred steps from the church founded by Markos, a man they claimed had known Jesus in Judaea and wrote what Timon called a gospel about what Jesus said and did. Timon was often there helping put together baskets of food for widows and orphans.

But even if he wasn't there today, Lusario could leave word that he'd be sailing to Carthago in a week. If his friend was in Alexandria, they'd pass on the message before the sun rose tomorrow.

Lusario held the door open as a gray-haired woman with basket full of bread passed through.

As soon as he entered, the man at the counter set aside the cloth with which he was polishing a brass urn. He offered a merchant's smile. "May I help you?"

"Timon wasn't at the library or the lecture halls today. Has he gone upriver or something?"

The polite smile turned into a friendly one. "Are you Timon's architect friend?"

"I am. I need to talk to him." Lusario rubbed the back of his neck. "I was hoping he was here."

The counterman's smile broadened, then he stepped to the curtain behind him and pushed it aside. "Timon. Your scholar friend is here."

Timon emerged from the back room, brushing flour off his hands. "Lusario? Zenon's lecture didn't send you to the library today?" His smile dimmed. "You look worried. Is something wrong?"

"I have to go back to Carthago in a few days."

Timon came around the counter and rested his hand on Lusario's shoulder. "What happened?"

"Caelus got a letter from his father telling him to come home. So, I just reserved passage to Carthago in a week."

The tinkle of three small bells announced the arrival of a customer. The counterman tipped his head toward the curtain, and Timon nodded.

"We can sit and talk back there."

Lusario followed Timon through the curtain and past shelves of brass lamps and boat fittings to a small table with three chairs in the back.

After pulling out a chair for Lusario, Timon settled into the one opposite him. "Tell me everything."

"Caelus's grandfather was the one who supported him coming here. His father was never happy about it. He told them it would take three years to become an architect, but he didn't know how much we'd have to learn. His grandfather agreed to three years, and it's past that now."

"So, he wants Caelus to stop before you finish?"

"Maybe. It doesn't say that in so many words, but the tone of it…" He sucked air through his teeth. "If Caelus's grandfather was still alive, I wouldn't be too worried. But it's Master Volero who'll decide if we get to return. Caelus is paying six months' rent to hold our room and not taking everything, but he doesn't know whether he'll be able to convince his father we need to stay longer."

Lusario closed his eyes and hung his head. "I lost everything I'd planned on when Diokles didn't take me back to Cyrene, but being an architect with Caelus would have been even better. Now that's at risk."

Timon took a deep breath and quickly released it. "I'm so sorry to hear that. I'll be praying for you both."

A shrug and a sigh were Lusario's response. "I suppose that couldn't hurt."

Timon's chuckle raised Lusario's eyebrow. "There's nothing a man can do that could help more. God can work all things together for good for those who love Him."

"But I don't love him. I never made the decision to follow your Jesus." Lusario leaned back in his chair before crossing his arms. "Becoming a Christian is too risky for a slave if your master isn't one, too."

Timon leaned forward to rest crossed arms on the tabletop. "Some risks are worth taking, and that's one of them."

"That's a matter of opinion." A wry smile accompanied Lusario's shrug.

"I was about to go home." Timon stood. "Walk with me?"

With a nod, Lusario rose and followed Timon through the curtain to the sales room. The counterman raised a hand in farewell before handing a goose-shaped brass lamp to the Greek woman who had two others set aside already.

After the door closed behind them, they walked south to Canopic Street and turned east. Silence hung between them until they reached the library.

"Maybe you'll get to come back." Timon rested his hand on Lusario's upper arm. "But if you want me to get what's left behind in your lodgings to you in Carthago, I can do that. I'm sure Achilleus would pay for the shipping if Caelus will arrange to repay him."

Lusario's head drew back. "Last time I went to Carthago, you were optimistic about my future. You said your god told you to be. So, you think he won't help me this time since I'm still not his follower and not likely to become one?" He hadn't meant to snap at Timon, but his words came out harsh.

Timon stopped and raised both hands. "I can't say until I pray and ask Him about it. He's not a puppet who does what I want just because I want it. Jesus said God gives rain to the just and the unjust. I know He works all things for good for those of us who love Him, but sometimes He does it for someone who doesn't follow Him yet." He nudged Lusario. "I still have high hopes for you."

Lusario's eye-roll was the answer his friend deserved. He wasn't in the mood to get into that discussion right now.

"I'd love to see you two start your business here in Alexandria, but only God knows what the future holds." Timon offered his usual smile. "Still, whatever that is, I'll always be praying for you."

Praying to his god. That was Timon's answer to everything. But his god would have to be real for that to do any good. Lusario had seen no convincing proof of that.

"Caelus thinks it would help convince his father to let us stay if he could show that he'll make money as an architect. Why don't you ask your god to make someone give us a commission to build them something? That's the kind of rain we need right now."

"I can do that." Timon nudged him again. "What will you do if He does?"

"I suppose we can talk about what's appropriate if it happens and if it convinces Master Volero to let us stay."

"That sounds fair." Timon bounced his eyebrows. "I'll be ready when you are."

They reached Lusario's town house. He raised his hand to knock, then paused. "We'll be at Marinus's lecture on China. Will I see you there?"

"You will. So, I'll only say goodnight, not goodbye. I'll save you a seat if I get there first."

"I'll do the same." After a light tap on Timon's upper arm, Lusario knocked his regular pattern on the town house door. As the door swung inward, he turned back toward his friend. "See you soon."

Timon raised a hand in farewell and strode down the street toward the Achilleus town house.

As Lusario strolled through the peristyle to join the other servants before dinner, a deep sigh escaped. He'd meet his friend for one more lecture, but would that be the last time?

# Chapter 4

## SAFE HAVEN



*Arsinoe Estate of Theodoros, son of Stephanos, evening of Day 2*

Sore neck, sore back, sore feet—walking for miles with the bundle on her head had Neferu at the brink of exhaustion. The sun was only three handbreadths above the horizon when she finally reached the farm where marriage had taken her once-close friend. But seven years was a long time apart. Would she be welcomed or told to leave?

*God, please help me find Corinna and let her welcome me. I'm afraid to spend the night outside somewhere with no one to protect me from whatever or whoever lurks in the darkness.*

A woman with a basket of dried fish on her head trudged toward her. Too many years had furrowed her cheeks and taken the light from her eyes.

Neferu lowered the bundle from her head and clutched it in her arms. "Where does Corinna, wife of Theodoros, live?"

The woman pointed toward a large house with a cluster of smaller buildings around it.

Neferu blew out a long, slow breath. Only a few hundred steps more, and she could rest.

"Thank you." She moved the bundle back onto her head, and it almost fell before she got it balanced.

"Be careful there, child."

Neferu stared at the weary eyes framed by deep wrinkles. Did she mean careful with the bundle that threatened to topple or careful at Corinna's house?

A handsome Greek on a spirited black horse trotted toward them on the road from the house. The old woman turned and hurried as best as she could toward the farm buildings on the other side of the road. Neferu darted off the road as he bore down on her without slowing. A disdainful glance was all he gave her as he nudged his horse into a faster trot that shifted into a canter as he swept past her.

When he was out of earshot, Neferu turned her gaze back toward the old woman in time to see her disappear behind a run-down building.

Be careful. Good advice no matter what awaited her. Even if this wasn't a safe haven for long, surely she'd be able to spend at least tonight while she figured out what to do next.

Flat stones fitted together like pieces of a puzzle fronted the double doors set in the mudbrick wall of Corinna's home. Someone had recently swept them, so Neferu set down her bundle and raised her hand. She drew it back to knock, then paused.

*God, please let Corinna be glad to see me. Let her want me to stay here and serve in her household.*

Her knuckles struck the door.

The grating sound of a bolt being drawn back tensed her shoulders. The door swung back to reveal an Egyptian youth. His gaze swept from her dusty sandals to her hair made unruly by carrying the bundle. He'd taken her measure and, in his mind, labeled her slave.

He tipped back his head to look down his nose. "Your business?"

"I'm here to see Corinna of Arsinoe."

Disdain curved his lips. "The Mistress isn't seeing anyone."

"She'll see me. I have an urgent message from an old friend she knew when she lived in Arsinoe." Neferu tipped her head back to match his move. "She will not be happy when she learns you turned away the messenger."

His eyebrow lifted, and he scanned her again. Then he shrugged and opened the door enough for her to pass. "You can wait in the courtyard while I let her know you're here."

She scooped up her bundle and entered what might be her new home. If only God would make it so.

He pointed at a spot on the floor, and she set the bundle there. "Stay here."

Beside a row of planters, a girl was cutting off spent flowers. The youth spoke to her in words too quiet for Neferu to hear, but she scurried up the stairs to the balcony and disappeared into what was probably the women's room.

Followed by the nervous girl, Corinna stepped out onto the balcony. As she leaned against the railing, her bulging belly declared her almost ready to deliver.

Corinna's mouth fell open, then closed. Her lips started to turn up, then froze. As quickly as the almost-smile appeared, it faded, replaced by straight lips. She straightened and assumed the superior calm expected of a wealthy mistress. With a flick of her fingers toward Neferu, she directed the girl's eyes toward the courtyard.

"Bring that one and what she's carrying up here." Then she turned and entered the room from which she'd come.

The girl descended and stood in front of Neferu. "You heard the mistress. Follow me."

Neferu's heart beat faster with each step up the stairs and along the balcony. What did Corinna's coldness mean?

As she stepped into the women's room, an imperious Corinna pointed toward the corner. "Put the bundle there." Her pointing finger swung back on Neferu. "You, come here."

"You." Her focused gaze snapped the girl to attention. "Return to your work and close the door on your way out."

After a deep bow, the girl left.

As soon as the door closed, Corinna stepped close. She pulled Neferu into as good a hug as was possible with a baby bulge that size.

"Nothing could be better than seeing you here after so many years. How long has it been?" Delight danced in her eyes.

"Not since the evening before your wedding…seven years ago."

"Seven years, but it seems like forever." Sadness washed across Corinna's face. "Never seeing you again was not my choice. Theodoros has always insisted I stay here, even when he's not home, instead of going back to Arsinoe to visit my family and friends without him."

"He ordered you to stay here alone?"

"He follows the Greek way of isolating women to protect them." Corinna shrugged. "Father has come a few times, but he never brought Mother or any news of my friends." She looked at the floor, then raised her eyes to Neferu. "Father told me a good wife does exactly what her husband wants in all matters. I was not to disobey and give Theodoros any excuse to divorce me. Father would not welcome me back into his house if I ever tried to leave on my own."

Neferu took her hand. Corinna had expected such happiness from marriage to the man she'd described as more handsome than Apollo and as muscled and strong as Ares. Was the handsome, arrogant Greek who almost rode over her Corinna's husband?

Corinna forced a smile. "So, why have you shown up here after all this time with a bundle on your head and looking like a slave?"

"I'd just finished packing the oils for the temple when the wab priest who buys from us showed up at the shop. Someone had told him I was a Christian, and he told Uncle he couldn't send any oils to the temple as long as I was rejecting Sobek as my god. He said I had to deny Jesus and return to worshiping Sobek or leave my uncle's house immediately to restore the ma'at so he could buy from Uncle."

Corinna's eyes widened. "So, you just left?"

"I had to. The temple buys more than three quarters of what we sell. Uncle and the rest of the family would starve without that temple money."

Corinna clutched the braided gold chain around her neck. "What are you going to do? How will you live?"

Neferu searched her old friend's face. Would Corinna grant her request?

*God, please open her heart to receive me, even though it's been so long.*

"I was hoping you could take me on as a servant for a while."

Corinna nibbled her lower lip. "If my husband was here, I'd have to ask him. But he won't be back for a few days. How long, he didn't say." She drew a breath, then sighed. "He never does."

She raised her chin. "But while he's gone, I can make my own decisions about a few things." A spark of the independence Neferu remembered so well lit her friend's eyes. "My baby is due within a couple of weeks. Among the metropolites of Arsinoe, many get a nanny for their first child when a second one is born. My Jason is six now. He's ready to start learning to read and write."

She fingered the large ruby set in her gold filigree ring. "He's very smart, but his father won't let him go early to the tutor his friends use for their sons."

Neferu tried to mask her surprise. Why would a father not want his son well educated? Any smart boy from an important Greek family was expected to write well and be a skilled orator.

But that strange decision by Corinna's husband offered the perfect reason for Corinna to want her service.

"I could be both nanny and tutor for him. Father taught me everything Jason would need to learn before he's ten. If I can work for you for a while, I could teach him."

Corinna twisted the ring as her smile grew. "I'd love that." She rested her hands on her belly. "But I don't have money of my own to pay you what a tutor charges."

Neferu echoed Corinna's sigh, but relief, not regret, inspired it. This could be the perfect refuge while she waited for someone to replace Sasobek so she could return home.

*God, if this is where you want me, please show me a way.*

A slow smile curved her lips. Normally, she wouldn't risk what she was about to propose, but this was Corinna.

"I could become your bondslave, and you wouldn't need to pay me with money. There was a man who sold himself for five years to get the money to pay off a debt before the judge ordered him to be sold to pay it. Father drew up the contract, and I made the extra copy for the man selling himself. If he could somehow get enough money to repay his owner, he could buy himself back before the five years ended. His owner could also cancel the contract and free him at any time."

Neferu touched Corinna's hand. "I could draft something for me to belong to you for a limited time. You'll give me room and board and whatever else I'll need as a tutor in exchange for…four years of service. Then we could do a new contract if we want me to continue helping your children."

Corinna stroked her cheek. "Mother didn't have to ask Father's permission for everything she did, and Theo rode out today without telling me anything about where he was going or when he'd return. He didn't tell me not to get someone to help with Jason." Defiance lit her eyes as her shoulders squared. "So, I should be able to get what my son needs, even if he thinks Jason isn't worth anything."

Neferu's eyebrows rose before she thought to stop them. "Why would any father think that?"

Hurt, then anger flared in Corinna's eyes. If Neferu could take that "why" back, she would.

"My boy came early, so Theo wasn't here when Jason was born. He would have exposed him." Corinna's mouth twitched. "He's not what Theo wanted."

Neferu reached to massage her neck but lowered her hand before it got there. At least the Egyptians who followed the old gods never discarded a baby to let it die, like the Greeks and Romans did. They tried to raise every child, no matter how flawed. Not what Corinna's husband wanted? Should she ask what he thought was wrong with the baby?

Corinna pointed at the corner of the women's room. "Put your bundle over there for now. I'll have our steward put a trunk for your things in Jason's room. Let's have you meet Jason, and then you can draw up our contract if you still want to be his nanny and tutor."

Corinna led Neferu down the balcony stairs and out the kitchen door into the vegetable garden. A girl of about ten was on her knees, weeding the onions.

"Where is Jason?"

The girl looked up at Corinna before pointing toward some animal sheds. "He went that way, Mistress."

"Find him and send him to me."

"Yes, Mistress." With a quick tip of her head, she headed out in search of Corinna's boy.

Corinna led Neferu to a bench under an olive tree and lowered herself onto it with a grunt.

"He'll be as dirty as a farm hand when he comes. I've given up on reminding him he's the young master of his father's workers, so he has to maintain a certain decorum. Whenever he disappears, he's always somewhere with the herdsmen. One of the old shepherds is so good to him, like a grandfather would be. Voskos explains things and lets Jason try doing what he's just shown him."

"My uncle was like that when I was small." Neferu's throat tightened. After her mother died, Uncle Peduhor let her help him with the oils while Father was at his scribal booth in the marketplace. A vision of him smiling at her as he sniffed a new scent she'd created pricked her heart. When would she see him again? Would she have to stay away so long that she'd never be with him before he died?

In the distance, a small boy came out of the stable beside the girl who'd been sent to fetch him.

"There he is." The oppressive heat of the day still lingered, and Corinna wiped her forehead. "He loves the donkeys. Some come to him like pets. Gaidaros lets him help brush them when they've finished hauling things for the day. I can't tell who enjoys it more, Jason or the donkeys."

With a skip and a jump, the boy cleared the narrow trench that carried water to the garden from the farm's irrigation ditch.

"He's almost seven now, so it's not a mother's attention he needs. He needs a man to show him things. He gets that from our workers." She lowered her eyes. When she raised them, an unshed tear lurked in each. "His father doesn't do anything with him. He doesn't want Jason where his friends will see him."

Neferu watched the boy who looked like any other she'd seen from a distance.

"Theodoros wanted a son his friends would admire as being just like himself —handsome, strong, smart. Jason isn't…perfect like his father wanted." Corinna clenched her jaw. "One of his eyes looks milky, and it drifts to the side. If Theo had been home when Jason was born, he would have ordered him to be taken out for the dogs to eat." She drew a deep breath. "But Jason came three weeks before we expected, so his father hadn't returned from his trip to Alexandria."

A triumphant smile curved her lips. "I sent a messenger to Theo's father telling him he had a new grandson and asking what he'd like us to name him. By the time Theo returned, his father had written his delighted congratulations, and he chose Jason as my boy's name. Once his grandfather had named him, Theo couldn't throw him out like garbage."

Corinna's smile turned sad. "He never forgave me for forcing him to keep Jason." Fire lit her eyes. "But I'd do it again in a heartbeat. My son is my greatest treasure."

Neferu touched Corinna's hand. "I would have done the same."

When Jason reached their tree, he cast a quick glance at Neferu, then lowered his chin so she could only see the mop of black curls atop his head. But with a father who wanted no one to see him, how could a little boy be anything but shy?

"Jason, this is Neferu. Her father was a scribe, and she can read and write, too. If I decide she should live here, she'll teach you."

The small boy's head tilted back so he could look up at Neferu. "She will?"

"She will. She knows about everything a boy your age should learn. She'll teach you other things a Greek boy like you needs to know, too." Corinna pushed the errant curls back from his forehead. "Would you like that?"

His rapid nod accompanied a shy smile. "I want to learn everything."

"Will you work hard to master everything she shows you?" Corinna's proud mother's eyes said "I love you" to him without a single word.

"Very hard. I'll be the best at everything." The delight faded from his face, only to be replaced by too-old eyes. "Maybe if I'm better than all the others, Patéras will be proud of me."

Corinna pulled him into a hug. "I will be so proud when you work hard and do your very best."

She raised an eyebrow at Neferu.

With one quick nod, Neferu signaled her approval of their plan.

Corinna turned Jason toward the donkey sheds and patted his backside to start him down the hill. "You can help Gaidaros with one more donkey. Then come clean up for dinner."

Jason looked across his shoulder with an impish grin, then trotted downhill.

"So?" Corinna asked, but her smiled declared she already knew the answer.

"I would love to be Jason's nanny and tutor. I can draw up the contract right now."

# Chapter 5

## The New Bondservant

Neferu followed Corinna back through the kitchen to the inner courtyard. Her friend raised one finger as they passed Theodoros's office; then Corinna stepped in and opened a desk drawer. When she returned to the courtyard, she carried some sheets of papyrus, a bottle of ink, and some pens.

"In the women's room, there's a table where I eat when Theo is entertaining his men friends." She lowered her voice. "I don't want anyone coming into Theo's office and finding you writing the contract there. It could be bad if he knew you served as legal scribe for me."

Neferu pointed at Corinna, then herself, then back at her friend. "We two are all who need know, but if you ever tell him, please warn me as soon as possible."

The arrogant man who almost rode her down was not one she'd want angry with her while she lived in his house.

As Neferu drafted a contract like the one she had copied for Father, Corinna leaned against the window frame, gazing toward the stables.

"You coming—I'm sorry you had to leave your family, but I'm so glad you came to me. Jason will finally start learning what every Greek boy should at his age. It's up to me to make certain Jason is cared for." She rested her palms on her enormous belly. "If I give Theo another son, I'm not sure he will even give Jason enough inheritance to live on. So, I made a will that leaves everything I own to Jason. I got the scribe who wrote it to file a copy at the records office in Arsinoe."

Neferu stared at her friend. What kind of man was she married to if she trusted him so little?

Corinna came from the window to stand beside her. "So, I want you to write the contract so it's clear it's with me and that you're only meant to serve Jason, not Theo." She rubbed her forehead. "Not that I expect him to do anything to you, but I don't want Theo to think you belong to him instead of me. He has a Roman friend who tells him any woman he owns is meant for his pleasure whenever he wants it. He tells me he doesn't do that here, but I've heard the houseslaves talking…" Her voice faded away into a sigh.

"But as soon as I give him a perfect boy, he'll be happy with only me again." Her smile was sad. "He wants more sons than his brother has. They've always been rivals."

"Uncle Peduhor says boys are what a man needs for his business, but girls make a house a home. If you have daughters, I can teach them, too."

"There's only Jason." Sadness coated those words. "I almost had two other boys…" The deepest sigh escaped. Her hands rested on her belly once more, and her warmest smile reappeared. "But I've never felt better, and this little one has been so active. I expect he'll be fine."

Neferu nodded, but she kept her gaze locked on the Greek letters her pen was forming. To be recognized as a legal contract, it must be written in Greek or have a Greek certification that it was official on anything written in Demotic Egyptian.

She bit her lip. How had her friend endured losing two babies? Corinna had always wanted a large family. Seven years, yet none of Corinna's girlhood dreams had been fulfilled.

She cleared her throat. "So, since you don't have any money other than what Theodoros gives you, I'm making the contract for room and board, clothing, and women's sundries."

"Not having my own money—it's not as bad as it sounds. He believes I should be protected like a Greek noblewoman. He doesn't like me to go anywhere away from the house and the nearby grounds, so I seldom need any money. When I do get some, I put most of it away for Jason someday."

Neferu wrote the final sentence and drew two lines long enough for their signatures below it.

She handed the sheet to Corinna. "For four years, I will be your bondservant to serve as tutor and nanny for Jason. You will provide housing, food, and clothing while I serve, which is worth about a drachma a day. If I wish to leave, I can ask for you to release me from the remaining term, and you decide whether to continue or end the contract. Because you're giving me no upfront money, I don't have to pay you anything more than the services I already performed. If you want me to leave before the four years end, you may not sell me, but you and I can agree to cancel the rest of the contract."

Corinna scanned the papyrus and placed it on the table. "Where do I sign?"

She handed Corinna her pen. "Here, where it says owner."

After Corinna signed, Neferu took the pen to write beside "bondservant." First, she wrote her name in Egyptian and then again in Greek, as if the scribe had translated her name into Greek after she signed. If Theodoros looked closely, she didn't want him to realize she'd written the whole document.

"I'll make a second copy for each of us to sign, and then maybe your steward can witness them."

As Corinna watched her make the copy, she laid her hand on Neferu's shoulder. "Now that's done, let's go down and eat. I'll get Kosmos to sign as witness after dinner."

Neferu tapped where Corinna should sign the second sheet, then handed her friend the pen. "As nanny and tutor, won't I be eating with the servants?"

Corinna handed back the pen. "When Theo is here, yes. But when he's gone, you'll be eating with me. It will be only me and Jason, and it will be good to have a friend to talk with again."

As they strolled side-by-side toward the balcony stairs, Neferu glanced at her friend. Corinna felt her gaze and answered it with a beaming smile. It was almost as if the past seven years had never happened.

*Thank You, God, for leading me here. Corinna wants me, and Jason needs me. You truly can work all things together for good.*

*Night of Day 2*

A night bird called outside her window as Neferu lay on her back, staring at the ceiling. She'd been watching a small patch of moonlight move across it for what seemed like hours.

The bed was barely wider than her shoulders. She could span the whole chamber with stretched-out arms. But as a bondslave of Corinna, at least she had a room to herself and a chest under the bed for the few treasures she'd brought with her . The women who were the permanent property of Theodoros slept on bunks, four to a room barely larger than her own.

Seeing Corinna again, receiving so warm a welcome, and becoming Jason's tutor—God had brought something good out of the upheaval in her life.

But her heart was still bleeding. When Sasobek forced her to choose between Jesus and the gods of Egypt, he had taken the last of her family from her. She'd only been six when Mother died in childbirth, and her baby brother hadn't survived. Since Father died eight years ago, Uncle Peduhor had treated her like a daughter. Would she ever be with him and her cousins again?

A tear escaped the outer corner of her eye and trickled down. She caught it just before it reached her ear.

But if she hadn't left, the whole family would have suffered for her faith. Only by leaving could she buy them time to someday recognize the truth about what Jesus had done and accept God's love and forgiveness.

At least she wasn't homeless and alone. She shuddered at that thought. If Corinna hadn't been able to take her in, could she have found Phoebe? It had been five years since they shared tears and hugs before Phoebe climbed aboard the riverboat. It shoved off and headed upriver to another town where Phoebe and her husband would share the Good News.

Neferu's sigh echoed in the darkness.

Would she ever see them again? If only she knew where they were. Joining them in their mission to tell the good news to as many as possible—could anything be better? But any messages they might have sent never reached her. Had their letters been lost, or had they paid the ultimate price for serving their Lord?

*Thank You, God, that Corinna is as happy to have me here as I am to be with her. Please let this be my new home until I can return to my old one.*

How would Theodoros react when he discovered her there? Did he know that Corinna's best friend had become a Christian? That she even considered becoming one herself? He came from a well-to-do family, with an uncle who helped run his nome's capital city. Having a Christian wife could affect his standing in the Greek community. Had Corinna been foolish enough to tell him about Phoebe's faith and that her cousin's whole family in Alexandria believed?

Corinna's father had arranged their marriage before she decided about Jesus. Making Theodoros happy and giving him many children had been what she wanted most. But she hadn't done either.

Before they wed, Corinna's father warned her that he expected her to be a good Greek wife, subservient to her husband in all things as her mother had been to him. She couldn't come back to him if the marriage had problems. But would he relent if Corinna told him the truth about what Theodoros had done to her and his grandson?

Neferu rolled from her back to her side. The bed seemed a little bigger as long as she didn't bend her knees too much.

What should Corinna tell Theodoros about her when he returned from his trip? How would he react when he learned she was Jason's new tutor? Would he question whether an Egyptian woman even knew enough to tutor anyone?

If he ordered her to leave, would Corinna stand up to him and insist Neferu wasn't his to command? Would he use Corinna signing a contract by herself as the excuse to divorce her and toss her out? Toss them both out. And what would he do with Jason?

*God, I think you told me to come here. Surely, I'll be able to stay for a while, at least until you show me what else I should do. Please make me stop worrying about things I can't control. Let me be a blessing for Corinna and Jason.*

She drew a deep breath and let it out slowly. *Please protect us all.*

The warmth of God's presence surrounded her. Her heart stopped pounding, and her breathing slowed. The muscles she'd tensed unwittingly relaxed.

She served the one true God, and He would watch over her. She only had to trust Him, and somehow everything would work out as it should.

# Chapter 6

## LOOKING FOR CLIENTS

*Alexandria, Day 3*

Even if Lusario had passed out from the heat at the back of the lecture hall, he would have remained standing. Marinus's lecture about the first map of China and the people of that land had proven too popular for the room it had been assigned. Caelus, wearing his toga, had managed to get a seat in the middle of a row more than halfway back from the podium. But many who normally sat near the front were forced to the rear. Slaves like him were ordered off the seats to make room for them. Those who stayed had been packed tightly together like amphora in the hold of a ship, and the air was heavy with human scent.

But it had been worth the discomfort. He'd been able to hear every word, but he wasn't next to his friend, as they'd hoped. Timon stood on the far side of the hall near Achilleus. But at least they could discuss it later in the cool, fresh air outside.

Before the lecture, he and Caelus had looked for Zenon in the suite of rooms near the lecture halls where he kept an office. They'd searched the library for him, but no one had seen him in either place. Now he knew why. Zenon must have been among the first who came long before the talk was scheduled to start since he sat in the front row near the podium.

The moment the talk ended, the scholars at the front surged forward to talk with Marinus. Zenon didn't join them. Before Caelus could work his way out of the row where he was sitting, the old architect had disappeared out a side door.

Lusario waited outside the entrance for Caelus to emerge.

His master tapped his upper arm. "I'm glad we waited to board a ship until after that. Can you imagine how exhilarating it must have been for Marinus to take that journey? I'd like to see the royal architecture of China someday." He fingered his lip. "Or India. That would be closer. I'm sure there would be unique motifs that our clients would love."

"Undoubtedly." Lusario nodded his agreement, but was that something Master Volero would ever allow? Simply getting to finish their training in Alexandria would be enough to satisfy him.

"Over there." Caelus waved his hand toward Timon and Achilleus as they appeared in the doorway. "I'm going to the gymnasium and the baths now to see if anyone I know there can tell me about someone who might need a designer. You can spend that time with your friend, if you want."

"I'd like that." Lusario's smiled, but only to mask the pain. In five more days, they'd be on the ship. This might be his last time with Timon.

With a flick of his hand to send Lusario to his friend, Caelus strode away.

Lusario was halfway there when Timon spotted him. Quiet words exchanged with Achilleus ended with a nod, and Timon came toward him, smiling.

"I'm glad you were still in Alexandria for that lecture. It might be the best we've heard this year."

"It might be the last, too. We'd hoped to ask Zenon before Marinus spoke if he could help us find something, but he wasn't anywhere he usually is. I saw him up by the podium, but Caelus couldn't reach him before he left." Lusario tightened his lips. "Without someone like him recommending us, I don't see why anyone would hire us."

"Maybe because you would cost less?"

Lusario snorted. "People with enough money to hire an architect want proven value for what they spend. They'd be taking a chance most wouldn't take."

Timon rested a hand on Lusario's shoulder. "It's still a few days before you sail. Don't assume all is lost yet. I'm praying for you both."

"So, now you've asked him about this. I don't suppose he's answered."

"Not yet, but I told you He's not a puppet. I don't expect Him to tell me His plans ahead of time. I'm asking that you'll be able to finish what you started. Whether and how that happens—that's up to Him." He nudged Lusario. "But I will keep asking until that's clear. I'd like to have you around at least long enough for you to decide to follow Jesus, too."

One corner of Lusario's mouth lifted. "That choice is too risky. You wouldn't hide what you believe if it wasn't."

"The reward outweighs the risk. Life is always risky." Timon shrugged. "Every decision to go a new direction brings with it hazards, but eternity with Jesus versus a longer life here and then eternal darkness…" The slight smile vanished from Timon's lips.

"But if you're wrong about your Jesus, that won't happen."

Timon's gaze bored into him. "But even if I were wrong, which I'm not, I would have enjoyed this life with brothers and sisters in Christ and peace and joy in my heart. If you're wrong, you will have cheated yourself out of true happiness in this life and plunged yourself into outer darkness in the next. Seems like any man who's smart about placing his bets would choose as I have."

Lusario frowned. Timon was smart, but no smarter than he was. Ending what might be one of their last conversations with an argument where neither would yield—that wasn't what he wanted.

"I've never been a betting man, but if I were, I'd need to see proof before I'd bet as you have. Let's see if your god delivers a solution to my problem before I decide anything."

"Sounds fair." Timon's eyes lit like they did when he placed the winning token in tabula.

Achilleus turned from the men with whom he'd been speaking and raised his hand.

Timon tipped his head toward his master. "Time to go. I'll try to see you again before you sail."

"Good. I should see how Caelus is doing at the baths." Lusario tapped Timon's arm. "See you later."

Lusario turned and walked away, but he glanced back over his shoulder. If Caelus could only find someone to hire them, that next conversation wouldn't have to include goodbye forever to the finest friend he'd ever had.

But if Caelus failed…

At the gymnasium, Caelus sat on a stone bench in a shady recess and leaned his back against the wall. He'd found several of his fellow students wrestling, jumping, running, and playing ball in the open grassy courtyard, but not one of them knew anyone who was looking for a builder.

The number of Alexandrian men he knew of his father's age, men who would have both land and money for something he might design—those he could count on his fingers. Aemelius Regillus, the wealthy cousin of a colleague of his father, had befriended Caelus since the day he arrived. He might have known a potential client. But as luck would have it, he'd gone to Carthago for a visit.

But there were several bathhouses near the gymnasium, and he might find someone there. He'd start with the biggest and work down.

The third one he entered was built in the Greek style with many terracotta hip-baths along the wall of the circular room. Off to his right, with a youth pouring hot water over his head, sat Zenon.

With a smile and a curl of his hand, the older man called Caelus over. "I've never seen you here before. Young men like you seem to favor Roman-style bathing."

"I do, but I'm not here to bathe today." Caelus bit his lip. How can a man ask for help without sounding desperate? Especially when desperation truly was gnawing at him.

"Hmm. I've seen you tired before, but that's worry written on your face." He stood, and Caelus offered his hand to steady him as he stepped out of the tub. Zenon took the towel from the attendant and toweled his face, chest, and hair. Then he slipped into the offered robe. As he tied the cloth belt, his brow furrowed. "Come with me, and we'll talk about it."

He led Caelus from the *tholos*, through a short passageway, and into the changing room.

"Do we need a private place for our talk?"

Caelus had never noticed before how much Zenon's eyes were like his grandfathers.

"No. I've been asking others for help at the gymnasium. I haven't found anyone who can."

Zenon settled onto one of the stone benches and patted the place beside him. "Then sit and tell me."

"I got a letter from my father." Caelus drew a deep breath and blew it out. "He ordered me home for a visit, but while I'm there, he'll decide whether I come back and for how long." He rubbed his jaw. "It was Grandfather I convinced to let me study to become an architect. Father didn't think it was worth doing, and he wasn't happy that I went around him for permission. Of course, Grandfather was paterfamilias then, and he had to approve anything important like living in Alexandria."

He dropped his gaze to the floor. "But he died a year ago, so Father controls everything now. He has the right to order me home, and I must obey. I told them I could master all I needed in three years, but I didn't know what was required until your first lecture. Grandfather would have understood and given me more time, but Father…"

His shoulders drooped. "If I were to bet on this, I'd bet he won't let me finish what I started because he doesn't believe it truly will open another line of business for the family."

He fixed his gaze on Zenon's sympathetic eyes. "But if I have a commission to build something, anything, that shows I can make money doing this, I think I can convince him to let me and Lusario return to finish our training. I've had Lusario learning everything with me from the beginning because he's going to be my right-hand man. If I can get Father to free him at thirty, he'll become my partner. I know the two of us together can make a name for ourselves."

Zenon steepled his fingers and rubbed both sides of his nose. "It's a shame you're a Roman. It's good for a man to listen to his father, but to be totally under his control…" Zenon's lips tightened. "But, as you say, your father has the right to command you as much as he does Lusario."

He slapped his thighs. "You two are among the best students I've had. I'd hate to see you quit now. As you say, being paid for a design before you even finish would prove to any man of business that it would be wise to let you continue."

"That's what I think, but I need to find someone who'll hire me."

Zenon fingered his lower lip. "I don't know of anyone looking to build right now. I can ask around to see if I can find something. But with so many established architects in the city looking for projects, I wouldn't expect someone to be eager to hire you. Many architects who could go elsewhere and do much better stay here because they don't want to leave Alexandria."

"It wouldn't have to be anything big, and we wouldn't have to be paid much. We just need something to show Father that proves there's money to be made if we're are allowed to finish our studies."

Zenon rested his age-spotted hand on Caelus's upper arm. "I can't guarantee success, but I'll look for something for you. When do you leave?"

"Lusario bought passage for us on the *Zefyros* in six days."

"Drop off your address here and your father's address in Carthago at my office. If I find something, I'll let you know. If it is after you leave, I can send a letter to tell you." He shrugged. "Who knows? Even if your father has decided to keep you there, he might change his mind."

Caelus closed his eyes and tipped back his head. When he looked at Zenon again, the smile on his mentor's face triggered one of his own.

"Thank you, Zenon. This means a great deal to me. To both of us."

Zenon flicked his hand toward the door. "I have a bath to finish. Go tell your future partner I'll do what I can. He's probably more worried than you are."

As Caelus passed through the doorway, he looked back. Zenon's smile had been replaced by a slight frown. If Zenon said he would try to find something, he would. But that downturned mouth proclaimed his doubt that he'd succeed, despite his kind words of encouragement.

Caelus had exchanged all his Roman money for Alexandrian coins when he came through the harbor customs office three years ago. As the Ptolemies had required before Augustus made Egypt his personal province, no coinage from any other land was allowed in. The emperors had continued the practice, and no Egyptian coins left the province. He'd be trading his drachmas for denarii before they sailed for Carthago. After this visit with Father, would he ever hold Alexandrian drachmas again?

# Chapter 7

## Something to Show Father

*Alexandria, Day 4*

At a table near the lecture halls, Caelus stirred the steaming bowl of lentil stew, but even the tantalizing aroma of onions, cumin, and coriander didn't entice him to take a bite.

"How can you eat like there's nothing wrong?"

Lusario swallowed and reloaded his spoon. "For most of my life, there's always been something wrong that I couldn't fix. I think better with a full stomach. Even if the problem remains, at least my hunger is gone." He set the spoon back in the stew. "I'm as worried as you are about this. Maybe more. I want to be an architect with you, not a household slave."

"I'll grant that you have more to lose if Father keeps us from returning." He released a sigh.

"And maybe I have more faith in your ability to get Master Volero to see how much he'll gain by letting you finish with Zenon and then start the business." Lusario raised the full spoon to his lips.

One corner of Caelus's mouth lifted. "I wish I could be as confident. If only I could go there with proof that someone will pay us to do this."

A hand on Caelus's shoulder made his head turn. "I haven't seen you around this week."

Fundanus settled onto the bench next to him. "I've been out of the city visiting my father. Why the long faces?"

"I got a letter from Father three days ago telling me to come home for a visit. Except he didn't really mean visit. He wants to get me involved in running the family businesses and to prepare me to serve on the city council, like he does. He'll want me to stay once I'm there."

Fundanus sniffed the stew, then raised his hand to summon the young man serving the diners. "Bring me a bowl and some bread." Then he fixed concerned eyes on Caelus. "But surely if you show him some of the designs you've already drawn, he'll see you'll be a great architect after you finish here."

A soft snort was Caelus's reply. "Yes, but being good at something isn't the same as making money with it. Not in Father's eyes. I told him and Grandfather that it would take three years to become an engineer. But I had no idea how much was needed until Zenon's first lecture. It's past three years now, but we still need a few more months. Maybe even another year."

A bowl of stew appeared before Fundanus, and he gripped the spoon. "That doesn't seem unreasonable. Returning to Carthago in a year should be soon enough." A smile followed his first taste.

"But a big part of learning anything is doing it with someone to advise you who knows more than you."

Caelus stirred his stew, then took a small bite. Lusario was right to be eating it.

"I'd like to do a few builds here where I can show Zenon what I've designed and get his opinion on how I plan to build it."

"So, how are you going to convince your father?" Fundanus blew on the spoon before slipping it between his lips.

"Father has a good eye for a business opportunity. All it might take is someone hiring me now to design something, no matter how small. With that commission in hand, I can argue that Lusario and I are worth betting on to do even better in the future…if we're allowed to finish with Zenon. If I was making money with what I've learned so far, Father wouldn't be thinking I'd spent my time playing at something just because I enjoyed it. He'd think it was a real business venture, like I told Grandfather, and let me stay to develop it."

"How are you going to get that first commission?" Fundanus tore off a piece of bread and popped it into his mouth.

"I asked Zenon yesterday if he could help us. He didn't know of anyone, but he said he'd try to find someone. Unfortunately, all the people I know here are scholars, who don't hire professional builders, or students like us."

"I might have the solution to your problem." Fundanus filled his spoon again. "I have a cousin who works in the city records office. Maybe he's heard of someone who could use an architect."

Caelus leaned forward then slumped back. "It's worth asking, but even if he gives me a name, I'd need someone they know and respect to introduce me."

Lusario scraped the last spoonful from his bowl. "The people you spend evenings with—do any of them have family estates nearby?"

"I've never been invited to visit one, so I don't know." With his elbow on the table, Caelus rested his cheek on his fist.

"Father's older brother was stationed up the Nile for a while when he was in the legion." Fundanus dipped some bread in the stew. "He liked it so well that he bought land there. His town house is in Alexandria, but he has an estate near the Faiyum outside a nome capital. Maybe he knows someone."

Caelus straightened. "Can you arrange a meeting tomorrow? That would leave a couple of days to talk with whomever he suggests."

"I'm not sure. He goes back and forth between the estate and the town house. Father said something a week ago about him coming downriver. So, if he's in the city now, I can."

Caelus nudged Lusario. "Looks like Fortuna might be smiling on us for a change. With the drawings we've done and a commission for a building project, I'll have something to show Father that should convince even him that we should return."

Caelus raised a stew-filled spoon as if in a toast, first to Fundanus and then to Lusario. Father always said acquaintances often saw what you missed yourself. Friends helped you see what you hadn't. True friends walked beside you to make sure all turned out well. The solution to their problem might be the friend sitting next to him.

*Corinna's home outside Arsinoe, Day 5*

At the table in Jason's bedroom off the balcony, Neferu closed the wax tablet that Jason had used for practice and set it aside. "I couldn't ask for a better student. In only three days, you've learned all twenty-four letters, and you can write both forms of each. That's forty-eight letters. I've never seen anyone learn them all that fast."

Jason set the brass stylus beside the tablet. "I promised Mitéra I'd work hard to be the best at everything."

Neferu took a fresh tablet from the small stack under the table. "Well, you're the best I've ever seen at learning all the letters so quickly. Shall we go show your mother?"

He picked up the stylus, and Neferu led him along the balcony to the women's room.

When they entered, Corinna lay on the couch, eyes closed and hand resting on her swollen belly. At the sound of their footsteps, she opened her eyes. With some effort, she swung her feet off the couch and sat up.

She directed her warmest smile at Jason. "You look pleased about something."

His smile turned into a grin. "Neferu said I should show you what I can do."

"What would that be?"

Neferu handed him the tablet and pointed at the couch. "Sit by your mother and show her what you've learned."

As he wrote each letter, first the capital and then the lower case, he said its name. When he finished, he kept his head lowered over the tablet as he glanced sideways at his mother.

"Writing every letter so quickly? And so perfectly formed." Corinna beamed at him.

"There's more." Neferu pointed at the tablet. "Write your name."

He bent over the tablet, and with great care to make each letter perfect, he wrote the words. When he finished, he raised his head. "It says Jason, son of Theodoros."

Corinna stood and took the tablet from him. She walked to the window and held it up in the brighter light to inspect it. "It does, and it's written so well. I couldn't do it better myself." She closed the tablet and hugged it to her chest. "I'm so proud of you."

Jason squared his shoulders and beamed at his mother. "Neferu said she'd never seen anyone learn that fast."

Corinna summoned Jason with a curve of her fingers. When he was within reach, she drew him toward her for a quick hug. His squirming made her release him before he got a good one. "You've always been quick to learn anything. Any mother would be delighted to have so smart a son."

"Maybe Patéras will let me show him when he gets home." Uncertainty dimmed the boy's good eye.

"Maybe he will. We can show Kosmos this evening. He'll be very pleased that you learn so quickly." Corinna rested both her hands on Jason's shoulders and leaned over to reach his eye level. "Would you like to help Gaidaros with the donkeys before dinner?"

A grin lit Jason's face. "Yes, Mitéra."

She turned him toward the door and gave a gentle shove. "Don't get too dirty."

Without looking back, he trotted out the door.

"He has a different idea of what is too dirty than you or I do." She rolled her eyes. "But that's probably the way with all boys."

"My cousins needed reminding, too." Neferu's smile turned wry. "Not that they always listened."

Corinna rested her hands on her bulging stomach. "What will you teach him next?"

"He knows the letters and their sounds, so we can start working on reading. Something that a clever boy would enjoy. Is there a scroll of Aesop's Fables?"

"We can look." Corinna fingered her lip. "Actually, I'll ask Kosmos to look for us. There's a scroll cabinet in the *andron*, but Theo doesn't like any woman who's not a slave to go in the room where he entertains his men friends. He'd be angry if he learned I got into that cabinet. I—"

Corinna raised her eyebrows, then blew out a relieved breath. "He just kicked.

Sometimes he doesn't kick for a while." Her eyebrows dipped. "It's a great relief each time he does. It tells me he's still alive."

Neferu's head drew back before she could stop it. Still alive?

Corinna rested both hands on her stomach. "I know it might be a girl, but I'm going to keep saying he." Her gaze shifted to the door where Jason had disappeared. "Theo told me I better have a perfect boy this time. Since Jason, I've lost two babies. My second son came a month before he was expected. The midwife said he was already dead before the pains started. I was sick a lot while I carried my next boy. He never moved as much as Jason, but the midwife said some babies simply rested more. He came when he was supposed to, but he stopped moving a few days before he was born. He never opened his eyes or took a breath."

Corinna's jaw clamped. Her eyes looked too moist.

"Theo insisted we try again right away, and it was only a few months before I was with child again. He hasn't touched me since I told him I carried our fourth child."

She wiped at the corner of her eye. "But everything seems to be going so well. I've felt good the whole time." She placed her hand on her belly. "I feel him kicking so often. I'm sure this baby's fine."

Even though she started to smile, it quickly faded. Her shoulders drooped. "But if it's a healthy boy, Theo will treat him as his firstborn son, even though Jason is six already. I'm glad the Romans let women have wills, just like men do. Jason will get everything I own, even if Theo cuts his inheritance to almost nothing as soon as he has another son to be his heir."

"What if it's a girl?"

"I don't know what he'll do if I fail to give him a perfect son this time. His brother has two healthy boys, and they've always been so jealous of each other."

Neferu took her hands. "Would you like to pray with me for you and your baby?"

With her toe, Corinna traced the dull red line woven into the rug. "I haven't prayed for a long time. Not since my marriage. I didn't pray for any of my babies. I got pregnant so quickly with Jason that I just assumed everything would be fine."

She glanced at Neferu before tracing the dark brown line next to the red one. "After that, I didn't think God would listen to my prayers because I turned away from Him to marry Theo. Jason's eye and how Theo's been since he was born… it felt like God was punishing me for that choice." She pulled one hand free and flicked away an escaping tear. "The love of a man meant more to me than the love of God. Now I don't have either."

"That's not true. God has always loved you." Neferu squeezed the hand she still held. "Nothing you've done, nothing you could do would ever make Him stop loving you."

"I'd like to believe that." Corinna tried to smile but it was only a pale shadow of the ones of their girlhood. "But how can you be so sure?"

"Trust Him, and see what happens. He'll show you if you give Him a chance."

After staring into Neferu's eyes too long to be comfortable, Corinna reached for Neferu's free hand. As soon as she held it, she bowed her head.

Neferu cleared her throat. "Father, I thank You for leading me here to Corinna for a place to stay. Thank You for our years of friendship and our love for each other. Thank You for the blessing of Jason, for the smart, special boy that he is and for the chance to love him and see him grow into a fine man."

Corinna squeezed Neferu's hand, and Neferu returned the squeeze.

"Be with Corinna as she brings her new baby into the world. Let him or her be everything Corinna has been hoping for, a precious new life to nurture and love, as she has Jason. Let this little one be strong and healthy, and give Corinna fulness of joy as she holds her newborn baby and gives You thanks for the miracle of new life in her arms."

She tipped her head back, feeling God's warm presence in the room with them. "Please let Corinna know deep in her heart that You love her even more than she loves her own child, that You've never stopped loving her, that You always will. Open her eyes and heart to see and feel that love and return it with joy. Give us both peace in Your presence and courage through whatever we face. In the name of Lord Jesus, I offer this prayer."

As Neferu spoke the amen, Corinna whispered it as well.

Neferu began to release Corinna's hands, but her friend gripped them harder.

"Do you think He heard you, that He'll do what you asked?" Corinna bit her lip.

"I know He heard us, and I know He'll always do what's the very best for us, even if I can't understand what He's doing at the time." Neferu's quick squeeze relaxed Corinna's grip. "Remember how Phoebe told us God can work all things together for good for those who love Him? I've just seen Him deliver on that promise. Being forced to leave Uncle's house with almost nothing, not getting to say goodbye to the people I love, not even knowing if you'd still be here...that was horrible. But being with you again, getting to help Jason...it would never have happened without it."

Corinna's shoulders sagged. "But I turned away from Him. I can't say that I ever loved Him because I wanted this"—her hand swept the room—"more than what Phoebe told us about Him. So, why would He want to give me anything?"

"Remember how Phoebe's husband told us that Jesus said God the Father is kind even to the ungrateful and evil? You were only a girl obeying your earthly father when he pressured you to marry Theo. But God loves to give us another chance to do better when we're ready to try. I know because He's given me so many of them."

Corinna offered a weak smile, but uncertainty lingered in her eyes. "Perhaps. Let's go find Kosmos. I'd like him to get that scroll for you to see if it's what you want for Jason tomorrow."

Neferu followed her friend out of the women's room. As Corinna waddled down the balcony ahead of her, one thing was clear.

It wasn't just for her own safety or for Jason's schooling that God had brought her to this place.

Her smile grew as she started down the stairs. She'd dreamed of sharing the gospel with others and seeing them come to faith, like Phoebe had with her. The first person God had chosen for her to lead to Him was her childhood friend.

# Chapter 8

## A New Life



*Corinna's estate near Arsinoe, Day 6*

The sky had brightened from its predawn gray to a soft blue. Neferu still lay on her bed, eyes closed, sharing the newly born day with God. As always, she began with praising Him for all He'd created and thanking Jesus for paying for her sins. She thanked Him for Corinna and Jason and the sanctuary and purpose she'd found with them.

As she began lifting up other people to God, she had so many to pray for.

For some, she had no way to know how her prayers were being answered. Had Sasobek let Uncle Peduhor send the oils and collect the money that would feed the family? She'd overseen the household for Uncle. Who was taking care of everyone now? Would her banishment disrupt her oldest cousin's plan to take a wife soon?

For others, she would know when Corinna's husband returned. Would Theodoros be angry with Corinna for hiring her? Did he dislike Jason so much that he wouldn't let her teach him? Was Sasobek right that her beauty tempted men too much? Would Theo ignore her because she was Corinna's servant or try to treat her like one of his?

She rubbed her forehead and stared at the ceiling. With so many changes, she'd let prayer turn to pondering and pondering to worry.

*God, I know I need to lay all these problems at your feet. I shouldn't dwell on them until I start to worry myself. I can't do anything while You can do everything. Help me trust you to work all things for good. Please strengthen my faith so I always turn my cares over to you.*

A knock on the door made her jump. When someone pushed it open, she raised up on her elbow.

One of the housemaids stood in the doorway. "Mistress Corinna wants you. The baby is coming."

"I'll be right there." Neferu swung her feet off the bed and slipped them into her sandals. When she entered the courtyard, the midwife stood by the kitchen, speaking in low tones with the cook. Neferu bounded up the stairs to the balcony, then into Corinna's bedchamber. Corinna might want some words in private, and there would be no chance for that when her birth pangs grew closer.

When she entered the room, Corinna stood by the window, gazing toward the stables. She turned with a smile, then flicked her hand toward the door. "Leave us."

Her lady's maid bowed and slipped past Neferu, resentment at being replaced simmering in her eyes.

A curl of Corinna's fingers drew Neferu to her side.

"So, it begins." She scrunched her face as a pain came and went. "Please keep Jason away from the house when the birth gets closer. He'll be frightened by my screams. He's seen lambs and kids being born, and their mothers don't suffer. He'll worry when it hurts so much more for a woman."

"We'll work on a few words in the garden, and then I'll take him down to Gaidaros and the donkeys. The stable should be far enough away."

"Stay with him to make sure he doesn't sneak back here."

"I will. The next time he sees you, you'll be holding his little brother. He keeps telling me about all the things he'll teach him. He'll be a wonderful big brother."

Corinna opened her arms, and they exchanged hugs. "I'm so glad you're here. For me and for Jason."

"I'll get him up for breakfast now, and we'll go outside until the baby comes. Send word when I should bring him to you."

The heavy steps of the midwife approached down the balcony. Neferu squeezed Corinna's hand and left to gather her charge. The midwife was one of the best in the area, and she'd be praying for an easy delivery and a healthy child. It should be a glorious day.

Neferu leaned on the mudbrick wall that made part of the donkey corral. As Jason brushed one of the donkeys, Gaidaros came to stand beside her.

"They're almost like pets."

A chuckle rumbled in the donkey handler's chest. "Not that one. Pikraménos is a biter and kicker with some of the workers. It's how he got his name. Jason just has a way with animals. When he's older, he'll have no trouble with the master's stallion"—he lowered his voice—"if he lets the boy ride him."

Neferu responded with a whisper. "Why wouldn't he? Doesn't every elite young man ride?"

"They do. Most men start teaching their sons before this." Gaidaros whispered as well. Then he shrugged.

"Neferu!"

She turned to see a housemaid running toward them. The girl was panting when she reached the wall. "Mistress wants you to come now."

"I'll get Jason."

"No. She said come quickly and alone."

Neferu's heart rate rose as she looked at the girl's grim face. "Stay here with Jason."

She lifted her tunic to her knees and jogged up the hill.

*God, please! Don't let her lose another baby.*

She was breathing heavily when she entered the courtyard and went up the stairs two at a time. Corinna's scream tore into her as she trotted along the balcony and entered the room.

Drops of blood were falling into the puddle beneath the birthing chair. Should that be there before the baby came?

She knelt by her friend and took her hand.

Corinna shivered. "Something's horribly wrong." Her grip turned viselike. "Watch over Jason." Her voice tapered off to a near whisper. "He has no one else."

"I will." Neferu fought to hold back tears. "Like he was my own."

"Tell him I love him most of all." Corinna's lip quivered. "I don't want to leave him all alone."

"He won't be. I'll be here for him. I'll love him like you would."

Corinna released her hand and gripped the wooden arms again as another scream tore through the room.

Her dearest friend's hand trembled when she reached out again. "I see death coming…I'm so scared."

Neferu drew Corinna's hand to her cheek. "Remember what Phoebe told us? You can still choose Him. He's waiting for you with open arms the moment you do." With her free hand, she pushed a sweat-soaked strand of hair back from Corinna's forehead. "Death only opens the door."

Corinna's gaze locked onto Neferu. "Why didn't I listen then? What I thought I wanted…" Her voice trailed off. "Jason's the only good thing from it all."

"It's not too late." Neferu rested her forehead by Corinna's ear. It wasn't safe for the midwife to hear. "Tell Him you believe right now, and He'll claim you as His own."

Corinna drew a shuddering breath. Her eyelids closed, and she blew it out slowly. After several deep, slow breaths, her eyes opened.

She gave Neferu a peaceful smile. "I did, and He has."

Another cry rent the air as Corinna bore down again. Ragged breathing followed.

"One more time. I see the head." The midwife moved into position to catch the baby.

Corinna's scream turned into a victory cry as the baby slipped free into the midwife's waiting hands.

"It's a boy."

Neferu stared at the blood-stained infant. He wasn't moving. Where was the piercing wail newborn babies were supposed to make? The midwife slapped his bottom. Still nothing. She slapped again. Then came a sound that was more whimper than cry.

The midwife placed him on the small table beside the birthing chair and rubbed him with a rag to clean off the bloody fluid. She tied off the cord and cut it. When she lifted him and turned, Neferu's breath caught. He was too pale, too quiet.

Corinna stretched out her arms and wiggled her fingers. "Give him to me. Please, there's not much time."

When the midwife placed him in Corinna's arms, his eyes stayed closed.

His mother's lips brushed his forehead, and the tiny eyelids opened. "Look at him. His eyes are so beautiful. He's…perfect." She closed her eyes, tipped her head back, and whispered, "Thank You, God."

Eyes still closed, she rested her cheek on his damp hair and sighed.

The midwife's lips tightened, and she looked at Neferu. The slightest shake of her head said it all.

The afterbirth fell to the floor with a sploosh. On the floor beneath the chair, the puddle of blood grew wider. Neferu's hand flew to cover her mouth as the red fluid kept spreading.

Corinna released a shuddering sigh, and her body slumped.

The midwife caught the baby as his mother's lifeless arms released him. She blinked hard and sniffed; then she shrugged. "She's gone, and he's not going to make it either, just like the last two. But at least she'll never know."

As Neferu stared at Corinna's precious boy, his eyelids drifted shut, and his body went limp.

Everything blurred until Neferu swept the tears away. *Please, God. It can't end this way.*

She held out her arms. "Please, let me hold him." Cradling the tiny body, she settled into in the wicker chair and drew him closer to her breast. Eyes closed, silently she cried out to the only One who could change this. Phoebe had asked God to heal, and a dying girl's fever had broken. *Please, God, like You healed her, I beg You to heal him. Don't let Corinna's sacrifice of her own life for his be for nothing.*

When she opened her eyes, Jason stood in the doorway, staring at his mother. How long had he been there? Tears streamed down his cheeks, but no sound came from the lips squeezed so tight she could barely see them.

His anguished eyes turned from Corinna to her. He needed her arms around

him. He needed to know his mother had said she loved him most of all. He needed to know he wasn't all alone, that she would love him, too.

Then a soft gasp pulled her gaze from the heartbroken boy. A tiny hand
reached toward her. Shuttered eyes opened. The ashen complexion of Corinna's
little one warmed to a rosy glow.

His cry started soft and swelled until it echoed off the walls.

The midwife swung around and stared at the pair of them. Her eyebrows rose,
then dipped. "What did you do?"

Neferu shook her head. "I didn't do anything."

She stroked his cheek as his lusty cry filled the room. She didn't—God did
it all.

The midwife strode to her side, and Neferu handed over Corinna's new son.
God had healed him, and the midwife knew what to do now. It was Jason who
needed her.

He still stood in the doorway. She knelt before him and drew him into her
arms. Silent tears turned into sobs as he buried his face in her tunic.

She looked over her shoulder at the midwife. "Do you need me to help?"

The midwife still held Corinna's now-perfect son. "No. But tell your steward
your mistress died. He'll need to find a wetnurse right away."

Neferu led Jason onto the balcony, away from the scene of blood and death
that tore at her own heart.

Forlorn eyes looked up at her. "If I'd been perfect, maybe I would have been
enough. Father wouldn't have made her keep trying for a better boy. Maybe
*Mitéra* wouldn't have died."

Neferu dropped on one knee and pulled him close. "This isn't your fault. You
were always more than enough to her. She told me so many things about you that
made her proud. Your mother just told me she loved you most of all."

She eased him away from her but left her hands on his arms. "She wanted me
here to teach you what a smart boy like you needs as he grows into a fine man.
She just asked me to watch over you, and I promised I would. As if you were my
own son."

She pushed back the curl that always seemed to fall onto his face. "Your little
brother will be so blessed to have you to teach him things as he grows."

Beyond the pain, hope lit a spark in Jason's eyes.

"I can tell him about her." His gaze dropped to the floor, then returned to her
eyes. "Father won't."

"You can, and he'll be glad you did." She took his hand. "We need to find
Kosmos so he can get someone to feed your little brother."

With his free hand, Jason swept the tears from his cheek, then wiped it on
his tunic. She scooped him up and he wrapped his legs around her waist. Then

he buried his face in her neck, and she felt the wetness as his silent tears flowed again.

With Corinna gone, what lay ahead for him? What lay ahead for her? It had been safe to bind herself to her friend for a while, but who would own that contract with Corinna dead? She'd only written the standard conditions. Why hadn't she thought to add that Corinna's death would free her?

What would Theodoros do when he came home to find his new son born and his unwanted wife dead? Would he still let her care for Jason, like she'd promised her dearest friend? Would he insist he was her new master and force her to do something else, as if she were really a slave?

She spied the steward by the stable and headed toward him. With each step, Jason's weight dragged on her more. She'd have to put him down soon. But somehow she'd find a way to mother him, as Corinna asked, and she'd teach him all she knew so he could make his own way, no matter what his father did.

At least she'd try.

*God, I know You can work all things for good, but how can anything good come from this?*

As the sweet boy in her arms began sobbing again, she couldn't stop her own sobs from blending with his.

# Chapter 9

## No Longer Needed

*Late afternoon of Day 6*

In the estate office, Kosmos sat at his desk, pen in hand as he checked the accounts of the olive harvest. For a man like him, work was the best antidote to grief. But each time he heard the new baby cry, he thought of the special woman who died giving him life.

One of the gardeners appeared in the doorway.

Kosmos finished the last entry before looking at him. "Yes?"

"Master Theodoros just rode in. He's at the stable now."

A nod sent the gardener back to the vegetable plot.

He replaced the wax plug in the ink bottle and headed to the stable. The young master's trips were welcomed by everyone, but they all knew to act happy at his return. He'd learned years ago to mask his emotions when speaking with Theodoros. But how does a man who's grieving the death of a kind young woman he'd watched over for years hide that grief from the brute who hated her?

Theodoros had dismounted when Kosmos reached him. He clasped his hands at his waist and summoned a respectful smile. "Welcome home, Master. We didn't expect you for another week. I trust your trip went well."

"It did. I came back early so that wife of mine will have no chance to do what she did the first time."

Kosmos drew a deep breath. The shorter he could make this conversation, the better. "You have a new son, but Mistress Corinna died giving birth this morning. She is laid out in her room awaiting the wagon that will take her to be mummified."

Not even a flicker of regret showed in Theodoros's eyes. "So, that's the end of it." Theodoros's face remained impassive. "Is this one perfect?"

"He is. The midwife thought the baby was dying, but the new nanny Mistress Corinna acquired to tutor Jason knew how to do something that revived the baby."

"He almost died, yet you say there's nothing wrong at all?" Theodoros's eyebrows lowered.

"The midwife said he's as healthy as she's ever seen now."

"Where's my son?"

"Sleeping. I got a wetnurse to tend him while he needs milk. They're in the room next to Jason's."

"I want to see him to be sure."

"Of course." Kosmos swept his hand toward the house. "After you."

When they passed the gardener, he stood and bowed his head. "Welcome back, Master."

Theodoros merely glanced at him. Then his gaze locked on Neferu and Jason, sitting together on a bench with her arm around the boy.

"You." At Theodoros's call, both looked at him. "Come here."

Jason stopped six feet from his father with Neferu close behind him. His eyes were red and puffy, but he raised his chin. "Welcome home, Patéras."

His voice started strong but quavered at the end. He lowered his head.

Theodoros only glanced at the boy before he focused on Neferu.

"So, you're the one who knew more about reviving a baby than the midwife. My wife was a worthless fool, but it appears that she did one good thing in making you Jason's nanny. What's your name?"

"Neferu." She looked into his eyes as he rubbed his lip.

His gaze raked her as if appraising a prize horse. "Egyptian for beauty. Whoever named you chose a fitting description. You'll do well serving when my friends dine here."

One corner of Theodoros mouth lifted, and Kosmos's stomach clenched. He'd seen that look too many times when a pretty young woman stood before this master.

Neferu cleared her throat. "I indentured myself to Mistress Corinna only to tutor Jason."

He flicked her words away with his hand. "A bondservant is no different than a slave, and I'll decide what your duties are now." His nostrils flared when he glanced at Jason. "I have no interest in the boy, but part of your duties can be teaching him. But you will serve me whenever I want you to, like I expect of all my female slaves."

Neferu's jaw twitched as her eyes blazed. If she spoke what she was obviously thinking…

"Neferu." Kosmos's commanding tone made her head turn toward him. "Take Jason to help Gaidaros with the donkeys until dinner."

The flames in her eyes cooled. "Yes, Steward."

She wrapped her arm around Jason's shoulders and led him away.

Theodoros crossed his arms as he watched her mother the boy. "How did Corinna find that one?"

"They knew each other as children. Neferu is well qualified to tutor. She reads and writes Greek and Egyptian. She taught the boy the alphabet and how to write his name in only two days."

"So, she'll be more eager to serve the boy than to serve me as long as he's here." He covered his mouth with his hand and rubbed his cheek. Then he turned to Kosmos. "Send Jason to his grandfather tomorrow. He named him. He can raise him."

Kosmos longed to speak what he truly thought of that command. But he was only the steward, and Theodoros was his master. "I can send word to Master Stephanos tomorrow for someone to come get him."

"Father might not want the boy enough to do that, but once Jason's there, he'll keep him. He chose Corinna for me, and he wouldn't let me divorce her to get a better wife. Her death solved that problem. It's only fair he take in her son."

Theodoros rubbed his jaw. "I want that boy gone tomorrow. It's easy enough to get to the river estate, and any of the men can take him. I only let him stay here to keep Corinna trying to give me a better son. But now I have one, and she's dead. So, I no longer need him. Besides, my next wife will give me more sons, ones I can be proud of.

After years of serving an arrogant, short-tempered man, Kosmos could conceal his thoughts from anyone. But he had to clasp his hands behind his back and grip as hard as he could to hold back the blistering words he longed to heap upon Theodoros's head.

"Very well, Master. I'll escort him myself. Sending a mere servant could displease Master Stephanos. Even though he's never seen Jason before, he'll expect us to make certain his grandson arrives safely."

Theodoros snorted. "Father will be as disappointed to have that half-blind boy in the family as I have been. But you're probably right that you should take him."

"I'll attend to it tomorrow. But this evening there are some documents left by Mistress Corinna that you need to read."

"Documents?" Theodoros's eyebrows lowered.

"Yes, Master. She had prepared a will and filed the original in the city records. A copy is in the strongbox. She said you would need to read it right away if she died."

"Do you know what's in it?" Theodoros's frown deepened.

"She never spoke to me about that, and she sealed it with wax to keep it private."

"I'll look at that first, and then you can update me on the estate."

Kosmos answered with a nod and followed Theodoros into the house.

Corinna never spoke to him before she did it, but she'd had him read the will before she sealed it. Everything she owned, including Neferu, had been left to Jason. It was all he could do not to smile as he imagined how angry Theodoros would be. In death, she had outmaneuvered him, and no one deserved that more.

◆

As Neferu walked away from the loathsome man who had broken Corinna's heart and tried to crush Jason's spirit, she blew out a breath through pursed lips. Kosmos had stopped her just in time. Challenging a man who thought he owned you was foolhardy, even if you were a bondservant, not a slave.

Or a wife. He'd kept Corinna away from everyone she loved for years. Was that only the punishment for keeping Jason, or had he controlled her like a child from the start?

They'd reached the donkey stable, and Gaidaros sat mending harness. He looked up when she leaned on the corral wall.

Anger flared in his eyes when he looked at the dejected boy beside her, and he glared at the house of the man who made Jason feel worthless.

"Kosmos said Jason should help you until dinner."

He came to the wall and cupped Jason's chin. "I could use the help of the best donkey wrangler on the estate."

A trembling smile was Jason's response.

Gaidaros lifted him over the wall. "Time for you to start learning to mend harness. There's always plenty of that to do at harvest time."

Neferu moved past the stable to where she wasn't visible from the house and sat on a brick bench under an olive tree. Staying away from Theodoros as much as possible, especially if she was alone, seemed wise.

Gaidaros stood at the workbench and patted the benchtop beside him. When Jason joined him, he wrapped an arm around the boy's shoulders for a quick hug. As he began showing Jason what to do, her charge listened just as intently as he had to her lessons.

Corinna's love for her son had strengthened him against the cruel neglect of his father. How was she ever to do the same when Theodoros thought she was only his property?

Had she written her contract with Corinna so it limited her duties to serving Jason as nanny and tutor? Did that contract really make her a slave of Theodoros?

The animal hunger as he looked at her—she'd seen that same lust simmering in Sasobek's eyes when he trapped her against the wall. But the wab priest had no power to force her against her will. What if she actually belonged to Theodoros now? She shivered at the prospect. What was he planning when she served his male friends at their dinners? What would he expect tonight?

*God, what am I supposed to do? How can I protect both of us from that horrible man?*

Staying out of Theodoros's sight could keep both of them safer. Jason could eat with her and the other servants. His father wouldn't want Jason dining with him, anyway.

Tonight, she would spread a pallet in Jason's room instead of sleeping in her own chamber. With the way he'd been clinging to her since his mother's death, she would do that even if Theodoros wasn't a threat.

She squared her shoulders. Coming here had seemed like an answer to her prayers for her own safety. But Corinna had finally turned to Jesus as her savior, and Jason still had someone to help him realize he was more than enough. Someone who had lost everyone she loved and understood his broken heart.

Eyes closed, she tipped her head back. *Strengthen and guide me, Lord. Please help Jason get past the pain of losing his mother, and work this out for good for both of us.*

# Chapter 10

## Experience Required

*Alexandria, early morning of Day 6*

Breakfast was over, and Caelus sat at his desk, staring at the papyrus Fundanus had just given him.

Lusario stood behind his shoulder. "So, that's all Fundanus's cousin found for us? Two Greeks and one Roman?"

Caelus's tapped the third name with his finger. "We'll have our best chance of success with Lucius Aemelius Rectus."

"Why?" Even after serving Caelus for three years, the way a Roman mind worked could still surprise Lusario.

Caelus rubbed his lip. "Fundanus said Rectus's great-great-grandfather was Prefect of Egypt under Claudius. So, since his family is still here after almost ninety years, I'd expect them to have both land and money for building something."

"But the wealthier Greeks have ties to the land going back to Alexander." One corner of Lusario's mouth lifted. "So, why would he be a better choice than the Greeks?"

"Connections." Caelus turned to face him. "He's an Aemelius. Aemelius Regillus said to come to him if I ever had a problem I couldn't solve. He'd be trying to help us now if he hadn't gone to Carthago. Regillus is second cousin to Grandfather's friend Paternus. They served together on the council for years, and Paternus asked Regillus to find us lodgings before we came. Rectus might be Regillus's cousin, so he should at least talk with me."

Lusario rolled his eyes. "A cousin of a second cousin of a friend of your grandfather—is that a close enough connection to get him to see you?"

"It might be. I don't know what it's like for you Cyrenians, but we Romans take extended family ties seriously."

What it's like for Cyrenians—Lusario stared at Caelus. How should he know? His own father was born to a slave in the house of some Greek who later sold him to tutor the sons of Lusario's old master. His own mother had been a kitchen slave in that household, but she died without ever telling him who her people were.

But Caelus's words triggered a slight smile. Caelus often seemed to forget he was only a slave. Becoming architects together could make him a freedman, maybe even a Roman citizen if Master Volero waited until he was thirty to free him.

The smile faded. If Caelus didn't get to return from Carthago, that dream would vanish like smoke on the wind.

"Fundanus's cousin included the address of Rectus's town house." Caelus stood. "I think it best to go in toga and join him for the salutation. I'll ask to speak with him last so we can talk as long as he wants."

With Caelus's arms extended, Lusario wrapped the toga around him, adjusting the folds so everything hung as it should.

He stepped back to admire his handiwork. Good enough for an orator or an honored guest at an elite dinner. But what really mattered was what Caelus would take to show Rectus.

Caelus opened the scroll cabinet and withdrew two rolled-up drawings. "I think we're more likely to persuade him to hire us with something small-scale. The gazebo and the terraced waterfall for a peristyle garden are good possibilities."

Lusario placed them in the satchel. "Let's add some of the larger designs that prove we're able to do more than you'll show him. He might ask."

"Good idea." Caelus transferred three more rolls from cabinet to satchel. He tapped Lusario's arm. "I have a good feeling about this. Let's go."

Lusario followed Caelus along the balcony and down the stairs. Their first attempt to get a client might succeed, or it might fail. But a man could only win if he entered the race and then did his best to take the prize.

*The Rectus town house*

When Lusario knocked on the door of Rectus's town house, the door slave opened immediately. He bowed as Caelus walked in as if he owned the place, and Lusario followed. When they entered the atrium, Rectus's secretary glanced at them, saw Caelus's toga, and came over.

Lusario stepped forward. "Caelus Publilius Martinus to see Aemilius Rectus. Master Martinus is a friend of Titus Aemelius Regillus."

With a sweep of his hand, the secretary directed them to two empty chairs where others waited their turn for an audience. "Master Rectus will see you shortly."

Caelus lifted his chin, projecting authority like any elite Roman would. "Take me in last. Our conversation might take some time."

The secretary's eyebrows rose. "As you wish."

The *tablinum* door opened, and a middle-aged man in a toga came out. With a slight bow of his head, the secretary left them to escort the next client in.

One by one, five more paid their visit to Rectus, and then it was their turn.

A curl of the secretary's hand summoned them to join him as he opened the door. "Master Rectus, this is Caelus Publilius Martinus."

On a raised platform across from the doorway, Rectus sat on a wooden chair with the legs of a lion and a river scene carved across the back. On the wall behind him, ancestral portrait masks and a couple of busts fixed unseeing eyes on those who came for an audience. One might be the former prefect of Egypt, but Lusario couldn't tell.

"So, Caelus Publilius Martinus, you come as a friend of my cousin. How is he doing these days? I haven't seen him in a while."

"He and his family are visiting Carthago, but I saw him recently at a dinner at his home. I've dined with his family often since I came from there three years ago to study architecture with Zenon. He admired some of my designs the last time we were together. His wife took special interest in all of them. She has friends who have been making some changes to their town house, and she loved my design for a garden gazebo. She told Regillus that it would be wonderful to have one just like it in their garden. She was eager to tell her friends about it and kept insisting I should be talking with others who might want to build one, too."

As Lusario stood behind Caelus, ready to hand him the gazebo drawings, he dropped his gaze lest Rectus read his thoughts. Every word Caelus spoke was true, but there was more to everything he'd said. Regillus had asked Caelus to bring some of his designs the next time he came to dinner, but that was only because he liked Caelus, not because he wanted to hire an architect.

Lusario had laughed with Caelus at where that led with the wife and daughter. Now fifteen and ready for marriage, their daughter had dined with them. She hadn't even moved close enough to the couch where he'd spread the plans to glance at them. It was the importance of Caelus's father in Carthago and the size of their estates and other businesses, not the beauty of his drawings, that excited her mother's enthusiasm. Marrying her third daughter into a rich Roman family, not building a gazebo, was Regillus's wife's goal, and she'd be willing to do one to get the other.

Regillus ended the discussion by telling her it would take up too much space where he'd rather have fresh vegetables and herbs growing. But when she pressed the point, he had agreed that if they had an estate close enough to Alexandria to spend a lot of time there, it would be a pleasant addition.

That twitch of the corner of Rectus's mouth—was that impatience with a story that seemed irrelevant or suppressed laughter at Caelus's attempt to prepare an older, wiser man for a question that would get a quick no?

"My wife and Regillus's Cornelia are cousins." Rectus crossed his arms. "She hasn't mentioned that change to the garden at Cornelia's." One corner of his mouth lifted. "But, if Cornelia has a garden gazebo, she's going to want one, too. Are you building it while Regillus is in Carthago or waiting until they return? Cornelia's a woman with strong opinions, and she'll insist on sharing them if she's watching you build."

"They left before they made a decision." Caelus's smile turned wry. "She especially liked the gazebo design and another for a terraced waterfall. Regillus will tell me which she wants when they return."

Rectus pursed his lips to erase the start of a condescending smile. "It's not wise to let a wife see something that she might want before you look at it yourself." He tipped his chin toward Lusario. "Does your man have your drawings in that satchel?"

"He does." Caelus turned and winked at Lusario as he handed over the satchel.

Rectus waved his hand toward a side table. "Show me what you have."

Caelus unrolled the gazebo plan first. As he pointed out key features, Rectus rubbed his jaw. A one-sided smile formed as Caelus ended the presentation.

"Show me the waterfall."

When Caelus finished, the corners of Rectus's mouth turned down as he slowly nodded.

"Very nice. After you've completed the build for Regillus, I'd like to see it."

Caelus's jaw twitched. "That could be some time. He didn't say exactly when he'd be returning. So, I could build one for you while he's gone."

A soft snort was Rectus's reply. "I only hire people who've proven they can do what I need. Can you show me something you've built already?"

Caelus's jaw twitched. "I don't have a complete project to show you right now."

"Come see me again when you do. Regillus might be willing to be your first client, but experienced builders are all I hire myself."

"Even the finest architect had no experience before his first project." Caelus took his hand off the drawing, and it halfway rolled itself up.

Rectus stepped away from the table. "And his first project was unlikely to be as good as his latest. But if what you do for Regillus meets with my approval and my wife loves it, I might be willing to be your second client."

Caelus moved away from the table and handed Lusario the satchel. A tip of Caelus's head, and Lusario returned the plans to the bag and slung it from his shoulder.

"I understand, and I'll look forward to meeting again after I have something built to show you."

"You do that." Rectus waved his upturned hand toward the door. "Greet my cousin for me if you see him before I do when he returns. *Vale*, Martinus."

"I will. Vale, Rectus."

Caelus led Lusario through the atrium and out into the street before his social smile turned into a frown. "Zenon warned us, but I'd hoped for something different. Will everyone hire only experienced builders? If we never get that first job, we'll never be experienced."

"He's only the first one you asked. As you told him, even the finest architects had a first build. If they did it, I'm sure you can, too." Lusario shifted the satchel on his shoulder. What felt light with anticipation felt heavy after disappointment. "Maybe we should try one of the Greeks Fundanus's cousin listed now?"

Caelus's shoulders sagged. "Not yet. I knew how to approach a Roman I didn't know personally. I have no idea how to ask a Greek to hire me."

He raised his chin, and his back straightened. "But there must be a way, and maybe Zenon can give me some advice on that. Let's find him. There's no time to waste."

As Caelus headed back the way they'd come, Lusario matched his master's stride, but he couldn't match Caelus's determined expression.

If Zenon knew how, why hadn't he told Caelus before? Or had he simply not wanted to tell two of his most diligent students that they had wasted their time studying with him after all?

*The Great Library, afternoon of Day 6*

Lusario stared at the unopened scroll as he sat at a table in a corner of the library. He needed something, anything to provide distraction from the gnawing feeling deep in his gut that he would never see this place again after they sailed for Carthago.

He and Caelus had looked everywhere they could think of for Zenon, but he was nowhere to be found. Caelus finally gave up and left with a couple of friends to go to the gymnasium to work off the tension that comes with looming defeat.

With the deepest sigh, Lusario unrolled the scroll that was one of so many recommended by the old architect. Maybe there was no point in reading it, but he had kept going to lectures when his last young master planned to make him a menial slave forever or send him to the mines to be worked to death.

Dwelling on the next loss that was coming only caused pain. Study gave enough pleasure to let him forget about it for a while.

He startled when a hand rested on his shoulder. When he turned to find Timon, he managed a sad smile.

"How are things going?" Timon settled into the chair across from him.

"Not good. We haven't found anyone who will hire us yet. People want experienced builders so they can see something they already built, but you can't get experience without someone taking the risk of hiring you. Caelus thought we might get hired by a cousin of the Roman we stayed with when we first got here."

Timon put an elbow on the table and leaned his cheek on his closed fist. "Who are the cousins?"

"Aemilius Regillus rented the room at the town house before we got here, and he still has Caelus come eat with him every couple of months. Rectus is his cousin. He said he'd be willing to be our second client, but not our first. If Regillus was in town, he might be able to find someone to hire us or even do it himself. But he's in Carthago. He won't be back before we have to sail there, too."

Timon offered a hopeful smile. "Maybe Caelus can talk to him there and get a commission back here."

"Maybe, but Caelus is afraid his father won't be swayed by that. It could look like Regillus is only hiring him to help out a friend, not because he thinks Caelus is good enough to make a business out of it." Lusario's mouth turned down. "And he'd be right."

Across the room, Achilleus raised his hand. Timon waved back and stood. "I have to go. But I'll ask the fellowship to pray that you find something before you have to sail."

"You do that." Lusario barely kept a skeptical smile from escaping. Nothing would come of those prayers.

"I will." Timon tapped his upper arm with the back of his hand. "God can turn what looks destined to end badly into something good. Achilleus and some others joined me in praying last time, and look at what happened."

Lusario nodded slowly, and Timon hurried across the room to catch up with the Christian who was also his master.

He watched Timon open the door for Achilleus, then walk beside, not behind him, as they left. His friend and the other Christians would pray. But as long as he could explain everything he saw as a fortunate turn of natural events, he'd continue to doubt that prayer to any god would do anything.

# Chapter 11

## Time to Leave

*Theodoros's estate, early morning of Day 7*

After a night divided between imagining what Theodoros might do to her and Jason and asking God to protect them from all of it, Neferu had never been so exhausted. When three soft taps on the door were followed by it slowly opening, her heart raced like a hare being chased by a jackal. She sat up and pulled the top sheet of her pallet up to her chin.

A head peered around the door's edge. It was only Kosmos.

When he curled his fingers, summoning her into the hall, she crept out the door, leaving Jason, who had finally cried himself to sleep, alone in the room.

Kosmos pulled the door shut behind her. A large trunk sat on the balcony, and Kosmos carried the chest she'd kept under her bed

"When you weren't in your bedchamber, I figured I'd find you with Jason."

"I couldn't leave him to grieve alone. And after what Theodoros said…"

Kosmos's quick smile raised her eyebrows. "That won't be a problem. I gave Master Theodoros the copy of Corinna's will after you took Jason away. It clearly states that everything she owned now belongs to Jason. The indenture contract bound you only to Corinna, and he agreed that you belong to his son, not him."

She closed her eyes and blew out a slow breath. "After I forgot to include a statement that would free me upon her death, I was afraid he really would own my contract. I'm so thankful I can take care of Jason, like I promised Corinna, at least until he's ten. But how I'm going to protect him from the horrible things that man says"—she rested her hand on the closed door—"I have no idea."

"You won't have to worry about that for long." He set down her chest. "Master Theodoros has commanded that the two of you will leave for the main estate where Jason's grandfather lives as soon as possible. He said Corinna tricked his father into naming a baby that should have been put out for the dogs, so Master Stephanos can take responsibility for the boy."

He tapped the large trunk with his foot. "As soon as you get this packed, I'll be escorting you there."

Neferu's eyes widened. As soon as she packed the trunk? "But Jason will want to say goodbye to his mother at her funeral."

"I understand, and I wish the boy could. But his father won't permit it." Kosmos looked across the courtyard at the door to Theodoros's bedchamber off the other balcony. "And you don't want to subject Jason to what the master might say if he stays. Master Theodoros does not want Jason in his house. He will be marrying again as soon as he can arrange it, and he doesn't want the father of any girl he finds desirable to refuse him because he fathered a one-eyed boy. Most don't even know Theodoros has a six-year-old son."

Neferu's jaw dropped. "How can that be? Surely his friends remember when he was expecting his first child."

"I don't know what he told them. Maybe he lied about the boy surviving. From the beginning, I was told not to talk about him with anyone who didn't live on the estate. He will be telling them his wife died giving him Menander. He'll pretend to be sorry he lost her."

"Poor Menander, to have a father like that." Neferu bit her lip. It was true, but she shouldn't have said it aloud.

"But he'll treat Menander well. He says he's never seen a finer baby, and any young woman who sees him would be eager to mother him. I expect he'll command everyone here to never mention Jason to Menander or to the next unfortunate woman who marries him."

"Leaving before Theodoros can say unspeakably cruel things to Jason is wise." She looked at the closed door beside her. "Jason planned to tell his brother about Corinna. He'll be so disappointed to leave his little brother. Do you think Theodoros will let the boys be together someday?"

"Does the sun rise in the west? That's about as likely." Kosmos rested his hand on her arm. "I'm glad you came when you did. Jason deserves much better than he would get staying here. Maybe his grandfather will see what Corinna saw, what I see in him." His gaze rested on the door as he sighed. "Many of us will miss him, but it's for the best."

"He'll want to say goodbye to Gaidaros…and the donkeys."

"Voskos, too. I sent someone to bring him in from the flocks. Bring Jason to the servant's breakfast when you get packed. I'll have them there."

"While he's still sleeping, may I get a few things from Corinna's room for him?"

"What things?" Kosmos crossed his arms. "Master Theodoros told me to oversee anything you take from this house. He said every piece of jewelry he gave Corinna was only lent to her, so they will stay."

"But there are a few pieces of jewelry that I know she had before her marriage.

Please let Jason take those. A couple of faience necklaces, some bracelets, and some earrings, nothing of great value."

Kosmos swept his hand toward the room. "What she brought into the marriage should be Jason's."

She paused with her hand on the door. Corinna's body was behind it. Would she be under a shroud or lying there where Neferu couldn't help seeing her?

She'd been too little to remember much about when her mother died, but Father had lain for viewing before the mummifiers prepared him for burial. It wasn't how she wanted to remember her friend.

Kosmos rested his palm against the door. "Mistress Corinna has been taken away already." He pushed, and the door swung into the room. "Gather what you think Jason should have."

A cabinet carved with ibis and papyrus stood in one corner, and she withdrew a red linen sash from one of the drawers. From the jewelry box on the dressing table, she took the few pieces of jewelry Corinna had before her marriage and wrapped them in the cloth.

From the drawer of Corinna's desk, she removed a rectangular reed basket with a matching lid. Corinna had put an extra copy of her indenture contract there with a few other papers.

"Let me see if there's anything that Master Theodoros will need to keep." Kosmos removed the papers, one by one, as she stood beside him.

A copy of her friend's will lay atop a letter from Corinna's mother that she sent the first month that her daughter was married. It told her how to be a good wife and mother. Neferu's jaw clenched. Too bad Theodoros's father hadn't taught him how to be a good husband and father.

Her own unsigned note that she'd sent to Corinna just before the wedding lay at the bottom. It asked for God's blessings upon her without saying which god. Neferu had left out God's name so Corinna wouldn't have to explain anything to Theodoros if he saw it. Her friend knew which God Neferu served.

After she added the sash of jewelry to the letter box and replaced the lid, Kosmos picked it up.

With his free hand, Kosmos fingered his lip. "Master told me to dispose of her clothes. I'll sell the more expensive ones, but take some of the plainer tunics for yourself. I don't know what Master Stephanos will provide for you."

Asking for Corinna's jewelry had been easy, and Kosmos had given it readily. But how to bring up the next question—she drew a breath through her teeth before starting.

"Corinna told me that she left everything she owned to Jason, that she had been setting aside any money she got for him. Shouldn't we take it now and have his grandfather look after it until he's grown?"

"If she had any, the will didn't say anything about how much or where she put it."

Neferu's hand shot up to cover her mouth. Corinna said she had saved up to provide for her boy because his father wouldn't. Had Theodoros found some way to take even that from the son he despised?

"Is there no money for him at all?"

Kosmos's eyes saddened, then he shrugged. "Master Theodoros said Corinna left nothing with monetary value except your contract. All he has will belong to Menander and his future sons. He said to let the one who named him provide for Jason."

"But what if his grandfather is just like his father and cuts Jason off?"

"As I told Master Theodoros when he asked, if there is any money, she never gave it to me to put somewhere. I would have kept it in the strongbox in my office. But you're welcome to take the two wooden boxes of old sandals and belts that Corinna stored in Jason's room." The twitch of his mouth accompanied a wink.

"So, I should put those into the larger trunk with Jason's things?"

"You should. His mother ascribed great value to the strangest things sometimes."

"Then I'll look after those carefully for Jason to have when he's grown. His own future wife might want them."

A wry smile lifted one corner of Kosmos's mouth. "I'm sure any woman worthy of him will."

He started to turn from the desk, then paused. The wax tablet where Jason had shown his mother how he could write every letter and then signed his name stood open at the rear, as if it was a work of art to enjoy each time she sat there.

Kosmos picked it up, and a sad smile curved his mouth as he touched Jason's name. "I'll keep this." He closed it and set it in the cabinet with the fine linen tunics he would be selling.

His mouth straightened. "Take some plain ones, and let's go."

# Chapter 12

## FAREWELLS

With a few folded tunics in her arms, Neferu followed Kosmos back to the trunk. He placed the reed basket in it and took hold of one handle. She put in Corinna's tunics, closed the lid, and took the second one. He pushed open Jason's door, and they carried it through the doorway.

Jason still lay on the bed, curled up to make himself as small as possible. Neferu sat on the edge beside him.

"Jason." She placed her hand on his arm and patted gently. "Time to get up."

His eyes, still puffy after a night of broken sleep, opened slowly. They widened when he saw Kosmos.

"What's wrong?" He sat up so quickly that his pillow fell to the floor.

The steward ran his fingers through Jason's hair. "Nothing. You're old enough to visit your grandfather now, and this is a good time for you to do it. So, I'll be taking you and Neferu to Master Stephanos's estate. It takes a day and a half, so we'll leave this morning."

"But what about Menander? Mitéra would want me to look out for him."

"While you're with your grandfather, I'll look out for him for you." Kosmos pointed to the trunk. "Be sure to take anything special with you so you'll have it while you're there. Neferu needs to pack right away, so do what she asks to help her."

Jason's brow furrowed. "Will I be gone long?"

Kosmos's strained smile accompanied his shrug. "How long hasn't been decided yet. Your grandfather will make that decision. I'm sure he'll want to have time to get to know you well before you return. Get up and help Neferu with the packing. Then come down and eat with me."

Kosmos moved Neferu's chest into the room. When the door closed behind him, she opened the chest that held Jason's clothing. After she transferred everything to the trunk, it was still only half full.

Jason knelt beside the small stable with its dozen wooden animals. He swung open the gate of the sheep pen and made the ram and two ewes walk out. He stroked the yarn mane of the horse and scooped up the donkey to hold it against his chest. "Voskos made all these for me." He picked up the lamb. "I don't remember when I didn't have this one." His lip quivered as he looked up at Neferu. "Can I take them all?"

"There's plenty of room."

"For the stable, too? Gaidaros made it."

Neferu knelt beside him. The stable was made of tiny mudbricks set on a thin sheet of stone left over from some building's floor. She lifted one corner. It weighed more than everything else she'd put in the trunk combined and would cover a quarter of the trunk's bottom.

She opened her mouth to say no, but the hope in Jason's eyes stopped her. Somehow, she had to make room.

"We can try." She took everything out of the trunk and spread one of the tunics on the floor. After centering the stone base on the fabric, she lifted it and lowered it into the trunk.

"Bring me your pillow."

When he handed it to her, she ripped open the end to reach the fleece stuffing. As she placed each animal in the stable, she padded it with some of the fleece. When she finished, she tucked the tunic around it. It filled a quarter of the trunk, but if she couldn't get her tunics in, she'd leave them behind. In the days ahead, the gifts from the men who loved him would be far greater treasures than any gold in the two sandal boxes.

Jason wrapped his arms around her. "Thank you."

The next thing that went into the trunk were the two boxes holding Corinna's old sandals and treasure under their false bottoms. The trunk was filling up fast. She lifted one end. It was heavy, but not so heavy two men couldn't carry it.

After packing some of Jason's clothes around the boxes, she added some wax tablets and styluses, the unused sheets of papyrus from Corinna's desk and some pens, and the Aesop's Fables scroll in case Stephanos didn't have anything a young boy could read. Kosmos knew she had it, so no one should accuse her of stealing.

She filled what little space remained with another of Corinna's tunics. Jason would soon grow out of what he wore now. Surely Stephanos would provide what his grandson needed, but she might have to make do for a long time with what she brought.

She closed the trunk and slid the latching bars into place. "Let's go eat."

As she started down the balcony, two men came up the stairs to meet her. "Are the trunks ready?"

"They are. A big one and a small one in Jason's room. Are you loading them now?"

One nodded, and they moved past her to vanish into his room.

She led Jason down to the kitchen and outside to the table and benches where the servants ate. When she passed through the doorway, Voskos and Gaidaros stood beside Kosmos, and all looked grim. But the moment Jason appeared behind her, each forced a smile for the boy. The shepherd and donkey wrangler sat on the bench facing the stable and pastures, leaving a space between them. When Voskos patted it, Jason slipped in beside them.

Neferu filled three bowls with porridge and handed each one. Voskos wrapped an arm around Jason's shoulders, and all three ate in silence. What was there to say when three hearts were aching and the final farewell was only moments away?

She joined Kosmos sitting a short distance down the table from them. As she stirred her own bowl, the thought of eating anything made her gag. But who knew when the next meal would be? She needed her strength for Jason's sake.

Jason stirred his porridge, but he ate hardly any. Too often, he reached up to wipe away a tear before it escaped.

After too long a silence, he cleared his throat. "When I'm a grown man, I'll be back to see you. Patéras can't stop me then."

The men exchanged a look before Voskos spoke. "We'll be looking forward to that."

Neferu bit her lip. Gaidaros was young enough, but would Voskos ever see him again?

Kosmos finished eating and stood. "It's time."

The two men followed his lead, and Jason stayed between them as they moved away from the table.

He scanned the donkeys in the pasture, and his gaze settled on one. "I'll see you when I return, but I'll never see Pikraménos again." Jason wiped first his eye, then his nose.

Gaidaros's blinks came too fast. "You might. He's young, and donkeys live a long time. They remember people they like, too. I expect Pikraménos will be as glad to see you as I will."

Jason wrapped his arms first around Voskos, then Gaidaros. When he stepped back, his eyes brimmed with tears. The haunted look that he wore as he stared at Corinna reappeared.

"We have a long way to travel today. Let's go." Kosmos squeezed Jason's shoulder before walking away.

Jason's lip trembled, and he wiped the corner of his eye. Then he clamped his lips as tight as he could and raised his head. Pain and anger twisted his face before he turned away. As he started toward the wagon that would take them to the boat, his shoulders drooped, then started to shake.

On the other side of the garden, Theodoros sat on his stallion, watching them with arms crossed. Then he reined away and nudged the horse into a trot.

Anger like she'd never felt before surged through Neferu like the Nile in full flood. She gritted her teeth, then forced her jaw to relax. God said that vengeance was His, and He would repay. After all Theodoros had made Jason suffer, she hoped God repaid him soon.

*I know I should not be thinking that. You said to love our enemies, to pray for those who persecute us. I'll try to do it, like You want me to. I do thank You for delivering me, for delivering both of us from Theodoros.*

Perhaps Jason's grandfather would see past his milky, wandering eye to the bright boy who was skilled with animals and appreciated any kindness shown to him. But no matter what his grandfather did, it could hardly be worse than what would happen here.

On the road ahead, the trunks awaited them in a wagon drawn by two mules. A saddled mule stood beside it. Kosmos lifted Jason into the wagon, then helped her climb in. She sat on one edge of the bench with Jason between her and the driver. As soon as they were settled, Kosmos mounted and nudged his mule into a trot. The driver snapped the reins, and the wagon lurched as the mules began pulling.

Neferu kept her arm around Jason's shoulders, but he twisted more than once to look back to where Voskos and Gaidaros stood. Then the road curved, and the house blocked his view. He slumped against her, and she turned her head to look away. If he saw she was fighting tears, he'd never be able to hold his in.

With the mule team at a trot, it took almost no time to reach the canal that would take them to the main branch of the Nile. Just ahead, a boat as long as five or six men was tied up front and back to mooring posts that kept it parallel to the shore. Two planks set side by side had one end on the boat and the other on the levee. Together, the planks were wide enough for two people to pass each other. Sixteen Egyptian men sat under a nearby tree.

"We're going on that boat?" Jason took Neferu's hand before he turned his gaze on Kosmos. "Are they all going, too?"

"We are. Last night I sent for this boat to be waiting for us." Kosmos smiled down at him. "Those men are the crew."

Jason's eyebrows rose. "So many? What do they do?"

"There's a pilot who stands at the front. He tells the helmsman at the back how to move the steering oar to stay where nothing blocks the boat's path. That changes with the inundation each year, so he watches carefully. In some places, the canal becomes shallower than the boat needs, so he can also check the depth with a long pole to make certain the boat will clear. The others will row."

The wagon reached the shore and stopped. When they climbed down, one man rose and came toward them. Kosmos tied his mule to the back of the wagon and met him halfway.

Neferu squatted by Jason to put her eyes at his level. "I've seen carvings of riverboats on the temple walls near home, but I've never been this close to one.

Look at that pole at the rear. It's taller than any of the men. And the paddle that's attached near the top with the big leaf shape in the water—we'll get to watch how the helmsman uses that to steer."

Jason's grip on Neferu's hand tightened. "I hope the crocodiles aren't hungry. I don't want to get eaten."

Neferu swept the curls back from his forehead. "It's a big boat, and I'm sure Kosmos hired men who know what they're doing. We'll probably see some along the shore, maybe even swimming in the water. But they could never get up so high onto the boat with us. We'll be perfectly safe sitting on the bench under that canopy toward the rear."

Some rowers carried the trunk and chest across the gangplank. With ropes, they secured them to the deck just ahead of the canopy.

The axle creaked as the wagon started back to the compound, and Jason turned to watch. As his last tie to what had been home rolled away, he swallowed hard. Then he turned back to face the boat and squared his shoulders.

As the rest of the rowers took their positions on the rowing benches, Kosmos summoned them with a curl of his fingers. He kept his hands on Jason's shoulders as they crossed the gangplank.

When they were seated with Jason between her and Kosmos, the helmsman and pilot laid the planks along the deck between the rows of rowing benches. Then each untied their end from the mooring posts, and the crew moved the boat away from the shore.

As the rhythmic movement of many oars started them toward the Nile, Kosmos patted Jason's leg. "We'll reach your grandfather's estate in a day and a half. You'll be seeing many new things as we go. If you have questions about any of them, just ask." He smiled down at the too-quiet boy. "There's no better way to learn."

There was plenty of room on the bench, but Jason pressed himself into Neferu's side. Unshed tears filled his eyes before he answered with a silent nod.

# Chapter 13



## A Chance to Say Goodbye

*The Latinus town house, Day 8*

While Caelus lingered in the triclinium over a breakfast with the elite students, Lusario had wolfed down some breakfast at the servants' table and returned to their room to finish packing. The first volume of Vitruvius, some complicated notes taken during an engineering lecture, and a selection of their drawings and construction plans had already been placed in the chest that would go with them. Along with the medium-sized traveling trunk that held Caelus's toga and some clothing for both of them, it would make the trip to Carthago under their bunks in the ship's cabin.

Lusario knelt by the next chest and spread the fleece in the bottom, wool side down. Next went a layer of wax tablets, their leather-bound notebooks of papyrus sheets where he'd combined their lecture notes, and the codices and scrolls that belonged in the library of every engineer and architect. It was almost full when he laid one of Caelus's older tunics across the top of the stacks and tucked it in around the edges.

With a thud, he closed the lid that fit so it would keep out any rain or sea water hitting the top and slipped the hasp over the metal loop. The padlock made a satisfying click as he turned the key to make it secure.

One down, two to go. These three would remain behind, locked in the room for which Caelus had paid six months' rent to hold it for their return.

Or perhaps only to protect the treasures in these chests until word arrived to follow their owner home to Carthago, never to be used again.

He closed his eyes and shook his head, trying to rid himself of that depressing thought. It was too soon to assume Caelus would fail.

After adding the fleece to the second trunk, Lusario placed his small chest of notes from his first stay in Alexandria in one corner. He'd risked the wrath of his last vicious master by sneaking it onto the ship they took to Carthago three years ago, but it was safe to leave it here with Caelus's possessions. One way or another, he'd be reunited with it. But that was more likely to be in Carthago than in this room that had been the best home he'd ever had.

Lusario startled at the knock behind him. When he glanced over his shoulder, Timon stood in the doorway, his usual smile of greeting missing.

"I'm leaving town this morning. Achilleus has been called immediately to his grandfather's estate, and I'm going as well. His great-grandmother is dying, and the whole family is gathering to say goodbye and for the funeral celebration. So, since I can't be at the wharf to say goodbye tomorrow, I came today."

"Celebration?" A snort escaped before Lusario thought to stop it. "There are some people whose deaths bring relief and even gladness to their families, but most wouldn't admit that by calling it a celebration."

On the balcony outside the room where Lusario had known both despair and great expectations, the voices of two of the renters with rooms past Caelus's grew louder as they approached.

Timon lowered his voice to a near-whisper. "We all share the same faith, and we know who is waiting to welcome her when she dies. We can celebrate that even as we grieve her leaving us for now. She was kind to all who knew her, whether free or slave."

"When Caelus's stepgrandmother died, he said the same about her." With his thumb, Lusario massaged his palm. Caelus was a Stoic, not a man who let emotion overpower him, but he'd shed as many tears at the news of her death as he had when his grandfather died six months later. "She helped him convince his grandfather to send him here even though Master Volero wasn't keen on the idea."

He cleared his throat. "I'm glad you came to tell me." He looked away and drew a line on the floor with his sandal. "I would have wondered when you didn't come to the wharves."

"I'd never choose to miss a chance to say goodbye to you." He tapped Lusario's arm and offered a weak smile. "A man's best friend deserves at least that." The smile vanished. "I'll be praying for God's best for you, and that includes you becoming a brother, like me. Let me know how things turn out when you can. A letter to Philip at the shop will always get to me the next Sunday."

"I will."

After drawing a deep breath, Timon opened his mouth, then paused before uttering his next words. "If you can't return, I can arrange the shipping of whatever you left behind to Carthago."

Lusario crossed his arms. "It looks like all your prayers fell on deaf ears, and your offer proves you've accepted that fact. Last time I left here, you said your god let you know things would turn out better than I expected."

"God hears every prayer." Timon's gaze turned intense. "And He always responds with what's best for us. His answer might be yes, no, or not yet. But for those who love God, all things work together for good in the end, even if I can't see how that could be in the midst of the storm. I'll keep praying for God's best for you."

Lusario snorted. "What's best for me…each time I think that's about to happen, Fortuna has other plans. I guess I shouldn't expect anything different. What I wish were only goodbyes-for-now keep turning into farewells."

Timon's dramatic eye-roll would normally have made Lusario smile, but not today. "I know you Stoics don't believe Fortuna has a role in this or anything else. I'm not ready to say this is farewell forever. Maybe there's a reason you have to leave for now that neither of us can see. That doesn't mean you won't be back someday. Or that we'll never see each other again somewhere else. I'll keep praying for you as long as I live."

Timon cleared his throat. "I told Achilleus I'd meet them at the canal as soon as possible. We've hired a boat to take us all to the estate. I need to go."

One corner of Lusario's mouth rose. "Well, maybe your god will decide to listen, and I'll see you again. If not…" He slapped Timon's upper arm. "It's been good while it lasted."

"It's been the best." Timon nodded and gave him a tight-lipped smile. "God be with you, my friend."

Lusario returned the same sad smile and nod. Then the friend who'd been like the brother he never had turned and walked away.

He stepped onto the balcony and watched Timon until he disappeared through the arch separating peristyle and atrium. With drooping shoulders, he reentered the room to finish packing the scrolls, codices, and notes they would be leaving behind.

Three years ago, Timon had come to the ship when they both thought he'd never return from Carthago. Was this truly their final farewell or only a see-you-later kind of parting?

It felt too final, and he clenched his teeth to stop the tears before they could start. A Stoic must face any loss with courage and self-control.

At least this time he'd be leaving with a master who was his friend, not his enemy.

Still, saying goodbye to a man who'd been his closest friend for more than four years—it was too hard. It hurt three years ago when he was dragged off to Carthago by the young Roman who hated him. When he'd returned after only a couple of months—that stroke of luck still amazed him.

But it hadn't surprised Timon as much because he'd been asking his god to give Lusario something better than he expected. It had been better, but what lay ahead?

Nothing seemed to shake his friend's belief in the Christian god's power. Nothing stopped him from claiming that Jesus was that god's son and cared

enough to die for him. He'd done his best trying to convince Lusario that the Christian god was the one true god for all people everywhere.

Timon had done his best, but his best wasn't good enough. Lusario had no intention of being anything but a Stoic, like Caelus and Caelus's father, the two men to whom he owed his life.

It was up to Caelus to convince Master Volero that they should return. Until Caelus failed to do that, Lusario could tell himself that they'd be returning and everything he'd been wanting, everything he'd been preparing for would finally become his.

And the best friend he'd ever had wouldn't be gone from his life forever.

# Chapter 14

## A New Home?



*Thmoinepsi on the Nile, Day 8*

It took a day, a night, and a few more hours to come down the canal from Arsinoe, pass the small branch of the Nile that went to the nome capital of Heracleopolis Magna, and finally join the main Nile. The rowers leaned into their task and maneuvered through all the boats traveling the river to reach the harbor town of Thmoinepsi on the eastern side.

The pilot guided them toward the shore until the front of the boat ran aground on the muddy bottom at the river's edge. He tapped one of the rowers on the shoulder as he walked toward them, and the man stood.

He took a satchel from a hook on one of the canopy supports and draped it across his chest. "Wait here. I have something to deliver in the town. Joba will fetch some bread and dates for everyone while I'm gone."

Pilot and rower walked to the bow, leaped forward to land on dry ground, and strode toward the buildings lining the shore.

With hesitation, Jason stood and inched closer to the edge of the boat. He peered into the water.

"It's so dirty. I can't see anything."

Kosmos moved over beside him. "It's always like that during Inundation. That dirt will settle out on the land and make it grow better crops."

A dragonfly darted past them and hovered over the water. Without warning, a fish broke through the surface, and the dragonfly vanished into its mouth before it disappeared again with a splash.

Jason scurried back to Neferu and wrapped his arms around her waist.

"It's only a fish." She gave him a quick hug.

"I know, but I was looking right where it was, and I didn't see it coming. It could have been a crocodile. They can jump to take someone off a boat."

Kosmos placed his hands on Jason's shoulders and squeezed. "It's good to watch carefully, but the crocodiles big enough to take any of us don't come that close to the boats in the harbor."

Jason looked up at Kosmos and saw his smile. His arms fell away from Nefe-ru, and he returned to his place nearer the water. "Do you think the fish is still hungry and will do that again?"

"Perhaps." As Jason fixed his gaze on the water once more, Kosmos's smile faded.

The rower returned and distributed bread and dates to all onboard. They had scarcely finished eating when the pilot returned. He motioned for them to return to their seats under the canopy, and the rowers manned their oars.

As they pulled away from the shore into the swift current, Jason took her hand. "What if Grandfather doesn't want me either?"

"Worrying about the what ifs before we know…you don't have to do that. That's why I'm here. I expect he'll be delighted to have you with him after he gets to know you. I think he'll see all the wonderful things about you that I do."

Kosmos patted his leg. "Master Stephanos is much wiser than your father. I expect you'll enjoy living at the main family estate."

The shadow of a massive sail on a large ship coming from the north passed over them.

Jason gasped. "It's so big!"

"It is, but a big ship needs a big sail to pull it upriver against the current." Kosmos pointed at their mast, where the yard holding the top of the sail was still touching the yard at the bottom. "Our ship has a sail, too. If we were going upriver, the men would raise it up to catch the wind when we move out onto the river. But we're going downriver toward Memphis, so the current will carry us. The rowers will help us go faster than the current, and they'll take the boat to shore when we reach the landing near your grandfather's estate."

As the boat sped north, propelled by both current and men, Neferu glanced at Jason, wide-eyed and watching the different boats. Many carried passengers, but whether going upriver or down, most of those probably had chosen their own destination and had someone eagerly awaiting their arrival.

*God, please let Kosmos be right about Master Stephanos. Please let him welcome Jason and soon love him like he deserves.*

*Stephanos's estate, late afternoon of Day 8*

The sun was two handbreadths above the horizon when the pilot pointed at a pair of tall sycamore trees on the riverbank, and the helmsman steered the boat toward it. As they had at Thmoinepsi, the rowers ran the bow of the boat ashore near one of several tall mooring posts.

Neferu nudged Jason's shoulder. "We're almost there."

"I wish we weren't." Jason glanced at her, then looked away before wiping the corner of his eye.

"I'm sure it will be much better than you think." She patted his leg and got a trembling smile in return.

Kosmos strode to the bow and jumped, landing on half-dried mud. He picked his way past scattered puddles of river water to approach a man who had beached a reed fishing boat. "Where is the estate of Stephanos?"

The man tied the rope attached to the bow of his boat to a different mooring post. "You've found it. I serve Stephanos."

"I'm Kosmos, steward of Theodoros, son of Stephanos, and this is his grandson Jason from the Arsinoe estate. I need help getting the boy and his trunks to the house where Stephanos lives."

The man pointed at a cluster of buildings on a low hill about a quarter mile away. "Master Stephanos lives there. I'll go tell Steward Akhom you're waiting here with the master's grandson." He slung a large net bag containing several fish over his shoulder and headed for the stone blocks that served as stairs to the top of the twenty-foot levee that rose about thirty feet back from the river's edge.

Kosmos followed and stood atop the embankment, arms crossed as he stared at the estate compound.

Still on the boat's bench, Jason slid over close to Neferu. "I hope Grandfather isn't too disappointed in me."

"He won't be." She kissed the top of his head. "Sometimes it takes a little while for someone to get to know you, but I'm sure he'll soon be very glad you came."

*God, please let that be true. Please don't let Jason suffer at his grandfather's hand like he did with his father.*

When it seemed long enough for the fisherman to have reached the buildings, she stood. "Let's join Kosmos up on the levee. We can watch for whoever is coming."

Jason ran between the rower's benches and leaped off the bow. As Neferu followed, he scurried up the steps to stand beside Kosmos. When she joined them, Kosmos pointed where the levee ended.

A man on a mule came from behind the compound and turned his mount onto the levee, which was topped by a grassy path wide enough for two carts to pass.

When he reached them, he reined in but didn't dismount. "I am Akhom, steward of Stephanos of Thmoinepsi. I was told you claim to have brought Master Stephanos his grandson. He and young Master Horion have gone downriver, and it might be a few weeks before they return." He rubbed his jaw. "But Horion's sons stayed here, so"—he tipped his head back to look down his nose—"who are you and why are you really here?"

Neferu barely kept her jaw from dropping. How could this steward not know Stephanos had one more grandson?

When the steward stopped, Jason had hidden behind Neferu. Now he moved enough to see past her, but he held her tunic so only half his face, the half with the good eye, showed.

Kosmos squared his shoulders and matched the tilt of Akhom's head. "I am Kosmos, steward of Stephanos's Arsinoe estate. I send him frequent reports. If you look at the signet seals on documents from that estate, you will see that they match the ring I am wearing. As Master Theodoros commanded, I have brought Jason to his grandfather."

Akhom glanced at Jason, who remained half-hidden behind Neferu. "Why has the boy come now?"

"His mother died birthing Master Theodoros's second son, and the master decided it was a good time for the boy to live for a while with his grandfather."

The steward's eyebrows rose. "Second son? I did not know Theodoros still had an older son. I thought the sons of Master Horion were the only living grandchildren."

Neferu's anger flared as if someone had poured oil on the ashes of a dead fire and tossed a burning torch onto it. How could Theodoros have been telling people Jason was dead? Why did Jason have to hear that his father pretended he didn't exist?

"He does, and one to be proud of. An unusually bright boy. He's a very quick learner, curious about everything. A natural with animals. Even our hard-to-handle donkeys do whatever he asks. He's more than ready to learn to ride, even as small as he is."

Kosmos looked over his shoulder. "Neferu."

She moved up beside him, but Jason stayed mostly hidden behind her.

"Neferu is Jason's new tutor. Mistress Corinna found her to teach and look after Jason after the new baby came. Neferu has a bondservant contract for four years with the mistress. Since Mistress Corinna left all she owned to Jason, he owns that contract now. I'll give you a copy before I leave."

Akhom tipped his head for a better look at Jason, but the boy stayed half-hidden behind her. "His tutor? He hardly looks old enough."

"He's six, but as I said, he's unusually bright." Kosmos rested his hand on Jason's shoulder, but Jason still kept half of himself hidden. "Neferu has only started to teach him this week, and within two days he'd learned all the letters and could sign his name."

Akhom raised his eyebrows. "That is four years ahead of when Horion's oldest son began." A warm smile curved Akhom's mouth. "Jason, I welcome you on behalf of your grandfather. Master Stephanos is not here today, but we expect his return in a few weeks. He will be delighted to learn that Theodoros's son is visiting."

Kosmos wrapped his arm around Jason's shoulders and drew him into full view. "And Jason will be delighted to finally meet his grandfather and the rest of his family."

Akhom's head drew back, and the smile turned into a frown.

Jason stepped behind Neferu again. When she reached behind her, small fingers took her hand and held on.

Akhom pushed his cheek out with his tongue. Then a noncommittal smile returned. "So, I see why Theodoros never brought him when he came to visit and why he has now sent you in his place. Master Stephanos's reaction would not b—"

Kosmos held up his hand. "Master Theodoros lacks his father's wisdom to see much deeper than what appears on the surface and to value far more than what the eye can see. I share his mother's opinion that Jason is an exceptional boy destined to make his grandfather proud. Master Stephanos will recognize that as well and be pleased that Jason has come to live with him."

Akhom smiled down at Jason, who was peeking from behind Neferu again. "Master Stephanos is wiser than most men."

He turned his gaze back on Kosmos. "Live with his grandfather? For how long?"

"Master Theodoros is convinced his own father will do a better job of raising Jason to manhood. It was, after all Master Stephanos who named Jason when he was first born."

"I see." Akhom forced a smile. "Well, nothing can be decided until the master returns. I will let him know his grandson will be awaiting his arrival. Some surprises are better received in a letter than in person."

Akhom pointed toward the boat. "Have them bring up whatever you brought for your stay here. I have a cart coming to take it to the villa."

The pilot stood, arms crossed, at the base of the levee. At Akhom's words, he returned to the boat. Three rowers brought the trunk and chest and set them at the top of the stairs.

"I need to return first thing tomorrow, and I'll be using the same boat." Kosmos glanced toward the pilot, who stood on the bow with arms crossed. "Can you arrange for the crew to be fed and provided with what they need for the night?"

"I will take care of that."

Kosmos waved at the pilot. A few words to his crew, and they began preparing the boat for the overnight stay.

At the sound of wagon wheels, Neferu turned to find a donkey pulling a cart toward them. Near the top of the stairs, the pathway widened enough to turn a cart.

The cart had almost reached them when it stopped. The man walking beside it pulled on the lead attached to the donkey's halter. But instead of moving, the donkey leaned back and brayed. Human curses joined the donkey's protest. The man hauled back his arm and began hitting its rump with a short leather strap. The loud slap from each blow made Jason cringe beside her. The donkey laid his ears back and brayed another protest, but after several hard strikes, it started walking again until it reached them.

As the rowers loaded the trunk and chest, Jason slipped from Neferu's side to join the donkey. After a few soft words, he rubbed the beast's cheek, like he used to do with Pikraménos. The donkey leaned into his hand, and its eyes partly closed.

Jason glanced at the cart man, but his hand moved to the donkey's neck and continued rubbing. "What's his name?"

"Peísmon." The man crossed his arms and glared at Jason.

"Is he?"

"Is he what?"

"Stubborn, like you named him."

The man snorted. "I didn't name him, but aren't they all?"

"Depends on who's asking them to do something."

"You think you can make this one behave, boy?" The man's lip curled into a sneer.

Jason stroked the donkey's nose. "Probably."

"Neheb." Akhom's voice carried an edge. "This is Master Stephanos's grandson. Show him respect."

Neheb bowed his head. "I beg pardon, Steward." He cast a resentful glance at Jason.

"Jason enjoyed doing things with the donkeys at the other estate." Kosmos rested a hand on Jason's shoulder. "Our donkey wrangler thought he did better than most of the men. It would be good for him to continue that here, as his studies allow."

Akhom rubbed his jaw. "I see no reason for him not to, at least until Master Stephanos returns."

Jason shot both stewards an appreciative smile before returning his attention to Peísmon.

"Whoever tends the master's horses, perhaps he can begin teaching Jason to ride as well."

Akhom raised one eyebrow, but a nod followed.

"Can I lead him to the villa? I won't have to hit him." Jason's quick glance at Neheb was met by a frown.

Akhom raised his eyebrows at Kosmos, who nodded his approval of Jason's request.

"If he will obey you, that is fine." Akhom's straight lips relaxed into a smile as Jason turned the cart and waited for the command to head home.

"Neheb." Akhom pointed at the boat. "Ask the pilot what he needs to feed his crew, and take care of getting it here."

Neheb dipped his head. "Yes, Steward."

As Akhom began their stroll along the levee, Kosmos walked beside him.

Neferu walked behind them with Jason and his new donkey friend. "I'm glad Kosmos asked about the donkeys. I'm sure you'll be as big a help here as you were there."

"Me, too, but it won't be the same. I miss Gaidaros." He fixed sad eyes on her. "And Pikraménos."

She squeezed his shoulder. "I know. I'm sure he's missing you, too. But Peísmon already likes you, and I'm sure the donkey wrangler here will enjoy your company as well when he gets to know you." She raised one finger. "And you'll start learning to ride. I expect you'll be as good with horses as you are with donkeys."

Jason's smile was fleeting, but it looked happier than any she'd seen since Corinna died.

*God, please let this be a place where Jason's heart can heal. Let Stephanos see him as the special boy he is, and let Jason know he still has a home and family who will love him.*

# Chapter 15

## Unexpected Opportunity

*Eunostos Harbor, Alexandria, morning of Day 9*

The *corbita* Lusario would be taking with Caelus to Carthago floated stern-first by the edge of the quay. Last time he'd boarded a ship heading west, his future look bleak. He'd lost everything he had, everything he dreamed of becoming when he didn't return to his old master in Cyrene. Newly the slave of a Roman who hated him, he expected nothing but misery and death within a year.

The future wasn't so dark this time. He belonged to a fair master and served a friend, but if they couldn't return, his dream of designing buildings with Caelus as a free man would vanish like smoke on the wind.

Caelus stood beside him, arms crossed as they watched two rows of men carrying crates and sacks up the gangplank and retuning empty handed to get another load.

"I hate to do it, but I suppose we might as well board and get the trunks put in the cabin." He turned his gaze on the giant lighthouse and released the deepest sigh. "If I know my father, we won't see the Pharos again. You'll be writing Timon to ship what we're leaving here to us, and we'll never get to use any of it."

"Maybe not." Lusario dredged up a hopeful smile, even though he didn't feel like it. "Maybe you'll convince him to let you finish. If not, maybe you can find something to design in Carthago."

Feet shuffled behind them, and Lusario glanced at the two men pulling the handcart holding their trunks. An impatient frown curved the taller one's mouth, but he quickly erased it when Lusario looked at him. Postponing the inevitable kept them from unloading and seeking another paying customer.

"The *Zefyros* doesn't leave for a while. I can have the trunks put on board, and we can stretch our legs before we spend a couple weeks with no chance for that."

"All right." Caelus scrunched his eyes and rubbed his forehead.

By a curl of his fingers, Lusario summoned the cart men to follow. The first mate stood by a rough podium a few feet from the water's edge. His eyes kept shifting as he watched the progress of the dock hands and made entries on a wax tablet.

"Excuse me." Lusario stopped in front of him.

With a flick of his hand, the first mate ordered him to move aside to not block his view of the loading. "What?"

"We would like to put our trunks in our cabin room and then leave for a while."

A quick nod from the mate, and he stepped forward to pull a man out of the stream of bearers.

"Take one end of that large trunk"—he pointed at the handcart—"and take those two to the cabin."

The dockhand nodded and did as told. With one cart man on the other handle and the second carrying the smaller chest, the three merged with the stream of men on the gangplank and stepped down onto the deck. As they moved away from the railing, even their heads disappeared from view.

"When do we need to be back at the ship to board?"

The first mate shot a glance his way. "Two hours." He took a step forward. "You. Stop."

At the point where men carrying sacks turned into men with crates, the first mate checked the labels on the first two, wrote something on the tablet, then started the line again with a wave of his hand.

As Lusario turned to rejoin Caelus, the two cart men came down the plank in the line of men carrying nothing on their shoulder.

Lusario summoned them and handed each a chalkon, the smallest Alexandrian coin. He'd held out a few when he exchanged their Egyptian coins for Roman coins. Not enough to buy food or drink, but enough to say thank you to a slave for doing the real work their owner had been paid for. The few that would be left he could give to someone on the wharf before they boarded.

◆

Caelus's shoulders drooped as they started back toward the causeway dividing the Eunostos and Great Harbors. He turned to watch the lighthouse as they strolled.

A nudge by Lusario directed his gaze forward. "Fundanus is coming. Who's the man with him?"

Caelus squinted for a clearer view. A Roman the right age to be Fundanus's father walked beside his best friend in Alexandria. "I have no idea."

Fundanus raised his hand high and waved. When Caelus returned the gesture, a curl of Fundanus's hand and arm summoned them. They had barely reached the two men when—

"Caelus Publilius Martinus, this is my uncle, Titus Vibius Latro." He tapped

Caelus's upper arm. "This is the man I've been telling you about, Uncle. He's been studying to be an architect for the past three years with Zenon. I've seen many of his drawings, and they are amazing."

Latro offered a social smile, like Caelus had received a thousand times from his father's colleagues.

"Zenon is called the best architect in Alexandria, and he says Caelus is more than ready to design buildings and direct their construction." Fundanus tapped Caelus's upper arm. "If I had something I wanted to build, Caelus Martinus is the man I'd hire to do it."

"I know how demanding that can be." The eyes of Fundanus's uncle warmed, but was that friendliness or laughter? "I'm about to have a villa added to an estate I recently bought upriver. I want to build a Roman-style house there, but not strictly Roman. It should have Greek and Egyptian motifs as well. When I return from my trip to Ephesus, I'll be starting that."

Fundanus raised his hand in a broad wave, and a well-dressed woman in her early forties strolled toward them with three maidservants and a bodyguard following. "My Aunt Tranquilla is coming."

When Tranquilla reached them, she rested her hand on Latro's arm, and he gave her the smile of a man who enjoyed his wife's company.

Caelus's heart rate ramped up. Father always said you never knew when a friendship would bear unexpected fruit, and this tree might be ripe for picking.

"Have you hired the man who will design and build it for you?"

"Not yet." He patted his wife's hand. "Women care more about the details of a house, and Tranquilla hasn't decided exactly what she wants."

"May I submit some plans for your consideration?" Caelus held his breath. Latro's next words might determine his future.

"I'm planning to use a local builder who built a new house for a neighbor. It turned out fine."

Latro's headshake made Caelus suppress a sigh. But victory was seldom won in the gymnasium or on a gameboard by a single move. Grandfather always said a good business man could see beyond a customer's words to find what he really wanted.

"Your villa could be much more than fine. It could be a monument to the greatness of your family for generations to come and set a higher standard for any others looking to build. We have been training with Zenon, who was a protégé of Tryon, who learned from Heron himself. His designs include the best of both old and new."

The twitch of Latro's mouth revealed his silent laughter at Caelus's bold claim. "An impressive pedigree for your instructor, but building in the real world is a far cry from what a scholar imagines it to be. Have you been to the Faiyum?"

"We have visited many important buildings within a day's travel from Alexandria, but we haven't had the opportunity to go that far upriver."

A patronizing smile curved Latro's mouth. "Each building must be tailored to the land where you build it. If you've only traveled in the Delta, you lack the necessary knowledge about the area in general and the site in particular."

"I agree that every site requires careful evaluation, and I would very much like to visit the Faiyum to do so." Caelus's nod and smile were born of watching Father address the council. He claimed that partly agreeing with a man could be the first step in leading him to agree to your proposal. But was Latro ready for the proposal that could keep them in Alexandria?

"Would you be willing to hold off on hiring the local man until after I visit the site and draw up plans for what will most assuredly be the finest house in the region? It could be Roman or Greek or Egyptian or a blend of any of them if you want."

Tranquilla's head tilted as she contemplated him. Then she graced him with a warm smile before turning to her husband.

"Titus."

Latro turned his gaze upon her. "What?"

"I'd like to see what a young man who's been trained by the leading expert might suggest. Something that blends the best of each architectural style might be better than any in its pure form. It truly could set the new standard for everyone who matters."

"It might." Latro rubbed his jaw before directing a slow smile at Caelus. "We're on our way to Ephesus to visit Tranquilla's family." He pointed to a ship five berths west of theirs. "It's time for us to board. But you're welcome to go upriver to look over the site and draw a proposed design. We'll be gone for a month. But when we return, I'll need to start with construction right away. So, you'll need to have any plans ready and waiting for me to be considered."

Relief surged through Caelus, and he barely stopped what would seem an unprofessional grin. "I'm sure I can find your land on my own with proper directions. I'll have exactly what you'll need to make that decision when you return."

"Then come with me." Latro swept his hand toward the waiting ship. "I'll write out clear directions when we board. I own a dozen riverboats based at Hermopolis on the Canopic branch. I'll include how to find them and hire one of my captains. They all know where to take you and will make certain you get off at the right place."

Caelus turned to Lusario, who had waited silently behind him. "Get our trunks unloaded and write a message to be delivered to Father by whoever meets the ship." He slapped Lusario's upper arm. "Explain why we aren't arriving as he expected and tell him I'll be writing more later."

# Chapter 16



As the party walked past the *Zefyros*, Lusario turned aside. The first mate glanced at him and waved him toward the ship. Only half a dozen men carrying crates still waited to board, with the first standing by the podium as the first mate wrote on a tablet.

Lusario made his way up the gangplank and along the rail to the cabin door. A workbench with cabinets above and below it stretched along one side. On the opposite side were rooms, each about five feet wide. The door of the first room, labeled Captain, was closed, but the other five stood open. A blend of voices from those who'd already boarded came from the rooms.

The second room was empty. As he walked by the next three, he glanced in to find one married couple and the others a mix of wealthy men and manservants. The last held a woman with two small children.

His brow furrowed. The empty one must be the one he reserved, but neither the trunk nor the chest could be seen. He returned to it and knelt to look beneath the lower bunk. Nothing but some dust.

When he exited the cabin, the first mate stood by the open hold, closed tablet in hand.

"Excuse me." Lusario's quiet words drew the mate's gaze. "There's been a change of plans. Our departure has been delayed, and I need to get our trunk and chest off the ship."

The mate's nod was accompanied by him calling out two names. When the men came out of the hold, he pointed at Lusario. "Get his trunks back to the wharf."

As the crewmen headed toward the cabin, Lusario cleared his throat. "They aren't in our room."

The mate's eyebrows plunged. "Not in your room?"

He brushed past Lusario, disappeared into the cabin for a moment, and came out wearing a black scowl.

The first's mate's quiet string of obscenities would have raised the eyebrows of most of Caelus's friends. "I told the ones carrying them to put them in the cabin. Nothing came off after they went on, so they're here on the ship somewhere. Did you check all the rooms?"

"I did. They aren't there."

The first mate's lips tightened enough to disappeared. "If they aren't there, then they're in the hold."

Lusario stared at the gaping hole in the deck as the last man carrying nothing emerged. "How do we get them from there?"

A laughing snort was the mate's first answer. "You don't. Not until this ship lands in Carthago. The crates that were about to be loaded when I gave you the dockhand were headed there. Your trunks are buried behind those crates and the cargo that gets unloaded at ports between here and there."

Lusario crossed his arms. What was in the trunk was easily replaceable. The scrolls, notes, and drawings in the chest were not. "Caelus Publilius Martinus needs at least the chest before you sail."

The first mate straightened to his full height. His fists settled on his hips. As he tightened the fists, his arm muscles bulged. "But he's not going to get it. Not until the ship reaches Carthago."

"We won't be going to Carthago now, so he won't be there to get them."

The first mate leaned over and spat. "Rich ones like him are always met at the ship. Aren't you expecting that?"

"Yes…" If only Caelus were beside him. The mate wasn't going to help a mere manservant.

"Then they can pick it up for you."

Lusario rubbed his lip. The first letter had named the ship and when they'd arrive. Surely someone would be there to get the trunks.

"Very well. I'll write a letter explaining why we're not on the ship and what's happened with the trunk and chest, and your captain can give it to them when you arrive. If you make certain to get Caelus Martinus's baggage to his father's men, that should be sufficient."

"Anything more won't happen."

"Do you have what I need to prepare that letter?"

The first mate pointed up the quay. "No, but there's a scribe two or three blocks that way. Write what you want and get it to me or the captain."

Lusario offered a quick smile, and it doused some of the fire in the mate's eyes.

"Don't take too long. We're almost ready to sail." The mate turned and went down the stairs into the hold.

As soon as his feet hit the wharf, Lusario quickened his pace to a trot. He was breathing hard when he reached the scribe's shop.

The clerk at the front counter startled when he snatched open the door and strode in.

"I need a sheet of papyrus, pen, ink, and sealing wax." The man stared at him. "In a hurry. I have to catch a ship that's about to sail."

As the clerk sprang into action gathering what he needed, Lusario twisted the brass ring that Caelus had given him. The raised pattern of a Greek temple adorned the surface. It would be better to seal it with Caelus's signet, but most didn't look at the seal before they opened a letter. It would still make the letter appear more important to anyone not looking too closely.

The clerk handed him a pen and placed an ink pot before him. He sliced a sheet of papyrus from a larger roll and held it without offering it. "That will be two obols."

Lusario blanched. After giving the chalkons, worth a quarter obol each, to the cart men, did he have enough Alexandrian money left?

He reached into the purse hanging from his belt and pulled out all his remaining coins. He dumped them on the counter and sorted them. A denarius or two of mixed Roman coins. Only seven chalkons.

"I already exchanged almost all our money for Roman coins. Do you accept those?"

"No."

"But this is all I have, and I don't have time to get more before they sail."

The clerk shrugged. "Two obols."

"How big a sheet of papyrus plus the other things can I get for seven chalkons?"

The clerk set the full sheet aside and sliced off a shorter sheet. It was about three quarters as long as the first, but it would have to do. Lusario dipped the pen and began the most important letter he'd ever written.

> *Lusario, secretary to Caelus Publilius Martinus, to Volero Publilius Martinus, honored father and master, greetings.*

Whether that was the proper way to start—Lusario had no idea. He'd never written a letter like this before.

> *Master Caelus had planned to be coming to you on the Zefyros, as he wrote you earlier.*
>
> *But he is now expecting a commission to design and build a villa upriver for Vibius Latro. Since construction will need to begin in a month, he will be making the site visit immediately and preparing some alternative designs for Latro to choose among upon his return from Ephesus.*
>
> *It will be the first of many designs for the new architectural*

*business he will be starting when he completes his studies with Zenon, the most renowned architect in Alexandria.*

*I am writing this for Master Caelus because the Zefyros is about to cast off and he is still in conversation with the owner of the estate aboard the ship that is taking Latro to Ephesus.*

*Unfortunately, a trunk and chest that Master Caelus was bringing to Carthago were supposed to be stored in the cabin room reserved for him. Instead, they were put into the hold. Hence, they will be making a voyage to Carthago on the Zefyros, even though Master Caelus will not. The chest contains important documents and scrolls, so please be sure to collect it as well as the trunk before leaving the wharf.*

He was almost out of room. But the most important information was there.

*As soon as Master Caelus knows the details about when the construction will be completed, he will be able to give you an expected time for his arrival. He looks forward to enjoying the pleasure of your company during that future visit.*

*Master Caelus and I hope all will continue to be well with you. May the gods guard your safety.*

"Sealing wax, please."

The clerk moved a small oil lamp in front of him and handed him a slim candle of red wax. Lusario flipped the papyrus, wrote "Volero Publilius Martinus, his steward, or whoever meets the Zefyros for him" near the bottom edge, and rolled it up. He lit the candle, let three drops of wax fall on across that edge, and pressed his ring into it.

He bolted out the door and trotted back to the ship. The gangplank still rested on the edge of the wharf.

A sigh of deep relief escaped. The first mate might not have ordered the plank put out again for him.

He strode up the plank and stopped. The cover over the large opening to the hold was in place and lashed down. He'd barely made it.

A crewman approached frowning. In a language Lusario didn't recognize, he was ordered to do something, but what? Still speaking words that made no sense, the man pointed toward the wharf.

Lusario scanned the deck. No captain, no first mate.

"Does anyone speak Egyptian? Or Greek? Or Latin?" He switched between languages as he asked.

The crewman glowered and pointed once more toward the gangplank.

Another man walked by on the other side of the hold cover.

"You there!" Lusario raised his voice as he waved his hand.

The man paused, pointed at his own chest, and raised his eyebrows.

"Yes. Please come over here." With a curl of his fingers, Lusario invited the second crewman to come.

He repeated his question. The crewman stared at him, as if thinking about it. "Yes. Greek."

Lusario's shoulders lowered to their normal position. Without realizing it, he'd tensed up enough to raise them. "I have something to give the captain or first mate."

The man's brow furrowed, then relaxed. "Captain, first mate not on ship now."

Lusario held out the papyrus. "This is for the captain to give to Volero Martinus's people who will be meeting the *Zefyros* in Carthago. The trunk and chest that should have been in Caelus Martinus's room are in the hold. Volero Martinus's men should claim them. This letter should also be given to them."

"Trunks from Caelus Martinus's room. Letter to Martinus. Yes."

"The one the captain is to give this letter is written here." Lusario pointed to the writing by the seal.

"Trunks. Letter. To Martinus. Yes."

Lusario offered the letter, and the man took it. Then he went to the cabin and disappeared inside. When he came out, the letter was no longer in his hand.

Lusario drew a deep breath and released it slowly. Would Master Volero be angry when Caelus wasn't on this ship? Would the explanation in the letter smooth things over until Caelus could report their first architectural success?

Only time would tell. But the end of their dream had at least been postponed for a couple of months. If Caelus accomplished all he hoped with this first commission, what had been the dream for both of them could still become reality.

# Chapter 17

## More of the Same?



*Stephanos's estate, morning of Day 9*

In his room off the balcony, Jason leaned on the windowsill and looked east. "I can see the boats on the river. Big ones with sails like the one we saw."

Neferu lifted the stable out of the trunk and placed it against the wall next to the bed. Then she joined him at the window. "What a great view. And look over there." She pointed across the vegetable garden.

"Donkeys." Jason smiled up at her. "Can we go see them before we start my lesson today?"

"I don't see why not. Akhom said you could help with them." She stepped away from the window. "I need to ask him something. I'll be right back."

He knelt by the stable and began to free the animals Voskos had made him from the protective wads of fleece. As he finished each one, he placed it in its stall.

"What's that?"

He startled at the voice so close behind him. Standing a few steps away with arms crossed was Karpos, the cousin who was only two years older than him.

Jason stood, still holding one of the ewes. "It's a sheep one of our shepherds made for me."

As fast as a striking snake, Karpos snatched it from his hand. "This ugly thing is supposed to be a sheep?" He sneered. "How could a shepherd think this was a sheep?"

Jason clenched his teeth. "He's a better shepherd than any you have here." He held out his hand. "Give it back."

"Take it from me." Karpos held it high above his head, and no matter how hard Jason tried, he couldn't jump far enough to reach it.

Karpos hurled it overhand against the wall by the stable, and Jason bent over to retrieve it. He blew out a relieved breath when a quick inspection showed it wasn't broken.

When he knelt by the stable to put it into its stall, Karpos hauled back his foot, took aim at the mudbrick wall, and started the kick that would surely break it.

But his bully cousin hadn't counted on Jason's reflexes. As the leg swung forward, he grabbed Karpos's ankle. Then he rose and rammed his shoulder into his cousin's gut before shoving as hard as he could.

Arms flailing, his cousin fell backward. He landed hard on his butt and whacked his head on the floor. With a cry mixing pain and fury. Karpos rose, fists clenched.

Jason had watched many playful wrestling matches between the young men who worked his father's estate. This wasn't play. Still, he clenched his own fists and went into the half-crouch the men had used in their fights.

Deep in his gut, anger flared from smoldering coals to leaping flames. What he had to do was clear. If he backed down now, Karpos would never leave him alone. Even if he lost the fight, his cousin would know he was no weakling to be bullied without cost.

"Go away and leave me alone." The pain and bitterness that Patéras's rejection and cruelty had inspired since Mitéra died fueled his outrage. What had happened in Arsinoe would not happen here. Not if he could help it.

◆

When Neferu reentered Jason's room, he stood between Karpos and his stable, fists clenched. Karpos faced him with a jutted jaw and matching fists.

She stepped between them. "Karpos, you should go do whatever it is you normally do in the morning. Your help isn't needed for unpacking."

Karpos glared at her. "I'll do whatever I want, wherever I want."

Neferu crossed her arms. "No, you won't. You'll go do what you're supposed to be doing wherever you're supposed to be doing it."

He rammed his fists onto his hips. "You'll be sorry when my father gets home. No slave of his can tell his sons what to do."

Neferu drew herself up to her full height. "I'm Jason's, not your father's, not your grandfather's. I'm about to start Jason's lessons for the day, and perhaps you should go find your own tutor and do something useful with your time."

"I do whatever I want. Our tutors can only tell Stephan what to do and only if Mother approves." If eyes could throw daggers, she'd be bleeding. "I'm telling her what you did." Muttering, he stomped down the balcony.

Jason bit his lip. "He threw the ewe against the wall. She didn't break this time, but she could have. He tried to kick down the stable, too." He turned pleading eyes on her. "How can I keep him from coming back and breaking things?"

The trunk had a hasp with a ring as thick as Jason's little finger and a hinged plate with a notch that went over it. For the trip, it was held shut by a short, curved metal rod. But it had no lock, and neither did the door. So, how was she to keep that bully from making Jason as miserable as his father had?

"Don't leave the room before I return." She took a wax tablet from the chest and handed him a stylus. "Practice writing the alphabet and your name, and I'll go ask Akhom that question."

She found Akhom talking to a gardener outside the front door. When the man said "yes, Steward" and headed around the side of the house, she approached him.

"What is it?" He faced her and crossed his arms. "I told you I had already spoken with our donkey wrangler about the boy spending time helping him."

His straight lips and cool eyes didn't invite her to make another request, but for Jason's sake, she'd risk his irritation. When she and Jason joined Kosmos and him for dinner last night, the two stewards seemed to enjoy talking together. But Jason had remained silent, and neither man gave any indication they would welcome her joining their conversation. So, she'd said almost nothing as well.

"A problem I hope you can help with, Steward."

"What and how?"

His tone made her swallow hard. A steward's loyalty was to the master of the estate. Would he listen to the bondservant of a young boy who wasn't yet an official part of the household?

"While I was speaking with you, Karpos tried to break the only toys Jason brought with him. They were made by two of the men who spent many hours teaching him things." She massaged her palm with her thumb. "When I returned to Jason's room, I found the boys facing off with fists, ready for a fight. I told Karpos his help wasn't needed unpacking, and he left. But Jason is afraid he'll come back and break what the men he loves gave him, just out of meanness."

Akhom's expression hadn't changed as she spoke. His cool, unreadable eyes stayed focused on her face. Another deep breath, and she forged ahead.

"I told him I'd ask you if there was a way to keep Karpos from getting at his treasures. Something he can lock where he or I can keep the key."

"Your traveling trunk cannot be locked?"

"It could, but we don't have a lock." She fought the urge to bite her lip. "Kosmos didn't expect we'd need it since we weren't leaving it anywhere."

A sudden turn of Akhom's head took his gaze off her. He took a step past her, then squared his shoulders and stood still.

The thuds of hooves and the creaking of a wagon caused Neferu to turn.

A Roman-style carriage pulled up, and Akhom opened the door. He held out his hand, and a woman in her mid-thirties took it.

"Welcome home, Mistress Zenobia."

With a wordless glance at Akhom, she stepped down. Her gaze locked onto

Neferu, raking her from face to feet and back. Her mouth settled into a frown and disdain filled her eyes.

"Did Horion tell you to buy this one?"

"Theodoros has a new son, Mistress. Menander's mother died in childbirth, and Theodoros has sent his older son, Jason, for his first visit to his grandfather." Palm up, he extended his hand toward Neferu. "Neferu is his tutor."

Zenobia tilted her head to look down her nose at Neferu. "Theodoros bought a woman tutor? She doesn't look old enough or smart enough to be one." Her gaze shifted to Akhom, and her brow furrowed. "I thought Theodoros's first son died shortly after birth."

"It appears not. Jason is six now. It will be good for him to get to know his cousins and the rest of his family."

"No one gets a tutor for so young a child." Her frown deepened. "How long a visit?"

"That remains for Master Stephanos to decide. It will likely be a long one."

"Where have you put them?"

"Jason has a room near your children. Neferu will be with the housemaids."

"Before my husband and his father return, move her to one of the farmworker cottages away from the road to the village. She'll be less in the way there."

"Very well, Mistress."

With chin held high, Zenobia turned and strolled toward the house. The door opened before she reached it, and the youth who opened it stood at attention, then bowed deeply as she passed.

Neferu rubbed both her arms. Staying out of the way of that one was a good idea. Other than when Zenobia was first examining her like a bug she'd like to squash, the Greek woman didn't even glance at her.

Akhom's gaze remained fixed on his mistress until she entered the house. Then he turned worried eyes on Neferu. "Until Master Stephanos returns, I would advise that you study in Jason's room, not the public areas. Master Stephanos has no wife now, so Mistress Zenobia has charge of the household. With Jason's eye, it will be better if he spends very little time around her. She is not known for holding her tongue about the defects of others or for welcoming those who are better than her in some obvious way."

Was Zenobia's hostility toward her because she didn't like pretty women in her household? She looked like so many other Greek women in their thirties, being neither pretty nor ugly. She wasn't a woman men would turn to watch, but elite Greek men kept their wives mostly at home and entertained without them, so not many would get the chance to watch, anyway.

Should she ask Ahkom if that was the reason? Was Jason's uncle Horion like his loathsome brother, a seeker of women beside his wife?

"What she says to me doesn't matter. What she says to Jason…" She tightened her lips and shut her eyes. How much was safe to say to a steward she didn't know? When she opened them, Akhom was looking at the door again. "I don't want him to suffer here like he did with his father."

"A valid concern. There is an empty cottage near the river among the workers. Jason should spend most of his time as you direct. If you would rather teach him there, I will arrange for a table."

"Do you think that wise?"

Akhom cleared his throat. "Someone will bring a table and chairs." He rubbed under his jaw. "Anything Jason especially values would be better kept there as well. The cottage will not lock, but I will get you a lock for Jason's trunk. It will be up to him to keep his treasures locked up when he is not using them."

"Thank you, Steward."

"You may call me Akhom." His lips twitched, and a fleeting smile appeared. "There is a second bed in the cabin. Whether Jason sleeps there or in the main house until Master Stephanos returns…I leave that to you to decide."

"Thank you, Akhom."

He raised an eyebrow, silently asking what for.

"For caring about Jason."

With a flick of his fingers, he pushed her thanks aside.

"Leave a good tunic or two in his balcony room. Zenobia might want him to dine with her boys. Karpos is eight and Stephan eleven. She expects them to look like future masters, not children who play with servants. I will send someone shortly to take you and your trunks to the cabin."

"As you wish, Akhom."

She didn't try to thank him with words again, but surely her smile spoke as clearly as any words.

He waved his hand toward the door to dismiss her, but a twitch of his mouth as he almost smiled was better than most saying "you're welcome."

# Chapter 18

## First Commission



*Alexandria, morning of Day 9*

Lusario strode up the wharf to where Caelus and Fundanus stood, watching Latro's ship being towed out by rowboats.

Caelus slapped him on the shoulder, grinning like a hyena that had just feasted on a gazelle. "We have our first commission."

"He hired you?"

After the past week of failing to find any job, no matter how small, had Caelus actually secured something Zenon himself would want to build?

"Well, not officially, but Tranquilla is excited about having her villa reflect a unique combination of Rome, Greece, and Egypt, and no local builder will be able to create that like we can. If my mother set her heart on that, Father wouldn't think it worth the grief it would cause him if he didn't give it to her. So, a trip upriver to see the building site should guarantee that our design will outshine any opposition."

Lusario glanced at Fundanus and found him nodding. "So, when do we leave?"

With eyebrows raised to ask the question, Caelus turned to Fundanus. "What's reasonable?"

"Pack today and leave tomorrow. It takes most of a day to get to Grandfather's estate near Naucratis, so if you leave early, you'll reach the city in time for dinner." Fundanus raised one finger. "You'll need to pay a river toll there and a few other places. But Latro's captains do that every time they go upriver or down, so they'll know what to do."

They started back along the quay, three abreast with Caelus between Lusario and Fundanus. When they reached the causeway that led to the lighthouse, Lusario cleared his throat. Leaving early tomorrow might sound reasonable to a master, but arranging the details always fell to him.

"Since you've made the start of this journey, where do I go to buy passage?"

Fundanus pulled at the edge of his eye. "To get to the Nile, I start with a boat that goes south on Lake Mareotis to a canal that takes you over to the river near Hermopolis. I change to a Nile boat there. It's only a short distance upriver to Naucratis."

A few more blocks, and they reached the lecture halls.

Caelus tapped Lusario's arm. "Let's find Zenon and tell him." He bounced his eyebrows. "Maybe we should tell him to sit down before we do."

"You don't need me now, so I'm going back to the town house." Fundanus took a step, then looked back. "I'll take Lusario to the lake harbor to book your passage after lunch."

As their friend who'd solved their seemingly unsolvable problem walked away, they turned into the courtyard between library and lecture halls. Zenon should be in his office. After sharing the news with their mentor and friend, preparations for the journey could begin.

Back in their room, Lusario knelt by the wooden box that would protect their most valuable surveying tool while they traveled. With its set of calibrated brass circles and geared semicircles that let the angle between them be finely adjusted, the *dioptra* would let them measure angles and distances to precisely lay out the future building site. After placing it in the fleece-lined box, he tucked several pieces of fleece around the different parts to thoroughly pad it.

Using diagrams from Zenon, Caelus had hired an expert in working with brass to make it. He had spent more than twice what Lusario cost and considered it a bargain. At Lusario's suggestion, he'd had the rod that held it at eye level made in several pieces, with ferrules at each end that made it straight and rigid when fully assembled.

Lusario closed the chest's lid, secured the straps that held it shut, and placed it beside the bag of rod sections. Still kneeling, he looked up at Caelus, who stood beside him, arms crossed as he watched.

"This and our drawing materials are going to fill a quarter of the trunk. The boat captain said not to plan on more than one. There isn't always room."

"I'm sure we can get everything we need in it." Caelus nudged Lusario's shoulder. "You're good at fitting a lot into a small space."

Caelus lifted one of their *decempedae* from its usual place on the floor next to the wall. He ran his hand along the smooth, hardwood shaft of the ten-foot rod that was fitted with brass ferrules at each end. They were designed so one end could mate with its companion rod and lock into place for a twenty-foot measuring rod. With the second rod held in place, the first would be disconnected from one end and moved forward to lock onto the other end to precisely measure thirty feet. And so it went for whatever distance one needed to measure.

"It was kind of Zenon to give us one of his measuring ropes so we wouldn't have to try to find and buy one before we could leave, but we'd normally be using these to lay out a building. Anyone watching how fast you and I work with them could see we're professional builders. A rope…to someone who's never seen an architect at work, it would just look like a rope." Caelus frowned. "Maybe we should take these instead."

Lusario placed the padded box holding their dioptra in the trunk and set the bag of rods beside it. "But we don't know what kind of boats we'll be taking. Who else will be passengers, how baggage is stored…it would be so easy for one of them to get broken, and then we'd have no way to measure site dimensions." Lusario hefted the leather satchel holding Zenon's rope. "This fits anywhere, weighs only a few pounds, and there's no way we can break it."

Caelus took it and flipped back the flap. Inside lay a hundred feet of rope with a knot every foot with a brass cylindrical bead pressed against it and held in place by a wrapped strand of twine. Stretched and coated with pine tar to keep it from changing length, its coils filled the satchel with a faint odor of pine.

He fingered one of the cylinders, where the engraved line marked the exact position of the beginning of the next foot. "You're probably right. The bronze division beads do give it a unique look."

He closed the flap and wrapped the cords around the two small cleats before leaning it against the trunk. He tapped the wooden box lying next to the roll of papyrus. "There might be nowhere handy to buy inks and such. Do we have enough?"

Lusario held up his first finger. "Three ink bottles and six pens for drawings." As he named each item, he raised another finger. "Two styluses and three wax tablets. Heracleopolis is the nome capital. If we need more, we can find it there. There's only room for one trunk on the boat we'll take up the canal to the river. We still have to fit clothes and everything else in here."

"So, this won't fit." Caelus fingered the folded toga laying on his bed.

Lusario picked up the tunics that lay beside it. "I think you can safely leave it. You shouldn't be meeting many Romans who would be impressed by it, and it could be an invitation to thieves. It makes you look too rich." He tapped the narrow red stripe on the top tunic. "So does this."

"We'll get better treatment in most places if I'm obviously Roman. Besides, the steward is more likely to believe we came at Latro's request if I look like I'm a wealthy friend of his nephew. He didn't have time to send a message that we'd be coming before he sailed."

From the drawer in the small table beside his bed, Caelus withdrew a sheathed dagger that Lusario had never seen before. "Latro said traveling the river was safer than walking through Alexandria after midnight. But he always travels with a bodyguard, so I doubt he watches as closely as you and I have to." He pulled the dagger from its sheath and fingered the sharpened edge. "So, I bought another dagger while you were arranging passage."

He held out the blade, and Lusario took it. "You'll be wearing one all the time, so pick which one you want. I'll take the other. Being armed sends a message we're ready for trouble. That's usually enough to keep someone from starting any."

Lusario rubbed his lip. Almost since they got off the ship from Carthago three years ago, he'd been wearing the one Master Volero sent with them. The new one wasn't as expensive looking.

"I'll take the new one. It looks like a bodyguard's weapon, not something a master would wear for show."

Caelus's chuckle raised Lusario's eyebrow. "Taurus is Father's best bodyguard. Grandfather bought him from the arena for when he traveled with a lot of money. He's scary even to look at, and he'd be rolling his eyes at you choosing it for that reason." He tapped Lusario's shoulder. "You look like a scholar, not a fighter, but no one could have taken better care of me than you have."

Lusario returned the smile of friendship that Caelus gave him. He'd been bought to watch over Caelus in Alexandria, and he always did his best to serve a master well. But even if he were free, even if he were rich himself and answered to no one, he'd do anything for Caelus. But not because Volero Martinus owned him.

Because he counted Caelus a true friend.

# Chapter 19

## A Promising Beginning



*Stephanos's estate, Day 9*

Neferu had finished repacking the trunk when a knock on the doorframe made her turn. A man dressed for field labor stood in the doorway with the youth from the front door in tow.

"Akhom sent me. What goes?"

"The trunk and the chest."

The worker took one handle and pointed at the other for the youth to grip. She picked up the chest and followed them onto the balcony.

As Jason walked beside her, Karpos stood in his bedchamber door, arms crossed, glaring at Jason.

Jason raised his chin to look down his nose at his cousin, perfectly mimicking the haughty expression she'd seen on Theodoros. Then he slowly turned his head away, conveying the indifference of an elite man toward those he thought inferior.

It would have been a knife into Corinna's heart to see it.

The dogs of Arsinoe that belonged to no one had two choices. Cower before those who threw rocks and kicked them or growl, snap, and sometimes bite. But even a dog that had always trembled could bite without warning. Once it discovered that biting ended the cruelty, it was dangerous to abuse it again. But sometimes it would bite even when no one was hurting it.

Was Corinna's sweet boy, who'd survived six years with a heartless father, going to become a man just like him?

*God, show me what to do to make him strong without him becoming hard. Please bring men like Gaidaros and Voskos to fill the hole that leaving them punched in his heart. Strong men who'll teach him that gentleness and strength are both found in the finest men.*

At the cart, the man donned a shoulder harness. As he pushed on a horizontal rod at the end of the yoke pole and leaned into the harness, he started the cart toward the levee.

They followed him back down the path they'd come up the day before. But they walked past the landing toward a cluster of cabins for the field workers. Made of mudbrick, a mix of one- and two-room cabins lay before them.

Her guide led them past most of the cabins to one at the edge of the cluster. It had a single room, but with a small window facing the river, the door ajar, and a few openings near the roof on both sides, a cooling breeze blew through it. A tidy garden lay between her new home and the edge of the levee that held back the flood waters.

A second cart pulled by a donkey waited in the shade cast by a date palm. Akhom watched, arms crossed, as a man carried a chair into the cabin. The cart also contained several baskets with cheese, dried fruit and vegetables, small bags of wheat, olive oil, wine. Another held plates, cups, cookpots, and utensils— enough to let her prepare meals for herself and Jason.

Jason walked on to look over the side into the wagon, but she stopped beside the steward.

"So much food?" After one glance at his face, she turned her gaze on the cart. If she were to guess, it would be that Akhom wasn't accustomed to servants questioning anything he did.

He turned unperturbed eyes on her. "You should see to Jason's breakfast and lunch yourself. Dinner as well when no one comes to escort him to the main house."

Under an olive tree in front of the next house over, an elderly woman stood with her arms wrapped around herself. But when Akhom fixed his gaze on her and nodded once, she came forward.

"This is Menmet. She will help you settle in here." Akhom spoke Greek, as he had since she met him. Then his gaze turned to the woman and he shifted to Egyptian. "This is Neferu."

Neferu offered her warmest smile. "It's my pleasure to meet you."

Her words in Egyptian brought a smile to the old woman's lips and warmth to her eyes.

"I speak Greek, too." Menmet's smile broadened as she swept her hand toward the adjacent houses. "I will take you to meet others. They will be pleased to see you here, like me."

Neferu pointed toward Jason, who'd moved from the cart to the donkey pulling it and was stroking its nose. "Jason is Master Theodoros's son. He has come to get to know his grandfather. I am his nanny and tutor."

The woman's gaze flitted to Akhom, then returned. "I am alone now, and I would be delighted to cook for the three of us if you give me the extra food."

Although the old woman's eyes and smile were friendly, not forced, each glance she gave Akhom revealed the idea had come from him. Was it a good thing that he was trying to keep Jason away from his nasty cousin? Or was there more to it than first met the eye? What could Neferu do but accept with thanks?

"Thank you for the invitation. We would be delighted to join you. When I'm not actually teaching Jason, I can help."

The last of the baskets had been carried into the house, and the donkey man gripped the animal's lead. Jason stroked its cheek one more time and stepped back. His shoulders sagged as his new friend walked away.

Akhom tipped his head toward Jason. "I will check on the young master later. Menmet will show you where to find the donkey stable. Koshari is expecting him." After a fleeting smile, he headed back toward the main compound.

"Come." Menmet walked with short steps, not the longer strides of a younger woman. With Neferu beside her, they strolled toward Jason at the base of the date palm.

"Koshari is my nephew." She pointed toward Jason. "Is his father coming soon?"

Menmet's nose had twitched before that last question. Somehow, Neferu wasn't surprised. It was too easy to imagine Theodoros was like Karpos as a boy.

"No. He sent Jason to live for a while with his grandfather." Neferu rubbed the back of her hand. How much should she say? "Probably for a long while. Master Theodoros is often away, and raising Jason doesn't interest him."

The old woman touched the side of her eye. "Because of this?"

"Yes. Jason's mother just died giving Theodoros his second son, and he thought it a good time for Jason to meet his grandfather. Jason is very smart and good to everyone, like his mother was."

"Young Theo was smart. But good…" Menmet's shrug said it all.

Silence fell between them. Menmet cast Neferu a furtive glance after almost speaking against Stephanos's son.

"I knew Jason's mother when we were girls. She was always good and kind. Jason is like her, not his father."

They had reached the shade of the palm. "Jason, this is Menmet. She lives next door to our cabin, and she has invited us to join her for meals when you don't have to go to the main house."

Jason kicked at the ground, stirring up a small cloud of dust. "I don't want to eat with Karpos."

"I don't expect you'll have to very often." Neferu tousled Jason's hair. "Menmet's nephew is the donkey handler. She's going to take us to meet Koshari."

Menmet pointed across the field to another small hill with a cluster of mud-brick buildings. "Over there."

Jason slipped his hand into Neferu's, and his shy smile appeared. "I liked the donkey who brought us things today."

Neferu gauged the distance across the field. For her, it was an easy walk of no more than an eighth of a mile. For an old woman, it was a long way. "If you'll point out where the stable is over there, Jason and I can find it by ourselves."

A grateful smile curved the elderly woman's lips as she pointed. "There on the side away from the river. It's easy to find when you get close."

"Then we'll see you later this afternoon."

"Stay on the levee. The field is barely dry enough for plowing and has just been planted. Menmet placed her age-spotted hand on Neferu's arm. "I'll plan for three."

It would have been shorter to walk across the field to the opposite hill. Jason was eager to take the shortcut, but she kept him beside her on the raised path. After depositing its rich load of nearly black soil on the fields, the water was going down. It was almost low enough to remain within the normal banks of the Nile. In some of the higher fields at the Arsinoe estate, the soil had been dry enough to plow and plant. Since it only took a few days for the wheat seed to sprout in the sun-warmed, rich soil, a few fields showed that bright green cast of newly sprouted grain. The fields here that were farthest from the Nile had the same.

But in this field close to the river, walking straight across would leave their feet caked with mud and their sandals ruined. So, they took the longer way around, sticking to the path atop the levee.

They had scarcely started down what seemed the main street of the estate work buildings when a donkey's bray revealed where Koshari would be.

Jason's grin started, then faltered. "What if he doesn't want me around?"

She squeezed his shoulder. "Gaidaros would roll his eyes if he heard you say that. He told me you were as good as two helpers. When Koshari gets to know you, I'm sure he'll agree."

When they rounded the corner of the stable, three long, hairy faces with tan noses and soulful brown eyes turned toward them. From behind the mud-brick wall that made the corral, three donkeys contemplated them as they approached.

An Egyptian man in his late thirties stood facing backward beside a gray donkey. He slid his hand down the beast's foreleg, wrapped his hand around its lower leg, and lifted the foot. With a special knife, he cleaned the sole of the hoof. After slipping that into a sheath hanging from his belt, he took a long-handled pair of clippers from his belt loop and worked his way around the hoof, nipping away parts of the rim of the hoof as he went. Then he smoothed it with a coarse file.

Jason tugged on the sleeve of Neferu's tunic. "Gaidaros did that to all the donkeys." Neferu bent slightly to hear his whisper better. "He let me hold the tools for him."

As the man set the foot down, he looked up. "Jason?" He straightened. "Akhom said you would come."

Jason tipped his face down, as he'd done when he first met Neferu, to hide his eye. Then he nodded.

"Menmet told us where to find you. We'll be living in the cottage next to hers."

Koshari's eyebrows lowered. "Not the main house?"

"Jason will have to be there sometimes, but mostly he'll be with me." She placed her hands on Jason's shoulders and moved him ahead of her toward the donkey wrangler. "I'm Neferu, Jason's nanny and tutor."

Koshari's slow nod accompanied his silence.

"Jason loves donkeys. At Master Theodoros's estate, he helped take care of them, and everyone said he has a special way with them."

When she paused, Koshari remained silent. Except for a few glances at her, his gaze remained fixed on Jason.

"Akhom said he could help you like that here."

Jason drew in the dirt with his sandal, keeping his face pointed down.

More silence was followed by Koshari drawing a deep breath and releasing it slowly. "Do you know how to brush them well?"

Jason looked up at him, hope lighting his eyes. "I like that best. Gaidaros had me help with that when they came back from the fields."

Koshari tipped his head toward the shed. "Brushes are in there. You can start on those three."

Then he stood, arms crossed, watching Jason as he began brushing the first donkey.

"What's his name?" Jason glanced at Koshari but kept brushing.

"Sekhem."

"Is he?" Jason scratched under the donkey's chin when it turned and looked at him.

"Is he what?" Koshari moved to the other side of the donkey he was tending and lifted its foreleg.

"Powerful." Sekhem's eyes partly closed as Jason kept scratching.

A wry smile lifted the corner of Koshari's mouth as he straightened and released the donkey's leg. "He's strong and works hard when asked."

Neferu moved closer to Koshari and lowered her voice. "Akhom asked Menmet to prepare dinner for us, but I'd like to go back and help her. I'll come back and get him in a little while so he won't be in your way."

"Don't bother. I'll have plenty of donkeys needing brushing when they come in from the fields. He can do for me what he did at the other estate. Not everyone is so eager to work"—he turned his smile on her—"especially with me. I'll bring him back to Menmet's house at dinner time."

"I'll be teaching him in the mornings, but can he come here most afternoons?"

"What's fine with Akhom is fine with me." He reached for the donkey's foreleg and pulled out the knife.

Neferu waved at Jason before heading back toward the cabins. But when her back was turned and he could no longer see, she lifted her eyes to the heavens.

*Thank You, God, for this promising beginning. Let this become a home where Jason can be loved and happy again.*

She followed the levee parallel to the river until it branched off at the cabins. In the distance, the villa sat amidst date palms, looking over the farmlands. A promising beginning except for Zenobia and Karpos. Whether it would fulfil that promise depended on Jason's grandfather. What would happen when he returned, only God knew.

*Neferu's cabin, late evening of Day 9*

The soft, rhythmic breathing of the small boy on the second bed blended with the faint conversations of workers by a distant fire. Neferu lay on her back, watching the moon-shadows move slowly across the ceiling.

Akhom seemed less approachable than Kosmos, but under that unemotional exterior was a man who saw the threats to Jason and did what he could to decrease them. He tried to help her fit in, too. Maybe someday she'd know him well enough that she could thank him for getting Menmet to ease her way into life among the workers.

When she confessed that she'd always lived in a city so she'd never had a vegetable garden and had no idea how to care for one, Menmet had placed an arm around her shoulders for a quick hug. Then she showed how to use a hoe to keep down weeds and promised to teach everything else Neferu should know. Best of all, she'd introduced her to a handful of women who weren't working the fields. Because Menmet was everyone's friend, Neferu had been accepted as one of them.

Koshari had done exactly what Jason needed to feel at home, putting him to work like Gaidaros had. During dinner, Jason had regaled them with stories about his new donkey friends. One was even stubborn like Pikraménos.

She rolled onto her side and rested her ear on her hand. Moonbeams from the doorway fell upon the table and two chairs Akhom had provided. Tomorrow she would continue Jason's lessons. When his grandfather returned, maybe seeing how bright Jason was would help him see past one bad eye to the whole boy who would someday make him proud.

Except for the near-fight with Karpos and the suspicions of Zenobia, it had been the best day for both her and Jason since Corinna died.

Jason was delighted that he wouldn't have to eat every meal with Karpos. But for a grandson of the patriarch to be excluded from eating at the family table created a strange feeling in the pit of Neferu's stomach.

Why had Zenobia done it? Was it targeting Jason or her? Neferu meant beauty, and God had given her a face that fit her name too well. It was far better to be ordinary and not draw unwanted attention from men.

And hostility from women. Zenobia wanted her out of sight where her husband wouldn't be tempted, and Akhom had immediately arranged it. Did that mean her husband was too much like Theodoros? Would Horion be hostile like his wife? Or even worse, too friendly. What could she do if the oldest son of Stephanos's family wanted too much of her company for all the wrong reasons? Or if Stephanos was just like his sons?

But it couldn't be worse than living with Theodoros. He'd agreed that her contract with Corinna made her Jason's, not his, but only God knew whether he would have found reasons to send her into Arsinoe.

Uncle Peduhor's livelihood depended on Sasobek thinking she'd been cast out. Near Arsinoe, there was always the risk someone might see her and tell him. Or even worse, Sasobek himself might see her. Coming to this estate on the main course of the Nile got her far enough away that their paths should never cross.

A sigh drained her lungs.

Uncle Peduhor, her cousins—she missed them every day. But perhaps she could send Uncle a letter, carefully worded so only he would know who sent it. Then he could reach her if, for some reason, they needed her.

A slow smile formed. Maybe she'd hear it was safe to return home. But for now, caring for Jason made this home enough. He'd already lost his mother and all the people he loved at his father's estate. She was all he had left. But in four years, he'd be ten. Surely by then his grandfather would appreciate how clever he was and love him for both his courage and his kindness. Jason wouldn't need her anymore.

*God, I thank You for getting us away from Theodoros and safely here. Help me to guide Jason and teach him all that he needs to learn. Please keep Zenobia, her nasty son, and her husband from hurting either Jason or me. Thank You for Akhom and Koshari and Menmet and their kindness toward both of us.*

Her smile broadened. *Thank You for bringing me to Corinna and Jason when they needed me most. A mother can never be replaced, but let me become enough for Jason so he will know how much he's still loved. Give me wisdom to know both when and how to show him how much You love him, too.*

Relaxing in the warmth of God's presence, Neferu drew the thin sheet up to her chin and fell asleep.

# Chapter 20

## Heading Upriver

*Alexandria, evening of Day 9*

"So, we won't be going back to Carthago for a while." Caelus leaned against the doorway of the house steward's office. "We're starting up the Nile tomorrow to compete for our first commission to build a villa near Heracleopolis Magna. I expect we'll be back in about three weeks. I won't know our future plans until then."

"May Fortuna smile upon your trip and give you your first commission." The steward's voice sounded like he expected their success. But why wouldn't he? He'd looked at some of their recent designs and said they were the best he'd ever seen.

Caelus raised one hand to acknowledge the steward's comment before joining the elite lodgers in the triclinium.

Fundanus waved to greet him, and Caelus reclined in his usual place near his friend.

The serving girl placed the first course of sliced purple carrots and a white dipping sauce before them.

"Everything packed and you're ready to go?" Fundanus shook out his napkin and spread it in front of him.

"Ready and eager. Lusario got everything except the rope satchel into one trunk." Caelus dipped his first slice and took a bite. "So, what do you think your aunt will find most impressive?"

"I've never been to the estate, so I don't know what's around it that she'll want to outshine. But in their Alexandrian town house, she likes statues in the pools, and the place always smells of flowers. So, maybe the peristyle garden is most important?"

"I haven't been back to Carthago since Mother took over Grandfather's town house, but she used a lot of flowers to decorate at our estate. So, maybe floral mosaics where Tranquilla is most likely to spend her time? And paintings of flower gardens on the walls. There won't be an upstairs women's room like in the Greek houses, but wherever she's most likely to have her looms…that should be a good place to focus."

"I suppose you could give her more than one design to choose among. If they all look impressive, she'll have to pick one of them. Or they might make her think of something similar that's exactly what she wants." Fundanus squeezed the back of his neck. "Uncle isn't very particular about decorations. This would be easier if your designs only had to please him."

"But if it weren't for Tranquilla, we wouldn't have this chance to design anything. Any man who wants peace with his Roman wife should be wise enough to let her decorate their home." Caelus raised his goblet. "To Tranquilla, her desire to impress her friends with something unique, and her husband's willingness to fulfill her desires. She probably saved us from going home in defeat."

Fundanus chuckled as he raised his goblet to drink the toast.

But Caelus wasn't joking. If he'd learned anything from growing up with his own mother, it was that women had ambitions beyond that of their men, and some would do whatever it took to achieve them. If a man wanted peace at home, he'd be wise to accommodate his wife's desires whenever he could.

Today he'd learned something Zenon never thought to teach them. Never again would he assume that persuading a Roman husband was the only way to be chosen to build.

*Alexandrian river port on Lake Mareotis, morning of Day 10*

As the pilot tied the final knots in the ropes that secured their trunk to the deck, Caelus stood on the dock between Lusario and Fundanus. He drew a deep breath and blew it out through pursed lips. The corbitas and even the smaller ships that carried cargo along the coast seemed up to the task. But this boat…

Six other passengers had joined them to go across the lake to the mouth of the canal that would take them to the Nile. Add to that eight men on oars, a helmsman steering with the long wooden rudder, and a pilot by the post in the front. Between each traveler's baggage and so many people to cram onto the three passenger benches, the boat would ride low in the water after all had boarded.

Fundanus nudged him. "They know what they're doing. They do it all the time. Once you're off the lake, there are no waves, and the wind is low enough today that there aren't even waves on the lake. Some of the Nile boats are even smaller, and they have masts. The wind pushes them upriver against the current, and they float or row coming back."

"If you say so." Caelus glanced at Lusario, whose slight frown revealed misgivings about the boat like his own.

"I've made this trip to Naucratis to visit Grandfather at least twenty times since I met you. I've never seen a boat get into trouble yet. When will you be back?"

"Three weeks or so. Before we talk with your uncle, we'll show our designs to Zenon. He thought we could figure out the site in half a week to a week, then draw the plans in another week or so since we can divide up the work between us. It's the beauty of the drawings that convinces most people, and we're both good artists. He'll check our plans for the amount of materials to complete the build. Heron did that for Tryon, and Tryon did it for him when he built his first villa. We have to get those numbers right. Enough to make a profit, but not so much that the cost seems too high."

The pilot clapped his hands, and all eyes turned on him. "Take your places."

Fundanus slapped Caelus's shoulder. "See you in three weeks. Uncle should be back a few days after you return, but I'll leave a message at his town house about when you'll be back with the plans, in case he returns early.

As Lusario joined the line of passengers at the gangplank, Caelus responded with a nod and a smile. "Take care of yourself."

"Always. May the gods smile on you and keep you safe."

Caelus strode down the plank and settled onto the bench beside Lusario, where he'd saved the end seat for him.

Fundanus raised a hand in farewell, then crossed his arms and watched their journey begin.

After a wave in response, Caelus turned to Lusario. "I'm still amazed how this all worked out."

Lusario rubbed his lip. "I'd almost lost hope. Who would have thought Fundanus would show up at the last moment with an uncle with a villa to build?"

"Sometimes Fortuna smiles"—Caelus lowered his voice to a near-whisper—"whether you believe in her or not."

Lusario's soft snort was the answer he expected. They were both Stoics, and neither believed the Greek or Roman gods were more than stories created by their ancestors. But when everything fell into place like this had, it was still the right thing to say.

As the oars rose and fell in perfect synchrony, droplets of water dribbled from their tips, sparkling like jewels in the sun. With each lifting of the oars, his nervousness drained away.

In one month's time, they'd be more than architects-in-training. They'd be paid professionals, and the new business he'd promised Father and Grandfather would be a reality.

*Hermopolis Mikra, Canopis branch of the Nile, afternoon of Day 10*

With a handcart following behind him, Lusario worked his way through the stacks of cargo and clusters of people to where Caelus sat on their trunk by the dock where the canal boat left them. He held out his hand, and Caelus passed him the satchel that held their measuring rope.

"The booth where Latro's boats sell passage is back there." With Caelus beside him, Lusario led them back to the booth.

The booth man looked up from writing on a papyrus sheet when Lusario stopped. "We're seeking passage to Vibius Latro's estate near Heracleopolis Magna. He told us to take one of his boats. Is this where we arrange passage?"

The man set down his pen. "It is. What do you need?"

Caelus stepped up to the counter. "A boat that can leave today or tomorrow. We'll need it to stop a few places as we're going upriver and spend several hours to a day at each."

The man crossed his arms and leaned on the counter. "Most of Master Latro's boats are hired now for carrying sacks of grain and the new date crop to the port at Canopis. Some carry passengers, but they would be too big and cost too much for what you propose, anyway. To stop like that, you'll have to hire the entire boat and pay for it to wait for you where you choose to stop. There's only one boat small enough for what you want, and it just went upriver to Heracleopolis. Five days up, four days back, so it will be here in eight or nine days."

Caelus sucked air between his teeth. "We don't have eight days to wait."

"Flavius Constans has two small boats like you want, and you could rent one of them." He scrunched his nose. "But not for tomorrow. One went upriver two days ago, and the other took some Romans downriver this morning and will wait to bring them back. So, the soonest would be four, maybe five days."

Caelus massaged the back of his neck. "Nine days going up and coming back, three to four days for Naucratis, Babylon, and Memphis, figure eight days or so at the estate. We can't add another five to nine days to that and make it back before Latro."

"There are others renting boats here. Perhaps you can find one elsewhere." The man shrugged, picked up his pen, and focused once more on the papyrus.

From the corner of his eye, Lusario saw an Egyptian had stopped to watch them, his head tipped as if to hear all their words. When Lusario focused his gaze on the man, he came over.

"Do you need a boat to go upriver?" He spoke accented Greek.

Caelus turned to face him. "We need transport to Heracleopolis Magna."

"I can help you." The Egyptian's smile was that of a merchant and didn't reach his eyes. "For two hundred and fifty drachmas, it is a five day trip to Thmoinepsi. From there you take a canal boat for the final few miles to the nome capital."

Lusario moved closer to Caelus, but the Egyptian only glanced at him before fixing his gaze on Caelus again.

Lusario moved still closer. "That seems high."

"It's not." The Egyptian crossed his arms. "It is the usual rate for six rowers, pilot, and helmsman with three drachmas for each rower, ten for me and eight for my helmsman. That's thirty six drachmas a day plus fourteen for the boat owner. So, only fifty drachmas a day. But that is the same for one passenger or four. For you two, only twenty-five drachmas apiece, only one hundred and twenty-five drachmas for the trip for one. Truly a bargain."

Caelus leaned toward Lusario. "Perhaps that's not too much. I'm more concerned with time than money." Caelus turned back to the Egyptian. "We will want to pause the journey a few times to look at the ancient temples and tombs. We'll want you to wait for us. What would that cost?"

"Another fifty drachmas for each extra day, as if we were rowing or sailing the river. You will be paying for the boat's time, not the distance traveled."

Caelus rubbed his jaw. "That seems reasonable. I'd like to get to Naucratis today, if possible. We plan to spend tomorrow looking around that area. It is the oldest Greek city in Egypt, so it should be worth the time."

The Egyptian shook his head. "We cannot leave today, but we can leave very early tomorrow. I have to gather my crew. We have just returned to Hermopolis rowing hard to bring some Roman officials down quickly from Memphis, and I told my men they had the rest of the day off."

"As soon as the sun is up tomorrow will do."

"Half an hour after, and my crew will be here. It is only an hour or two to Naucratis."

"So, we'll be spending tomorrow there and continue upriver day after tomorrow. When we get to Babylon, we'll be spending a day at the pyramids and their temples. Another day or two at the tombs and temples by Memphis, then on to Heracleopolis Magna."

The Egyptian's smile was broad, and finally his eyes almost matched it. "To Thmoinepsi. It is the port on the Nile where the canal to the nome capital heads west. My boat is not suited to that canal. But there are many canal boats making that trip. So, five days travel and three days for you to look around…that will be four hundred drachmas." He held out his hand. "You pay me four hundred drachmas now, and you will have the finest trip up the Nile you could ever wish to have."

Lusario cleared his throat, and the Egyptian turned satisfied eyes toward him before raising his eyebrows. "You have a question?"

"We will pay you half in the morning when we board. The other half at journey's end."

The Egyptian straightened as his smile stiffened. "But paying upon arranging passage is what we do on the Nile."

"But it's not what is done in Alexandria. We will have your two hundred drachmas for you tomorrow when we sail."

The Egyptian stared at Lusario, then raised his eyebrows at Caelus.

"Half tomorrow when we board, the rest at journey's end." Caelus offered a polite smile. "We look forward to the trip upriver with you... if you will do as in Alexandria."

"We will do as in Alexandria." The Egyptian shrugged. He pointed toward a boat with a canopy near the rudder post, seats for six rowers, and a mast between the benches and the pilot post at the bow. "I am Temhotep, son of Siamun. We will be there waiting a half hour after dawn."

As Temhotep walked away, Caelus rubbed his jaw. "Since we have to spend the night, maybe we should ask him where we should stay."

Lusario crossed his arms and stared at Temhotep's back. "No. I can't be certain, but I think he is overcharging us. Not by much, but some. There's a better place to ask."

He led Caelus back to the booth where they started. "When Latro spends the night here, where does he stay?"

With his fingertip, the booth man drew a quick map on the counter as he gave them the name of a decent inn that served good food. Plus, they would be able to hire a cart there to bring their trunk back to the dock.

As they followed his directions to the inn with the trunk in the handcart behind them, Caelus furrowed his brow. "Why did you put off paying until tomorrow? You paid ahead for passage in Alexandria."

"No ship captain wants to risk being banned by the harbormaster for stealing from passengers like that, and Fundanus often used that canal boat." Lusario glanced over his shoulder before continuing in Latin. "Until we know a man can be trusted, it's unwise to let him know how much you have and where you carry it. We should put the amount we'll be paying for the boat in one of our purses. Maybe add a few drachmas more so Temhotep won't know how much we're taking with us."

He lowered his voice to a near-whisper. "We're carrying almost two thousand drachmas to cover expenses, and that's enough to tempt even men who are mostly honest."

"I see your point." With his eyebrows lowered, Caelus began scanning the people around them.

"Another thing." Lusario kept his voice low. "Enough Romans live in Alexandria that many speak some Latin. But away from the city, it's Egyptian and Greek. Did you hear any Latin where we hired him?"

"No. It was almost all Greek except for a few words I didn't understand."

"Tomorrow ask Temhotep something easy in Latin and see if he understands. If not, we can speak privately even with the boatmen present. He's Egyptian, and his crew probably is as well. They'll understand at least some Greek, but I don't plan to let any of them know I speak Egyptian. It's safer to know what those serving you think without them knowing you do."

Caelus chuckled. "I'm impressed that you take your bodyguard responsibilities so seriously. That level of caution probably isn't needed, but it won't hurt to be careful."

Lusario massaged his palm. For all his brilliance, Caelus was naïve about how dangerous it could be to trust a man until he proved himself untrustworthy. Then it was too late.

"I'd rather be too careful and not need the caution than to assume all is safe only to discover it isn't."

"So, I have a real bodyguard after all." Caelus slapped Lusario's arm. "Your frown won't make grown men quake like Taurus can, and you're not gladiator-trained. I don't expect you'll ever have to win a knife fight to save me. But I've watched you training at the gymnasium. You'd do well enough to keep us alive if it ever came to that."

Caelus bumped Lusario's shoulder, triggering Lusario's wry smile.

"You jumped off a merchant ship to keep me from drowning. Keeping you alive is the least I can do to repay you, whatever it takes."

"I taught you to swim so I won't have to do that again." Caelus nudged him once more. "And if I ever fell in, you'd return the favor."

"Probably." Lusario's mouth twitched as Caelus chuckled.

It was every slave's duty to protect his master from harm. But Caelus was much more than his master. They'd have to kill him before he'd let anyone hurt his friend.

# Chapter 21

FIRST STOP ON THE JOURNEY

*Naucratis on the Nile, Day 11*

The morning was scarcely half over when Temhotep guided the boat to a berth in Naucratis. While Lusario went ashore to find a handcart, Caelus remained on the boat with the trunk and satchel.

"What do you plan to do here?" Temhotep leaned against the canopy post.

"After we get a room for tonight, we'll look inside some of the public buildings in the city center. Then we'll view some of the villas outside the city."

The pilot settled on the bench beside him. "The estate houses usually are not right on the canals. You will not get close enough to see much."

"We'll rent some horses." Caelus scanned the dock. Lusario was taking longer than he expected to find a cart. "Or mules if we can't find those."

Temhotep crossed his arms. "You will find donkeys mostly, but maybe a few mules. Only the rich ride horses, and they have their own."

"A mule is not as good as a stallion with spirit, but it's good enough when nothing better can be had." Half a block away, Lusario appeared from between two buildings with a man pushing a cart behind him.

Caelus stood. "Where will we be spending tomorrow night?"

"We can reach Terenuthis in the afternoon if we start by an hour after dawn. That is if the toll-takers move the boats through quickly enough."

"Toll-takers?"

"You do not know about the tolls?" Temhotep raised his eyebrows, but from the look of his eyes, was that surprise real or faked?

"Here, Babylon, Memphis—all have garrisons of the Alexandrian Fleet that patrol the river. You have to be inspected and pay tolls many places. For the two of you with your trunk, that will be eight drachmas each." He held out a hand. "But I can pay the toll for you ahead of time today. Then you will not have to wait in line while several merchant ships are inspected ahead of you. That can take half

111

a day." Palm up, he shook his hand slightly. "They will give me a receipt that will let us bypass the slower line of big boats."

Caelus reached into his purse and withdrew three silver tetradrachma coins, each worth six bronze drachmas. "Get the receipt, and we'll be back here by an hour after dawn."

"I will have one of my crew come to take you where the boat is." Temhotep's fingers wrapped around the coins, then opened as he offered his palm again. "Nothing is free on a river patrolled by Romans. There will be a two-drachma fee for beaching the boat overnight."

Two more drachmas dropped into the pilot's palm.

The handcart stopped beside them, and Temhotep removed the ropes that tied the trunk to the deck. "I can take you to an inn my passengers like. Plenty of good wine and food. Pretty serving girls, too." He bounced his eyebrows. "Anything a young man like yourself might want."

"I have the name of one from our last innkeeper."

Temhotep drew his head back. "But what can an innkeeper in Hermopolis know of the best places to stay in Naucratis? He has probably never been here, but I know both cities."

"He assured me it was as good an inn as his own. I prefer to go there."

"As you wish." Temhotep shrugged. "But I do know the good places in the cities I visit often." A trace of resentment colored his voice.

"I'm sure you do, and I'll be asking your advice as we go upriver."

Words meant to soothe Temhotep's irritation produced a stiff smile instead.

Lusario and the handcart man boarded. With one on each end of the trunk, they carried it across the gangplank and deposited it in the cart.

Caelus slung the rope satchel from his shoulder. "Until tomorrow."

Temhotep's tight-lipped smile might as well have been a frown. His eyebrows dipped as he nodded once. "Tomorrow." He pointed downriver. "I will beach the boat down there somewhere, in case you need to find me earlier."

"Very good." Caelus offered a friendly smile, and Temhotep's face relaxed.

When Caelus stepped off the plank, two of the rowers pulled in the first board and laid it on the deck between the rower's seats. When they stowed the second board, they sat and gripped their oars. As Caelus watched with arms crossed, they moved into the current and headed downriver to an area where many boats lined the shore before running the bow aground.

Lusario stood beside him and held out his hand. "He didn't seem pleased with you."

"He wanted us to stay at a friend's inn with women for hire. He didn't like me saying no." Caelus shrugged. "So, do you know where the inn we were told to use is?" He handed the satchel to Lusario.

"I found it first and rented the handcart there. Good locks on the doors, and I got a room on the first floor where the innkeeper can see it from the front counter. He said he keeps an eye on the rooms he can see. He knew of a stable where we can rent mules, too."

"Temhotep thought we'd want an inn with pretty girls for young men to enjoy." One corner of his mouth rose. "We don't need that kind of entertainment on this trip."

"Probably a good place to get your purse lightened or stolen completely. My old Cyrenian master went to those places. He always came home drunk and with too little in his purse. Maybe Temhotep gets a cut if he sends people there."

"He said he knew good inns in all the towns he visits."

Lusario rubbed his jaw. "He might know both good and bad, but we should check any out carefully before we stay at one."

After going about six blocks, Lusario knocked on a door in a courtyard wall. Above it hung a sign, written in Greek, that pronounced it the Inn of Chnoúbis, Great God of the River. A carving of a man with a ram's head stood beside the name.

Caelus pointed at the sign. "Chnoúbis? That's an image of Khnum."

"Greek city, so a Greek name for the Egyptian god." Lusario shifted the satchel. "Alexandria's a Greek city. So is Naucratis. As we go south, I expect more Demotic writing than Greek."

"But you read both, so that won't be a problem." Caelus tapped his arm. "Father had no idea how important that would become when we came here three years ago."

A brawny man who looked Greek opened the door and left one hand on it to keep it from opening too far.

Palm up, Lusario held his hand out to Caelus. "Publilius Martinus has a room here tonight."

A silent nod, and the doorkeeper swung the door wide. They led the handcart man into the courtyard before the door closed behind them.

Several small rooms lined the right wall of the courtyard. More rooms came off the second-floor balcony that encircled it. To the left, a half-wall separated the first room from the brick pavers that lay between several raised beds filled with flowers and food plants. Two date palms provided shade. A larger room with dining tables of different sizes overlooked the garden.

From within his tunic, Lusario withdrew a key hanging on a chain. He unlocked the first room on the right and helped the cart man move their trunk inside.

He set the satchel on the upper bunk. "Let's go rent the mules. Then we'll be certain to have some when we finish looking around the agora and forum. We don't have to be back here at any particular time since the dinner will be stew and fresh bread."

"Just as the innkeeper in Hermopolis described. Bring a couple of tablets in case we see something needing notes so we can make papyrus drawings tonight."

As Lusario got what they would need from the trunk, Caelus glanced across the courtyard. The innkeeper sat at the counter, and he raised a hand to show he was watching. With a lock, the innkeeper, and a guard on the door, it was as secure as the town house in Alexandria.

With the tablets in a small bag slung from his shoulder, Lusario stepped out of the room and locked it. He slipped the key and chain inside his tunic and waited for Caelus to lead the way.

Caelus tapped his friend's arm as he passed and got a broad smile in return. It was an excellent start on this journey toward the career of their dreams.

*Evening of Day 11*

When Caelus and Lusario returned from their ride through the countryside, the innkeeper stood on the balcony above their room, handing a key to an equestrian Roman and his wife. He raised a hand in greeting and descended the stairs to stand beside them.

He placed a hand on his chest. "I'm Hermos, owner of this inn. Did you enjoy your ride?"

"We found it very worthwhile." Caelus's words triggered the innkeeper's friendliest smile.

"What did you see?"

Caelus glanced at Lusario. Such interest from a stranger was unusual.

"We looked at how several estates were laid out. I had read about different ways to build a levee, but it was good to see the real thing and what was planted on them to stabilize the soil. Some of the villas were on high ground that was man-made. But levees still protected them and the workers' cottages. I hadn't thought of making the top of a levee broader and lining it with cottages as if they were along a city street."

Hermos's nod accompanied another broad smile. "Different kinds of levees are everywhere. They control where the Nile waters renew and water the land."

"But that's all very different from the way we do it near home in Carthago. Our lands are watered by rain, so we don't have to plan for the land being flooded."

"But it is the flood that makes Egypt wealthy. The Inundation brings rich new soil and life-giving water to the fields. A gift from the gods that makes life predictable and secure. It is why my inn bears the name of Chnoúbis, the god who guards the source of the Nile. With Hapi as the god of the Inundation, he gives life to all Egypt. He makes children of clay and places them in each mother's womb." He grinned at them. "My fourth child grows inside my wife now."

Caelus mirrored his smile. "Our congratulations on your coming child."

The innkeeper beamed at them both.

Lusario cleared his throat. "You sent us to a good stable. We prefer horses, but it was good they only had mules. I heard one of the men we passed tell his companions we looked ripe for picking. For good horses, they might have jumped us."

Hermos's gaze shifted between Lusario and Caelus, stopping on Caelus before he rubbed his lip. "You look like a man of wealth. Such men know the risks and travel with their own bodyguards. Where will you be staying next?"

Caelus glanced at Lusario and got a shrug in return. Probably no harm in telling him.

"Terenuthis, then Babylon and Memphis. Anyone who goes up the Nile should see the pyramids, but we plan to examine their mortuary temples and tombs for the statues and carvings."

Lusario shifted the bag slung from his shoulder. "You were recommended by the innkeeper in Hermopolis. Several customers had praised your inn to him. Do you have a recommendation of where to stay in any of the cities we'll be visiting?"

"I can't tell you a good inn to use. I've never stayed in any of those cities, and my guests have never spoken of any they recommend." One eye narrowed, then he nodded as if finishing a discussion with himself. "But if you don't mind, I have some advice to keep a man safe when he has no bodyguard to protect him."

A subtle shake of Lusario's head stopped Caelus before he claimed the man who excelled as architect and secretary was his bodyguard as well.

Lusario crossed his arms. "We welcome anything you think would be good for us to know."

Those words drew a quick nod from the innkeeper. "I don't mean to offend with any of my questions. If my own son was traveling like you, I'd want someone to tell him how to stay safe. First, your trunk…are you carrying something of unusual value in it?"

Caelus glanced at Lusario, who nodded his approval. "It wouldn't have much value to anyone else, but it's invaluable to us. We had a dioptra specially made in Alexandria. It lets us measure angles and distances without moving from one spot. That and the measuring rope in the satchel are how we'll lay out the site for a villa we hope to build outside Heracleopolis Magna. They're not worth a lot of money, but they can't be replaced except in Alexandria. We have to be back there in three weeks to convince the owner's wife she can't resist what we've designed."

A knowing nod was Hermos's first response. "Then I will tell you how to keep what you are bringing with you safe. I kept an eye on your room, but most innkeepers wouldn't. Some even have extra keys that will let them enter to see if there is something worth taking. If there is more than one floor, don't stay at street level. A room on the second floor with windows that are high and small—it might be hotter, but it will be safer for both you and your tools."

He rubbed under his jaw. "When you are sleeping, you should block the door so anyone trying to enter will make enough noise that you'll hear the thief before he gets in. You should also sleep with your daggers beneath your pillows."

Caelus glanced at his self-appointed bodyguard and found him nodding as the innkeeper shared his wisdom.

"Babylon is where the Nile meets Trajan's Canal to the port on the Red Sea where ships from India unload their cargo. Too many people only passing through usually means more thieves to take advantage of opportunities.

"So, in Babylon, Memphis, any other town where you plan to leave your trunk while you explore, you should hire a guard. There will be small garrisons of the Alexandrian Fleet at the docks, and that's a good place to ask for where to hire honest guards."

"We can do that." Caelus's glance at Lusario drew a nod. Until they reached the estate, where Latro had said they could ask the steward to give them lodging, his right-hand man would take care of it.

"You stayed with the mules you rented here?"

"We did."

"So, no one had a chance to steal them. You will want to rent donkeys to ride to the tombs and temples. You should hire a man to go with you and watch over the donkeys, or you could end up on foot a long way from the river. Being out after dark is never good, and it could take a long time to get back to the city from some of the sites. You might not get back at all."

He paused, as if he'd said all he intended.

"Thank you for advising us like a father would, Hermos. We'll do as you suggest as we go upriver. When we come back to Alexandria, we'll be stopping in Naucratis again." Caelus offered his most appreciative smile. "I'll be telling the innkeepers to recommend you to all their customers coming here, and we'll definitely be staying with you again."

"Thank you for that, and if you find good inns, I'll look forward to hearing so I can tell guests who ask. Do you know when you'll be back? I can make certain I have a room for you."

"If all goes well, about twenty days."

The innkeeper tipped his head toward the dining room. "I need to check on my diners. Tonight's stew is one of my own favorites." He licked his lips. "You will always be welcome here. If I don't see you again this evening, I wish you a peaceful night's sleep."

"May you have the same, Hermos."

Lusario unlocked and entered their room, and Caelus followed. But he cast a glance at the dining room, where the innkeeper was talking with two older Greek men. He would be more than happy to tell anyone how Hermos, owner of the Inn of Chnoúbis, ran the finest inn in Naucratis and treated guests well.

# Chapter 22

PART OF THE FAMILY

*Stephanos's estate, Day 11*

When Neferu squeezed his shoulder, Jason looked up with eyebrows raised. Then his lips curved into his biggest smile.

"You've done an excellent job of remembering the letters. I only had to remind you of two of them. And you wrote your name so clearly each time. I've never seen anyone do so well at your age." She picked up the wax tablet and closed it with a snap.

"Can I go help with the donkeys now?"

"We'll have some bread and cheese with Menmet, and then I'll take you to Koshari."

She pointed at the trunk holding his stable and animals. "Please lock it and give me the key. I'll watch over them while you're working."

"I'm glad we have our own house." His smile flipped into a frown. "I don't want Karpos breaking anything." He turned the key in the lock and handed it to her.

As she draped the chain around her neck, she gave him an encouraging smile. "Menmet said he almost never comes to the workers' village."

He took the hand she offered, and they strolled next door. Menmet stood by a loom under her canopy, guiding a shuttle between the warp threads.

"Lunch is ready." She waved her hand toward a bench under an olive tree. Two clay plates sat near its center. One held bread. Chunks of cheese and some dried dates were arranged on the other.

She lowered herself onto one end of the bench, picked up the cheese plate, and offered it to Jason first. He took some of each and moved to the far end of the bench. He waited to eat until Neferu had seated herself between them and taken a portion for herself.

Menmet leaned forward to look at Jason. "Koshari stopped by this morning to make sure you would be coming. He said it's good to have such an eager helper."

Jason blushed as he tore off a bite of bread. "I like him."

"I'll be taking Jason over after we eat. It's nice to share lunch with you."

Jason's vigorous nod drew Menmet's smile. "It's nice to have a young one around again."

When they'd eaten everything, Menmet returned to her loom, and Neferu carried the plates into the house. Then she walked along the levee path with Jason bouncing beside her. That drew her smile. Even though he listened carefully and tried hard to do what she asked of him, only donkeys excited that much enthusiasm.

When they reached the donkey corral, no one was there. Jason scurried ahead and entered the storage shed. Muffled voices, one high and one low, reached Neferu's ears. Then man and boy emerged with Koshari's hand resting atop Jason's shoulder.

"Thank you for bringing my helper." Koshari offered a friendly smile. "I'll bring him back to Menmet's when he's through."

Neferu strolled along the edge of the levee, watching the workers in a field that was dry enough to plant. Spaced out across the field, several men and women walked with cloth sacks of seed hanging from their shoulders, dropping grains of wheat as they walked. Soon bright green shoots would appear. Later, taller, darker leaves would look like rippling water when breezes blew across the field. Finally, the green would turn to gold, and the harvesters would cut the stalks of wheat to take to the threshing floors.

Every year in unending cycles, God would bless Egypt with more than enough food to feed her people and plenty of grain to feed Rome.

Her nose twitched. Sasobek would claim it was Khnum and Hapi, the two main gods of the Nile, who made Egypt the envy of the world. But it was God Almighty, the creator of the heavens and the earth, who gave the bounty because of His love for people. All people, not just good ones.

It wasn't in the writings of Markos that she loved to read and copy, but Phoebe had taught her what Jesus said about loving her enemies.

Bless in response to cursing. Do good to those who hate you. Pray for those who persecute you. For God makes the sun to rise on the evil and the good. He makes the rain fall on the just and the unjust. He makes the river flood the land of both good and bad men.

*God, that teaching is too hard. Somehow, it doesn't seem fair.*

She'd prayed for protection from Sasobek, but never for the man himself. She didn't want to see good come to him. The sooner he was no longer priest, the sooner she could go home. If she heard one of the crocodiles that he fed ate him instead of the offering, would she be able to keep from smiling? Even if she could control her mouth, what would her heart do where none could see but God?

And Theodoros? He wasn't her enemy, but he had been Corinna's and he still was Jason's. It was hard not to hate him for his years of cruelty to that precious little boy. How could he have told his father that Jason was dead?

Jason longed to do something that would make his father proud of him. But since he learned Theodoros was so ashamed of him that he pretended he was dead, what could she do to keep Jason from hating the father who despised him?

*God, help me to change my own heart so I can help him with his. I can't do it without the Holy Spirit's help.*

As she approached Menmet's cottage, a man was talking with her neighbor. Menmet nodded several times, then pointed toward her. He approached at full stride.

"Mistress Zenobia said Theodoros's son is to eat with her and her children tonight, and make sure he doesn't smell when he comes."

At last! It was the first step toward making Jason part of the family, and she couldn't stop what started as a smile from turning into a grin.

"When should he be there?"

The man rolled his eyes. "For dinner."

"Of course, but what time is that?"

"An hour before dark."

"I'll have him there. Thank her for the invitation." It was tempting to add "but he'll smell like the donkeys" and see if the invitation would be withdrawn. But Zenobia didn't look like the kind of woman who would appreciate either a joke or too forward an answer from a servant.

Aesop must have some fable about the wisdom of silence when words would be like oil poured on embers. The leaping flames that followed could do worse than singe. They could catch you on fire and kill you. It was a lesson to make certain Jason read soon and took to heart.

When they left the cabin for the walk to the main house, Jason pulled on her hand to get her going faster. But as the house loomed ahead of them, he slowed.

"I don't want to see Karpos again." He stopped moving. "Can we go back?"

"No. Your aunt is eager for you to join the family for dinner, and we already said you would. Besides, you didn't bring anything Karpos could be jealous of, like he was with the beautiful things Voskos and Gaidaros made for you. I expect he'll be quite pleasant at this dinner."

Neferu pasted on an encouraging smile. Whether Zenobia was eager or not—

she had no way of knowing for certain. But she'd probably control her son's behavior even if she wasn't.

"I'm scared of meeting Stephan."

"You shouldn't be. He might be nothing like Karpos. He might be very nice. Don't assume bad things about people until you know them."

When they reached the closed doors to the courtyard, Neferu raised her hand and knocked. The door swung inward, and a young doorkeeper stepped forward to block the way.

"Mistress Zenobia said you weren't to come in. You should go back to the workers' village. You won't be needed until after dinner."

Panic lit Jason's eyes, and his hand slipped into hers. She gave it a quick squeeze. "Then I'll leave him with you to escort him to his aunt."

She bent over to put her eyes level with Jason's. "Enjoy your time with your family. I'll see you later."

With her hands atop his shoulders, she turned him and gave a gentle push. He took several steps forward, but he turned to watch her until the doorkeeper broke their eye contact by closing the door.

For a long moment, she stood on the threshold, resting her hand against the door.

*God, be with Jason this evening. Let his aunt and cousins begin opening their hearts to him to make him truly part of this family.*

With a sigh, she started home to eat with Menmet. In a couple of hours, the dinner would be over, and Jason would be playing with his cousins. Before dark, a servant would escort Jason back to their home. Until then, she'd be praying for Jason to start feeling he belonged here with the cousins who would become his friends.

# Chapter 23

## THE COUSINS



*After dark, Day 11*

The moon had risen nearly full. It sat low above the horizon, casting long shadows as Neferu sat on the bench with Menmet, waiting for Jason to come home.

She'd expected him no later than dusk. He should certainly have been home well before dark. Was he sleeping in the main house that night, and no one had thought to tell her?

Her gaze swept the parts of the levee that she could see from Menmet's house. No servant walked there with a small boy at his side. "He should be here by now. Do you think Zenobia kept him there overnight?"

"Since he hasn't come home, where else would he be?" Menmet patted Neferu's hand where it rested on her thigh. "I wouldn't worry. I'm sure he's fine."

Neferu stood. "With the full moon, there's plenty of light tonight. I'm going to the house to make sure he's still there."

Menmet smiled the knowing smile of a mother. "You do that if it will make you feel better. But watch for snakes. They hunt in the grass on the levees at night."

"I will." She gave Menmet an appreciative smile and started toward the levee.

As she stepped onto the well-worn path, she nibbled her lip. She hadn't been allowed to enter the house when she took him. Would the doorkeeper let her come in so she could go to his room to check on him? If Jason wanted to go back to their cabin, could she take him, or was Zenobia expecting him to eat breakfast with the family as well?

She half expected to meet Jason coming back before she reached the big house. But he still hadn't appeared when she reached the carved courtyard doors.

She knocked and waited. No response. But that wasn't surprising because it was already dark. No one would be expected to arrive without invitation this late.

Three more knocks, harder this time, and still no one appeared.

She was about to knock a third time when the door opened to reveal the youth who told her not to enter the last time.

"I've come to see if Jason is spending the night."

"I don't know." Indifferent eyes accompanied his shrug. "Stephan and Karpos took him out the back door when Mistress Zenobia went upstairs for the evening. I haven't seen him since then."

"Is there another way to his room than up the main stairs?"

"No."

She drew air between her teeth. So, he hadn't gone to his room. But if he wasn't in his room, where was he?

"Which way did they go?"

He pointed to a door at the far end of the courtyard. "Through there to the kitchen."

Without asking permission, she stepped past him and scurried along under the balcony. With Zenobia in her chamber or the women's room off the balcony above her, she'd never be seen.

She pushed the kitchen door open and stepped inside. An older woman glanced over her shoulder as she placed a stack of plates on a shelf.

"Excuse me."

The woman turned to face Neferu. "What?"

"Have you seen Jason?"

The woman squinted at her. "Jason?"

"Master Theodoros's son. He's six. Karpos and Stephan would have been with him as they passed through here. Which way did they go?"

"Come." After a tip of her head toward another door, she led Neferu into an herb garden lush with fennel, coriander, garlic, cumin, and thyme. "I was scraping leftovers onto the waste pile when they came out that door." She pointed in the opposite direction of where Neferu and Jason were living. "The boys went that way."

"Where does that go?" Neferu nibbled her lip. Why would they be taking Jason the wrong way?

"To the levees that divide the fields." The woman shrugged. "The biggest one follows the river but others come off it."

"Did the boys come back yet?"

"Stephan and Karpos did."

"How long were they gone?" Neferu willed her heart rate to slow. Where was Jason if they returned alone?

"Maybe half an hour."

"Thank you." After one deep breath, she strode down the levee path. "Jason!"

No reply.

"Jason!"

She quickened her pace to a trot until she reached the first levee that branched off.

"Jason!" She cupped her ears to catch the faintest response as she stopped to catch her breath.

Which way did they go? It was still getting darker and harder to see. But the dirt on the levee top wasn't soft enough for them to leave tracks, anyway.

*God, please guide me to him. Please don't let him be hurt when I find him.*

Left on the main levee or right on the branch? She closed her eyes and waited.

Then she went left. It felt like the right way to go, like God had shown her the way. Where each new levee branched off, she did the same. The answer kept being the main levee.

By now, the view of any lights at the main house was blocked by the rows of olive trees and date palms along the edge of the still-brown field. But in the distance, a few pinpoints of light revealed where the worker houses were.

"Jason!"

"I'm here." At last, a faint voice answered her call. She turned onto the branch levee from which the high-pitched voice seemed to come.

At last, she reached him. He sat in the dirt, staring across the field.

She squatted beside him. "Are you all right?"

He turned his face toward her. Even in the moonlight, his puffy eyes revealed that he'd been crying. "They said they wanted to walk me home a better way than I came. We went out a different door. I didn't know it was a trick."

He wiped the corner of his eye, and the sniff pricked her heart. "It seemed like we'd walked too far. When I said that, Stephan pulled my tunic over my head and spun me around. He pushed me down, and when I got up and could see again, they were gone. I didn't know which way to go. So, I stayed here."

"That was wise. You made it easier for me to find you." Neferu stood and held out her hand. "I know the way home. Let's go."

Jason took her hand before he stood.

"Why did they do that?" His lip quivered before his jaw clenched.

"Because no one has taught them the right way to treat people." Neferu squeezed his hand. "But they'll probably stop doing that sort of thing if they see it doesn't upset you. They think they did something that would frighten you, but you and I are simply going to walk home. You don't need to be afraid."

"I think they're just mean." He raised his chin. "I'm not scared."

"That's good." She pointed across the fields to the distant cluster of cabins. Tiny points of light flickered where people had lit lamps or small cookfires. "Now that it's dark enough, you can see where we're going. All we have to do is walk along the levees until we get there. So, if they ever do something like this again, you'll know how to get home to me all by yourself, just like a young man would."

She took a step and swung their arms as they walked. After they'd gone a few feet, she pointed at the sky. "It's a beautiful night for a walk with the moon almost full. It's like God put a lamp in the sky so we can see easily for walking home."

"Koshari said Khonsu was god of the moon and protected baby donkeys and lambs from jackals. But we brought the two new babies and their mothers into the corral anyway. Koshari has a dog there that keeps jackals away. I should have asked Khonsu to protect me."

Neferu barely stopped herself from sucking her breath through her teeth. She glanced at the small boy beside her. Jesus told his disciples to let the children come to him because the kingdom of God belonged to them. Corinna had trusted her to care for her most precious treasure, to love him and teach him what a man should know. Nothing was more important than knowing the one true God and what Jesus had done for everyone who believed.

"I worship the God with real power." Palm up, her hand swept the sky. "He created the sun, the moon, the stars." She pointed toward the field beside the levee. "He made the land, the river, the animals. Everything you see around you, alive or not."

"The donkeys?" Jason lifted his head to meet her gaze. "They're my favorite animals."

"Especially the donkeys, and he made each one different and special." She bit her lip. Jason's grandfather would worship the Greek or Egyptian gods or some mix of the two. Would he insist Jason must do the same? Would he send her away because she didn't? Even if he didn't care what she worshiped, would he take Jason from her if she taught the boy the truth?

"But that's not something you should tell your cousins or anyone else here. Not yet anyway. They aren't ready to hear it. It could be dangerous. It will be our secret until I tell you that it's safe to share it."

"I like secrets. Mitéra used to tell me things Patéras shouldn't know. She'd place her finger on my lips and say, 'Our secret.' I always kept those to myself."

"We'll have our secrets, too. You can tell me anything, and if you say it should be our secret, it will be. You can ask me anything you want. I'll always tell you the truth, and I'll do my best to protect you. When it's something only we two should know, I'll say that it's our secret so you know for sure."

He tipped his head back to gaze into her eyes, then nodded.

"Before they played that trick, was the dinner nice?"

Jason shrugged. "I liked the food. Karpos kicked me under the table once, but I wrapped my legs around the chair legs, and he couldn't reach me then. Aunt Zenobia pretended he hadn't done anything. She spoke to me a little, but sometimes she looked at me like Patéras did." He lowered his head. "Stephan seemed nice until he tricked me." When he looked at her again, he lowered his eyebrows. "I won't trust him next time."

"That's wise for now. But I expect things will get better as they get used to you being here." She tousled his hair. "Some boys take more time to welcome someone new. They just need to get to know you first."

He fingered the corner of his bad eye. "If I didn't have this eye, it would be easier." He kicked at the dirt. "I hope Grandfather doesn't…"

His voice trailed off. Neferu would give anything to promise him that it wouldn't matter to Stephanos, but she couldn't. Akhom planned to write about Jason coming, so Stephanos wouldn't blurt out something cruel because he was surprised. But if father was like son, he'd soon say something that would pierce his grandson's heart.

"Kosmos said he was a man who would see all the good things about you once he knows you well. Akhom agreed that he was a wise man." She pulled him against her for a quick side-hug. "Any wise man would be proud to claim you as grandson, so I don't think you should worry before he meets you."

A hopeful smile accompanied Jason's slow nod.

They passed the main house without getting too close and finally reached the spot where the boat that brought them had landed. She stopped. "Which way now?"

Jason pointed toward the distant lights from the cabins. "There, but we go straight down this path a little before it turns back that way."

"Very good! Do you think you can lead us home now?"

Vigorous nods and a smile were his answer. He dropped her hand and started walking. She hurried to reach his side. She'd teach him tomorrow about looking ahead to see any lurking snakes before he took each step after dark. But for tonight, she'd let his confidence grow as he led them home.

*God, please protect Jason from the snakes that crawl on their bellies and those on two feet. Protect me as well. Please show me when and how to tell him more about You, and let him learn to believe in You with the strong faith of a child. Thank You so much that Corinna believed before she died so we can someday be together again.*

With a full moon to light the path and God to guide the way, she would help Jason navigate life in this household with nasty cousins and an aunt who didn't want him there. With God's help, Jason would grow into the strong, brave, kind young man that Corinna had hoped he would be.

# Chapter 24

## A Warning Worth Heeding

*Morning of Day 12*

Sitting beside Jason at the well-worn table in Menmet's cabin, Neferu stirred the wheat porridge that her neighbor had made for their breakfast. Last night was eye-opening about what Jason faced here with his cousins, and she hated what she'd seen.

What could she do about it? Should she tell Akhom what they did? The steward had placed her and Jason with the workers. She'd thought he'd done it because Zenobia didn't want a woman as pretty as she was in the house to tempt her husband. But was part of it to protect Jason from Karpos? From Stephan as well?

Could Akhom do anything to correct the boys, or would that make Zenobia angry? Even if he had the authority, would Zenobia learn it was due to her complaint? Where would that lead?

Jason scraped the last spoonful from his bowl. "I like your porridge, Menmet. It's different from at home."

Menmet patted his shoulder. "Did you want more?"

With a grin, he held out his bowl.

Neferu fingered her hair. The cousins thought their mean trick had left Jason alone and afraid. Before he saw them again, he needed to know what to say to them about it.

"Did you enjoy our walk in the moonlight listening to frog calls?"

"I did. Especially the ones with the low croaks."

"Can you still tell me how I chose which levee was the one we should walk to bring us home?"

"You looked for the light from the lamps and fires, and we went toward it."

"Very good! So, do you think you could walk from where they left you back to our house by yourself now?"

"I think so."

"So, when you eat dinner with them again, you can say how pleasant it was to walk in the moonlight with the frogs singing to each other."

He grinned at her. "Stephan thought he would scare me." Jason wrinkled his nose. "He didn't, and I like walking at night. Can we do that again?"

Menmet raised her eyebrows. After her warning about snakes, it wasn't likely she'd want to stroll with them.

"We can, and I'll teach you how to watch for the snakes that like to hunt mice. Some of them have bites that could make us sick, and it's hard to tell after dark if it's a safe snake or not. So, it's important to watch out for all of them."

Jason nodded as he swallowed a big bite of porridge. "Like some dogs are mean and some are friendly. Voskos told me how some that are nice with people might still like to kill sheep."

"Yes." Neferu drained her cup of water. "It's true of people, too. Some are always mean, some are always nice, and some are nice only part of the time. Right now, Stephan is like the third kind."

She scraped the bowl one last time and licked her spoon. "But a truly good man is nice all of the time, as much as he possibly can be, anyway. You want to be like the good men, not the mean ones. Give Stephan and Karpos time to do the right thing before you get angry with them. And don't be mean like they are. As far as it's up to you, be at peace with everyone."

Jason's smile had vanished. "Voskos and Gaidaros are good men. I want to be like them."

"They are, and that's a fine goal."

The corners of his mouth rose again. "Koshari is a good man, too."

"He certainly is good to you." Neferu stood. "Time to go back to our house. I'll take you to Koshari after lunch. Studies first, then donkeys."

His lips twitched as he glanced sideways at her. "I like donkeys better."

"I think most little boys do, but the more you learn, the more you'll like to study." She ruffled his hair. "Your grandfather will be pleased with how much you've learned before he comes home. You can be proud of how fast you're learning."

His mouth drooped. "Mitéra always said she was proud of me." A tear tricked down his cheek until he wiped it off. "I hope Grandfather will be, too."

Neferu pulled him into a hug. "He should be if he's as wise a man as Akhom says he is. Now, let's go work on your letters. When you know those perfectly, you can start to read. Someone who reads can travel all over the empire without ever leaving his own home."

She led him out the door and headed for their cottage. A steward knew his master well, but he was supposed to speak well of the man, even if he wasn't what he should be.

*God, please let Stephanos see past his eye to the smart, precious boy behind it. Please let Akhom be right that Stephanos is a wise man.*

*Dinnertime of Day 12*

Neferu sat on the bench in front of her house, waiting for Jason. No summons for dinner with Zenobia and her boys had come, so tonight would be filled with tales of new donkeys and food eaten with a friend.

She stood when Jason reached their house with Koshari at his side. The donkey handler's frown was almost a scowl. Was it Jason he was angry with or someone else?

When Jason looked up at him, the scowl flipped to mirror Jason's smile.

"Neferu." Koshari dipped his head before offering a tentative smile.

"Can Koshari eat with us?" Jason's happy voice suggested all was well.

"Not tonight. Menmet only made enough for the three of us. She didn't plan on four, five really because hard-working men need twice as much food as Menmet or I do."

Eating with any unmarried man was not something she wanted to start. As they worked on their looms that afternoon, Menmet told her that Koshari was a widower. His wife had died of a fever after bearing their son a couple of years earlier. The baby didn't live long after his mother died, and his sister was raising his young daughter with her family.

Sasobek had wanted her as a replacement for his own dead wife, and his injured pride when she didn't leap at the chance to marry him might have inspired his attack on her. She had four more years as Jason's bondslave, so she wasn't free to marry anyone or even to leave if a man became so fond of her that she shouldn't stay. She didn't want any man who wasn't a follower of Jesus, anyway, but that was too dangerous to reveal to discourage anyone.

Koshari's ambiguous smile as he gazed at Neferu made her uneasy.

Then he shook his head. "I always eat with the men without wives at the men's lodge, and they expect me." He tousled Jason's hair. "I'll see you tomorrow. Go help Menmet."

When Jason disappeared through Menmet's door, Koshari turned his gaze on Neferu. "I want to talk with you where Jason won't hear."

"Of course." She led him onto the pathway, in the open but out of earshot of anyone. She tilted her head, clasped her hands, and waited.

"Jason told me what Stephan and Karpos did. You did well turning what they meant to hurt him into teaching him how to find his way home alone. But you need to know what can happen when Stephan or Karpos gets angry with someone."

His gaze swept the area around them. "One of the shepherds who was my good friend saw Karpos and Stephan keeping a newborn lamb from drinking from its mother. They didn't stop when Amasis told them to, so he grabbed them by the neck of their tunics and dragged them away. He told them not to come back until they could treat the animals like they should.

"They cursed him and said they were Horion's sons. That they could do whatever they wanted. Then Stephan made a fuss about having his knife stolen. He or Karpos hid it in Amasis's chest in the men's lodge, so my friend got fired."

He massaged his hand. "Zenobia wanted him charged with theft and punished, but Akhom suspected the boys had lied. He recommended only firing, and Master Stephanos listened to Akhom instead of Horion's wife. She took her anger out on the house servants for at least a week."

He pointed at Neferu. "You need to be very careful about getting the boys angry with you. Master Stephanos won't be back for a few weeks, so Zenobia could get her way if she decided she wanted to hurt you. Jason needs to be careful, too."

"I got Karpos angry at me the first day. He tried to break some things that were gifts from a couple of workers who treated Jason like a son. Jason stopped him, and I walked in to find both boys with fists clenched, ready to fight. I told Karpos to go do what he was supposed to instead of bothering Jason, and he said he'd tell his mother."

"He probably did. That's not good."

She tightened her lips. Was that why the doorkeeper told her not to enter?

"Well, what's done can't be undone. I'll do my best to look out for Jason, and I'll tell him to be careful about doing anything that they could twist into a lie to get him sent away. He has nowhere else to go."

Koshari's head drew back. "Couldn't he just go back to his father at the Arsinoe estate?"

She scanned all around them and found no one watching. "Will you promise you won't tell anyone what I'm about to tell you? I'm not sure anyone here knows."

His frown deepened. "I won't do anything to hurt Jason."

Concern for his little helper shone in Koshari's eyes. It should be safe for him to know.

She drew a deep breath and held it. It would be good to have someone else who cared about Jason watching out for him.

"We're here because his father has never wanted him. He would have exposed him because of his eye, but his mother got Master Stephanos to name Jason before Theodoros could have him killed. He wanted nothing to do with a son with a bad eye, and he made sure Jason knew it. He even let people here think Jason had died. When Jason's mother died giving birth to a healthy son six days ago, his father got rid of him by sending him here. Even with Karpos and Stephan being mean to Jason, it's a better place than what used to be his home."

Koshari clenched his teeth. "Jason's a fine boy. Any man should be proud to call him son." He flexed his jaw to relax it. "Anyway, now you know to be careful of Zenobia's boys until Master Stephanos returns."

"And after he returns?"

Koshari shrugged. "Being careful is never a bad idea." He massaged his palm with his thumb again. "Tell Jason I'll see him tomorrow. I have something new to teach him."

He smiled down at her. "I'll see you, too."

Then he turned and headed farther into the workers' village.

She watched him until he stepped between two cabins and vanished.

Her shoulders sagged.

*God, what am I going to do? The cousins like doing cruel things, and their mother backs them in it. She doesn't want me here for fear her husband will want me. Koshari might decide he wants me, too, but I only want a man who follows You. I want to take care of Jason, like I promised Corinna, but what if Zenobia or Stephanos makes that impossible?*

*It feels like I'm a river pilot without rowers or helmsmen, trying to avoid the sandbars and dead trees that hide near the surface before they upset the boat. I don't even have a rod to probe the water ahead or an oar to avoid the dangers I might see. Please keep Jason and me safe until Stephanos gets home. Please make him glad to have Jason here. I don't know what we will do if he tells Jason to leave.*

As God's warm presence surrounded her, the panic drained away. She only needed to see where to place her foot next, not the end of the path. As she walked in faith, God would make clear the way.

# Chapter 25

## Rich Young Roman

*Naucratis, morning of Day 12*

Lusario scraped the last spoonful of rosemary-seasoned porridge from the clay bowl. It was barely past dawn, but a hot breakfast had been ready, as promised. In a sack on the table beside him, a lunch of cheese, bread, and dried dates prepared by Hermos's cook awaited. The trunk stood in the handcart in the courtyard, and in a few moments they would lead the cart man back to the boat that would take them upriver.

In a few hours, they would reach Babylon, and Lusario would ask at the dockside garrison where he could hire an honest guard and find a good inn for two nights.

Hermos strolled over to stand by their table. "Almost ready to leave, I see. I wish you safe travels and abundant success in your business when you get there. I hope to see you in about three weeks. I might be thanking you then for recommending me at your next three inns."

Lusario tipped his head back to smile up at the innkeeper. "I think you will. A wise traveler should always ask for recommendations, and we'll be sure to praise you to the other innkeepers. I especially appreciate your words of wisdom on how to stay safe. I'm all Caelus has as a bodyguard, but no one would think I look like one."

"An unarmed man who watches carefully to avoid trouble is safer than an armed man who walks into danger thinking he can defeat anyone. May you be favored by Tyche with safe travel and great success in whatever business you seek. I expect you will."

Hermos shifted his gaze to Caelus. "But for you, young Roman, I'll say may Fortuna smile on all that lies upriver for you. If you come this way again, remember my inn and return."

"If we get the commission, I hope it will lead to many future occasions for staying here."

The Roman couple entered the dining room.

"You will excuse me, please. Other guests await my service." With a tip of his head, Hermos headed toward them.

Caelus took the payment for breakfast and lunch from his purse and added three more drachmas to the stack of coins. "A much-deserved gift for his helpfulness." He spoke too softly for Hermos to hear.

Hermos raised his hand in farewell as Lusario picked up the food sack and followed Caelus into the courtyard.

With the inn's handcart being pushed behind them, they headed back to the river. When they reached the dock where they'd landed, one of Temhotep's rowers was waiting. He led them along the river to the beached boat.

Temhotep lounged under the canopy, and he flicked his hand toward them without rising. Two of his rowers carried the trunk aboard and tied it to the deck, like before.

Not until Caelus and Lusario boarded and approached the canopy did he rise.

"If you had stayed at the inn I suggested, this might be too early after an enjoyable night. But at least we will leave on time."

"I'm more interested in business than pleasure this trip." Caelus tipped his head back slightly. "Being punctual is always good. I was pleased to see your man waiting for us, as you said he would."

Temhotep's mouth twitched, but he said nothing more as he moved forward to the pilot's post.

The rowers maneuvered them into the middle of the river, then worked their way over to the western side. They bypassed several piers where larger boats were being inspected and pulled up to a small dock where a man in uniform stood.

Temhotep handed a piece of papyrus to the soldier, and they moved back to the center of the river. He gave a hand signal, and two of the crew raised the sail. It billowed out in the wind, and the next leg of their journey south began.

*Terenuthis, late afternoon of Day 12*

As they approached Terenuthis, it stretched along the west bank of the Nile. But on the northern end of the city, two temples of very different style rose ahead of them.

Caelus nudged Lusario as he lounged on the bench. "Striking view with the Egyptian pylons near the river and a temple with Greek columns to the west of it. Tranquilla said she wanted something that blended the best of three cultures. I can picture that as a landscape on a triclinium wall where the dishes served reflect the three cultures as well." He stood. "Temhotep should know something about them."

Caelus strolled past the rower's benches to join Temhotep by the pilot's post. "Those temples—which gods are worshiped there?"

Temhotep gave him a sideways glance before focusing once more on the water ahead of them. "The one nearer the river is for Hathor. The first Ptolemy built it. The other one is for Apollo."

"It's a striking view coming in from the north."

"It is." Temhotep kept his gaze focused on the water a short distance in front of the boat.

"We'll want to visit both after we arrange lodgings for one night. Do you know of a good inn? What I mean by good is a place that a Roman official traveling with his wife would approve."

Temhotep cast him a quick glance before watching the river again. "I have carried rich men upriver before. I will take you where they stayed."

"Anything else here we should see?"

"West of here they mine the natron that is used to make glass throughout the Empire. Much of it goes downriver from this port. There is enough money in it for many to live like a prince. You will see more than mudbrick buildings here."

"I've seen natron. My grandfather had a glass foundry near Carthago. My cousin owns it now. Even selling the raw glass pays well, and the special pieces her glassblowers make...each is a thing of beauty and worth what she charges for it."

Temhotep glanced at him, and a slight frown was his only comment. Then he clapped his hands. "Lower the sail."

The crewmen who'd hoisted the sail hours earlier now lowered it as the others prepared to extend their oars. When all were seated again, the rowers bent to the task.

Caelus had stayed by Temhotep as the boat switched from sail to oars. "I want to speak with someone at the port garrison as soon as we land."

"Why?" Temhotep's word was more challenge than question.

"To find where I can hire an honest guard. We'll be leaving the trunk in the room while we visit the two temples."

"A guard? You will not need that." Temhotep dipped the sounding rod into the water to check its depth.

"The innkeeper in Naucratis said we did. When something can't be replaced this side of Alexandria, only a fool would leave it unguarded."

Temhotep's mouth tightened; then he shrugged. "Then I will take you to the garrison to find your guard. Since you are going to Apollo's temple, there are two Roman baths next to it. I hear you Romans go to one every day, even if you did nothing to make you sweat or get dirty."

"In Alexandria, that's often true. I don't expect that this far into Egypt, but when the opportunity presents itself, we'll gladly take it."

They were a quarter mile from the first dock for large cargo boats when Temhotep pointed toward a stretch of shore where the bows of several boats the same size as his rested on the shore. The helmsman pushed on the rudder. He called out something in Egyptian, and the rowers on one side reversed direction to make a sharp turn.

Caelus bent his knees and braced for the sudden stop that was coming. After the soft swish of the bow sliding across the silty sand, he returned to Lusario, who stood by their bench with the satchel on his shoulder.

Temhotep followed him back to the canopy. As he untied the ropes holding the trunk, he spoke two names. The rowers belonging to them stowed their oars and came to take the handles on the trunk ends.

"The inn you want is not far from here."

Near the bow, the two front rowers angled the planks from the deck to rest on the ground just above the waterline.

Temhotep strode down the gangplank and kept walking.

As the rowers with the trunk followed him, Caelus raised his eyebrows and got a shrug and slight frown as Lusario's response. Then they hurried after the still-walking pilot.

In a few blocks, they reached an open gate into a courtyard that smelled of fresh-baked bread and flowers.

Temhotep pointed toward an obviously Greek man sitting on a bench beside a counter. "The owner of this inn fit for a Roman and his wife. I will take your man to the garrison now. My men will come in the morning to get you and your trunk and bring you to where the boat is."

"The boat is moving?" Caelus raised one eyebrow.

"Maybe. The river patrols sometimes tell smaller boats to move to make room close to the docks for larger ones. But they keep their two drachmas no matter where they put us."

He held out his hand, and Lusario dropped two coins into his palm.

A wry smile raised one side of Temhotep's mouth. "Do not worry yourself about it, young Roman. You bought passage to Thmoinepsi, and I will get you there as expected."

After Lusario paid for their second-floor room, Caelus took the key and led the rowers upstairs. He pointed where he wanted the trunk at the foot of the bunk beds, and they left.

When he returned to the balcony, Temhotep leaned against a column that supported the balcony across the courtyard. When he saw Caelus at the rail, he straightened. "I will take your man to the garrison now. I will send my men for you early tomorrow, so be ready."

Caelus tightened his grip on the railing. It wasn't Temhotep's place to be telling a man who'd hired him when to be ready, even if that was what he'd asked for himself. "Early tomorrow, as I requested. We'll be waiting."

He reentered the room and closed the door. From beneath his tunic, he pulled a chain holding its key, then unlocked the trunk.

A small desk and chair stood by a barred window. After taking a papyrus, pen, and ink from their box, he sat and spread the sheet before him. It was time to sketch the river with the two temples in the near distance as they approach from the north. That scene would be good to paint on a wall where the blending of Egyptian and Greek culture was a theme.

He'd finished the drawing when Lusario appeared in the doorway.

"I have a guard in the courtyard. He'll remain there to watch our door until we return for dinner."

"Excellent." Caelus stood. "A visit to the temples and one of the baths in is order." He lifted the sketch and waited for Lusario's nod of approval. "Before we retire, we can sketch what we might want to propose to Tranquilla for her walls or perhaps a floor mosaic."

He stood, and Lusario drew out his own key to the trunk to relock it.

Caelus handed the room key to Lusario and tapped his upper arm. "These Greek-built temples should prove interesting, but tomorrow we'll see far greater sights that have amazed those who see them for more than two thousand years." He bounced his eyebrows. "Tomorrow we reach Babylon."

# Chapter 26

## BABYLON

*North of Babylon, Day 13*

It was early afternoon when Caelus's arm shot out, pointing at the triangular shapes in the distance. The Great Pyramids! Like the Pharos Lighthouse in Alexandria, they were among the great wonders of the world.

He turned on the bench to face the helmsman. "How far away are they?"

His words were Greek, and the answer was a shrug. So, he rose and worked his way forward, past the rowers to join Temhotep.

Arms crossed, Temhotep leaned against the pilot's post, scanning the river ahead of them. He glanced at Caelus when he reached the bow.

"How far to the pyramids?"

Temhotep turned his gaze on the sail. "With this wind, less than two hours."

"We'll be looking around Babylon during what day remains after we get there, then cross the river tomorrow to visit the *necropolis*. What should we see on the east side of the river?"

As he rubbed his jaw, a slight frown curved Temhotep's mouth. "A squadron of the Alexandrian Fleet is stationed here, based in the legion fortress built under Augustus. He had three legions based here to make sure Egypt obeyed him after he captured our final queen." His mouth twitched. "Cleopatra Thea Philopator. She killed herself so you Romans could not drag her in chains through Rome before you butchered her."

Caelus's head drew back. That was a hundred and fifty years ago. Why should it bother Temhotep now? "She waged war on Rome and lost." He shrugged. "I've never been to Rome myself to see a triumph, but that's what's always been done. Rome isn't the only one that executes defeated enemies. The pharaohs did the same."

Temhotep's eyebrows dipped. "It is not what the winning king does that make the difference. It is how he does it."

He forced a cool smile. "Just north of the fortress, the Canal of the Pharaohs enters the Nile. Trajan repaired it, so it bears his name now. Boats from the gulf ports, where the ships from India bring their cargo, enter the Nile there. They pay customs taxes in Babylon." One corner of his mouth lifted. "There will be tolls and landing fees for you as well. Ten drachmas for the toll, four drachmas for two nights on the shore."

"Lusario will pay you when we get to the inn."

"Does he carry all your money? He always pays, like he is the rich one."

Caelus's eyes started to widen before he stopped them. Why was Temhotep asking that? "He's my secretary. Stewards and secretaries usually do that."

"Some rich men pay themselves." Temhotep shrugged before turning his gaze back on the river.

Caelus returned to the canopy and settled next to Lusario. "Two hours or less to Babylon, depending on the wind." He switched from Greek to Latin. "He's noticed you always pay. He asked if you carried all the money."

Lusario rubbed his mouth. "What did you tell him?" His words were Latin as well.

"Stewards and secretaries usually pay. I didn't tell him who had the money."

"Wise choice." Lusario rested his hand on the hilt of his dagger and shifted on the bench. "It's probably just curiosity, but I don't like the question."

Caelus nodded, then turned his eyes toward the distant pyramids. It was probably only curiosity. Babylon awaited, and a full day exploring the temples and tombs that he'd heard so much about lay ahead of them. He'd enjoyed the trip so far, but tomorrow might be the best day ever.

*Babylon, late afternoon of Day 13*

As the rowers maneuvered the boat past the entrance to Trajan's Canal, Caelus contemplated the long row of boats waiting their turn at the toll stations on the north bank. Near the south shore stood the legion fortress, declaring to all that whatever was once Egypt's was now Rome's. Caelus didn't have to see Temhotep's face to know that fortress inspired a scowl.

Temhotep pointed toward an empty dock, and his crew brought the boat alongside it.

"The inn you want is close to the public buildings on the other side of these warehouses. You will get off here, and we will take the boat upriver a half mile to land it. But the boat cannot stay here long enough for you to get a cart, and you will not find the inn without me." He rubbed his jaw. "If you take your trunk with you here, my boat will be short two rowers while they carry it."

He made his smile friendlier than usual, but his eyes stayed cool. "You could leave your trunk on my boat this afternoon. I can have two of my rowers bring it to the inn this evening and back to the boat in the morning. My men guard the boat when it is beached. They will guard your trunk as well. You do not need to spend the extra money on a guard." His smile turned wry. "Besides, how do you even know you can trust the guards you hire?"

"I trust the optio at a garrison. Besides, I'll be using some things in it as soon as we get in the room."

Temhotep shrugged. "Then follow me to a hotel suitable for a rich Roman with his wife."

Caelus crossed his arms. "And a garrison. We'll be staying for two nights so we'll have all of tomorrow to explore the temples and tombs on the west bank."

"As you wish, young Roman." A sneer started to form, then vanished.

At a break in the warehouses lining the quay, Temhotep led them through a passageway. Where it opened into the street, he pointed at a soldier standing at parade rest. "There is your garrison."

Lusario entered and, after a few moments, returned smiling. "I have two recommendations. Either can provide a guard to be at the inn this afternoon while we look around and to return tomorrow for as long as we need him. So, we can stay as late as we want to look at the pyramids and temples of Khufu, Khafre, and Menkare."

"That should be enough to more than fill a day." Caelus turned to address Temhotep. "We'll want you to take us across the river to the necropolis early tomorrow, so someone who knows where the boat is will need to come find us before we finish breakfast."

Without a word, Temhotep signaled his men and led them further into the city.

When they reached the inn, Temhotep held the door while the rowers followed Caelus and Lusario into the courtyard. The sounds and smells of the street vanished as the door closed, replaced by the gurgle of a fountain and the scent of flowers.

The innkeeper rose from the wicker chair by the door to his office and approached, smiling. When Lusario met him halfway, they strolled together to the desk for payment and the key.

Temhotep moved closer to Caelus. "You could still let us take your trunk back to the boat with my men to guard it while you look around. No extra charge."

Caelus's lips tightened before he thought to stop them. How many times did he have to say no before Temhotep stopped asking? "I prefer to leave it here."

Temhotep's eyes narrowed, as if he took Caelus's refusal as a personal insult.

Lusario rejoined them with a key in his hand. "But we appreciate the offer." Without being asked, he took four drachmas from his purse and handed them to Temhotep. "For the landing fees."

Temhotep took them, then shook his hand, palm up. "The toll will be ten more."

Lusario doled out the extra money.

Temhotep slipped the coins into the purse that hung from his belt. "Since you plan to use something in there"—he nudged the trunk that his rowers had set down—"perhaps it is better to hire a guard for today." He raised his eyebrows and smiled. "But you still could save the cost of a guard tomorrow if we take the trunk with us. I or some of my men will stay on the boat to guard it for you while you look at old buildings."

With arms crossed, Caelus barely kept from rolling his eyes. "The expense of the guard isn't a problem, and the trunk will stay in our room."

As Lusario started up the stairs to unlock their door, a quick flick of Temhotep's hand told his rowers to follow.

When they returned to the courtyard, Lusario handed the key to Caelus. "I'll arrange the guards now."

Temhotep straightened to his full height and raised his chin to look down his nose at Caelus. "I will send one of my men to fetch you as soon as you finish eating breakfast."

He spun and his men fell in beside him. He muttered something to them in Egyptian and left without looking back.

Lusario followed right behind them, and Caelus went to their room.

From the window, the view to the north was dominated by the fortress, but in the distance, the Nile was decorated with the large sails of cargo boats and small sails of boats like their own. It could be the perfect scene to paint on the wall of Latro's tablinum, if he began his day with a salutation, or a smaller office if he didn't. They would ask the steward if Latro needed a formal room for meeting clients, like Father had in Carthago. If there was one thing he'd learned on this trip, it was that Egypt away from Alexandria might be a Roman colony, but Roman rules of society barely applied.

He'd finished a rough drawing of the scene when Lusario appeared beside the desk.

"The guard is below. I told him to sit on the bench and keep his eyes on the door until we return. He'll come back by breakfast time to spend the entire day here tomorrow."

Caelus wiped the tip of his pen on a small rag. "Then let's go explore." He folded the cloth and capped the inkwell. "Did you hear what Temhotep said to his men as they were leaving?"

"I did. He hates the arrogance of rich men, especially young ones."

Caelus held up the drawing, and Lusario nodded his approval. "With how he feels about Rome, that doesn't surprise me. But what he thinks doesn't matter. He doesn't have to like me, just do what I pay him for."

Lusario massaged his hand. "I don't like being at the mercy of someone who dislikes and resents you."

A wry smile accompanied Caelus's shrug. "We're spending less than I thought we might for someone to take us exactly where we want and wait as long as we need them to. We paid him to stop where we say and to get us to Thmoinepsi quickly. As far as I can tell, he's done a good job of taking us upriver."

Lusario replaced pen and ink in their box and returned it to the trunk. "He is finding decent inns and not complaining about waiting while we study the best of what's been done before. But I'm glad we'll only be with him five more days. We'll hire someone else to return. Latro's steward can help with that. Since we can find the inns without help now, it won't matter who takes us."

Caelus handed Lusario the key and tapped his arm. "Let's go see if there's anything here worth sketching. Tomorrow we should take papyrus and ink with us. There should be more to see than we can remember to draw later."

"We'll leave the rope here and pack what we'll need in its satchel." Lusario closed the trunk and locked it. "And a couple of tablets to rest the papyrus on while we draw. We'll need the hard surface."

As they started down the stairs, Caelus glanced at Lusario. No matter what he asked for, his friend anticipated what they'd need and took care of it. Whether they got the commission or not, this trip upriver had been the best time of his life, and a big part of that was having a good man who shared the same dream at his side.

*A taberna near the docks in Babylon, evening of Day 13*

Temhotep and Narmer sat at a gouged and stained table against the back wall of their favorite taberna in Babylon, each with a cup of beer before him. The food was good enough to keep it busy, but it offered other services, too.

The servant girl had been pleasant enough when she took their order for bread and stew, but now she stood by the table where the captain of a large cargo boat and his first mate were eating. With a suggestive smile and flirty eyes, she leaned close enough to brush the captain's arm as she asked if he wanted anything else.

Narmer took a swig of beer, swished it around in his mouth, and swallowed. "Taberna women are drawn to men with money like flies to a honey jar."

Temhotep snorted. "Or flies to a carcass. It doesn't matter how ugly or old they are if they look like they'll pay well for what she's selling."

He cradled his cup in both hands. "They'd be wasting their time with Caelus Martinus. I tried to get him to stay with Seb in Naucratis so his girls could make him some money, and Martinus insisted on a rich-man's inn that a Roman's wife would approve."

Narmer drank another mouthful. "He looks rich, but it's always the Greek who gives you money."

"The money is Martinus's, and he has plenty of it." Temhotep traced the rim of his cup with his middle finger. "Those red stripes...only the richest Romans have that color."

"Neither carries a purse with a lot of coins. I wonder where they keep the rest of it." Narmer drained the last of his beer and raised the cup to ask for a refill. The girl glanced at him, then kept talking to the captain. "Maybe the Greek has a money belt under his tunic."

"It is more likely in that trunk they keep hiring the guards for." Temhotep traced a gouge shaped like the Greek theta. "I told the Roman we could watch it for him tomorrow while he wanders around the west bank. Free of charge, even. He would not even consider it." He wrinkled his nose. "He could not have hired anyone better than me to bring him upriver, but I get no respect from him. No trust at all."

Narmer snorted. "Well, you are charging them twice what it costs to beach for the night. The Greek is the suspicious kind. I half expected him to catch that."

"But most of us do that when we can." Temhotep clenched his jaw. "I am not paid enough for what I do. Neither are you."

With the back of his hand, Narmer wiped some beer off his lips. "You know, that trunk must hold something very valuable for them to keep hiring guards for it." He lowered his voice. "Something more than would be in their money belts. If something were to happen to them, whatever is in it would be ours."

Temhotep scanned the tables around them and quieted his voice to match Narmer's. "What are you suggesting?"

Narmer leaned forward and rested his arms on the table to get close enough to whisper. "Accidents can happen to anyone when they go on a journey." He shrugged. "We wouldn't know where to send what they left behind. So, it could become ours. They'd planned to take one of the Roman-owned boats, so I doubt anyone even knows they sailed with us. But if they ask...we let them off in Thmoinepsi, like they hired us for."

Temhotep massaged the back of his neck. "It would be risky..."

Narmer nudged his arm. "But no reward comes without risk. Would one like him have enough for us to start buying our own boat?"

"Hard to say. We might have to give some to the rowers for them to keep it secret."

With a shrug, Narmer swallowed the beer in his mouth. "They might be content to just start working for us if we pay more than that tight-fisted Greek we work for."

Temhotep picked up his beer. "I need to think about it."

The pretty servant girl picked up a tray holding their dinner and started toward them, directing her teasing smile their way.

Narmer leaned back in his chair. With his hand that rested on the table, he pointed at the girl. "Looks like the captain only wanted dinner, but at least she tried. We only have a few days left to do something, so don't take too long to decide."

# Chapter 27

## A Secret to Keep



*Stephanos's estate, midday of Day 13*

With lunch cleaned up and Jason by her side, Neferu left Menmet at her loom and strolled down the levee toward the donkey stables.

Jason took her hand and swung it. "I like Koshari. He lets me help with almost everything. But he'll be leaving soon."

Neferu nibbled her lip. Was there a lot of turnover in the estate workers? What if Jason couldn't have a close friendship with anyone without the risk of it ending almost as soon as it started?

"We'll miss him. Menmet will, too. He is her nephew. It's hard to leave family like her behind. But maybe his new job won't be far away, and he can visit."

"He's not leaving for good. Part of Grandfather's estate is too far away from the main house, so their donkeys don't come to the stable often. There's someone new who'll be taking care of them, and he's going there to teach them how to do it right. Especially how to make sure the mamas have their babies safely."

Jason's eyes lit with pride. "He didn't need to teach me. I already knew. I told him I could do everything here while he was gone. He said I knew enough to do it, but I needed to keep studying in the morning. One of the gardeners will be at the stable while he's gone, but he said I could stop by to see if Setne needs my help in the afternoon."

"We can certainly walk over to see, but we won't want to make Setne feel like you're checking on whether he does the job well."

"I know. I won't. It could hurt his feelings. Patéras didn't care if he hurt people." His smile dimmed. "He did it to me and Mitéra all the time."

"But he won't be doing it anymore." Neferu wrapped her arm around Jason's shoulders and pulled him close for a quick hug. "I think God has brought us to a good place for you to grow up. A much better place than with your father. God tells us we must treat other people like we want to be treated ourselves. It can be hard to do sometimes, but we should do it even when they do mean things to us."

"Mitéra was never mean." He looked down and kicked a small rock aside before focusing solemn eyes on her face. "Did she believe in your god?"

Neferu's heart missed a beat. How could she explain so that he'd understand? *God, give me the words to lead Jason to you.*

"Yes."

"But she never told me about him."

"Let me tell you why that was." She pushed a lock of hair back from his forehead. "Your mother and I were best friends before she met your father, even though she worshiped the Greek gods like Zeus and Apollo and I worshiped Sobek and some other Egyptian gods. Then her cousin Phoebe came from Alexandria, and your mother introduced me to her. Phoebe was teaching us both about God the Father, Jesus His son, and the Holy Spirit who stays with those who believe in Jesus. We were both excited about what we were learning."

She went down on one knee to put her eyes at his level. "I decided God was the one true god, and I stopped worshiping Sobek or any of the others, Egyptian or Greek. Your mother was almost ready to do that, too. But then she married your father. When she moved to his estate right after they married, your father didn't want her visiting old friends in Arsinoe. Greek men expect their wives to do exactly what they say, and she did her best to do everything he wanted."

Jason stared at the ground as he drew a line in the dust with his sandal. "But she kept me, even though Patéras didn't want her to. When he got mad at her, he'd say horrible things to her about tricking Grandfather into naming me so he couldn't get rid of a worthless baby."

Neferu rested her hands atop his shoulders. "You are *not* worthless. You never were. God formed you in your mother's womb, and you're as valuable in His eyes as every other baby that's ever been born. Your mother loved you. From the moment she saw you, she knew you were a treasure that she'd been given to love and protect. She didn't care that your father only wanted a boy who would grow up to be just like him. She refused to obey him when what he wanted was terribly wrong. Only God deserves our total obedience because He loves us and knows what's best for us."

She stood, wrapped an arm around him, and drew him to her side. "I could see from the moment I met you why she was so proud of you. We've only been together a few days, and I think you're the finest boy I've ever known. Her final wish was for me to look after you and love you like she would, and I'm so glad she asked me to do that. You make it so easy."

He squared his shoulders and raised his head, but a loud sniff revealed he was crying even before he swept a tear from his cheeks.

"I miss Mitéra." His voice quavered.

She wrapped her other arm around him and pulled him closer. "I miss her, too. But remember how she was learning about God before she married your father? She'd stopped thinking about God and what He wanted for her, but He never stopped caring about her. When I came, she had a chance to finish learning what she started, a chance to decide what she wanted to believe, whom she wanted to follow. Before she died, she told me she'd chosen God over all others. She felt Him with her as she was dying, and she's with Him in heaven now. I'll see her there after I die."

"I want to be with Mitéra again. Could I be with her, too?"

"Absolutely. All you have to do is decide to believe in God like your mother and I do. I'll tell you all about Him so you can. But it must stay our secret because it could make me be sent away if Zenobia or Akhom find out."

"I always kept Mitéra's secrets. I can keep yours, too."

She took his hand and started walking. "Good. Koshari is waiting for you now, so we better hurry. But we'll have lots of time to talk about God later."

Jason swung their hands as they strolled down the levee. With each swing, her smile grew.

*Thank You, God, for Jason taking this first step toward following You. Please guide me as I tell him more about You and share the joy of being one of Your children through what Jesus did.*

When they reached the corral, Koshari came out of the stable.

"How is my helper today?" He tousled Jason's hair. "Did you study hard?"

"I did. I tried reading a story Neferu wrote about a donkey, and she said I did well for my first time."

Koshari turned his gaze on Neferu, and a warm smile accompanied it. "I would like to hear that story sometime."

"As soon as Jason can read it all perfectly, he can share it with you."

She kept her smile lukewarm. The last thing she needed was for Koshari to look on her as more than Jason's tutor. He was a nice man, but he worshiped Egyptian gods. That was not what a Christian woman should want. Even if she knew a Christian man who wanted to marry her, everything had to wait until her contract was fulfilled.

*Late afternoon of Day 13*

The sun rested atop the western hills as Jason and Koshari returned home from the donkey sheds. When they neared the break in the brush on the river side of the levee, Jason's arm shot out, pointing at what he'd waited all day to show Koshari. On the edge of the shore, an area of sand had been cleared of any plants. Beside it lay a sleeping monster.

"Look at that crocodile. He looks twice as big as me." He looked up at Koshari's face and found only a smile. Maybe the beast wasn't as big as he'd thought? "Coming here, I thought one might jump up and take me from the boat, but Kosmos said that couldn't happen."

"That's a she." Koshari waved off a fly that had been bothering them. "That clear area beside her, that's her nest. She's guarding her eggs. She might be twice as big as you, but she's still a short one. They get much longer. So, I'd say she's young. That might even be her first clutch of eggs, but she still knows to guard it well."

He dropped to one knee, putting his face at Jason's level. "Whether she's there by the nest or not, you are to stay on top of the levee. She can hide in the water so you'll never see her. If you go down to shore level, she might go after you."

His eyes bored into Jason. "All along the river, the crocs lurk where the water is shallow, waiting for some animal to come for a drink. If Karpos or Stephan try to get you to go to the river's edge anywhere around here and they won't go first, don't go. Understand?"

Jason's eyes widened. "I won't."

Koshari stood and tousled Jason's hair. "Good. I don't want to lose the best helper I've had."

The biggest grin split Jason's face. "I'll be careful."

"Don't let Neferu go down there either." He placed both hands on Jason's shoulders. "You tell her about that mother croc tonight so she won't."

Jason's vigorous nod drew another ruffling of his hair, and they walked the final short distance to Menmet's house.

As they approached, Menmet scooped some cut-up carrots into the stewpot. "I was wondering when you would get here."

"Where's Neferu?" Koshari wrapped an arm around Menmet for a quick squeeze, then stepped back.

She pointed down the path to the main house. "She just went to find Akhom and ask him about something. Did you need to tell her something important?"

"No. It can wait. I'll see her tomorrow when she brings Jason." He lifted the spoon from her hand, dipped it in the stew, and took a sip. "Your stew is as good as I remember."

"I'm still adding to it, so it can't be. But it will be when I'm done." She took the spoon from him and tapped his shoulder. "Maybe I'll ask you to share it with us sometime when I make enough extra for a big man like you."

He turned his gaze toward the main house. "I'd like that." Then he turned away, but he looked back over his shoulder. "See you tomorrow, Jason. You remember what I said about staying on the levee."

Jason kept his eyes on Koshari as he strode away toward the men's lodgings. Jason turned back to Menmet when Koshari disappeared around a corner. "He's nice. I like him."

Menmet added a handful of herbs and stirred the stew again before taking a tiny sip from the spoon. "He likes you, too. We'll eat as soon as Neferu gets back. You could set the bowls out."

Jason flashed her a smile before heading into the house. As he gathered the bowls and spoons and placed them on the table, the smile faded.

He still missed Gaidaros and Voskos every day, but he'd miss Koshari now if they had to leave again. But maybe Neferu was right that her god helped them go somewhere good after Mitéra died and Patéras didn't want him. If he studied hard with Neferu and did everything Akhom thought he should, maybe Grandfather would like him enough to let them stay.

*Morning of Day 14*

Akhom stepped out of his office with a roll of papyrus on his arm. He would get a replacement the next time he went to Thmoinepsi. After stopping by Menmet's house to see how things were going with the new grandson, he had been surprised when the tutor came over and asked him for a roll that she could slice pages from or perhaps a stack from his desk drawer.

When he asked why, she said for Jason's stories. He was not ready for the scroll of Aesop's Fables that Kosmos had sent with her, so she was writing some at his level. She had gone to the main house to ask him yesterday evening and been turned away on Zenobia's orders.

That a boy of six would be reading at all was unusual, so he had Jason show what he could do. The boy had traced under each word with his finger before speaking it aloud, and he read the several-sentence story without error. Either Jason was extraordinarily bright, or Neferu was exceptional as a tutor. Or both.

With his middle finger, Akhom rubbed his lower lip. He had just fired the second of Stephan's tutors because Zenobia complained long and loudly that he was too demanding of her precious son, as the first had been. It was tempting to have Neferu take over, but would a spoiled boy of eleven even listen to a beautiful young woman when a forceful Greek man could not handle him?

He stopped the sigh before it escaped. Zenobia was marching toward him, down-turned lips and an angry squint making her often petulant face even less attractive. It was no wonder Horion traveled with Master Stephanos whenever the opportunity arose.

"Akhom. Surely Horion and his father have been gone long enough to take care of whatever business took them to Alexandria. They could at least send word about when they are returning. Have you heard anything and not told me?"

"Not since last week, and I read you your husband's message saying he hoped all was well with you and your boys. There was nothing about when they would be finished so they could return."

"You could write and ask."

"I already wrote to tell Master Stephanos about Jason's arrival and Menander's birth, and I expect to hear from him any day."

"That boy." Her snort was not as delicate as Akhom would expect from an elite Greek woman. "I invited him to dine with me and my boys. It's appalling that one like him should be a grandson of Stephanos. He acts like a servant with the way he keeps his head down and says almost nothing, but with that eye, I wasn't surprised. It's no wonder Theodoros didn't want him." She thrust her fists onto her hips. "But he shouldn't have foisted him off onto us."

Akhom cleared his throat. Correcting Zenobia required as much tact as he could muster, but after what Kosmos had told him about Jason, he couldn't let those words stand unchallenged. "His eye is cloudy, but that is all that is wrong with the boy." He raised the papyrus roll. "He is already reading simple things his tutor is writing for him. This is for her to write more until he is ready to read what your boy was reading with the latest tutor I need to replace. As fast as he is learning, that will not take long."

Zenobia's scowl deepened at the comparison of her eleven-year-old son to the six-year-old. But what Akhom already saw, Stephanos would probably see as well.

"I expect Master Stephanos will be glad Theodoros sent him here. The boy likes to learn, and he likes to help. Neferu tutors him in the morning, and he helps with the donkeys in the afternoon. Our donkey wrangler says he is as much help any youth would be. He likes the boy, and I expect Master Stephanos will like Jason as much as Koshari does."

Zenobia's eyes widened. "Don't be ridiculous. My Stephan is the finest grandson Stephanos could possibly have. Karpos will be just as impressive when he grows older."

"Boys often grow up to be like their fathers, and Master Stephanos is proud of both his sons. He has not had a chance to get to know Theodoros's son, but I am certain he will enjoy this new grandson as well as he does the two he knows. He will be pleased to have four grandsons instead of two."

He patted the roll of papyrus. "The tutor came to the main house for this yesterday afternoon, but she was not able to find me. I need to get it to her this morning for Jason's lessons. So, if you will excuse me..."

Akhom took a step back as he dipped his head, then turned and strode toward the workers' cabins before Zenobia could say anything. For the most part, Master Stephanos liked Stephan, but he thought Karpos was too much like his mother. From what he had seen of Theodoros's son so far, Jason was almost certain to become the favorite grandson before long.

# Chapter 28

## West Side of the River

*Day 14*

Caelus popped the last bite of hard-boiled egg into his mouth and wiped his lips with the napkin. The dipping sauce was as delicious as any that Father's chef had made in Carthago.

A good night's sleep on a soft bed and a tasty breakfast had him primed for the day's adventure among the tombs and temples.

"Can you believe we're actually here, seeing what Herodotus and even Alexander the Great saw?"

Lusario's bounced eyebrows were answer enough as he ate his last bite of goat cheese.

The inn's cook had prepared a sack of bread, cheese, and dried dates to take with them. It sat on the table beside the large waterskin that the innkeeper had said was essential for anyone exploring the area west of the river.

Temhotep entered and scanned the room before striding to their table. He turned the empty chair at their table to straddle it and sat. "I hope the beds were as soft as in the other inns fit for a Roman wife."

Caelus gave him a subdued smile. "The accommodations were as good as you said they would be."

Temhotep flashed a smile, but a challenge lurked in his eyes. "I told you I knew good inns on the river."

"You did, and you've found us some." Caelus tipped his head back and finished his drink. "We want a full day in the necropolis, so let's get going."

Temhotep reached across the table to pick up the roll that remained half eaten on Caelus's plate. He took a bite of the rosemary-laced honey whole wheat roll and smacked his lips.

"So, this is what the rich eat for breakfast."

Lusario slid his chair back. "I'll get the satchel."

Temhotep stood. "If you want, I can bring the boat up to a dock. You could take your trunk." He turned the chair back the way it was. "In case you need to get to something from it later." He waved his hand toward the guard, who already sat on a bench watching their door. "You can save the cost of the guard, too."

Caelus's mouth twitched as he scooped up the food sack and handed the waterskin to Lusario. How many times did he have to say no before it registered on this man?

"I've already paid for him. The trunk and the guard will stay."

Temhotep shrugged. "As you wish, young Roman. Then I will take you to the boat."

As soon as Lusario returned from the room with the satchel of papyrus, pens, and tablets, Temhotep strode toward the outer door.

Caelus raised his eyebrows at Lusario. Tightened lips and a shrug were the reply.

Temhotep was perseverant, if nothing else, when it came to pushing what he thought they should do. But as long as he took them where they wanted to go and reached Thmoinepsi when they'd been promised, what an Egyptian pilot thought didn't matter.

*West bank of the Nile across from Babylon*

After the boat worked its way across the river, yielding to the large cargo vessels sailing upstream, the swish of a boat keel sliding onto sand was music in Caelus's ears. Ahead lay the temples of the pharaohs who built the greatest pyramids of all, the ones that travelers from all over the empire came to see.

Their valley temples had been on the ancient banks of the Nile before floods and time moved the main riverbed. The mortuary temples at the base of the pyramids had seen centuries of offerings to the men that Egyptians worshiped as embodiments of their gods.

But no matter what thoughts the temples inspired in others, the relief carvings and painted walls would be inspiration for their own future designs.

Caelus left the canopy and walked past the rowers to reach Temhotep at the bow. "So…" His hand swept several men, each with a few donkeys, lounging under the palms near the shore. "Which do you recommend?"

Temhotep's frown accompanied a shrug. "I know the river and the towns along it, not the donkey men."

"Haven't you brought others to view the great pyramids?" Caelus matched frown with frown. "You know good inns where someone touring the Nile would want to stay. Why not this?"

"Others hired guides in the city to show them around. Donkeys to carry the Romans and rich Greeks are part of that." Temhotep's half-smile spoke a silent challenge. "But you know enough you aren't hiring guides, so you can find your own donkeys."

Lusario stepped up behind Caelus. "It won't be a problem. We can find someone good ourselves. We'll tell you who, and in the future, you'll have someone to recommend." Lusario's mouth curved into a wry smile. "Or warn against. Not everyone who offers a service is worth the money you pay him."

Temhotep's eyes narrowed. "You could not have hired a better boat to come upriver."

Caelus raised his hands to calm their pilot. "I agree that you've done a fine job of providing what we need. We'll be recommending the inns to others."

The tensed shoulders of the pilot relaxed. "I told you I knew the river towns. It is good you see that now." He waved his hand toward the donkey men. "Go explore, young Roman. We will be waiting when you return."

Lusario stepped aside to let Temhotep past as the pilot headed toward the canopy. A short jump put them on the shore. Lusario started toward the donkey men, but Caelus looked back before following. Temhotep and the helmsman sat on the bench, watching him with crossed arms.

He'd be recommending the inns Temhotep had chosen, but never the man himself.

Temhotep stood by the pilot's post, arms crossed, watching the Greek talk to first one, then another donkey man. When he reached the third, waving arms and pointing turned into money changing hands. The three mounted and rode toward the valley temple of Khufu.

Narmer came up beside him and nudged his shoulder. "Walk with me."

When they'd strolled far enough that the rowers couldn't hear their words, Narmer stopped.

"I can't believe he said that. He's as arrogant as older men who've maybe done something to justify their pride."

Temhotep glanced at the now-distant pair. "He's a Roman. They can't help themselves."

"That's no excuse. First, he refused to pay full passage until the end of the trip, as if you didn't know how to get him to Thmoinepsi. Now he accuses you of not knowing your business because you couldn't recommend a donkey man."

Narmer nudged Temhotep's shoulder. "Why are you holding back when what's in that trunk could make us owners of a boat, not just hired workers of a rich Greek? Without lifting a finger, he takes more than you or I work hard for, just because he's the owner. We might never get so good an opportunity again."

Temhotep scrunched his nose. "We don't really know whether there's a lot of money in the trunk. What if we kill them only to find there's not much there?"

Narmer snorted. "Two young men like them? They spend money like there's no limit to it. The inns you've taken them to—a single night costs as much as five or ten nights where we would stay. Those guards—they make as much as you or I do just sitting there watching a door. The stripes on the Roman's tunic—only the richest ones have that color. Have you seen money belts on either of them?"

"Well, no…" Temhotep drew a line in the sand with his sandal, then erased it.

"So where are they keeping it?" A fly that had followed them landed on Narmer's chest. One slap, and its carcass fell to the sand. "What will it take to prove they can spend that way because there's a lot of money in that trunk? Money that could be ours."

With the back of his hand, Temhotep rubbed his lips. "If we could just get a look inside to be sure…"

Narmer tapped Temhotep's shoulder. "I think I can open that lock if they leave even for a few minutes. Then we'll know."

Temhotep's slow nod triggered his helmsman's smile. "But first we have to get them to leave the trunk on the boat."

Three men stood with a group of ten donkeys in the shade of a cluster of palms, and Lusario had a choice. What with the cost of rich-men's rooms, guards, tolls, and fees to beach the boat, they'd already spent almost twice as much as he'd expected when they left Alexandria. Would he get a better price if he spoke Greek or Egyptian as he negotiated for three donkeys and a guide?

Enough elite Romans came to see the pyramids that they might know what Caelus's red stripes meant and charge higher prices. But when he'd been with Timon in the Egyptian quarter of Alexandria buying clothes or food for the widows, his friend always bargained in Egyptian to get a better deal. The rich-looking tunics their masters gave them didn't seem to affect the cost.

"Wait here until I call you." He left Caelus staring at the largest pyramid and strode toward the group.

When he approached the donkey men, all turned toward him wearing friendly merchant smiles. Three sets of eyebrows shot up when one man addressed Lusario in Greek and received an Egyptian reply.

One only had two donkeys. The one who spoke to him first had five and would only go with them if they rented all of them. But the third man had three and was eager to accompany them for an extra drachma beyond them hiring his three donkeys at four drachmas each.

He raised his hand to summon Caelus.

"I'm Lusario. What's your name?"

"Inyotef, son of Hebny."

"We're builders, and we're here to look at the valley and mortuary temples near the greatest pyramids of all Egypt. We especially want to see those that have the best relief sculptures on their walls. Can you guide us to those?"

"I can, with pleasure. We will start with the valley temple of the great Khufu." He pointed at the temple near the river that was connected by a causeway to the Great Pyramid.

"This is Caelus Martinus." Lusario held out his hand, palm up, when Caelus reached them. Switching to Greek, he continued. "This is Inyotef, son of Hebny. He knows these buildings well, and he'll be showing us the best reliefs in the temples here."

With a slight tip of his head, Caelus offered a friendly smile. "I look forward to that, Inyotef. Lusario and I work together to design buildings, and we hope to learn much from what we'll see here. We'd like to see as much as possible while taking time to look closely at the best work."

Inyotef motioned toward his animals. "Then let us go. Six temples wait for us."

He mounted and started his donkey walking with a slap to its rump. Lusario and Caelus did the same, and they headed toward the northernmost temple in the complex, the valley temple of Khufu.

◆

The sun was high in the sky when Caelus led Lusario out of the mortuary temple of Kaufre and back to the donkeys. "The valley and mortuary temples of Khufu, the mortuary temple of his son Kaufre—I'm not sure what I like best." He patted the satchel that hung from Lusario's shoulder. "The drawings we've made so far should be invaluable for what we'll propose to Latro. But it's time to eat."

Lusario untied the lunch sack and waterskin from his donkey's saddle. "They packed an ample lunch."

Caelus turned to their guide. "Inyotef, come join us."

With eyebrows raised, their guide touched his chest. "You want to share with me?"

"Of course. We couldn't be doing this without your help. And whatever is left when we return to the boat, you should keep for your family."

Lusario took the bread, cheese, and dried dates from the sack and spread them out on it. The three men sat and ate half. When all had eaten their fill, he returned the rest to the sack.

Inyotef stood and dusted the sand off his tunic. "Now we go to the mortuary temple of Menkaure, Khufu's grandson." One corner of his mouth lifted. "But first I want to show you something."

He led them back toward Khufu's pyramid, but he rode past it to a tomb built of stone with slightly sloping walls. It was larger than most of the mastabas, and the usual plain brick single-room chapel for the offerings for the spirit of the dead man was missing. Instead, a doorway in the stone wall opened into a tomb chapel.

"This mastaba belonged to Hemyunu, vizier to Khufu himself." Inyotef took a small torch from a sack tied to his donkey and lit it. "Enter the offering room at the back. I will stay with the donkeys."

Torch in hand, Caelus entered the first chamber. The dust on the floor appeared undisturbed, as if no one had passed through for some time. Through the doorway across from the entrance, what waited in the darkness?

Both gasped as they stepped through the second door and the flickering light played on the walls of the offering room. The smooth stone was covered with images so vivid they looked like they were just painted instead of being more than a thousand years old. Scenes of life of the ordinary people planting, harvesting, tending cattle, weaving, making bread and beer spread out before them.

Caelus looked over his shoulder at his partner. "Let's start sketching."

Lusario knelt by the satchel and took out papyrus, pens, ink, and the tablets to support the papyrus as they drew. One went left, the other right, working their way around the room, making quick sketches of as many scenes as they could before they ran out of papyrus sheets.

Lusario capped and stowed the ink vials and pens before carrying the still-drying drawings into the outer chamber.

When he finished, they stood shoulder to shoulder, gazing at the walls until the final flickers of the torch faded away and the room was swallowed once more by darkness.

After carefully stacking the papyrus sheets and placing them in the satchel, they stepped into the blazing sunlight.

A chuckling Inyotef met them. "The look on your faces…it reminds me of my son the first time I took him to see what travelers are seldom shown."

Caelus rested his hand on Inyotef's shoulder. "Thank you for sharing something so special with us."

"It is my pleasure." Inyotef gestured toward their donkeys. "Now we go to the mortuary temple of Menkaure, the great Khufu's grandson. There is still much more for me to show you."

In the next few hours, Inyotef took them to the mortuary temple of Menkaure, then his valley temple and that of his daughter Khentkaus, and finished their tour by the great sphinx and the valley temple of Kaufre.

When they reached the cluster of palms where they began and dismounted, Caelus tapped Lusario's arm. "Twenty-six drachmas."

When Lusario dropped the coins into his outstretched palm, Caelus wrapped his fingers around them and led his donkey over to Inyotef.

"For the best tour we could ever hope to have."

He held out his fist, and Inyotef placed his hand beneath it. When the coins fell on their guide's palm, a huge smile lit his eyes.

"Thank you, Caelus. If you come again, I will have more to show you that not everyone sees."

"I'll look forward to that, and I'll be telling anyone I know who's coming here to ask for you."

Lusario slung the satchel on his shoulder and handed the food sack to Inyotef. Then they headed toward the boat.

Temhotep and the helmsman sat on the canopy bench, but Temhotep returned to the bow before they boarded.

"Did you see all you wanted?" Temhotep leaned against the pilot post, arms crossed.

"There's still more to see, but for the time we had to spend here, I'm very satisfied." Caelus tapped the satchel hanging from Lusario's shoulder. "We used all the papyrus we brought."

"Perhaps you should have brought your trunk. Your man could have come back here for more."

Caelus's jaw clenched, but he said nothing. Temhotep's impertinence was best ignored. "Lusario found us an excellent man to provide the donkeys. Inyotef showed us even more than we'd hoped to see. He did such a good job that I paid him twice what he asked and consider it a great bargain. You can definitely recommend him."

The smile on Temhotep's lips didn't extend to his eyes. "Thank you for telling me. I will remember."

When Caelus joined Lusario on the canopy bench, the rowers shoved off and began the trip back to Babylon.

Lusario patted the satchel. "A good day today."

Caelus nudged his shoulder. "No, a great day. We're halfway there, and after what we learned today, we can easily make unique designs that are sure to please Latro's wife. That commission will almost certainly be ours."

# Chapter 29

## MEMPHIS

*Memphis, Day 15*

With a mix of smooth-faced and step pyramids arrayed to the west, the great city of Memphis loomed on the western bank of the Nile.

Lusario's gaze was locked on the nearby pyramids when Caelus's hand shot out, pointing downriver.

"Just look at it. Memphis. Capital of Egypt for thousands of years." Caelus grinned like a child with a new toy.

Lusario returned a smile. "With what's left of today and all of tomorrow, we should find plenty for inspiration."

Caelus intertwined his fingers on the back of his head and arched his back. "It was only when Alexandria became the Ptolemies' capital that it became less than the greatest city in all Egypt." Caelus nudged Lusario as they sat under the canopy. "Manetho wrote how Menes first united Upper and Lower Egypt and built dikes to protect this new capital from the flood. Herodotus wrote how the Persians during his visit took great pains to maintain the dams to keep the city safe. You can see how the Nile channel has been drifting eastward, and the city is on the west bank with the tombs now instead of the east bank like Babylon. I would never have expected a major river channel to move that much."

"Being on the same side of the river as the necropolis is good." Lusario chose Latin for his next words. "Temhotep won't have to wait with the boat for us. That must be boring. Maybe he'll be in a better mood after a day to do whatever he feels like."

Caelus rolled his eyes before his Latin reply. "But I'll still be a rich Roman to him, and he hates those. So, I'm not expecting anything to change."

With a hand signal from their pilot, the men who both rowed and handled the sail lowered the yard and roped the fabric in place. With oars extended, the crew aimed for the shore and eased the bow onto the sand. While two men positioned the gangplank, Temhotep joined them and untied the trunk.

"You will like the inn for Romans here. I have heard the cook is as good as what rich men have. But I suppose you are used to the finest food at banquets."

Caelus's glance at Lusario barely stopped short of another eye-roll. "I'm more interested in seeing the temples in the town and the buildings near the pyramids of Djoser and Snefru. We'll be spending two nights here to do that. So, you and your crew will have a free day."

"No day is free. It is the same fifty drachmas whether we are on the river or waiting for you."

Lusario stood, drawing Temhotep's gaze to himself before Caelus irritated the pilot more than usual. "He meant a day to do whatever you want, not a day we wouldn't pay for."

Temhotep's lips tightened. "I knew what he meant. Narmer." He summoned the helmsman with a curl of his fingers and tapped a rower's shoulder as he passed. They picked up the trunk and waited. Lusario shouldered the satchel and followed Temhotep and Caelus down the gangplank.

◆

When they reached the docks where several large boats were taking on cargo, Caelus scanned the area. A soldier at parade rest stood by an open door, and he pointed toward it.

"They made it easy to find the garrison."

Lusario shifted the satchel on his shoulder. "I'll ask about getting a guard while we're here."

At Caelus's nod, he strode toward the doorway and disappeared in the dim interior. Temhotep signaled his men to set the trunk down and crossed his arms. With resentful eyes, he watched Caelus without speaking.

It took only a few moments until Lusario came out, followed by a man wearing a large dagger. But for Caelus, the time with Temhotep staring at him crept like a snail on the wall of the atrium pool at home.

"This is Demetrios. He'll stay until after we eat and return before breakfast tomorrow."

In silence, Temhotep escorted them the remaining few blocks to the inn. While Lusario paid, he waited, tapping his foot.

"Second floor, third door." Lusario pointed at their room, and the men carried the trunk up the stairs. "The innkeeper told me where to rent mules here. It's several miles to the two pyramids of Snefru and the step pyramid that Imhotep built for Djoser."

Temhotep snorted. "For you, young Roman, maybe they will rent a fine stallion."

Caelus offered a cool smile. "A mule will do fine. Three mules and a man to watch them, like Inyotef did."

The tight-lipped smile the pilot returned was just as genuine. "If he pleases you the same, you can pay him double, too."

Lusario took a step toward them. "Inyotef was exceptional. I doubt another would be worth double like him."

The pilot looked at the helmsman and spoke softly in Egyptian.

When Lusario tensed beside him, Caelus glanced at his friend. What was wrong?

"The day after tomorrow, someone will come for you early." Temhotep signaled his men to leave, but before he followed them, his mouth curved into a half-sneering smile. "Enjoy your old buildings, young Roman. They may be your last. Most do not find much to see between here and Thmoinepsi."

When Temhotep strolled through the door and headed back toward the river, Caelus rubbed his jaw. "What did he say?"

Lusario's gaze had followed Temhotep. "I might be willing. Let's talk."

"Willing to do what?"

A shrug was Lusario's answer. "Maybe they're going to see a friend or find a taberna with more than food. They travel the river often enough to know what's here. I just didn't like how he said it."

"Well, whatever he's doing doesn't matter as long as he's ready to go when we are. I expect he will be. He's a decent pilot, despite his attitude."

Caelus slapped Lusario's arm. "Let's get the papyri and tablets. The Temple of Ptah awaits. Herodotus said the large alabaster sphynx by the south wall and the row of Ramesses's statues at the west entrance are extraordinary."

As they climbed the stairs, the guard settled onto a bench in the courtyard.

A wry smile curved Caelus's lips. At least this time Temhotep hadn't insisted he'd do as good a job as a paid guard and do it for free. It was worth a few drachmas to know their dioptra, drawings, notes, and money would remain safe while they were gone.

As they started back to the river, Temhotep took some coins from his purse and held them out to the rower. "Have the crew eat at the usual taberna but leave at least two with the boat while the others eat."

As the coins fell into his hand, the rower grinned. "Yes, captain."

When the rower was out of earshot, Narmer rested his hand on Temhotep's shoulder. "I feel like something better than that."

"The stew at The Ibis is good. We can talk there, too."

A block from the docks, they entered the taberna and settled in at a table by the back wall.

Temhotep signaled the serving girl, and she came for their order. "Two beers, two stews with bread."

As soon as the girl moved away, Narmer crossed his arms and leaned on the table. "So, how shall we do it?"

"I said I might be willing but only if we can be sure they have enough to get a boat of our own." Temhotep traced some Greek letters that were carved into the wine-stained wood. "We are only guessing about what is in that trunk. Is it a lot of money or something of great value only to a few people? Something that would be too hard to sell to get what it is worth. Maybe it is something so one-of-a-kind that trying to sell it would make people ask what happened to the one who owned it."

The serving girl brought their beers and headed back to the counter to serve a new arrival.

Narmer took a sip. "Not bad." He traced the rim of the cup. "Anyone who would recognize anything as the Roman's would live near Alexandria. That's far enough that I wouldn't expect any problem like that. But if you're too worried, we can sell it upriver in a nome capital. Or in Memphis on the way back down."

Temhotep swirled his own cup. "If we could just look in the trunk, then we would know."

Narmer opened his mouth to speak, then waited until the girl set their bowls and bread before them and left. "I only need a few moments with most locks to get one open. If it had a lock that's too hard to break into, he wouldn't be hiring a guard."

Temhotep tore off a piece of bread and dipped it in the stew. "So, we need a short stop where they get off and go far enough away for long enough that you could open the lock." He popped the morsel into his mouth. "That should not be hard to find."

Narmer pulled his bowl closer and inhaled its savory aroma. "And a place where the river traffic is light enough no one will see us become the new owners." He picked up his cup. "There should be many chances for that after we're south of Aphroditopolis."

Temhotep traced the letters again. "But first I need to be sure this will get us a boat of our own."

"If you get them to leave the boat long enough, I can get us into the trunk." Narmer took a swig of beer and wiped his mouth with his arm. "If I'm going to kill someone, I want to be sure it's worth doing, too."

# Chapter 30

## LESS THAN HONEST



*Necropolis at Memphis, morning of Day 16*

Behind Caelus, the sun rose above the massive pylons that formed the western entrance to the temple of Ptah. With the eight giant statues of Ramesses II arrayed on either side and a walkway lined with fourteen alabaster sphinxes leading up to it, they could hardly have found a more dramatic scene for a wall in Latro's future villa.

But today might yield even better. Senbi had brought the mules even before they finished their early breakfast, and it promised to be a day filled with architectural wonders and magnificent reliefs both inside and outside the buildings.

Senbi rode a short distance ahead of Caelus, but a swat to the mule's rump brought Caelus up beside him.

"So, do you know of anything unusual to show us? Something most people don't see?"

A smile accompanied Senbi's shrug. "I know almost nothing about the necropolis. The guides who show their visitors around hire our mules, and I only go along to care for them. You are the first I've taken who know how to guide themselves."

So, Senbi would be no Inyotef, but last night Caelus and Lusario had planned enough to see to make it a day to remember.

"We do have a lot we want to see. The Serapeum and its chapels, Djoser's step pyramid, and both the bent pyramid and red pyramid of Snefru with their mortuary and valley temples."

Sembi's eyebrows shot up. "That is a lot. Many split that into two days. But you said you only have one, so we will be riding maybe twenty miles today and trotting between your stops."

Caelus patted his mule's neck. "We're both horsemen, so set whatever pace you think we need to see everything."

Senbi urged his mule into a trot. Caelus dropped back beside Lusario, and they did the same. Near the end of the alley of human-headed sphinxes approaching the Serapeum from Memphis, Senbi slowed to a walk.

"Whatever you want to look at, tell me, and we will stop."

Caelus moved closer to Lusario so his words could be heard. "We already saw the embalming house for the Apis bulls near the temple of Ptah. Seeing the living animal…I don't care if we do or not. But there might be some different reliefs in the chapels and temples near the catacombs for the bull mummies."

The satchel, positioned against Lusario's back before they mounted, had shifted sideways as they trotted along the road. He repositioned it so it wouldn't bounce against the mule when a slap on the rear made it trot again. "We should probably look at the bull. When one dies, they choose the replacement to have the same pattern of black and white. So, we better make a sketch of one in case an Egyptian hires us who cares if we get that right." He reached back and patted the leather bag. "I brought plenty of papyrus sheets for us to sketch anything that looks useful. But we should buy more before we leave Memphis."

"Senbi."

Their mule guard turned and raised his eyebrows.

"We'd like to see the Apis bull and look in some of the chapels and smaller temples near the bull catacombs. Then we can move on to the pyramid of Djoser."

"Then follow me."

As Caelus urged his mule back into a trot behind Senbi, he glanced at Lusario riding beside him. It was good to have a partner in this great adventure. Whether they got the commission or not, their first trip up the Nile would be one to remember.

With arms crossed and legs spread, Lusario stared at the Step Pyramid of Djoser. "Manetho called Imhotep the 'inventor of the art of building with hewn stone.' No wonder Zenon in that first lecture said he was one of the greatest architects of all time. To be the first one to design a stone-faced tomb, to be declared Master Sculptor by Pharaoh Djoser while you live and be considered the god of medicine and healing two thousand years after your death…could a man ask for more of a legacy?"

One corner of his mouth curved. "Well, maybe not the god part. But in Egypt he's made equal to Asklepios, and people ask him for healing. It's no wonder the Ptolemies built a temple to Asklepios on the western edge of Memphis where visitors can see what Imhotep built. Did you see how many were there when we rode by this morning? Greeks and Egyptians."

Caelus rubbed his jaw. "But when someone is sick or dying, people cling to any hope they can. My grandfather always said that the wise man knows death is coming for everyone, and the Stoic faces it with courage and dignity. He resigns himself to it, even welcomes it when it comes, expecting it to be the end of him. It's like the chorus says in Seneca's *Trojan Woman*, 'There is nothing after death; and death is nothing—only the finishing post of life's short race.'"

Lusario glanced at Caelus, then turned his eyes back on the pyramid. It had been several months since his friend's grandfather died, but a trace of sadness colored Caelus's voice whenever he spoke of him.

Nothing after death—neither suffering nor reward. No hoped-for reunion in an afterlife. That finality of the separation was what he believed himself.

He tightened his lips to keep a wry smile from appearing. It would make Caelus ask him what was funny, but he wasn't laughing at what Caelus just shared. It was only the contrast between them and Timon.

His closest friend believed that he'd live forever with his god and his Christian friends. Was that only wishful thinking? He claimed Jesus proved the truth of it by rising from the dead. But was that a fact or a delusion embraced by those who didn't want to face the nothingness?

"The priests at the Asklepieions around the empire might believe what they do works. Or maybe it's just a way to get money out of desperate people. But I'll only believe a god can heal when I see it with my own eyes."

Caelus's amused snort was his first answer. "You and me both."

Caelus flexed his jaw to relax the muscles he'd tensed too many times since reaching Snefru's Bent Pyramid. The party of Romans who were preparing to leave as they arrived were the cause of it.

No, Temhotep was the cause. The Romans had merely told him the truth about what it cost to travel on the Nile. It wasn't their fault that the pilot who claimed to be the best on the river had been less than honest from the moment they met him.

The boat landing fee was one drachma, not two. The only places they had to pay tolls were Naucratis and Babylon. What else had the lying snake of a pilot overcharged them for?

It wasn't the amount of money. A few extra drachmas here and there were of no significance…except for the lies that had made him pay them.

He scowled at Lusario, even though he wasn't mad at him. "Temhotep thinks he put one over on us. Well, he'll soon find out he didn't. I'm going to demand a refund of everything he said we owed in fees that went into his own purse instead."

Lusario held up his hands, palms out. "Perhaps that's not the wisest thing to do. We only have two more nights on the river before Thmoinepsi. A few drachmas aren't worth the risk of making our pilot angry enough to do something worse than overcharge a little. It's never a good idea to anger a dishonest man that you still have to rely on to get to your destination." He rested one hand on Caelus's upper arm. "All together, it's less than fifty drachmas. He has found us good inns and done whatever else we asked of him."

Caelus drew a deep breath and held it before releasing it. "He has, but it galls me to be cheated that way. Father wouldn't put up with it if he found out someone was lying to him like that." The fire faded from his eyes. "But you're right about not saying anything until we're through needing his services."

Lusario lowered his hand. "At least we know what to ask a captain who might be taking us back to Alexandria. If he lies like Temhotep, we'll know to pick another boat."

"Grandfather always said that experience teaches a man how to avoid trouble, but it's getting in trouble that gives him experience." A wry smile leaked out. "But I don't think I'll tell Father how gullible I was."

"How gullible we were." Lusario looked away, then turned his gaze back on Caelus. "I should have caught what he was doing. That's part of my job as your secretary."

Caelus slapped his friend's arm. "You couldn't have done a better job of making this trip go smoothly for us."

He tipped his head toward Snefru's pyramid where the angle of its walls changed halfway up because they started out too steep. "It's embarrassing to be cheated, but it's nothing compared to what Snefru's architect must have felt when he knew everyone who ever looked at his work would see where he had to correct a mistake."

"But there's a lesson in that." Lusario traced the distant angle change with his finger. "Admitting and fixing a mistake can still make something that will stand for more than two thousand years." Palm up, he swung his hand toward the Red Pyramid with its walls rising at the angle that worked. "And he never made that mistake again."

Caelus nudged Lusario's shoulder. "I suppose I'll let the overcharging pass… for now. I still might ask for that refund in Thmoinepsi after we have our trunk on a cart we've hired and we won't be getting on his boat again."

"It will be safe to do it then, and I'll be there to back you up." Lusario pointed at the mortuary temple at the base of the Red Pyramid. "Let's go look before it's time to start back. You never know what's waiting until you get there."

Caelus fingered his lip. What did lie ahead? No man could know for certain until he got there. But Lusario would watch his back, no matter what.

# Chapter 31

## HARD QUESTIONS



*Stephanos's estate, late morning of Day 16*

Neferu held out her hand, and Jason gave her the papyrus. "You did a fine job today reading this first story about a donkey. Tomorrow, I'll have a new one about a sheep. Menmet's father was a shepherd, and she helped him as a girl. She said she has lots of stories you should enjoy."

She opened the box Akhom had provided and placed the sheet atop the half-written story. She'd have plenty of time to finish it and start another while Jason helped at the stable.

A pall of sadness spread across Jason's face. "I wish Mitéra was here so I could read her your stories."

"She would have loved that. She was so proud of you, and I can see why."

Contempt replaced sadness in his eyes. "Karpos is two years older than me, and he doesn't even know the letters."

Neferu stopped short of drawing a breath through her teeth. Jason's sweet countenance had changed so he looked less like Corinna and more like his father.

"Most Greek boys don't get to start learning until they're ten. I expect he'll learn fast enough then." She tousled his hair. "God tells us that envy and pride are two things we should set aside if we're His followers. Holding onto anger when someone does something mean to us is another. Being glad when something bad happens to them—that's wrong, too. We're called to forgive those who hurt us, even when it's hard. At least we're supposed to try our best to do it. God Himself will help us when we ask Him."

"I never heard anyone talk about a god like you do."

"Would you like me to tell you something about the God I follow? The God who gave your mother joy and peace when she decided to follow Him, too?"

Jason's eyes stayed fixed on her as he nodded.

"There are dozens of gods who are worshiped by the Egyptians, Greeks, and Romans. I'm sure you've already heard some of the stories about them. But those stories are only made-up tales. They didn't really happen, and those gods are just something people made up many, many years ago to try to explain why things are the way they are."

She sat in the chair to get to his eye level and took his hands in hers. "I worship the one God who's real. He came to earth as Jesus of Nazareth, and he opened the way for anyone who believes he's the Son of God to be with him in heaven forever after we die. To know him and feel him close while we're living. Jesus especially loves little children because they open their hearts and minds to believe in him best. He told his followers to encourage them to come to him whenever they wanted to."

Jason's eyebrows rose. "All children?"

"All children."

He touched the corner of his milky eye. "Even me?"

"Especially you. Your brother, too."

"I wish Patéras had let me stay with Menander. Mitéra said he'd be so lucky to have me as his brother." He wiped away a tear before it could trickle down his cheek. "She said he'd love me like she did."

She pushed a stray lock of hair back from his forehead. "I'm sure he would. You're easy to love. I know I do."

Jason lowered his face and watched his foot as he traced a circle with his sandal. "I'm glad he didn't die when Mitéra did. The midwife said he was dying. But you took him and then he didn't die." His eyebrows dipped. "Why didn't you tell her what you did?"

"I didn't do anything. I only asked God to not let him die, and He healed Menander."

He drew another circle before raising his eyes to her again. "Did you ask him for Mitéra, too?"

It was the question she'd dreaded. Why did God let anything bad happen to His people? God could work all things for good for those who love Him. But how could she ever explain to a little boy how his mother's death could bring good? She couldn't be sure herself that it would. So much hung on the choices his grandfather would make, and Stephanos wouldn't be asking God for guidance.

"I did."

"But she died. Why didn't he heal her, too?" The next tear was too fast, and it was halfway down his cheek before he caught it.

"I don't know. But did you see how happy she was as she died? She was joining Jesus where no one is ever sick and no one ever dies. She's with Him now, and someday when I die, we'll be together again."

"Can I go with you?" Jason bit his lip. "I don't want to be alone."

Her hands cradled his face. "God doesn't want you to be alone either. He wants you to know Him and love Him and be with Him forever. That starts here and now when we believe in Jesus, God's son. He came from heaven to show us how much God loves us, to teach us how we can love Him back."

Jason wrinkled his nose. "How can I love someone I can't see?"

"Do you love Gaidaros and Voskos?"

"Yes."

"Why?"

"Because they were good to me."

"They loved you, too."

"I know."

"Do they still love you, even though they can't see you now?"

"I think so." He looked away and shrugged.

"I know so."

"But they remember seeing me. How can anyone love someone they've never met?" His lips tightened before he slowly shook his head.

"My cousin's wife loved each of her children while they were still growing inside her. She hadn't seen them yet but she would have done anything to protect them. She already loved her babies with her whole heart before she heard their first cry."

"Did your cousin love them, too?"

"Men don't often say the words, but I know he did. His eyes lit up with love when he held each newborn child."

Jason pulled one hand free. "Maybe Patéras loved me before I was born. He didn't after he saw me. I heard Mitéra tell Kosmos one time that Patéras was so happy when she first told him I was coming, but that changed when he saw my eye." His lip quivered. "I tried to do everything I could think of to get him to like me, but I wasn't good enough."

She rested her palm on his cheek. "But God loves you, and He wants you to love Him back. His love is bigger and better than even a mother's love. He loves me so much that there's nothing I could do that would make Him love me more."

"You can't see him, so how do you know he loves you?"

"Jesus, God's own son, came to earth as a man to tell us about His love and to open the way for us to know Him and love Him. When I pray, I'm talking with Him." She placed her hand over her heart. "I can't see Him with my eyes, but I feel Him here with me." She patted her chest. "I know He loves me then, and I know He loves you."

Jason lowered his chin and stared at her feet. She waited for the next question until the silence became uncomfortable.

*God, please open his heart to hear and feel the truth of what I'm telling him. Guide my answers to be exactly what he needs to hear to come to You.*

She rose and moved her chair back by the wall. "Later, we can talk about this more. Menmet will have lunch ready for us. After we eat, do you want me to walk you to the stables and come get you before dinner since Koshari won't be bringing you home?"

Jason closed his tablet and lined up the stylus with the top edge. "No. I can get there and back by myself. And I'll stay on top of the levee, like Koshari told me. He reminds me each time we walk past the croc nest." Jason's smile came quicker than it had when they first arrived at the estate. "I always do what he tells me. And what you tell me. I won't say anything to hurt Setne's feelings, even if I do know more than him."

"Good. I'll be doing what Menmet tells me this afternoon. She's going to teach me what are the weeds in our garden and how to use the narrow, pointed hoe to dig them out without hurting the good plants. I never had a garden before, so I have much to learn, too."

She waved her hand toward the door, and he went out ahead of her. But before he reached the bench where Menmet waited with their lunch, he looked over his shoulder with a grin. "Next time he walks me home, I can read him your first donkey story. He said he never met someone who could write stories before, and he wants to hear them all. And maybe he can stay and eat with us."

"If Menmet makes enough for five, perhaps he can."

As Jason walked ahead of her, Neferu's shoulders slumped.

*God, please don't let Koshari start thinking of me as anything more than Jason's tutor.*

She nibbled her lip. Perhaps it was too late to ask for that.

*But if he has, please make him stop before he asks for more than I can ever give.*

# Chapter 32

## What Will Grandfather Think?

*Afternoon of Day 16*

Jason had milked the goat and put some of the warm, white liquid in a wide, shallow bucket. Koshari said that was the best way to feed an orphan donkey after it was two weeks old. Little Mikro had trotted over to greet him when he hung the bucket on the special wooden hook that Koshari had carved. It held the bucket at the height of the baby's head.

He scratched under the baby's chin. Gaidaros had told him almost every donkey loved that, and Mikro was no exception.

"Drink up, little one. I'll be back after I brush some of the others."

With a milk ring encircling his muzzle, Mikro lifted his head to look into Jason's eyes, then dropped it to lap at the milk again.

He'd just started brushing the first donkey when a chorus of excited braying startled him. Why were the mares with the new babies raising such a fuss?

When he came around the corner and could see the corrals, Karpos stood by Mikro's bucket, tugging on the little donkey's ear each time he tried to reach into the bucket for some milk.

Setne stood with his back to Karpos, his eyes scanning the fields as if nothing was going on behind him. Why wasn't he telling Karpos to stop?

Jason set down the brush and started toward Karpos. "Don't pull his ear. They don't like that. And let him finish his milk."

Karpos tugged on the ear again, as if he hadn't heard, then turned to face Jason with a sneer.

"It's not your donkey, and I'll do whatever I want to it." Karpos took the bucket off the hook and tossed the milk in the baby's face.

Jason marched over to him and snatched the bucket out of Karpos's hands. "He's Grandfather's donkey, and you have no right to be mean to any of Grandfather's animals."

Karpos wrinkled his nose. "You have no right to tell me what I can't do.

Mother says you don't belong here, acting like you're part of our family when Theodoros let everyone think you were dead. He wanted to put you out for the dogs or for someone to make a slave." Another sneer curled his lip. "You're nothing compared to us, and you'd better learn your place. Grandfather will be as disgusted by you as your father is, and you'll be lucky if he lets you stay here to take care of donkeys like a slave."

He slapped the side of Jason's head and shoved him to the ground. Then he bent over to pick up a rock and threw it at the tiny donkey, hitting it on the side of its head.

Gaidaros had warned Jason about terrified baby donkeys turning into statues instead of running from a predator, how their mothers would stand and fight a hyena or a dog pack until their baby came out of it and started to run.

Mikro stood frozen, eyes staring, milk still dripping from his chin.

With a bloodcurdling yell, Jason launched himself at Karpos, knocking him to the ground. He straddled the shocked cousin and dropped his butt onto the ample belly, pinning Karpos's arms against his sides. He hauled back his fist and rained blows on the screaming face.

He yelled a single word with each hit. "You...will...never...ever...hurt...my...donkeys...again."

Screams turned to blubbering words. "Stop! Stop! I won't hurt him again."

Jason had pulled back his arm for a final blow when Setne grabbed him under his armpits and dragged him off a writhing Karpos.

Setne tossed him to the side, but Jason got his feet under him before his body hit the ground. He landed in a crouch, like his wrestling friends at the old estate, and rose with his fists clenched.

Setne stepped between him and Karpos. "You!" Setne thrust a pointed finger into his chest. "Behave yourself and leave the young master alone."

Jason lowered his fists and backed away. He rubbed his knuckles as he stared at Setne. Karpos was totally in the wrong. Why didn't Setne see that? How could he take the side of anyone who deliberately hurt a baby donkey?

His jaw dropped when Setne glared at him before the gardener held out his hand to Karpos to help him to his feet. "Are you all right, Karpos?"

Karpos wiped his nose and screamed when he saw the blood. His hand shot out, his finger trembling as he pointed at Jason. "He tried to kill me!"

Jason's lips tightened. "Not this time, but don't you ever try to hurt Mikro again." Jason pointed toward the main house. "Go home and stay home."

With blood still dripping from his nostrils, Karpos stretched to his full height. "I'm going to tell my mother you attacked me."

As he'd seen the farm hands do with an unworthy opponent, Jason spat to the side. "Go ahead. When Grandfather gets home, I'll tell him what you were doing and how I stopped you. He'll be glad I defended his donkey. Now go away and don't come back."

Karpos spun and ran toward the main house.

Setne covered his mouth with both hands. "He's going to tell her I didn't keep you from hurting her spoiled brat." He glared at Jason. "What were you thinking? You just got us both in deep trouble with Mistress Zenobia. I could lose my place at the estate because of what you did."

Jason raised his chin and met glare with glare. "I promised Koshari I'd watch over the donkeys. When you didn't, I had to. Mitéra told me a good man keeps his word."

An eye-roll ended in a shake of Setne's head. "A smart man keeps his hands to himself and his mouth shut when Stephan or Karpos wants to do something. You'd better chose smart over good if you want to live here."

Jason's eyes filled with tears. "I only wanted to protect Mikro."

"Well, you didn't. Now he'll come back with Stephan and do something much worse to him."

Only one tear escaped, and Jason swept it away so quickly that maybe Setne didn't see. "Then I'll take him and the goat home with me. Neferu will help me protect him until he's big enough to protect himself."

"You think that will stop Karpos?" Setne rolled his eyes again. "You're Master Stephanos's grandson, so I can't stop you. But Koshari can't blame me for what happens if you do that. You tell him I warned you…if you're still here when he gets back."

Jason's chin quivered. Would he still be here when Koshari came home? Could his aunt send him away before he even met Grandfather?

He clamped his jaw and squared his shoulders. "I belong here as much as Karpos does, and I will save Mikro from him any way I can."

He stood by the corral wall and held out his hand. With a few soft clucks, he called to Mikro. The frozen donkey shivered, then came to him. He stroked under the foal's chin. When he opened the gate, the baby came out and leaned against him. He wrapped an arm around Mikro's neck. "Everything will be all right. I'll take care of you."

He turned to face Setne. "Will you help me get Mikro and the goat and the bucket home?"

Setne's gaze shifted to the main house in the distance. "You can make two trips. I want no part of this."

Jason's sigh was deep. Would Grandfather think he'd done the right thing or not?

He got a rope from the shed and tied it around the goat's neck before picking up the bucket.

"Mikro." He slapped his thigh twice, and Mikro trotted over to Jason as if his own mitéra had called.

"I might not come tomorrow. Mikro will need me to take care of him at our house."

With head high and his donkey friend beside him, Jason started home.

Mitéra always said a good man was brave in the face of danger and always tried to do what was right. No matter what Grandfather might think, what he had done, what he was doing now—both were right.

Zenobia stormed into Akhom's office and slapped the desk with her palm. The steward jerked back in his chair as his eyes widened.

"Do you know what that worthless son of Theodoros just did?"

Akhom set down his pen and crossed his arms. "It is afternoon, so he should be helping Setne at the stables while Koshari is training the new handler at the rented fields north of here. There are some mares with new foals there, and he trusts Jason to know what care they might need. The boy is a hard worker, and he knows much more about donkeys than the gardener who is filling in until Koshari returns."

Zenobia huffed. "Karpos just came from there covered in blood after that little monster tried to kill him."

"Tried to kill him?" Akhom's lowered eyebrows bespoke unbelief, not the anger the boy's attempt on Karpos's life deserved.

"Yes. Karpos's face was still bleeding when he ran home to me. His tunic was covered in blood, and his nose might be broken. He has red patches and swelling by both eyes. Jason tried to blind him."

"What did he say happened?"

"Theodoros's boy was trying to tell him what to do, so Karpos slapped his head and shoved him to the ground for such disrespect. Then Jason charged into him, knocked him to the ground, and kept punching his face until Setne pulled him off and made him stop hurting my son."

She rammed her fists onto her hips. "It's no wonder Theodoros sent that one-eyed beast here to get rid of him. But he had no right to make his problem our problem. Send that little monster back to his father *right now*."

With shoulders squared, she tipped her head to look down her nose at the steward. With Stephanos gone, she was head of this household. Whatever she wanted was what Akhom should do, and he should do it as quickly as possible.

Akhom rubbed the underside of his jaw as his too-calm eyes stayed focused on her without him uttering a word.

"Say something. When are you going to send Jason back to his father?"

He rested his forearms on the desk and clasped his hands. "Karpos has now learned a valuable lesson with no real harm to him. Picking a fight, even with someone smaller and weaker, could leave him knifed and dying at the feet of an enemy he had created by his own actions. Master Stephanos wants grandsons who command the respect of others, as he does himself, not bullies who throw their weight around to get their own way. Tell Karpos he is to stay away from the donkey stables until Master Stephanos returns."

He picked up the pen he'd set down when she entered. "He will have black eyes tomorrow, but those will fade in a couple of weeks. A bloody nose does not mean it is broken, but even if it is, that will heal, too. If you do not want to talk with him about not starting fights, send him to me, and I will."

Zenobia stared at the steward as he turned his attention back to the papyrus before him. Then, head high, she made a graceful turn and left the office.

Her too-fast breathing slowed, but as her composure returned, a horrible thought raised her heart rate again.

Akhom took the one-eyed brat's side and blamed her son for the fight. Would Stephanos do the same? Would Theodoros's son worm his way into his grandfather's affection like he had with the steward? Might he look on the new boy more favorably than either of her own sons?

Her jaw clenched. Jason could not be here when Stephanos returned. If Akhom wouldn't do anything to get rid of her sons' rival for Stephanos's affection and riches, she'd have to do it herself.

# Chapter 33

## BETTER LEFT UNSAID?



*Memphis, morning of Day 17*

With arms crossed, Lusario watched the helmsman and rower lower their trunk onto the deck. He'd made a wise choice in letting none of them know he spoke Egyptian. Whatever Temhotep said about them when he and Caelus weren't with them, it had tainted what the crew thought.

"I'll be glad to be rid of these two." The rower drew the back of his hand across his forehead, and it came away wet. "I'm tired of hauling this trunk back and forth to some rich-man's inn. What's in it that it's so heavy, anyway?"

"That's a good question." The helmsman went down on one knee to thread the rope through the first of several metal rings that were used to secure the trunk just ahead of the canopy. "We've never had two as young as these who wander off by themselves to look at old buildings and pharaohs' temples without a body-guard. But they hire a guard whenever they leave their trunk at an inn, as if it holds a treasure—that seems strange, too."

"Maybe it does." The rower shrugged. "But both of them wear daggers all the time, so they're probably safe enough."

A snort was the helmsman's first reply. "It's not the weapons that make a warrior, and a woman working the streets would be more dangerous than these two. Any robber can tell a weapon worn to use from one worn for show."

The rower's grin ended their conversation. The rower seated himself on his bench, and the helmsman slipped past the canopy to his steering oar.

Caelus boarded with Temhotep right behind him. But this time the pilot didn't go straight to the front of the boat.

With a friendly smile on his lips, Temhotep rubbed his jaw. "We passed something any builder should not miss, and it is only a little way downriver. The white limestone for many of the buildings you have been seeing came from the quarries at Troia. They have been used since Khufu built his Great Pyramid, and they still quarry there."

Caelus looked at Lusario and raised his eyebrows. Lusario's nod earned a grin in return.

"That sounds worth going back for. How far back are they?"

"Troia is not far. Less than halfway to Babylon." Temhotep leaned against the canopy pole. "It will be extra work for my men because they will have to row against the wind, but for you they will be willing to do it for only a little extra. A hemidrachma per man…only three drachmas for something few who travel the river stop to see."

One corner of his mouth lifted. "But for men who have seen the Temple of Ptah and the pyramids of Snefru and Khufu…what are three drachmas to see where their white limestone came from?"

Caelus glanced at Lusario "It's worth it. We didn't have time to stop coming upriver and still see all we wanted around Memphis, but we can spare a couple of hours now."

Lusario took three drachmas from his purse. "I trust you to get the proper coins to divide it among your rowers."

Temhotep's outstretched hand accompanied a fleeting smile. "Of course."

After taking the coins, he moved to the pilot's post and gave the command to shove off.

As they moved into the river's flow, the waterdrops dribbling off the synchronized oars glistened in the sunlight. With both oars and current driving it forward, the boat reached a speed Lusario had never seen when the wind drove them south.

He'd marveled at the size of the limestone blocks forming the pyramids and temples. Nothing he and Caelus would design would ever reach that scale, but there was no better place to learn how to transport and position stone slabs than from the men who carved up a mountain to create what builders would use.

*Troia, morning of Day 17*

As the Roman and his man disappeared into the quarry, Temhotep strolled back to Narmer, who already knelt by the lock.

With his foot, Temhotep nudged the trunk. "They might not stay long, so open it quickly."

He scooped up the satchel and set it on the bench. After unwrapping the two cords that secured the flap to a pair of small brass cleats, he flipped the flap back, exposing the contents.

He pulled a rope out and stared at what remained in the satchel.

Nothing. The satchel the Greek watched over so carefully held nothing but rope.

He felt for any hidden compartments or secret pouches. He found none.

After a few wraps of each cord around the small cleats, he set it back in the same place.

Narmer cursed softly under his breath. "It should open. I can feel the tumblers in it, but I can't get them to move. It's either too new or too old for me to get enough pressure on them."

"Maybe too old. The name on the brass plate…it looks too long to be how the Greek introduces him." Temhotep licked his lips. "There is nothing but a rope in the satchel, so everything must be in the trunk. The chains around both the Roman's and the Greek's neck hold a key. That will get us in."

Narmer stood. "So, somewhere this side of Thmoinepsi we should find the right spot. I'll make the first move, then you take care of the second one." He tapped Temhotep's arm. "Before you know it, we'll have a boat of our own."

*Peme, evening of Day 17*

The boat was still under sail as it approached the town of Peme. Lusario nudged Caelus and pointed toward the group of smaller pyramids. "Anything we want to see here?"

Caelus scanned the area, then shook his head. "These are Twelfth Dynasty—Amenemhat I moved the capital here from Thebes, but it's not likely we'd see much that's different from what we sketched already. So, let's just spend the night and move on. I'd expect more Greek influence in Aphroditopolis, and I'd rather see what's there."

When the rowers maneuvered the bow of the boat onto the shore, Temhotep strolled back to the canopy. "Not many stop in Peme, so there is no inn fit for a Roman lady. But I know an inn with decent food that is at least clean enough for one. But there is no garrison or guards for hire here, so you will have to guard your trunk yourself." He held out his hand. "Two drachmas for the landing fee."

"So Peme isn't an important port town?"

Lusario glanced at Caelus. There was too much edge on his friend's voice.

One corner of Temhotep's mouth lifted. "Peme is not an important town in any way I know. Only the local people ship their goods through here."

Caelus's eyes narrowed. "Why is a town with few port facilities charging the same landing fee as cities like Babylon and Memphis?"

Lusario rubbed the side of his nose. He'd warned Caelus about making an issue of the small overcharge before they were off this boat for good.

Temhotep's eyes narrowed, then relaxed as he faked a smile. "That is something you can ask the provincial governor when you get back to Alexandria. It does not seem fair, but what Rome requires, we have to do."

Caelus opened his mouth, but Lusario's nudge made him close it before speaking.

"Even Romans get tired paying of fees and taxes." Lusario's smile was just as fake, but perhaps Temhotep wouldn't notice. "Roman citizens can't even pass on what they own to their children without paying a tax on the estate. At least you won't have to do that."

A loud snort was Temhotep's first reply. "This boat belongs to another, and I make ten drachmas a day only when I am on the river. Men like me have no estate for Rome to tax. When a rich Roman dies, he has so much he can afford to give Rome its share."

He spun on his heel and tromped down the gangplank to the shore.

With two rowers carrying the trunk behind them, Caelus and Lusario followed. The pilot led them to a small mudbrick inn. It was nothing like what Temhotep usually found them. But the entryway had lockable gates, and the rear of the inn had a second floor.

Lusario rented a second-floor room, and Temhotep left without speaking as soon as his rowers carried the trunk up to it.

Caelus stared after him. "I assume he'll send them back at breakfast time."

"He will. He'll want the extra money from tomorrow's landing fees and maybe a toll charge where there isn't one." Lusario rubbed the underside of his jaw. "But it would be better not to make a point of that until we unload in Thmoinepsi."

Caelus rolled his eyes. "I know you said it was foolish to say anything yet, but it galls me to let him think he's getting away with cheating us."

"What matters most is getting where we need to be on schedule."

They climbed the stairs to find a small room with a bunk bed and a small table and chair by a barred window.

Caelus lifted a corner of the lower blanket and shook it. No billow of dust appeared. "At least it's been cleaned recently."

Lusario set down the satchel by the trunk. "We're on the second floor, the door locks, and the inn prepares food so we won't have to leave the courtyard where we can keep an eye on the stairs. All in all, not bad for a town like this."

"I can see the river from here." Caelus moved from the window and sat on the lower bunk. "It was fascinating how the quarries were partly underground with portions left unquarried to support the cavern roof. We need to sketch what we saw of the exposed quarry walls and the underground chambers. Either might be an interesting backdrop to a garden scene."

Lusario knelt by the trunk to get out pens and papyrus. But as he pulled the key from beneath his tunic, his hand froze. Around the keyhole, there were scratches in the brass that weren't there that morning. A quick survey of the satchel where it leaned against trunk revealed the cords had been wrapped around the cleats in the direction opposite of how he always did it.

Someone had looked in the satchel and tried to look in the trunk. Should he tell Caelus or not? Would Caelus be able to keep from challenging Temhotep over who tried to get at whatever was inside?

If he were a betting man, he'd bet against it. For an honest man like Caelus, nothing drew his contempt faster than a liar, a cheat, or a thief. Temhotep was all three.

He unlocked and opened the lid. Nothing appeared to have moved from where he'd placed it. A quick survey of the money belt confirmed nothing was missing. That was sufficient proof that Temhotep didn't get into the trunk. Now that he'd tried and failed, at least he should stop suggesting they leave it with him. And there was only one more night in Aphroditopolis and part of a day to Thmoinepsi before they could say goodbye to the dishonest pilot forever.

Since nothing was taken, the wiser course was to say nothing.

If his years as a slave had taught him anything, it was that the wiser course was much safer than the nobler one when a man like Temhotep was involved. Master Volero had charged him with Caelus's safety, and sometimes that meant protecting Caelus from himself.

*Aphroditopolis, afternoon of Day 18*

The boat stopped with its usual jerk after the rowers' final strokes propelled it into the shore. When Temhotep turned from his pilot post and sauntered toward them at the rear, Lusario rose and took enough steps toward him to keep Caelus from talking to their lying, thieving pilot. One more day, and he wouldn't have to worry about his honorable master speaking the words that could turn a man who already disliked him into a true enemy.

Temhotep looked past him to where Caelus still sat on the bench before focusing his gaze on Lusario. "This is a nome capital, so there will be another eight-drachma toll." He held out his hand. "And the usual two drachmas for the landing fee."

Lusario took the ten drachmas from his purse and dropped them into the outstretched palm. But was there really a toll here?

It made some sense that tolls would be collected in nome capitals, except Babylon wasn't one. But Trajan's Canal entered the Nile there, so maybe it was an exception. Temhotep always claimed he paid when they weren't with him. But if the Romans at Snefru's pyramid saw everything on their own trip upriver, their pilot had charged for four more tolls than Rome required.

"Tell the young Roman since this is a nome capital, I know an inn a Roman lady would like, so it should be fancy enough for him." His nose twitched at "lady."

"Good. As usual, we'll want to stop at the garrison to learn where to hire a guard."

"Of course. Follow me." Temhotep strode down the gangplank, then waited for them. The helmsman freed the trunk, and he and a rower took the handles for the trip to the inn.

The garrison was just off the quay where large cargo boats landed, but Lusario shook his head at Caelus as he emerged from it.

"The optio said he didn't know of anyone with guards to rent."

A sneer curled Temhotep's lip. "So, will you miss all the city has to offer to guard it yourself? You could have left it for my crew to watch until nightfall."

Caelus's mouth opened, but Lusario's nudge made him pause. "That's a matter for Lusario and me to determine. We don't need your suggestions."

"Whatever you wish, young Roman." The look in his eyes contradicted his accommodating words.

They walked the rest of the way to the inn in silence. Lusario rented a second-floor room, and Temhotep's men carried the trunk up to it.

When all descended, Temhotep's gaze raked Caelus. "My men will return at breakfast." With a flick of his hand toward the door, he led his crewmen into the street.

Caelus stretched his jaw to release the clench. "I know it's only one more day, but I don't know if I can stand that man even for so short a time."

Lusario rubbed his lower lip. "You can. A man can put up with almost anything when speaking could make the wrong man mad at you."

"Like when you belonged to Florus. I don't know how you bore everything he did to you. At least that will never happen again." Caelus rested his hand on Lusario's shoulder. "I'll be careful what I say to our pilot. At least until we're on the dock at Thmoinepsi. I wouldn't bet on what I might say then."

The innkeeper was leaning on the counter, but he straightened when Caelus approached. "Do you need something else?"

"Some information. What do travelers who stopped at the Memphis necropolis like to visit while they're here?"

"So, you liked the ancient temples there? Well, this city was once called Tpehwet. It means First of the Cows. Hathor has been a chief goddess of this area for centuries. So, there is an animal necropolis with many sepulchers of cows."

Caelus looked at Lusario with eyebrows raised. "We've been traveling for ten days, and I think what we want to visit first is a Roman-style bath."

The obviously Greek innkeeper chuckled. "I know of a small private one two blocks from here. Most who visit prefer the Greek style, so they will be glad of your patronage."

As they started down the street in the direction of the bath, Caelus lengthened his stride. "Let's not linger. A quick bath will do for me, and we can spend the rest of the day organizing our drawings and adding what seems missing."

Lusario scanned the people on the street around them. It was a decent part of the city, and the innkeeper had been lounging in the courtyard when they first entered. But without a guard, not staying out too long seemed wise.

"A bath, a good meal, and a comfortable bed are enough to expect from Aphroditopolis. And tomorrow, we can enjoy the hospitality of Latro's estate before we start the design work that Tranquilla won't be able to resist."

"I expect you're right. How could she after what we've learned?" Caelus pointed at a Latin sign announcing their destination. "So far, this has been the trip of a lifetime. Many would say Fortuna's brightest smiles were upon us when Fundanus came to the quay with his aunt and uncle. I call it incredibly good luck." He slapped Lusario's arm. "Whatever caused it, we'll make the most of the opportunity it's given us."

As Lusario followed Caelus through the gate into the Roman bath, a wry smile escaped. If their luck held, he'd soon be writing his father in Cyrene to tell him about being Caelus's partner directing their first construction project. But the first person he'd tell when they got the commission would be Timon. He might even tell Timon he wouldn't mind him asking his god to make sure everything went well while they were building. It would make his friend happy, even if there was no god listening to his prayers.

# Chapter 34

## FINAL DAY ON THE RIVER

*North of Thmoinepsi, Day 19*

When they boarded the boat, Lusario noticed something he hadn't seen before. A short club lay on the deck, mostly out of sight behind the upright rudder pole. The helmsman was looking at him with calculating eyes, but when he returned the stare, the man turned away to run his hand along the steering oar's handle down to where the paddle flared out at the end. Then he dropped to one knee, as if he were inspecting the underwater portion.

Temhotep called out the usual commands to rowers and helmsman, and they moved into the center of the river, where the sail billowed as the steady breeze filled it, pushing the boat south.

They had been traveling under sail for several miles, and the rowers lounged on their benches, oars drawn out of the water. In Egyptian, Temhotep called out to the helmsman. "Toward the shore."

The boat left the center of the river and veered toward the eastern bank. That was not something Temhotep had done before when there wasn't a large boat approaching from the south or they were coming into a port. The boat angled eastward, where two male hippos were fighting over a herd of females and at least a dozen crocodiles lounged on the shore.

In Latin, Lusario spoke as he pointed at the hippos. "I think we'll be getting a closer view of hippos than we've had."

"That should be interesting." Caelus's gaze followed Lusario's pointing finger.

"Crocodiles, too." Lusario lowered his voice. "Something's going on. Watch for anything odd at the front."

He turned his head as if to watch the shore, but it put the helmsman in his field of view.

Just ahead and with mouths wide open, displaying foot-long tusks, the two males charged and pushed mouth-against-mouth, until the larger twisted its head and drove one tusk into the other beast's muzzle. Trailing blood in the water, the

180

loser retreated. Then the winner turned and, with gaping jaws, challenged the boat that was only thirty feet from its harem of cows with their calves.

Temhotep, still facing forward, called out in Egyptian. "Here."

Seen from the corner of Lusario's eye, the helmsman leaned over and picked up the club. Lusario shouldered Caelus, then stood, gripping his dagger as he rose. "It's happening."

Wide-eyed, Caelus took his eyes off Temhotep and stared at Lusario.

The helmsman moved forward, club raised. Lusario drew his dagger and stepped toward his attacker.

As the helmsman swung the club sideways at his head, Lusario crouched, letting the club swing harmlessly over him. As he'd learned in bodyguard training in Alexandria, he rose, thrusting the blade up under his attacker's ribcage and into the heart.

When he pulled the dagger free, the helmsman toppled into the river.

The splash triggered movement on the shore, and the first crocodile slipped into the water.

"He's coming."

Lusario spun at Caelus's words behind him. Caelus stood behind the bench, dagger drawn, as Temhotep seized an oar from the farthest rower and strode toward them.

Lusario pushed Caelus behind him. Even with his fellow assassin gone, Temhotep had the advantage. A dagger was for close combat; it was no help when the enemy could reach you with an oar from six feet away.

But before the first swing of that oar, the boat shuddered, knocking all three off their feet. The gaping jaws of the hippo tore into the boat, ripping a chunk out of its side. The rowers scrambled away from the raging beast as it attacked again, tearing enough away that the boat began to fold in the middle. The hippo dove, then rose beneath the boat, flipping it and throwing every man into the river.

Lusario came up sputtering, but he'd held onto his dagger. He slipped it into its snug-fitting sheath. Caelus surfaced next to him.

Then came the first scream. One of the rowers flailed in the water, then disappeared beneath the surface.

Caelus gripped his arm. "Crocodiles. We'll never make it past them. So, we'll try for the other side of the river. Good thing I taught you to swim. Smooth strokes, feet under the surface. Don't splash more than you have to. Swim under the boat, and I'll stay beside you as we cross. Together now." He pulled in a deep breath and held it.

With the second cry of agony echoing in their ears, they dove together and swam away from the sinking boat and dying men.

Jason sat in the grass at the edge of the levee. When Mikro finished eating and went to sleep in the shade of the tree by Neferu's garden, she told him she could watch him while she worked there. She would stop Karpos if his cousin came to bother his baby, so he could go visit the donkeys at the stable for a while.

Except he didn't get that far. A herd of hippos had moved into the area across the river. Watching them was much more fun than listening to Setne fret over when Karpos would strike back and what his cousin might do.

It had already been three days, and no one had said anything to Setne about Karpos's bloody nose or bruised face.

Jason rubbed his knuckles that had done the damage. No one had yelled at him or even told him to be nicer to Karpos. Maybe nothing would happen after all.

Besides, it would only take a little while to check on the mothers and their new babies. He had plenty of time for both hippos and donkeys.

The baby hippos were the best, and sometimes they walked out of the water beside their mothers so he could see them well. But today a male hippo was defending them all from another male. With mouths wide open, they were pushing and shoving while the females tried to keep themselves and their babies out of the way.

He glanced at the bare area below the levee. In his own mind, he'd named the crocodile Scaly Zenobia, but he never spoke that aloud where his aunt might hear of it. The croc was sprawled on the sand next to what Koshari said was her nest. With eyes closed, mouth slightly open, legs stretched out beside her, she didn't look dangerous...except for those teeth.

Every time he went to the donkey stable, Neferu reminded him to stay on the levee. Koshari had warned him. Menmet had warned him. He wasn't going to forget what any of them said. So, why did Neferu keep reminding him?

Of course he would stay atop the levee where Scaly Zenobia could never reach him.

As the big hippos fought, a boat the size of what brought them to Grandfather left the center of the river and headed for shore. They were almost up with the hippos when the big male won, and his rival ran out of the water. Two men in white tunics with red stripes and blue bands sat under the canopy, like he had with Kosmos and Neferu.

Then the man by the rudder swung a club at the man with blue on his tunic. Somehow the blue-tunic man pushed the rudder man into the water.

And a crocodile slid off the bank.

Jason's hands shot up to cover his nose. If rudder man didn't get back on the boat....

The pilot took an oar from the front rower and headed toward the passengers.

But the big hippo charged. First, he bit the boat and made it rock back and forth. The three standing men fell to the deck. When the hippo pulled back, he'd taken a piece out of the boat. Two of the rowers were hitting at his head with their oars.

The hippo bit the boat again, and it was breaking in half. He ducked under the boat and rose up beneath it. The boat tipped over, tossing everyone into the water. The hippo kept tearing at the boat, and it was sinking fast.

Then the crocodiles that were resting in the sun past the hippos all slid into the water, and the screams began.

But the two men in white were swimming toward the center of the river, away from the angry hippo and hungry crocs. It was only moments before they were more than half way to him.

A movement to the left caught his eye. Scaly Zenobia stood, entered the water, and disappeared beneath its surface.

His heart raced.

Where did she go? Was she going after those men?

He spun and ran to get Neferu.

Neferu moved the narrow, pointed hoe along the row of onions, trying to maneuver it exactly as Menmet had shown her to kill the weeds but not the crop. She'd just finished another row when—

"Neferu, come quickly!"

Jason's panicked tone spun her around. Arms pumping, he sprinted toward her. His chest heaved when he reached her.

"What is it?"

"Two men…in the river…Scaly Zenobia…left her nest…I don't know… where she is."

She leaned the hoe's handle against herself and placed her hands on both his shoulders. "Take a deep breath, slow down, and tell me again."

"I was watching the hippos. The father hippo sank a boat, and everyone went into the water. The crocs went in, too, and I heard screams. Two men are swimming across to us. No crocs were chasing them, but she left her nest. She's in the water with them."

"Stay here." She gripped her hoe and ran to where Jason sat to watch the river.

Two men walked toward her, knee deep in the water with the red-striped man a couple of steps behind the blue-banded one.

Her pounding heart slowed. They had made it.

In Greek, she called to them. "Come up here away from the shore."

But instead of heeding her call, they stopped moving and looked up at her.

A ripple in the water behind them brought her hand to her mouth. "Run!"

But before she could say more, Scaly Zenobia tipped her head and lunged to grab the leg of the one with red stripes. He fell sideways as she straightened her head and backed up to pull him into deeper water. Even though she was only seven feet long and weighed no more than he did, he was doomed.

Then his companion dashed into the river past his struggling friend. He grabbed the croc near its tail and lifted its hind legs out of the water, stopping its backward motion.

The croc released its first victim, and with his arms and one good leg, he struggled out of the water and onto the sand, dragging his croc-savaged leg behind him. But he only got ten feet before collapsing.

Now the croc thrashed back and forth, throwing water everywhere, trying to reach the man holding it. He fought to keep his footing, but how long could he stand? The moment he fell or lost his grip, he'd be in the croc's jaws.

And no one would be there to help him. She looked at the pointed hoe still in her hand.

No one except her.

Using the hoe's handle to steady herself, she climbed down the large rocks that stabilized the levee. With one hand, she lifted her long tunic, freeing her knees for the sprint. In moments she was within striking distance of the croc's head. It reached back for the man, and its head stayed still as it snapped at him several times.

She lifted the hoe over her head and drove the blade into the top of its skull.

It bounced off as if she'd hit a metal plate. The only thing the blow did was turn the snapping jaws away from him and direct them at her.

She struck at the head again, aiming for an eye, but the croc moved too fast, and the hoe bounced off the skull again.

As she stumbled backward, it dragged the man who was restraining it toward her. But at least he slowed it down enough to let her get away.

Then the man released one leg and drew a dagger. He leapt onto the croc's back and drove the dagger into its eye, twisting the blade after he'd driven it in as far as he could.

The croc shuddered, then went limp.

He rested a moment astraddle the carcass, then pulled the knife out.

The immediate threat was over, but even a dead croc posed a danger, especially to the one who had killed it.

"Push her into the water so the others will eat her. I come from Arsinoe where the Great Sanctuary of Sobek is. If the priests of Sobek discover you've killed her, I don't know what they'll do to you. Then we must get your friend on the levee before those get here." She pointed at the river, where the surface of the water was broken by two large croc heads coming their way.

He rolled the body into the water and ran to his friend.

The man with blue bands got the red-striped man up on his good leg, and Neferu put the injured man's other arm across her shoulders. The climb up the rocky slope was difficult, but with the hoe to help her balance, they reached the top.

Splashing at the water's edge drew a glance over her shoulder. The two crocs who wanted to feast on these men had settled for their attacker.

Jason hadn't stayed at the house. He stood at the top of the levee, shifting from foot to foot. "Can I help?"

The weight of the injured man bore down on Neferu, but she couldn't stop helping yet. "Go find Menmet. She went to see Koshari's sister. You know where that is. When you get back, don't come into our house until I say. You should milk the goat and feed Mikro."

"I know. I'll run as fast as I can." He bit his lip and tipped his head toward the injured man. "Will he be all right?"

"We'll take good care of him now. Go get Menmet."

He scurried away.

A trail of blood marked where they'd climbed the levee, and the bitten man's head drooped.

"We've got to get the bleeding stopped." The croc-fighter's face was grim. "Please take us to someone who can do that."

"Follow me." She started toward her house. "What's your name, and who is your friend?"

"Lusario, and this is Caelus Publilius Martinus."

"I'm Neferu. I sent Jason for the woman who treats everyone's injuries and illnesses here. Menmet will know what to do."

Lusario scooped Caelus up into his arms, and his friend's head rested on his shoulder. "Hang on, Caelus. We'll get you fixed in no time."

"There might be no time left to fix me." The Roman's mouth curved into a wry smile before his face contorted with pain. "I saw what it did to my leg." He closed his eyes. "This might be it." His voice was barely above a whisper.

"Your leg's only broken and bitten some. I expect the estate physician can take care of that. Seneca's chorus doesn't apply to you yet."

Neferu stared at Lusario. He smiled at his friend as if the injuries were nothing. But he couldn't keep the fear from his eyes.

It seemed like forever until they reached her cottage with Lusario carrying his friend and her supporting his mangled leg. Blood coated her hands, and crimson drops marked their path. Caelus's eyes stayed mostly closed as he faded in and out of consciousness.

"Bring him in here and put him on my bed. Jason should be back soon with Menmet."

When Lusario lay Caelus down, not even a groan escaped him.

She almost rubbed her lip, but stopped short before making her own face bloody. If that bleeding didn't stop soon, Caelus Martinus would die.

Corinna had bled to death despite all her prayers, but would God save this poor man? Phoebe always said to pray, even when what she asked seemed impossible. After all, what were miracles if not God making the impossible happen?

"Would you please step outside and watch for Jason returning with Menmet?"

Lusario stared at her. "I'm not leaving his side."

"Do you want your friend to live?"

His eyebrows lowered as his head drew back. He probably thought her question crazy. "Of course I do. I just fought a croc to save him."

"Then you must step outside and not come back in until I call you."

His lips tightened, and he didn't move.

"Please. If you don't, I can't help him."

He rested his hand on his friend's shoulder. "I'll be right outside."

Whether Caelus heard or not, she couldn't tell.

As soon as he left, she placed her hand on the Roman's forehead. God heard her silent prayers for Menander. She didn't need to speak aloud and risk the Greek hearing her ask God to keep his friend alive.

*In the name of my Lord Jesus, I ask for Your mercy and healing for this man. Like You healed Corinna's baby, please heal him.*

God hadn't stopped Corinna's bleeding, but Phoebe always said that we should never be afraid to ask for what we needed. Only God knew the best way to answer our prayers.

*Please stop the bleeding before it kills him, too.*

A quick glance at his leg showed the flow of blood from where the bone stuck through his skin and from each oozing toothmark had reduced to less than a trickle. She pushed his wet hair back from his forehead, and he released a soft sigh. His eyes opened for a moment, almost focused on her, then closed.

*Thank You for sparing him, Lord. Now please show us what else to do to help him get well.*

She tipped her head back and lifted her hands. In whispered tones with a language known only to God, she gave thanks.

"Where's Lusario?" His eyes had opened again, more alert this time.

"He's waiting outside. I'll get him. Don't move. Your leg is broken, and we're not through tending it."

He gripped his thigh, and a deep groan escaped. "I won't be walking anywhere for a while."

As she stepped out the door, she glanced back at Caelus Martinus. God had stopped the bleeding, but as bad as his leg looked, he might never walk anywhere again.

# Chapter 35

## Helping Caelus

Lusario paced outside, and as he passed the window, he looked in. She was standing by the bed, her eyes focused on Caelus, her hand on his forehead. But Caelus hadn't moved, and his eyes remained closed. On his next pass by the window, she was standing with head back, hands raised. Whispered words he didn't recognize as Egyptian or Greek came from her lips.

An Egyptian woman speaking some incantation calling on an Egyptian god. That wasn't going to help his friend live.

He'd read some of Celsus's treatise, *De Medicina*, but not the volumes about animal bites or broken legs. Mentally, he kicked himself for that omission, but who would have thought he'd ever need that knowledge?

She came to the door. "He's asking for you. You can come in now. The bleeding has mostly stopped, but we still need to tend his broken leg."

In the distance, Menmet stepped onto the road with Jason holding her hand and pulling to hasten their progress.

"We can ask Menmet what to do next. I'm sure she's dealt with broken legs before."

"I'll stay with Caelus until she gets here."

◆

He disappeared into the cabin.

Neferu met Menmet at her gate, and they walked into Menmet's house together.

"Jason said the croc bit a man, and he has a broken leg." A slow shake of Menmet's head accompanied sad eyes. "If it is crushed as badly as most, we might be cutting it off to try to save his life." Her mouth drooped. "More often than not, death still takes them."

"It's his lower leg. The bones are sticking out, but I wouldn't say it's crushed. And so many punctures from the teeth. He bled badly, but that's mostly stopped."

Menmet's eyebrows rose. "He is very lucky then. Perhaps there is hope for him." She picked up a basket and opened a cupboard. "The first day, I should bind raw meat on the places that bleed a lot. But I do not have any, and Mistress Zenobia would not let her cook give me any for a stranger." She shrugged.

"But since his bleeding has already stopped, perhaps that will not matter. We still must clean the wounds well." She placed a small jug of wine in the basket and a jar of honey. "And splint it after we pull on the leg to get what is broken back where it should be."

From the chest beside the cupboard, she took a roll of linen strips, like the embalmers used to wrap a mummy, and three curved pieces of acacia bark that together could encircle a limb. "I use these for arms and legs. They keep the bones from moving while they mend."

She added them to the basket, and Neferu took it from her.

Menmet patted her arm. "Let's go do what we can for the poor man."

"His name is Caelus Martinus, and his friend who fought the croc to save him is Lusario."

"Jason told me you fought it, too." She placed her hand on Neferu's cheek. "I am glad it did not grab you. I do not want to see you join the *hesyu*. I do not think the 'blessed drowned ones' are blessed, like the priests of Sobek claim."

"I couldn't let them both die. I was afraid they would if I didn't help."

"I told Jason not to tell anyone you killed it. Some around here would rather see a person die than a croc."

Neferu held her gate open for Menmet, then closed it to keep Mikro in. "I know. I lived in Arsinoe, where the Sanctuary of Sobek is. I had Lusario put the croc in the river. Two others ate it for us."

Menmet looked over her shoulder as she passed through the gate. "We will do what we can to make sure no one but Scaly Zenobia dies today."

They found Lusario sitting on a chair by his friend. The smile on his lips didn't match the worry in his eyes. "The physician is here."

Menmet reached the bedside and looked him over. "Not a physician, but I have taken care of Stephanos's workers when they get hurt for many years. I know what to do for you. You are very lucky it was only a small female. A larger croc would have crushed the bones beyond healing, maybe even taken your leg off with that first bite."

She pointed at the table, and Neferu set the basket there. "But we need to clean your wounds first, and for that we must change the bed some. So that you will not be lying on a wet bed when I finish, we will pull the mattress off the head of the bed so your legs are only on the rope mesh. Then what I use to clean can just drip onto the floor for wiping up when I am done."

Lusario rose and looked at Neferu. "I can lift if you can pull."

She took her post at the head of the bed. Lusario lifted his friend, and she pulled the mattress until Menmet said to stop.

Dried mud from dragging himself up the shore still clung to part of his leg. Blood had stained it red near every tooth mark and around the break.

"Water and soap, then wine, then honey—it is what you need, but it will hurt." Menmet rested her hand on Caelus's shoulder.

He closed his eyes and clenched his teeth. Then he fixed his gaze on her. "Whatever you have to do, please do it."

"Lusario?"

"Yes?" Lusario moved the chair back from the bed and stood beside her.

"Hold him down, please. Neferu can help hold his shoulders."

She handed Caelus a thin piece of wood. "To bite to help with the pain."

"It's going to be that bad?" Fear flashed in Caelus's eyes.

"I am afraid so, but it will not last long."

Menmet's words made Neferu bite her lip.

He slipped it between his teeth. "I'm ready."

It took all Neferu's self-control not to cry as Menmet first cleaned the wounds with water and soap, then dribbled wine into every puncture, and finally applied honey to every break in his skin. Through it all, he bit the wood and stopped any screams. But beads of sweat coated his forehead, and his breathing raced as if he were being chased by a pack of starving dogs.

When Menmet set the honey jar on the table, Caelus's stiffened body relaxed. He took the wood from between his teeth. "Is it over?"

Menmet pushed a strand of sweat-soaked hair back from his forehead. "I wish it was, but I still need to set your broken leg. I wish I could tell you that it would not hurt as much, but that would be lying. We have to pull until the bone ends slip back inside and line up for healing."

He closed his eyes and tipped his head back. He tightened his lips until they were scarcely visible. "If it must be done, please do it quickly. I can't take much more pain." His voice broke on the last word.

"Neferu will hold your shoulders. I will hold your thigh, and your friend will pull until I say stop."

Lusario's eyes widened. "I've never done anything like that. Isn't there someone else at the estate who has?"

"We need to do it now. It needs a young man's strength, and you are the only one in the village this afternoon."

Caelus gripped Lusario's arm. "I know you don't want to hurt me, but don't let that stop you. Someone must do it."

Lusario placed his hand over Caelus's and squeezed. "Anything you need, if I can help…you can count on me."

Caelus replaced the wood between his teeth. "Let's do it."

Neferu slipped her hands under Caelus's shoulders and gripped under his arms. Menmet leaned on his thigh, and Lusario started to pull.

Caelus's scream rent the air, then silence filled the room. He had passed out, and Neferu's vision blurred. Watching the pain rip into him carried her back to Arsinoe, back to Corinna's room where every birth pain ended in a scream, and silence only came with Corinna's death.

*Please, God, let this ordeal be over. Let Menmet finish so Caelus can start to heal without hurting so much.*

"Stop." Menmet checked the open wound and felt his calf. "I think that is enough."

Lusario released Caelus's ankle and wiped the perspiration from his face with the back of his hand. "Now what?"

Menmet bandaged his leg with a long linen strip. Then she took the three linen-wrapped pieces of acacia bark, positioned them around the broken leg, and tied them snuggly in place with the linen strips.

"We will let him rest now. Tomorrow we will clean his wounds again with wine and honey." She put the jug of wine and the honey jar on a shelf above the counter.

"You did well for your first time." She patted Lusario's arm. "I will need your help each time. Can you stay with him until he awakes?"

"We've been working together for three years. Nothing but death would make me leave his side."

"That is good. I will be back to check on him later, but I will be next door. So, send for me if he needs me sooner."

Neferu picked up the basket. "We need to let our steward, Akhom, know what has happened. We have to ask him to let Caelus stay here at the estate while he recovers. I will take care of that."

Menmet dropped the roll of extra linen strips into the basket. "It would be good if he stayed here in your bed. Then I will be close when he needs tending. We can borrow a bed for you to put in my house."

"I want to stay here with him, if I can." Lusario ran his fingers though his hair. "I'm responsible for keeping him safe."

"We can make a pallet in here for you to do that."

Neferu stiffened. What Menmet suggested made sense, and she wanted to help any way she could. But that could be risky…for her.

Her gaze settled on the small chest that held all her possessions. Her copy of Marcus's writings was in there. It had no lock. If Lusario was a nosy man, what was to keep him from looking inside and discovering her secret? But Menmet couldn't read Greek, so no harm would come if she looked.

"I think that's a good idea. I only need to move my chest to your cabin as well. Jason's things can stay here. I tutor him at our table in the morning. We'll try to be quiet enough that we won't disturb Caelus."

The corner of Lusario's mouth twitched. "He'll probably welcome the distraction. I would. Nothing is harder than doing nothing when you're not used to it."

He pointed at her chest. "Shall I carry it over for you now? It's the least I can do after everything you've done to help us. There are no words that can express how grateful I am."

"We're glad to do it. Thank you for offering, but I can manage the chest myself." She handed the basket to Menmet. "I'll go find Akhom now, but if either of you need something, Jason will be here with his baby donkey. He'll get Menmet for you."

◆

Lusario leaned against the doorframe and watched the brave, beautiful Egyptian woman walk up the road toward the main house. She was the reason Caelus was still alive. The reason he was alive as well.

But what would happen next?

A soft groan drew him back to Caelus's bedside.

"How are you feeling?"

Caelus laid his arm across his forehead. "I never, not even in my worst nightmare, thought anything could hurt that much. I wondered why my mother screamed so much when my sisters were being born, but I think I understand it now. When you pulled to get the bone ends back inside…I couldn't have held in that scream if my life depended on it. I'm glad I passed out."

Lusario swung the chair back beside the bed and sat to get closer to Caelus's level. "Menmet said the worst is over. She will be using wine and honey again tomorrow to keep the bites and wound from infecting, but it shouldn't hurt as much. With the bones only broken, not crushed, they should heal."

"But then what? When that boat went down, we lost everything. The letter from Latro to his steward. The dioptra and rope, all our drawings…all gone. We have no money for passage back to Alexandria. We don't even have enough money for sending a letter to Fundanus or Zenon for them to send some money to get us home. Fundanus might be willing to come upriver with what we need, but we don't even know what to tell him so he could find us."

As he spoke, Caelus's words came faster, and his voice rose in pitch and volume.

"You don't have to worry about any of that. Between the two of us, we can remember enough of what we saw to make new drawings. We can even start while your leg is mending. Not having passage money doesn't matter yet. We can't go anywhere until your leg heals anyway."

"How long will that take?"

"At least six weeks, more likely eight. That gives me plenty of time to earn the money. Most jobs this far from Alexandria are done by hired workers, not slaves."

Caelus's breath caught, and he scrunched his eyes against the pain. "Then it might be wise not to mention you belong to Father. We're partners in this venture, and that's all anyone needs to know. You're Lusario of Alexandria while we're here."

Lusario blew out a slow breath. Passing himself off as a free man? If he did that of his own accord, he'd be breaking Roman law. But if Caelus ordered him to do it, would he be?

"If you think that's best, then I won't. I've done so many different things that someone could hire me for. I can build or be a scribe or a tutor or a valet. I could even be a kitchen worker or a house servant. I'm sure I can find work doing one of those or even something else. It's only four or five days to Alexandria, and passage on a boat carrying many passengers will be maybe one twentieth of what Temhotep's boat cost. So, I only need to earn thirty or so drachmas."

He rested his palm on Caelus's shoulder. "So, all you need to focus on is getting better."

"I'll try." Caelus placed his hand atop Lusario's. "Thank you for what you did…saving me that way."

"I was only returning the favor." Lusario shrugged. He'd do it again if Caelus needed him to.

"No. I only swam with the dolphins in the safety of the sea. You fought a crocodile to save me from a gruesome death. If you hadn't won, you would have died the same way. I can never repay you for that." Caelus placed his hand over his heart. "But I swear that I will do everything I can think of to convince Father to free you as soon as he learns what you did. Whether we get to start our business or not. You're the best man I know, and you deserve it."

Lusario felt the heat to the tip of his ears. He never thought of himself that way, but for Caelus to say it aloud…

"We will start that business, so I did it mostly for myself. Without you as my partner, I could never become the architect I want to be. The two of us together…we're much more than the sum of what we can do separately."

Without Caelus, he would have to return to Carthago to serve Volero Martinus however the man who owned him wanted. Once more he'd lose everything he'd dreamed of, everything he'd worked for. But that wasn't the reason he fought the croc.

To Caelus's father, he was only a slave to be sold when no longer needed. To Caelus, he was a man who mattered, and Caelus treated him like a true friend. He felt the same about Caelus, and that made Caelus worth dying for.

One corner of Caelus's mouth rose. "I guess we call it even, then, even though we both know I owe you more."

Lusario sat in the chair beside Caelus's bed, arms crossed, legs stretched out and crossed at the ankles. Despite the pain, Caelus had finally dozed off.

Sleep was the only way to get any relief when the slightest movement triggered a grimace or a groan. Rather than risk awakening his friend, Lusario sat as still as a hare waiting for a jackal to pass.

A soft tap on the open door drew his eyes. Neferu stood in the doorway, summoning him with a silent curl of her fingers. She was alone.

He rose and crept across the room. Caelus didn't stir.

Once outside, she led him away from the door to the shade of an olive tree, where Menmet waited for them.

Neferu's hand went to her throat. "Our steward isn't here. Stephanos owns several olive groves and vineyards that are some distance from the main compound. Akhom has gone to inspect them. He should be back late tomorrow."

She pushed a loose strand of hair behind her ear. "Until he returns and decides what to do with you two while Caelus recovers, Menmet and I have a plan."

"What do you propose?" His gaze bounced between the two women. Both were welcoming and kind. But Neferu's bravery was beyond anything he'd ever seen in any man or woman, and that name that meant "beauty" could not have fit her better.

"She knows where to borrow a cot for me to sleep on. It will be tight, but there's room to move that and Jason's bed into her house. But I will need to use the table and chair in my own house for tutoring Jason in the mornings. She will cook something for the five of us at least until Akhom returns."

"Do you expect that he won't let us stay while Caelus's leg mends?" Lusario rubbed his jaw. If the answer was yes, where could they go?

Menmet chuckled. "I have known Akhom since he came to the estate as a young man. You would not know it when you first meet him, but he has a kind heart. I am sure he will let us keep caring for your friend and you."

Lusario's hand dropped to the purse still tied to his belt. "I have a few drachmas that I could pay for the extra food that two men would need. When Caelus recovers enough that he won't need constant tending, I plan to look for work to earn passage money home. I speak and write Egyptian as well as Greek, and I know how to do many things."

"That is good. Now that Caelus is sleeping, I am going back to my loom." Menmet patted his arm. "Watch over your friend. Do not let him put weight on that leg. If he starts bleeding again, send for me."

"I will, and I thank you for everything you've done for him. I owe you more than words could ever convey for how you've helped us."

"You are welcome." With a smile that was what he'd expect from a loving grandmother, she turned and headed toward her house.

Neferu watched her for a moment, then turned back to him. "I have hoeing to finish, so I'll be in the garden behind the house. Jason will be tending an orphan donkey there as well. If your friend needs anything, just call, and Jason or I will come to help."

He cleared his throat. "I want to thank you for risking your life to save mine. Neither Caelus nor I would be alive without your bravery in coming to help me."

Her lips twitched, as if what he'd said was funny. "It's not the riskiest thing I've ever done, and I'm glad I was there to help you both." She lowered her voice to a whisper. "Remember, don't tell anyone we killed that crocodile."

One corner of his mouth lifted. "If anyone asks what happened to it, I'll tell the truth. It went back into the water."

Her mouth curved into a delightful smile that accompanied a nearly silent chuckle. "You could say that, and it would be true. I've heard about famous Greek orators who can make truth seem false and falsehoods seem true. I never expected to meet one."

"I'm not a great orator, but life has taught me both the wisdom of choosing a man's words carefully and the importance of truth."

"Hmm." She took the hoe from where she'd leaned it against the wall and stepped around the corner.

As he crossed his arms and tipped his head to one side, his gaze stayed fixed on where she'd disappeared. He was a good orator, although Caelus was better. Either of them would find it easy to recite a tribute to a woman with the courage, kindness, and beauty of Neferu of Arsinoe.

# Chapter 36

## What Next?



*Morning of Day 20*

After eating her own breakfast of wheat porridge at Menmet's table, Neferu led Jason to their own house and knocked on the frame of the open door. Jason stood behind her, peeking past so only his good eye showed.

Lusario sat on the bed, serving as a back rest so Caelus could sit up to eat without turning on his side to recline.

Caelus lifted a spoonful to his lips, then returned it to the bowl uneaten. From the tightness of his mouth and the fatigue in his eyes, it was obvious how hard he was fighting the pain.

"Are you through eating?" Neferu softened the question with a smile.

Caelus closed his eyes and answered with a silent nod.

"We are." Lusario reached around Caelus to take the bowl from his hands.

Neferu moved toward him, hands ready to take their dishes. "Before we start Jason's lessons, I'll take your bowls back to Menmet."

Jason stepped out from behind her. "I can do that."

He stacked Caelus's half-empty bowl with Lusario's empty one and headed out the door.

Lusario slipped off the bed and supported Caelus as he lay down again.

Neferu took a stylus and wax tablet from their shelf and placed them on the table. "I usually tutor Jason in the morning, and there isn't room to do it at Menmet's. I hope it won't disturb you too much. We'll try to be quiet."

Caelus's eyelids opened, and he turned his head to face her. "I'd rather listen to your tutoring session than lie here in silence, staring at the ceiling, trying to ignore every place where a tooth punctured my leg and the throbbing where the bones broke." He drew a breath and held it. His eyes scrunched, then he blew it out slowly.

"I've seen how Greek boys here in Egypt start learning to read when they're ten, but I started my own studies when I was seven. How long have you been teaching him?"

"His mother took me on as tutor and nanny eighteen days ago. I was to care for Jason after her new baby was born." She glanced at the door to be sure Jason wasn't back. "But she died giving birth. Her new baby is a beautiful, healthy boy that his father can show off to his friends. He plans to remarry soon, so he sent Jason here for his grandfather to raise. I was sent with him."

"Was he born with that eye?"

Neferu stopped her head drawing back before Caelus saw. That blunt a question was not what she expected from a total stranger. But blunt questions sometimes made sensitive conversations easier.

"He was. It's the only thing wrong with him, but his father doesn't want him around where others might see him."

Caelus's brow furrowed. "The elite Greeks in Alexandria are like most Romans. Why didn't he simply put an unwanted baby out to die?"

"He wasn't home when Jason was born. Jason's mother wrote to ask his grandfather what to name him. Once Master Stephanos chose his name, his father couldn't expose him." She dropped her gaze to the floor, then turned it back on Caelus. "Jason's father never forgave his mother for doing that. When she died, he said it was Jason's grandfather's fault he was still alive. So Theodoros sent him here for Stephanos to raise."

She picked up the stylus and rolled it between thumb and middle finger. "He'd let his father and everyone here think Jason died years ago. Master Stephanos didn't know he had another grandson until Steward Akhom wrote to him." She cast a quick glance at each man. The quality of their tunics proclaimed lives of wealth, and the wealthy didn't keep defective babies. "I don't know how he'll react when he returns and meets Jason."

Caelus's slow nod ended in a shrug. "My step-grandmother would have persuaded my grandfather to keep him, but she had a softer heart than most Romans and a knack for making him see how the good outweighed the bad. If you're teaching him to read at six, he must be smart. My father and grandfather both set a higher value on that than on how someone looks."

"Very smart. He's a sweet child, too, as you'll soon see." She cleared her throat. She hadn't meant to tell these two Jason's story this morning. But since the Roman asked, maybe it was a good thing.

"Jason will be back any moment, and I don't want him to hear us discussing him."

"Enough said." Caelus closed his eyes. A grimace followed. He gripped his thigh and held his breath, finally releasing it as a deep sigh.

Lusario stood by the head of the bed, gazing down at his injured friend. When he turned his eyes on her, sorrow and worry clouded them, as they had her uncle's when pain racked her father as death neared. Then he masked the emotions.

He picked up the chair to move it back to the table.

"I won't need it today." She offered an encouraging smile. "I often stand while I'm teaching. So, you can keep it there by the bed if you wish. If you want to get some fresh air, take a stroll or…whatever, I can watch over him while I'm teaching."

"I'll stay. I worked as a tutor in the school my father runs in Cyrene. Our students started at ten, like most Greeks, so I'm curious about how you teach a boy who's so young."

Neferu's hand went to her throat. Being watched by a man who'd tutored himself…what if he didn't think she was doing it right and said something to Akhom? But no gracious way to discourage him came to mind.

She was spared from responding by Jason appearing in the doorway. She patted the tabletop. "Take your seat, and let's begin."

Neferu held the tablet out before her, making a show of inspecting Jason's work. "You've done well today. You read the donkey story to me without error, and you've chosen the right letters to spell each of the short words I gave you." She closed the tablet with a snap. "Now it's time for a break so you can feed Mikro."

She pointed at Caelus, asleep on the bed, and placed a finger across her lips. He mimicked her action and slipped out of the house without disturbing the injured man.

She followed Jason out the door. Menmet should be at home. The estate's healer needed to know how much Caelus was hurting. Maybe she knew of something to lessen his pain.

"Neferu." Scarcely louder than a whisper, Lusario spoke her name.

She turned to face him. "Did you need something?"

"No. I just wanted to tell you I'm impressed with how Jason is doing. Some Roman boys start their schooling at seven like Caelus, but most of the Greeks wait until ten, like here in Egypt. Jason is doing as well as the ten-year-olds when they first begin their studies. Part of what I did at my father's school was write simple stories for the beginners to read. If you want, I can write some for Jason at the level of your first story and others that get harder for when he learns more."

She bit her lip. Her stories stayed away from the immoral tales of gods and demigods that the Greeks were so fond of. If Jason was to learn about the one true God, he didn't need exciting adventures leading him astray.

"What kind of stories?"

His head drew back. Had he expected her to accept his generous offer without questions?

"Whatever kind you want. I've spent many hours reading the great historians, so any topic is possible. Kings, empires, battles that decide who controls the land. I know Egyptian history as well, so stories about the ancient pharaohs. Maybe something about Alexander the Great and how he conquered the eastern end of the Mediterranean and the distant lands as far as India. The usual stories about the Greek gods. He probably knows some of those already so reading one will tie into his religion."

She fingered her lip. He said "his religion," as if it wasn't Lusario's as well. Phoebe had told her many educated Greeks and Romans went through the motions of worship but didn't believe in the gods they were worshiping. Was he one?

"Jason doesn't need stories about the gods. His mother just died in childbirth, and his father has never wanted him. So, stories about death and broken families and selfish, promiscuous gods wouldn't be good. But he loves animals. Do you know much about the things of nature? Birds and fish and livestock and wild beasts? I think he would like those. He's happiest when he's working with the donkeys."

His brow furrowed, then relaxed. Perhaps her objection did seem strange to a worldly Greek man, but Jason was still too young to understand why the Olympians and the gods of Egypt were only stories but God was real.

"I've read all of Pliny's *Natural History*. He wrote about many animals, from common ones Jason has probably seen to exotic creatures that a boy from the interior of Egypt might not think were real." He raised his eyebrows as he smiled. "Would stories like that suit you?"

"They might. Anything you want to write, I can read to see if it's suitable. I'm teaching in Greek now, but I'll be adding Demotic when I think he's comfortable enough with Greek writing." She turned her gaze on Jason where he stood under the tree past the end of the garden, petting his baby donkey. "This is, after all, Egypt, and an elite boy should be able to read and write both Greek and Egyptian. I can translate some of your stories to Egyptian for him to practice."

"What about Latin?"

She shook her head. "Very few here use that. But the Ptolemies were pharaohs for three hundred years, and most of them didn't learn Egyptian. So, people speak Greek well enough to get by, even if they can't read or write either language. My father was a scribe in Arsinoe to help people with that need."

Lusario raised an eyebrow at her. "I can do the translations, if you want. I've lived in Alexandria for more than five years, and during my first year there, I found it wise to learn Egyptian. We're alive because of it."

Her eyebrows shot up as she stared at him, triggering his chuckle.

"I don't normally mention it. But I figure a woman who fought a croc to save me can be trusted. You only need Greek in Alexandria. Maybe Latin if you want to impress the Romans. I know both well."

One corner of his mouth lifted. "But a wise man wants to understand the words spoken around him by people who don't think he understands them. I knew the helmsman and pilot were up to something because they thought they could speak secrets aloud with Egyptian words in front of a Greek and a Roman. Caelus and I used Latin the same way after testing to see if they understood it. But I never spoke Egyptian where they might hear me. I knew they were plotting something against us, and when it came, we were ready."

"But Jason said the hippo attacked your boat. That's why you swam the river."

"The pilot and helmsman were going to rob us and feed us to the crocodiles there. But I killed the helmsman when he attacked me, and the hippo overturned the boat before the pilot could use an oar to knock us into the water for the crocs. So, the hippo actually saved us on its side of the river."

Lusario's smile at her was as warm as any Koshari gave her and just as uncomfortable. "And then you saved us from dying on this side."

"Actually, you saved yourself from dying. I merely distracted Scaly Zenobia long enough for you to strike the killing blow."

He chuckled. "Who gave the croc that name?"

"Jason, but don't repeat it to anyone. His aunt would be furious if it got back to her."

"I won't, but only if you admit you saved us. If you hadn't distracted her, I would have eventually lost my grip, and she would have grabbed me before I could get a knife into her brain. Caelus could never have climbed the levee alone, so she or another croc would have caught and feasted on him."

"Well, however it happened, it's a good thing Jason saw her go into the water and came to get me before she could get you both. So, you really owe your lives to Jason."

"Since you won't admit it's you, I suppose he's the next best choice. The Romans say Fortuna smiles. The Greeks credit the Fates or Tyche or Agathos Daimon. The Egyptians call the one controlling their fates Shai or Shait, but they can't even decide if it's a god or a goddess. With so many choices, no one knows which is right or whether all of them are wrong."

Neferu offered a weaker smile than he probably expected. He was a skeptic with nothing to anchor him, but she knew they were all wrong. Only God had control over what happened to a person, and she gave thanks that He'd decided Lusario and Caelus should live.

◆

Lusario sat on a bench beneath the olive tree in Neferu's front yard, elbows on his knees, watching a row of ants carrying what looked like spilled flour back to their colony. She had asked for stories about animals, and he'd found the perfect topic. A queen with her workers, another rival colony nearby, each wanting to control the territory where they scavenged their food. He could make them like people with jealousies, ambitions, worries, loyalties. Maybe three colonies, where two join forces against another.

Caelus had been sleeping when he slipped out, leaving Neferu with her willing student copying part of the donkey story to practice writing. It felt good to take a break from sitting in the cottage while she was there in case Caelus needed something.

From the corner of his eye, he detected movement. A boy was skulking along the garden wall shared by Menmet and Neferu. He opened the gate and slipped in. As he scanned the area, his gaze settled on the fruit tree where Mikro was sleeping. With a smile that was too much like what his old master Florus directed at him before striking, the boy started toward the helpless donkey.

Lusario rose and trotted past the house to intercept him.

"What do you think you're doing?"

The boy was reaching for the donkey, but he jerked back at Lusario's challenge. He spun, and his mouth settled into a sneer. With two black eyes that had barely started to fade, he'd clearly been in a fight lately that he probably hadn't won.

He shoved his fists onto his hips. "This is my donkey, and I've come to get it."

The boy was dressed in a fine linen tunic and sandals with a complex woven pattern at the toes. Probably a son or grandson of the estate owner, but the way he sneaked in proclaimed that he knew he shouldn't be there.

Lusario tipped his head to look down his nose at the boy. "Are you Stephanos, owner of this estate?"

The boy raised his head to mimic Lusario's expression. "I'm his grandson. He gives me whatever I want, and I want this donkey."

"So, it's not really your donkey." Lusario crossed his arms and spread his legs, like the professional bodyguard he'd trained with. "Jason is also his grandson, and from what I've seen, the donkey prefers to be his. I'm watching Mikro for him today, and this donkey will stay here with me until Jason says otherwise or until Steward Akhom tells me it's yours, not his."

Lusario flicked his hand toward the main house in the distance. "Your tutor is probably looking for you. I suggest you go back to him before you get in trouble for leaving when you shouldn't."

"I don't have a tutor."

Lusario raised his eyebrows. "Really? A boy of your age hasn't started his studies yet? You look older than Jason, and he's with his tutor now. I wonder why you don't have one..." He shrugged. "So, maybe your nanny is worried about where you went. Whatever the case, there's nothing for you here."

The boy opened his mouth as if to speak, then covered it with his hand. Uncertainty lingered in his eyes. Then he turned and stomped off toward the large house in the distance.

Lusario rubbed the back of his neck. If Stephanos or his son didn't take that one in hand, he would grow up just like Florus. But if the patriarch of the estate approved of the brat's behavior and really did give him whatever he wanted, that did not bode well for Jason when his grandfather finally returned.

*Afternoon of Day 20*

One glance to make certain Caelus was sleeping, then Lusario left the house to stretch his legs for a while. He ran his fingers through his hair, and the gentle breeze of a fall afternoon felt refreshingly cool. Thirty feet away, Neferu stood under a canopy by Menmet's house, working at a loom. One corner of his mouth rose. This break might be more refreshing if it included some conversation with Neferu, the first woman he'd met who was brave enough to fight a crocodile, smart enough to be a tutor, and kind enough to take in two strangers in desperate need of help.

When he reached her side, she greeted him with a subdued smile. "How is Caelus doing?"

"No change. Constant pain when he's awake. Fighting it exhausts him, and then he sleeps deeply for a while. That's what he's doing now."

"I'm sorry. Menmet knows of something that might help with the pain, but she needs to find some lotus roots to make it."

"I appreciate anything she can do that might help."

She placed her shuttle on a tray at the top of the loom. "I can't help with that problem, but perhaps I can help with your need for passage money. Not me, exactly, but Akhom. Stephan's tutor just left, and he needs to find a new one. If you'd like to do that, Menmet or I can let him know you've been one."

Lusario rubbed his jaw. Tutoring in a school was different from working with one elite child. Who the father was and what the child was like…either could make it a pleasure or a nightmare. But it wouldn't be for long, and he could make enough for passage home by the time Caelus's leg was healed.

"Is Stephan the one who wanted Jason's donkey?" He wrinkled his nose. "I can see where a tutor wouldn't want to work with that one."

A fleeting frown accompanied a quick shake of Neferu's head. "That's Karpos, not Stephan. Karpos doesn't hide what he's thinking from anyone. Stephan is eleven, and he's a chameleon. He can seem nice, but then he does cruel things to Jason, especially when Karpos is with him."

"Hmph." Lusario leaned against the wall on one hand. "I helped Father tutor elite Greek boys from the time I was eighteen, and I've seen Stephan's kind before. I know how to handle him. So, yes, I would like you to tell him I'm available."

"I'll mention it when I see him next."

Lusario straightened. "I'd better get back to Caelus, in case he wakes and needs something. I'll see you at dinnertime."

Her answer was a smile and a nod. Then she picked up her shuttle and resumed weaving, so he headed back to take care of his friend.

## *Chapter* 37

### THE NEW TUTOR

*Late afternoon of Day 20*

Jason lifted the empty feeding bucket from its hanger on the garden wall. After he scratched Mikro under his chin, the now-full baby sauntered to the garden tree. He lay down beside its trunk, tucked his head in, and closed his eyes.

Menmet stood at her loom, sending the shuttle back and forth through the warp threads. He carried the bucket to the pitcher of water by her house and rinsed off the last of the goat milk, as Koshari had taught him. He set it on the bench and joined Menmet by her loom.

"Where is Neferu?"

Menmet kept weaving. "She went to get more grain and dried fruit so we will have enough to feed two men as well as the three of us." She glanced at the sleeping baby. "If you want to go watch the hippos for a while, I will watch your donkey." She tapped his chest. "But be sure you stay on top of the levee. It is a good place to nest, and another mother croc will claim it soon."

"I never saw another one around there." He shrugged.

"But Scaly Zenobia is not there to keep the others away. So, just because you cannot see a croc, do not think one is not there."

"I won't." He bit his lip and glanced at their house. "And I'll stay on the levee, as if she was still there."

He pointed at Mikro. "Please call Lusario if Karpos or Stephan show up. He stopped Karpos before he could do anything mean this morning."

Her chuckle raised his eyebrows. "I have scolded your cousins since they were smaller than you are for doing things they were not supposed to. They always stop and scurry back home." She tousled his hair. "I will take good care of your donkey."

"Thank you." He gave her a quick hug and started down the levee roadway.

He glanced back at Menmet and bit the corner of his lip. Last night, Neferu

203

told him to keep how she and Lusario killed Scaly Zenobia a secret. They couldn't tell anyone, or Neferu might be sent away.

It was good Koshari wasn't home yet. What if he'd let it slip out when Koshari warned him to stay away from her nest? He had to keep their secret, even from Koshari.

Nothing could be worse than losing Neferu, like he'd already lost everyone else.

*Evening of Day 20*

Lusario sat outside the house in the shade of the olive tree. From there, he could see Jason in the fenced garden with his baby donkey and Neferu helping Menmet clean up after dinner.

He rubbed his lip, and a deep sigh escaped. Caelus had eaten less than half of what Menmet served him. When he fell asleep and almost dropped the bowl, Lusario took it from him and slipped out to let slumber give its brief relief from pain.

Was it normal for pain to make a man lose his appetite, or was something more sinister happening to his friend? What should he tell Caelus if he asked when his suffering would end?

He startled when someone cleared their throat behind him. He twisted to find a middle-aged Egyptian dressed in an ankle-length tunic of fine linen. Clearly a man of authority, and probably the steward Neferu had been waiting for. He stood and turned to face the man.

"I am Akhom, steward of Stephanos of Thmoinepsi. And you are?"

Lusario dipped his head, then placed his hand over his heart. "Lusario of Alexandria."

The steward crossed his arms. "Neferu left a message that she and Menmet had taken in two men. She did not explain how you came to be here."

"Caelus Publilius Martinus and I were traveling upriver on a boat we had rented. It was attacked by a hippo, and we and the crew ended up in the water. When the crocodiles started feeding on the others, my partner thought the odds were better if we swam across the river. But as we were getting out of the river on this side, a crocodile grabbed Caelus."

He glanced toward Menmet's house and found Neferu and Menmet coming toward them. What happened to Scaly Zenobia was his doing, not hers. What the local priests of Sobek thought probably wouldn't matter for him and Caelus, but it might for her. Either way, her advice to conceal the killing was still wise.

"I was able to get the croc to let go, but only after Caelus's leg was broken."

Akhom raised one eyebrow. "Broken? A crocodile bite usually crushes and sometimes takes off the arm or leg."

"It was a smaller croc, only a little longer than my height. Menmet said that's why it wasn't crushed."

"I would like to speak with your partner now."

Lusario swept his hand toward Neferu's cottage. "This way. He was asleep when I came out."

The steward stepped inside and stopped beside Caelus's bed. His straight lips turned down in a frown.

Menmet touched his arm and whispered. "It would be better not to wake him. The bones were sticking out, and many teeth pierced him. His only relief from pain is sleep. I cannot find any lotus roots to make what could help."

Akhom leaned over to inspect Caelus's leg, and although his lips said nothing, his eyes and frown spoke volumes. Did he not expect Caelus to recover? After a slow shake of his head, he led the group outside and back to the shade of the olive tree.

"I have Neferu and Jason sleeping with me so the young man has a place to mend." Menmet rubbed the back of her hand. "I have been cooking for all of us since they came. Neferu helps, and I am happy to keep doing that."

"I saw the pallet you put together for your second guest." Akhom rubbed his jaw, then fixed his gaze on Lusario. "While your friend is trying to heal, you may stay in Neferu's cabin, and she and Jason will stay with Menmet. I will provide enough to feed the two of you for a few days while you tend him."

"I thank you. Our trunk was tied to the deck, so we lost all but a few drachmas in the river when the boat sank. But as soon as Caelus doesn't need someone at his side all the time, I'll be looking for work to earn our passage back to Alexandria."

"What do you know how to do?" Akhom crossed his arms.

How and where he could find work—Lusario had made it sound easy to calm Caelus's fear, but he had no idea himself. Was the solution standing before him?

"We were going upriver to evaluate building sites at a Roman-owned estate and design a villa that should please the owner's wife."

"I do not know anyone in need of an architect or builder." The corners of the steward's mouth turned down.

"But that's not all I can do. I worked as a tutor before going to Alexandria to study. After I met Caelus in Carthago, I returned to Alexandria with him to study architecture and engineering with Zenon, one of the best men teaching such things."

Akhom's eyebrows rose. "You have worked as a tutor? When and where?"

"My father had a school for elite boys in Cyrene, and I taught with him."

The steward's brow furrowed. "Cyrene? So, you're not Alexandrian?" His nose twitched. "Are you even Greek?"

Lusario squared his shoulders and raised his chin. If he could convince Akhom to hire him, Caelus would have somewhere to heal while he earned passage money. Caelus had ordered him to act like a free man. It was time to display the confidence, even the pride, of the elite students he'd deferred to for years.

"Of course, and I tutor as you would expect of a Greek scholar who has studied in Alexandria for five years."

The steward's straight lips curved into a slight smile. "Good. Master Stephanos's oldest grandson is eleven. Stephan is not an enthusiastic student. I have just released his second tutor because his mother was unhappy with the man's teaching style, so I need to find another who can deal with the boy and complete his training to prepare him for a final year in Alexandria. Finding such a man might take some time, given Zenobia's…active interest in her son's education. Would you be able to take over tutoring him while you are here?"

Unhappy with his teaching style? Lusario fingered his lip. If the mother was unhappy, was that because the tutor demanded too much of her child or too little? A boy who could be nice or deliberately cruel, a mother who spoiled him and his younger brother…not ideal, but nothing he couldn't deal with.

Lusario responded with a subdued smile. "I'd be happy to do that as soon as Caelus has recovered enough that he doesn't need me here full time to care for him."

Akhom's gaze shifted to the cottage door, then returned to Lusario. "Since you will be getting lodging and food, a drachma a day seems appropriate. He usually studies only half a day."

"I agree that would be appropriate. With it taking at least six weeks for a broken leg to heal, I believe I can tutor Stephan for two months for you."

The steward's smile turned warm. "Then we will plan on that arrangement." He offered his arm, and Lusario gripped his forearm to confirm the contract.

"I thank you for enabling me to care for my friend here and to earn what we'll need to return to Alexandria."

Akhom's mouth twitched. "Perhaps I will be thanking you if Stephan learns better than he has with the men before you."

Zenobia sat at the table, her boys beside her, as the servants cleared their dirty plates from the main course and prepared to serve dessert.

When Akhom entered, she dabbed her lips with a napkin. "You're back."

"I am, and all was well at the smaller farms. But I came to tell you that I found a tutor for Stephan for the next two months. That will give me time to find the right man who can complete your son's preparation for his studies in Alexandria."

Stephan wadded up his napkin and threw it onto the table. "I don't want another gray-haired old man who thinks the words of long-dead philosophers are the most important things in the world. They never did anything themselves."

Akhom shifted his gaze to Stephan, and his slight smile turned into a frown. "This one is different. Lusario of Alexandria is available because the boat he was traveling on was destroyed by an angry hippo. He and his Roman friend swam the river, and just below our levee, he fought a crocodile to save his friend."

Stephan sat up straight, eyebrows raised. "Really?"

The steward's mouth twitched. "Yes. He has agreed to tutor you for two months starting when his friend improves enough that he is not needed to watch over him. He will be returning to Alexandria in two months or so. But while he is here, a man like him will expect you to work hard and always do your best. Can you do that?"

Stephan's eager nod received a nod in reply. "Then I will tell him you will be ready when he is."

Karpos thrust his fists into his hips. "Why don't I have a tutor, too?"

Zenobia patted his shoulder. "It's customary to start your studies when you're ten, as Stephan did."

"But Jason has a tutor, and I'm two years older than him."

The steward raised his chin and looked down his nose at Karpos. "Your brother started when he was ten. That is the usual age. I see no reason for you to start early."

"But Jason has. If he can do it, why can't I? I'm smarter than him."

Akhom crossed his arms. "You are older than him. That does not mean you are smarter. I have seen him reading and writing. He is doing very well because he pays attention to his tutor and works hard to learn what she teaches." His nose wrinkled. "I do not think you are ready to do that. Until you are, there is no point in getting you a tutor. But when Master Stephanos comes home, you can ask him."

Zenobia moved behind Karpos and wrapped him in her arms. "It's obvious my son is much smarter than that boy his own father rejected. I'm certain Stephanos will see that and act accordingly."

"Hmm." Akhom shrugged. "When Master Stephanos returns, he will decide what each of his grandsons should be doing. Two of the boys will continue with tutors. Whether the third will begin...you can try to convince him Karpos is ready."

He tipped his head to Zenobia. "Since I returned later than usual, I still have a few things to check before retiring. So, I will leave you now."

"Of course." She flicked her hand toward the door, as if she was dismissing him. She returned to her seat, and the serving girl set a plate of pastries in front of her. She took one, and pushed the rest down the table where the boys could reach them. Between them, they would eat every morsel.

She bit the corner off and scooped out some of the fruit filling with her tongue. Theodoros's brat had already won over Akhom after less than two weeks at the estate. Would Stephanos be so easily swayed? How long would it take before Jason replaced Karpos in his grandfather's affection?

That boy needed to go, one way or another, before that could happen.

# Chapter 38

## Someone Else to Trust?

*Morning of Day 21*

Lusario carried the two breakfast bowls back to Menmet's cottage. There was too much left in Caelus's again.

When he entered, two smiles greeted him.

Neferu took the bowls, and both smiles faded.

"So, the pain still keeps him from eating." Menmet rested her hand on Lusario's arm. "Akhom found me some lotus roots." She pointed at a pitcher on the counter. "I started soaking them in wine to pull out the medicine that will help his pain. But it won't be done until tomorrow, so he'll have one more day with no relief."

A knock made them all turn.

A male house servant stood in the doorway. "Mistress Zenobia wants Jason to come for another family dinner. But she says that he is to clean up and get the stench of donkeys off him before he comes this time."

Neferu set the bowls on the counter. "I will attend to that before I escort him there."

He broke eye contact and cleared his throat. "Mistress Zenobia said the boy is old enough to get there unescorted. You are not to use bringing him to the house as an excuse to come there." Without waiting for a reply, he left.

Lusario moved to the door and watched the messenger stride toward the main house. He glanced down at Neferu when she joined him. "Doesn't it seem odd that she doesn't want you to escort her nephew to the house? He's smaller than many boys his age, even if he is smarter than most."

"Zenobia has wanted me to stay away from the main house since the first time she saw me." Neferu fingered her hair. "She doesn't like what I look like."

She lowered her gaze, and a blush overspread her cheeks. With the perfect symmetry and exotic allure of her facial features, that made her even more striking. He'd never seen a woman who fit her name better.

Any woman might feel some jealousy. With an eleven-year-old son, the mistress of this estate would be at least thirty, and any loveliness she might have had would be fading. If she had a husband irresistibly drawn to youth and beauty…

"Then Karpos complained to his mother after I kept him from breaking the toys that two men Jason loved at the old estate had made for him. I've been banned from the main house since then. If she learns that you didn't let Karpos do what he wanted with Mikro, she's going to be unhappy that Akhom hired you to teach Stephan."

A Greek wife unhappy with a steward's decision—Neferu's concern about that triggered a wry smile. He'd been a slave in an elite Greek household for most of his life, and the opinion of the mistress of the house rarely mattered.

"Akhom committed to hiring me for two months. He seems like a man who will honor a contract. Our deal included nothing about Zenobia having authority over me. With that name, I assume she's Greek. She's not a Roman wife, who could cancel what a steward arranged. So, nothing can change it without my agreement before her father-in-law returns."

"But she could make being in the house miserable for you."

Lusario's laugh raised her eyebrows. "She could try, but it takes more to make me miserable than what she could do."

Neferu bit her lip. "I do wish I could take him and wait to bring him back." She leaned sideways to where she could see Jason feeding Mikro in the garden. "Last time Zenobia had him to her 'family dinner,' Stephan and Karpos did something horrible to him."

"What did they do?"

"They took him onto the levees past the main house where he hadn't been before, covered his head, pushed him down, and left him there when it was almost dark. I kept expecting a servant to bring him home, but when it was fully dark and he hadn't returned, I went looking for him."

"How did you find him?"

"The doorkeeper told me he'd left with Stephan and Karpos heading away from where we live. They returned without him. A kitchen helper pointed out which way they headed when they passed her in the herb garden. So I went that way and found him sitting on the edge of a levee, so quiet and looking so small. As we walked back to our house, I taught him how to find his way home by looking for the lights of the worker's houses and following levees that brought him toward them."

"Is he afraid of his cousins now?"

His own gaze followed hers to Jason where he scratched under the chin of his contented charge.

"No. He wasn't afraid then either. He decided if he just waited there, someone would come find him sometime. But he was hurt. Stephan had acted like he wanted to be Jason's friend and then betrayed his trust."

"Then he learned a valuable lesson."

Sadness filled her eyes. "I suppose he did, but I hate seeing him hurt. But knowing how to find your way home alone—that is important."

"It is, but that's not what I meant. Never be too quick to trust anyone, even if they seem friendly, even if you should be able to trust them. A man who's untrustworthy in little things isn't to be trusted for bigger things. Even if he's trustworthy about some things, that doesn't mean he always will be. But when a man risks himself for you—that's a man you know you can trust."

"You speak like you have experience." When she turned her gaze from Jason to him, the warmth of her smile surprised him. "Caelus can certainly trust you completely."

"He earned my trust and loyalty by saving me from drowning in the sea."

Her gasp was what he expected. "He did what?"

"We were going up the coast to visit a Greek shrine to see how its gardens were designed, and I got knocked off the ship. He dove in to keep me from drowning until the rowboat came for us."

"And now you've returned the favor."

"That's what he says. But I would have fought the croc for him even if he hadn't done that. Since the day I met him, he's treated me like a friend." He gave her his warmest smile. "And a person who would risk drowning or"—he tapped her arm with one finger—"take on a croc with a hoe to save me has my trust and loyalty, no matter what happens."

She looked away. "When we treat others like we want to be treated ourselves, that naturally builds trust."

"Will you be starting today's lessons shortly?"

"I was just going to tell Jason is was time when you came."

"Caelus was sleeping when I brought the bowls, and I don't expect him to awaken for a while. While you're in the house tutoring, would you keep an eye on him?"

"I can do that."

"So, now is a good time for me to meet my future student…and his mother, if I can. Since she was the reason the last two tutors left, I'd like to find out what she expects of a tutor. Then I can satisfy at least part of it or maybe help her understand why, for the sake of her son, I will be teaching the way I do."

She stepped outside and waved at Jason. When he returned the wave, she curled her fingers to summon him. He took Mikro's feeding bucket from its hook and headed toward Menmet's house to rinse it.

"I hope your meeting goes well." She tipped her head back to meet his gaze with somber eyes. "Do not tell them you killed the croc." She'd lowered her voice to a whisper. "In Arsinoe, it's mostly Egyptians who worship Sobek, but some Greek families worship a mix of the Greek and Egyptian gods. But even if Zenobia only worships the Olympian gods, she might say something to someone Egyptian who will be angered by what you did. They might blame me as well. Even though I didn't really hurt it, I did try."

Lusario moved to her side so she would hear his own soft words. "I've lived with men where I had to watch everything I said. I never speak without considering possible consequences."

She took a step away from him. "Is Caelus one of those men?"

His laugh raised her eyebrows. "Caelus is one of only two men that it's safe to tell my true thoughts and to share my deepest concerns."

That was almost true. Timon was the one man he never had to worry about losing as a friend, no matter what he said or did. Caelus's respect was something he never wanted to lose, and that meant he sometimes held things back.

Her quiet sigh drew his gaze to her enchanting face. Was that loneliness he saw in those eyes? "It's been too long since I had a friend like that. Both of the ones I had are gone now."

"I'm sorry. Before I had one, I didn't know what a treasure it is. To have it and then lose it...that's almost too sad."

Neferu forced a smile. "Perhaps, in time, I'll make a friend here who is like that."

"It's not something I've seen myself, but I've heard some husbands and wives have that level of trust. Perhaps someday you will."

"I don't expect to meet a man here who would want me as his wife. But if I did, I doubt he'd be pleased to know my thoughts about the most important things in life."

Jason had reached the bench where he cleaned the bucket, and Neferu left Lusario's side to join the boy there.

One corner of his mouth lifted. To expect no man would want her—was she really that naïve about how men thought? She was the most beautiful woman he'd ever met, and living in the second greatest city of the empire meant he'd seen more women than most. Any man with even one eye couldn't fail to see that, and many would want to be able to show her off to others as their own.

But maybe the kind of man who would want her for that reason wouldn't be the type that cared what she thought as long as she stayed beautiful. Master Volero's wife Artoria had probably been gorgeous when she was Neferu's age. She was still a pretty woman, even after giving birth to Caelus and two almost grown daughters who had inherited her beauty.

But watching Volero Martinus dine with Artoria when it was only family made it obvious that her thoughts about almost everything were shallow and selfish. Her husband only paid attention so he wouldn't have to put up with her anger when she asked him about something she'd said and he hadn't heard it.

Yesterday Menmet had borrowed someone's tunic for him to wear while she washed his. Even with Caelus's bloodstains, the fine linen of his blue-edged tunic should tell Zenobia he wasn't an ordinary workman. Elite women paid attention to things like that, whether Greek or Roman. So, he would don it for this meeting before leaving Caelus.

When he met the mistress of the Stephanos estate, he expected the vanity of an elite woman. He knew how to play the part of a man of some importance to impress her. But would the mother of a son like Karpos merely be another Artoria, self-centered but basically harmless, or something far worse?

When Lusario knocked on the main house's door, a youth opened it partway, then froze, staring at Lusario's waist. Maybe it was the blood stains that remained after Menmet washed his tunic. But it could be the dagger that he'd used twice to keep himself and Caelus alive. When he'd worn it in Alexandria, no one did more than glance at it. Did a dagger look different once it had been used to kill? Or did he look different now?

"I'm Lusario of Alexandria. Akhom hired me to tutor Stephan for two months while I'm staying at this estate. I've come to meet my new student."

The youth opened the door enough to admit him. "Mistress Zenobia said she wanted to meet you the first time you came to the main house."

"As she wishes. I'm happy to talk with both her and Stephan."

The doorkeeper left him in the courtyard and disappeared into what was probably the kitchen. A woman with flour still on her hands came out, climbed the stairs, and entered the women's room off the balcony.

A boy starting his growth spurt burst through the kitchen doorway, walking so fast he was almost trotting.

"I'm Stephan, son of Horion. Akhom told us about you last night." He wrinkled his nose. "I'm ready for someone new. My last tutor…he complained too much when I didn't want to learn the boring things he tried to teach me."

"Lusario of Alexandria." He let a wry smile form. "I've never been accused of complaining about students or boring them too much for them to want to learn. But a true love of learning is the sign of a boy who will grow into a leader that others naturally follow. Leaders are willing to put in the work needed to master what I'll be teaching you."

He crossed his arms. "I'll begin tutoring you in a few days, and I will expect that of you, as I have of others I've taught."

Stephan's head bobbed up and down rapidly. "What was it like to fight a crocodile?"

"You heard about that?" Lusario laughed. "It was terrifying."

The boy's eyes widened. "You were afraid? But I thought you must be the most courageous of men to do that."

"Courage isn't the lack of fear. It's the determination to do what must be done even when it scares you half to death. If I had done nothing, my friend would have died. That was something I would do anything to prevent."

"Even die?"

"What we are willing to die for is the true measure of each of us. True friendship is worth the sacrifice of whatever it takes, even life itself."

The boy's slow nod was what Lusario had hoped for. Perhaps this one wouldn't be as hard to teach as the steward led him to believe.

A woman, probably in her mid-thirties, appeared on the balcony, dressed in a green *chiton* of fine linen with a necklace of garnets and matching earrings. She descended the stairs as if she were a queen entering an audience hall and approached him with a superior smile.

"I am Zenobia. Akhom told me last night that you would be available to tutor my son while we seek a superior tutor to take over his training. What is your name?"

"Lusario of Alexandria." With a slight sideways tip of his head while not lowering his chin, he acknowledged her words without sending a message of subservience.

From the moment she emerged from the upstairs room, she radiated her expectation of total dominance over any who worked in that household. He had to put up with that from Florus before Volero Martinus bought him. But he owed this woman who'd driven off two tutors in two years no such deference. Caelus said to act like a free man, and he would.

The boy who had tried to get Jason's donkey entered the courtyard from the kitchen. Grasped in his hand was a fruit-filled pastry, and he looked like he ate more of them than was good for him. His head drew back and his mouth curved into a scowl when he spotted Lusario. Then he marched over to his mother.

"That's the man who wouldn't let me have my baby donkey. Tell him I get whatever I want when I want it."

Irritation flashed across Zenobia's unremarkable features and disappeared as swiftly as it appeared. "This is Stephan's temporary tutor until Akhom finds a permanent one. You don't need a baby donkey. Those are for peasants. Your grandfather got you a fine horse to ride, and his stableman is teaching you how to ride it. So, hush."

Karpos crossed his arms, and he muttered as his scowl deepened. His mother ignored him.

Lusario's lips twitched at that exchange. He pitied the poor man who would be hired as Stephan's permanent tutor. Especially when Karpos started his lessons in two years. But that wasn't his problem.

He'd planned on telling Zenobia what he expected of a student and how he taught, but if Stephan was as receptive as he seemed, the lessons should go well for the next two months. Until she asked, perhaps it was better to say nothing she might want to argue about. Sleeping cats kept their claws sheathed and their fangs to themselves.

"I look forward to teaching your son, but I need to return to my business partner. With a newly broken leg, he still needs my help with many things. I'll start Stephan's lessons when that changes, probably in a few days. So, I'll leave you now." He offered Zenobia a social smile and received a condescending tip of her head. Then she turned and walked into the kitchen.

He passed through the entranceway and took the road to the workers' cottages. Given that he and Caelus could both have died in the river, their present situation was not too bad. A little over two months and they would be headed home to Alexandria. If Latro hadn't already hired his architect, perhaps they'd be passing this way again. But a distant view of this estate from their next boat to Thmoinepsi was as close as he'd want to get.

# Chapter 39

## Maybe Better?



*Afternoon of Day 21*

Neferu swung the hoe in short strokes, clearing the new weeds that had sprouted near her onions. If anyone had told her she'd be trying to kill a croc with it, she couldn't have held in the laughter. But there was nothing funny about what had happened.

*I thank You, God, that Lusario knew how to kill the beast once I distracted it. Thank You for sparing Caelus from so horrible a death.*

But it hurt to watch him in so much pain. Maybe the lotus extract would help tomorrow, but what could be done today?

Lusario came around the corner. His brow was furrowed, his mouth straight. It was the look he wore when Caelus wasn't watching him. But this time when his gaze met hers, his mouth curved into the friendliest smile.

He waved his hand toward Mikro where he slept under the olive tree. "Looks like you're watching the baby for Jason. Where is he?"

"He went to the donkey stables to check on the mares and their foals. Koshari asked him to do that while he's training the new donkey wrangler at another of Stephanos's estates near here. Jason knows more about donkeys than the gardener who's trying to do Koshari's work while he's gone."

"But he's only six."

"He helped Gaidaros with the donkeys at the Arsinoe estate. When you love something, you learn everything you can about it. He loves donkeys that way."

"I understand that. It's how I feel about designing buildings." He rested one hand against the wall and leaned on it. "I offered earlier to write some short stories that he could read. So, what kind of animals does Jason like?"

"He loved one of the shepherds at his father's estate. Voskos let him help with the sheep and carved him farm animals to play with. A ram, ewes, lambs." She placed her clasped hands atop the hoe's handle and rested her chin on her hands.

"So, sheep would be good. He made a horse, too, and Jason will be learning to ride soon."

Lusario rubbed his jaw. "I've always lived in cities, so I don't know much about sheep, except that's where wool comes from and some say sheep cheese is the best kind. But horses…those I know well. I like them fast and spirited."

She rolled her eyes, but her smile erased any insult in that. "I've never ridden one, but if I ever did, I'd want mine slow and calm. I lived in Arsinoe most of my life, so I'm no expert on any farm animal. But Jason is always grateful for anything special I do for him. He laughs when my donkeys do something a real one never would. I'm sure he'll appreciate your efforts, too. There's a roll of papyrus in the drawer under the shelf I keep the wax tablets on. Use some of that."

"A roll?" His eyebrows rose. "How big a roll? Enough to make many sheets for stories?"

"Yes. My father was a scribe, and I used to make partial copies of different documents for him to add the details while his customer waited. I know how much I'll need for the short stories I'm writing, and I slice that much off the roll."

"If Caelus and I can have some, we'll replace what we've used before we leave. I should earn enough extra beyond what we need for passage to cover that."

"What do you need it for?"

"We made many drawings of the carvings in the tombs and temples near Babylon and Memphis. They were in the trunk that sank with the boat. But we remember enough to start drawing the most important by memory." He ran his fingers through his hair. "Working on this will give Caelus something to think about besides the pain."

"Menmet has a tray that he could use as a drawing table on his lap, if he can sit up."

"He can when I help him. He's asleep right now, but he might like to start when he wakes up."

"If you'll watch Mikro, I'll go borrow the tray. Jason doesn't want him left alone in case Karpos comes back."

Lusario leaned his back against the wall and crossed his arms. "Karpos won't be coming. When I met his mother yesterday, he told her I wouldn't give him Mikro. She told her donkeys were for peasants, so Mikro isn't his. He didn't argue, but I think she's not a woman with whom many would choose to argue. She'd be even more dangerous to disobey."

"I'm glad he didn't get you into trouble with her, like he did me. She's given orders that I'm not to enter the house."

Lusario chuckled. "She came to meet me dressed like many elite women dress for a banquet. She probably doesn't want you inside because you'd be the most beautiful woman there, no matter what you were wearing. She's not the type to want competition in anything, but especially not that." His eyes turned appreciative.

She lowered her gaze and cleared her throat. "I'll get the tray now so you'll have it when he awakens."

Before he could answer, she walked away.

First Sasobek, then Koshari, now Lusario paying unwanted attention to something she couldn't help. But at least Lusario would be leaving in two months, never to return, and hopefully Koshari would find another woman to marry before her four years as a bondservant to Jason were over.

*God, thank You for giving me a believable reason for why I can't marry good men who don't follow You. Please keep them from wanting more from me than I will ever be willing to give. You have my heart, and Your love is all I'll ever need.*

*Morning of Day 22*

Lusario stood by Caelus's bed, watching his friend's chest rise and fall with each breath. It was time for breakfast, but Caelus's appetite hadn't improved at all in the last three days. It might even be worse.

A tap on the open door made him turn. Menmet cradled a cup in her hands.

"Can you wake him? It takes a day for what helps the pain to move from the crushed roots into the wine, and it is ready now. I would like him to drink this before he eats breakfast."

As she set the cup on the counter, Neferu appeared in the doorway holding two bowls. She set them beside the cup and left without even looking at him.

Odd. Why had she gone from that pleasant conversation yesterday afternoon to ignoring him now?

Menmet came to Caelus's bedside. "Give him the wine first, then the porridge. After he eats, come get me."

Lusario reached for Caelus's shoulder, but paused before touching him. "What are you planning to do?"

"Clean his wounds again with wine and honey. But before I dribble wine on each break in his skin and smear honey on everything, I want the lotus wine to make his pain less."

"I'll bring the bowls over when he's eaten."

As she looked down at Caelus, her lips narrowed.

"Perhaps you should just stay here. I can come back after we finish eating at my house."

With a single slow shake of her head, she turned and left.

Lusario stared at her retreating back. What made the woman who had tended everyone's injuries for years have such sadness in her eyes? What did she see that he didn't as he watched Caelus sleep?

With his fingertips, he pushed on Caelus's shoulder. It took three pushes before Caelus opened his eyes.

"Menmet brought something for the pain. She said to drink it first, then eat."

He helped Caelus into a sitting position and moved the pillow against his back to help him stay there. Then he handed him the cup.

With the cup just below his nose, Caelus sniffed deeply. "All I'm smelling is the wine, but I bet whatever she mixed in will make it taste worse than it smells." He gave Lusario a crooked smile. "I've yet to taste a medicine that was strong enough to do something that didn't pucker my mouth or make me want to gag."

Lusario mirrored the smile. "She didn't say you'd like it, just that it would make you feel better."

Caelus drew a deep breath and blew it out between pursed lips. "I'd be willing to drink the foulest liquid if it can make this pain go away." He raised the cup to his lips. "Here goes."

He scrunched his eyes before swallowing a big gulp. "Not too bad. Not good, but not as bad as it could be."

Without taking a breath, he drained the cup and held it out.

Lusario returned it to the counter and came back with two bowls. He handed Caelus his porridge and sat behind him to be a backrest while he ate his own breakfast.

If the lotus wine worked, he'd be asking Menmet for the exact recipe for making it. A man never knew when pain might become a brutal companion, and many would pay good money for anything that might help. If they ever got the chance to direct a construction site, their workers would be glad he'd learned that a lotus plant produced much more than a pretty flower.

A light tap on the doorframe announced Menmet's return. "So, how is my patient feeling?"

"It still hurts, but not as bad as it did. Your brew must be doing its work."

"Good. I will start now with the wine and honey. It will hurt, but not as much as the first time. It will speed the healing, and that is worth a little more pain."

"Easy for you to say, but I agree in principle. Like so many things, what sounds good before you start isn't so good while you're doing it."

"Will I need to hold him down?" Lusario moved closer to the bed.

"Maybe, but maybe not. We will only know when I do it."

Menmet patted Lusario's shoulder. "We will have to remove the bark so I can get to everything, so you can help me keep him from moving too much."

Caelus gripped his arm. "Don't worry about whether what you do hurts me. Remember, what matters is the end result, not what we go through to get there."

Lusario acknowledged the command with a nod, then turned his attention to Menmet.

"Just tell me what to do."

# Chapter 40

THE FIRST LESSON

When Menmet finally finished and the bark supports were back in place, Lusario knew one thing for certain. It was harder to watch a good friend suffer than it was to bear it himself. Each sucked in breath, each low moan spoke more than words ever could. When he let his gaze drift to the exposed leg, the skin around some bites was an angry red, and the first rinse of wine washed away the cloudy fluid oozing from them.

"I am done for today. Tomorrow I will use oil instead of wine, and that might hurt less." Menmet tightened the last knot holding the bark in place and straightened.

A deep sigh drained Caelus's lungs as his body relaxed for the first time since she started. "How is it looking?"

She forced a smile. "Some places are a little more red and swollen. But I have seen the same with dog bites, and those usually heal well."

When she turned away and Caelus could no longer see, her smile faded. Deep concern filled her motherly eyes as she turned her gaze on Lusario.

"I will let Neferu know we are done. She will bring Jason for his lessons. We thought it better for him not to see until it heals more."

Caelus placed his hands behind his head and settled into the pillow. "I'm feeling a little better today. You don't need to stay with me every minute. So, if you want to start your tutoring to earn our way home, I'll be fine."

"You're not ready to be alone yet." Lusario crossed his arms. Caelus's independent streak was mostly a good thing, but not when he wanted to do too much too soon.

Caelus raised one finger. "Ah, but I won't be alone. Neferu will be teaching Jason until lunchtime. So, you don't need to be trapped inside with an invalid when she's here."

He reached out and nudged Lusario's side. "She's easier on the eyes than you are, and her voice is more musical, too. Haven't you noticed?"

Caelus's wink was usually enough to trigger a grin or a roll of Lusario's eyes, but not this time.

"I have. Jason obeys her well, so she can probably keep you in line, too." Lusario gave Caelus the smile he wanted. "I guess I'll go to the main house and see if Stephan is ready to begin."

Jason bounced through the door with Neferu behind him and came to the bedside. "I told Mikro the last story you told me. His ears twitch when he likes something." He wiggled his ears with his fingers. "I think it's the best one yet. He wants to meet you soon. I hope you're feeling better today."

"Some." Caelus's smile was enough to fool the boy, but Neferu's solemn eyes revealed she knew better.

"Neferu, please tell this man he can leave me and go tutor for a while because you'll watch over me."

She offered a calm smile to each in turn. "Of course. And if Caelus should need more than I can do, I'll send Jason to get you."

"Very well. Time to start earning our passage home." He tapped Caelus's shoulder with his knuckles and headed out the door. There really was nothing he could do that Neferu wouldn't, and the sooner he started working, the sooner he'd have money for anything beyond the room and board Akhom was providing.

When he reached the main house, his first set of knocks brought no response. Likewise the second. But when he made a fist and pounded, a youth opened the door enough for him to step inside.

"I've come to see if Stephan is ready for his first lesson."

The youth bolted the door behind him. "I'll get him."

Karpos came out of the dining room and tromped over. "What are you doing here?"

"I've come for Stephan."

The boy tipped his head back to look down his nose, making the resemblance to his mother too obvious. "Stephan is doing something with me." He flicked his hand toward the door. "Go back and tend my donkey."

Adopting an amused look, Lusario scanned and then ignored the obnoxious brat. Relief that he'd been hired to tutor only Stephan turned into pity for the tutor who'd be starting Karpos's training in two years. But if he'd had to tutor both to earn passage to get Caelus back to Alexandria, he would have done it. It would only be two months, and a man could do almost anything for that long if he had to. He'd done so before; he could do it again.

"You heard me." Karpos shoved his fists onto his hips. Lusario looked past him to the kitchen where the doorkeeper had vanished.

With a snort, Karpos spun and marched toward the kitchen as well. Just as he reached it, Stephan came through the doorway.

"Let's go." Karpos slowed his steps, waiting for Stephan to follow.

"My tutor is waiting. We can do it later." Stephan sauntered toward Lusario instead.

Karpos grabbed Stephan's arm and tried to pull him into the kitchen.

Stephan gripped his brother's wrist and lifted the hand off his arm. "I said later." He shoved his little brother aside and headed toward Lusario again.

With a huff and a look that threw daggers at Lusario, Karpos stormed into the kitchen and disappeared.

Lusario met Stephan halfway across the courtyard. "My friend is feeling better today. So, we can start your lessons. Where do you study?"

"This way." With a curl of his fingers as invitation, Stephan led Lusario up the stairs and into a small room where a table with two chairs sat close to a window. A cabinet holding tablets, papyrus sheets, and a few scrolls stood by one wall, and a narrow rope bed for the future tutor was pushed against the opposite one.

Stephan stopped by the table, but he remained standing. "Do you always wear a dagger?"

"I do."

The boy fixed his gaze on the unadorned sheath and plain-handled dagger hanging from Lusario's belt. "Can I hold it? Some of the farmworkers carry knives when they're doing something that needs one, but I've never touched a dagger before."

Lusario drew it from its sheath. "You can, but it's not a toy. I keep the blade very sharp, so you need to be careful." He handed it to the boy.

Stephan gripped the hilt and made a few playful thrusts. "Do you know how to use it in a fight?"

"Alexandria is a big city. It can be dangerous at night, and we often come home late. So, I trained with a bodyguard."

"Will you teach me how to use one?"

Lusario snorted. "Not unless your grandfather or father asks me to. I doubt either will, even if you try to persuade them. You're far too young to use one wisely. A dagger is a tool for defending yourself, not a toy."

He held out his hand, and Stephan placed it in his palm.

"Have you ever stabbed someone?"

Lusario slipped the dagger into its sheath. "Yes, to keep someone from killing me and Caelus."

"Did you kill him?"

"Yes."

Lusario clenched his jaw. He hadn't meant to tell the boy. It just slipped out. He should never have had to kill a man. If only Temhotep had been honest. If only his helmsman hadn't tried to kill him first. They'd be at Latro's estate right now, selecting a spot to build, drawing up plans sure to delight Latro's wife, reveling in their first chance to do what they'd trained for.

But he'd trained in more than architecture, more than engineering in Alexandria. He'd trained to kill.

The bodyguard who trained him said there was no time to reflect on what you were doing in the middle a fight. Just do what it took to keep the one you were protecting alive. The first time was hardest, but if you survived that, it got easier each time.

He could still see the shock in Narmer's eyes when he thrust the dagger up into his heart. But that only lasted a moment. Life flickered out, and there was no emotion there when he pulled the blade free, leaving the shell of what had been the helmsman. As he turned to face the next attacker, he was ready to do it again to save Caelus.

But those dead eyes and the warm blood on his hand…he tried not to remember, but he probably always would. He didn't want do it again to see if it got easier.

He pressed his index finger into Stephan's chest. "But that is not something you are to tell your mother or Akhom or anyone else here. I'm an ordinary man who was faced with the choice of kill or die, and I chose to live."

"Can I tell Karpos?"

"No. Especially not Karpos. Your brother has no more self-control than an untrained puppy. He would be telling everyone, and being a killer is not a reputation I want."

He tapped Stephan's chest again. "Give me your word that it stays between you and me."

"I won't tell anyone. I promise." Solemn eyes accompanied Stephan's nod.

The boy probably meant it now, but would he keep his word?

Lusario took a wax tablet and stylus from the cabinet and handed them to Stephan. "Sit. I live my life by Stoic principles, and I'll be teaching you the wisdom of some Stoic philosophers. Your next tutor will be teaching you about many others. Learn their words, take them to heart, and you'll know how to live well as a man. They wrote in Greek and Latin, but for now we'll discuss Greek ones, since that's what you speak."

He crossed his arms and looked down at the seated boy. "I understand you're tired of learning what men who died hundreds of years ago taught. So, we'll start with a Stoic philosopher who was still alive when your grandfather was your age, Chaeremon of Alexandria. If your grandfather went there to study, it is possible he heard him speak."

Stephan's eyes widened. "Really?"

"Yes. Chaeremon was a man of both words and action. He served as an ambassador to Claudius when he was emperor and tutored the future emperor Nero while in Rome. He served as head of the Museion, the greatest school in the Empire. That's where I studied in Alexandria and where you will be going in a few years if you study hard and prove you are ready. He wrote a history of Egypt, a book on the interpretation of hieroglyphics, and another on comets. I have seen the original scrolls he wrote in the Great Library, where he was Chief Librarian as well. When you go there, you can see them, too."

Lusario tapped the wax tablet with his finger. "Prepare to write. I'm going to recite from one of his writings, and you will write down the words as I speak. Then we'll talk about what they mean."

Stephan sat straighter and slid his chair closer to the desk. Stylus in hand, he grinned at Lusario. "I'm ready."

# Chapter 41

## A Missing Son

*Carthago, Day 22*

Graptus, steward of Volero Martinus's town house, watched with arms crossed while the ship bringing Caelus home from Alexandria was pulled stern-first into the quay.

The gangplank was lowered, and several passengers disembarked. But Caelus was not among them. Two crewmen carried a few trunks out of the cabin and off the ship, and their owners claimed them. While some left right away or as soon as one or two trunks were delivered to them, a few well-dressed men lounged in foldable chairs under a canopy attached to the closest warehouse. Their menservants, some sitting on their trunks, waited for more baggage to come from the hold.

Like two streams of ants, dock slaves disappeared below deck and returned carrying crates, amphorae, barrels, and trunks up to the quay. A man looked at each and directed them to different wagons and carts or to the servants waiting for the rest of their masters' baggage.

When the last of the menservants left, one chest and a medium-sized trunk remained.

Graptus spoke to the two house slaves who'd brought the cart for taking Caelus's baggage home. "It says *Zefyros* on the stern, so this is the ship Master Caelus said he would be arriving on. Follow me."

He strode to the trunk and chest that sat alone where the other passengers' baggage had been. The trunk bore a brass plate near the keyhole. Graptus bent over to read it.

G. Publilius Martinus. It was one of a pair of his grandfather's trunks that had gone to Alexandria with Master Caelus. He peered at the chest and found a plate bearing the same name. Caelus must still be on the ship, but why would he tarry so long?

"Load these and wait for me."

He approached the man overseeing the ship's unloading.

"Caelus Martinus had passage on this ship, and as his father's steward, I have claimed his trunk and chest to take to the Martinus town house. But he didn't come off the ship with the other passengers."

The man shrugged. "Everyone I saw during the voyage got off. Maybe you missed him."

Unease gripped Graptus. "I watched the rowboats pull you in. I did not miss him." He rubbed his jaw. "I would like to speak with your captain."

The man pointed at the gangplank. "He's still aboard. Go ahead."

Graptus boarded the ship and approached a crewman who lounged against the railing. "Where is your captain?"

The crewman straightened. The words he spoke were neither Latin, like the question, nor Greek. But Graptus tried again in Greek.

"Your captain. I want to speak with him."

The man's eyes narrowed. "Captain. Speak." Then understanding replaced confusion in his eyes. "Come." With a curl of his fingers, he led Graptus to the cabin. He pointed at the room closest to the entrance. "Captain."

The captain sat at a desk by the window, stylus in hand, with a tablet open before him. Graptus cleared his throat, and the man turned in his chair.

"What do you want?"

"I came to take Caelus Publilius Martinus home. His trunk and chest were unloaded, but he hasn't left the ship."

The captain nodded. "He hasn't left the ship because he never got on the ship. When he failed to board on time, we sailed without him."

"Did he send any message as to why he wasn't coming on the ship that carried his baggage?"

"Not that I heard or saw."

The captain was turning back to his desk when Graptus cleared his throat. The captain frowned, but he looked at Graptus again.

"His father, Councilman Volero Publilius Martinus, will need to know what happened to him. What shall I tell him?"

"Tell him his son stayed in Alexandria." With a shrug and a dismissive wave of his hand, the captain turned back to the tablet.

Graptus retraced his steps along the deck and up to the quay. Why would Master Caelus have his baggage loaded if he wasn't planning to come on this ship? What had happened to keep him from boarding? Where was he now? Was he all right?

With each question, his breaths came faster.

When he reached the cart, he paused. "Take Master Caelus's things home and put them in his room. Do not say anything to Mistress Artoria or anyone else about him not coming off the ship. I'm going to see Master Volero at the council meeting."

As the men pushed the cart up the street, Graptus followed behind. They would take the cart straight to the town house. He must find Master Volero with the distressing news that Caelus had failed to board even though he'd told them to expect him and his baggage had arrived. How Mistress Artoria would be given the news that could make her hysterical…that was for the master to decide.

Volero Martinus stood at the front of the council chamber, listening to Paternus and Viator, two councilmen old enough to be his father, decide the order of business for their next meeting. It was gratifying that they now included him in these conversations, as they had his father before he died almost a year ago.

With the conversation finished, he turned to leave. Caelus was due home today, and that thought brought a smile. A smile that quickly faded.

Volero's father had sent his eighteen-year-old grandson off to finish his education in Alexandria, as his wife Artoria had insisted every elite young man should do. She wanted to impress her female friends with their son's scholarly brilliance and to increase his desirability as a husband for some important man's daughter.

One year would have been enough for that, but Caelus had wheedled three years instead of the usual one or two out of his grandfather by promising he could become an architect and start a new family business. But with Father dead and Caelus staying in Alexandria with no mention of completing those studies, it was time for his son to learn what it took to run the businesses they already had and to begin his service to Carthago, as all the Martinus men had before him.

But when Volero stepped out into the blazing Carthaginian sun, a grim-faced Graptus met him.

"You look like someone just died." Volero kept walking, and Graptus fell in beside him.

"I hope not, Master."

Volero stopped midstride. "What do you mean, you hope not?"

"Master Caelus's baggage came, but he and his manservant weren't on the ship."

"What happened?" Volero's gut clenched. How could Caelus not be on the ship where he'd booked passage?

"The captain said he never showed up to board, so they sailed without him."

"Did he know why Caelus didn't show? Was there some message for me explaining that?"

"No. I asked if there was any message, and he said none that he saw or heard. When I asked what I should tell you, he said to say Caelus stayed in Alexandria." Graptus rolled his eyes. "As if that was a sufficient explanation!"

"Is the ship still there?"

"It was when I came to tell you."

Volero reversed directions. "We're going to talk to that captain right now. He'll give me a better explanation, or…"

What would he do? If Caelus hadn't sent a message, how could the captain know anything?

But he still needed to know every detail the captain might have forgotten without being asked the right questions.

He lengthened his stride as much as a long tunic and toga would allow. Someone must know something about where Caelus was, and he'd make them tell him.

When the captain of the *Zefyros* heard the sharp rap on his door, he turned in his chair to find the Martinus steward. "I told you he didn't board in Alexandria."

Then a Roman, dressed in toga and long tunic with narrow red stripes, stepped past the steward. With his chin held high and his mouth curved down, he entered the room. "My steward said my son didn't board, but I'd like to know more about how that happened."

The captain stood. He was a tall man himself, and sitting gave an advantage to the elite Roman glaring at him. "As I told your man, when it was time for us to cast off, he hadn't boarded the ship."

His first mate appeared in the doorway behind the steward. The captain raised his hand to stop him entering. But it also signaled him to stay, just in case he was needed.

"Our passengers are all told to be on board an hour before we finish loading the cargo. It was at least a quarter hour after we finished when he still hadn't come. That was plenty of time to wait past when he'd been told to be there. If he'd sent a message asking for a short delay, maybe I could have waited." He shrugged. "But without one, I assume a passenger isn't coming, and we leave as scheduled. Other ships were waiting for our berth."

"So, he sent no message about why he wasn't boarding?"

"None at all. For whatever reason, your son stayed in Alexandria, like I told your man."

The Roman's eyebrows plunged, but at first he said nothing. He merely locked his gaze on something through the window. "So, I'll need to look for him in Alexandria."

"You will."

The Roman tipped his head in acknowledgement before turning and striding away with his steward in tow.

The first mate leaned against the doorway and crossed his arms. "That was… interesting."

The captain tightened his lips. "I don't know what he expected. I'd already told his steward there was no message about why his son didn't board after dropping off his baggage."

"There should have been."

The captain was turning back to his desk, but he swung around to face his first mate. "Why do you say that?"

"Because Martinus had decided not to sail with us, and his manservant came to get the trunk and chest that was supposed to be in their room." He rubbed his jaw. "They weren't. Someone had put them in the hold, and they were buried behind a lot of other cargo. His man was going to write a letter for you to give to whoever met them here. But he never brought anything back to me before we sailed."

"Humph. So, I was right when I told him to look for his son in Alexandria." One corner of the captain's mouth rose. "But I'm glad you didn't tell me this earlier. I'd have had to explain why something that should have been in the cabin was deep in the hold instead." He stretched to his full height and raised his chin, as Martinus had. "The noble councilman of Carthago didn't get his son delivered today,"—a broad smile formed—"but at least he got his baggage."

*Headquarters of the XIII Urban Cohort*

Walking as briskly as a toga allowed, Volero and Graptus entered the headquarters of the Urban Cohort near the Forum. When they entered, Tribune Acilius Glabrio's aide, Gaius Sartorus, sat at the desk in the antechamber of the tribune office.

Glabrio was tribune in command of the XIII Urban Cohort, which policed Carthago and the area for a hundred miles around it. As a hands-on commander of his troops, that responsibility kept him more than busy. But as the husband of Volero's niece Martina and a good personal friend, he would want to help find Caelus. No one Volero knew was more capable of finding a missing man.

Volero swallowed hard. During his first month in Carthago, Glabrio had proven he could find one who'd been missing for weeks, whether alive…or dead.

He started past Sartorus's desk, then stopped. "I need to speak to Glabrio immediately."

He turned to Graptus. "You can leave, but find something to do away from the town house. I don't want Artoria asking you about Caelus before I can tell her."

"I'll be at the baths if you need me. How long should I stay away?"

"At least an hour. Maybe two."

"Then I might visit the agora first."

A flick of Volero's hand sent Graptus toward the exit.

Sartorus's knock on Glabrio's door was answered with "enter."

The aide slipped inside, and when he emerged, Glabrio was right behind him.

"Volero. What brings you here still in toga?" Glabrio's eyes narrowed. "And looking like something bad has happened."

Volero took a deep breath. "Caelus was supposed to arrive today. His trunks did. He did not. I'm afraid something terrible has happened, and I don't know what to do."

His Stoic beliefs called for control of his emotions no matter what was happening, but his voice almost broke on "do."

"I can't lose a second son."

Glabrio raised his eyebrow. "Second son?"

"Martina never told you? He was a twin, and he should have been named Vopiscus, like other second-borns. But his brother died within a few hours, and Artoria insisted that was a horrible name to saddle a boy with, telling everyone he was only a second-born twin. She fussed and fussed that she should get to name him since I'd named our firstborn Volero. It wasn't worth fighting over, and she chose Caelus. Why she wanted to name him after a god of the sky…only she knows, but my father didn't object so he became Caelus."

Volero tightened his lips. "None of that matters now. Only his safe return does. But how can I find out why he's not here?"

"Centurion." Two fists striking chests and two voices in unison announced the arrival of one of the four cohort centurions. Dubitatus slowed his steps when he saw them, pausing as if he wanted to find out what was going on before turning into the office nearest Glabrio's.

"We'll discuss this in my quarters." Glabrio placed a hand on Volero's shoulder and guided him toward the narrow passage that led to the private rooms of the tribune in charge. "Can Sartorus join us?"

Volero nodded, and Sartorus closed the antechamber door before following them.

Glabrio directed Volero to one of the wicker chairs beside the tabula table. When he took the other, Sartorus stood behind him. "Tell me what you know."

Hoping to loosen the tension, Volero squeezed the back of his neck. It didn't help.

"I sent a letter to Caelus telling him to come home from Alexandria for a visit and to discuss whether he'd be continuing his studies there or beginning to take on responsibilities here. He replied immediately that he would be arranging passage, and he'd let me know which ship he'd be on as soon as he had. A week ago, I got that letter saying he'd booked passage on the *Zefyros* to arrive today."

He rubbed his lip. "I came out of the council meeting to find Graptus. He told me Caelus's trunk and chest arrived, but the captain had said he and his manservant never boarded the ship. I went to speak to the captain myself, and he told me the same thing. When Caelus hadn't shown up an hour and a quarter after they were supposed to board and hadn't sent a message about anything delaying him, the ship sailed without them. Then I came here."

Glabrio fingered his lower lip. "Did your son include an explanation in the chest or trunk?"

Volero opened his mouth, then closed it. "Graptus didn't say he looked for one before sending them to the town house. So, maybe the answer is there, and this is a false alarm. But I would have given the message to the captain to deliver, not worried my father by making him open my trunk before he knew where I was. I would expect Caelus to do the same."

"Then the first thing we'll do is check that baggage." Glabrio stood. "Let's go."

# Chapter 42

## ALL THEY KNOW

*The Martinus town house*

When they reached the town house, Volero led Glabrio and Sartorus to the small courtyard off the peristyle and up to the balcony.

"Caelus went to Alexandria before I moved here from the estate, so he never lived in this house. Graptus gave him the room that Martina used after Artoria replaced her as *domina* when Father died. She said it was even better than the family bedchambers off the peristyle. More peaceful, and the view of the harbor made her think about life's endless possibilities."

The trunk and chest sat in the center of the room. Glabrio walked past them to look out the window. "I never saw that view before. Your son should like it as much as my wife did."

Volero lifted the chest onto the bed and opened it. One by one, he lifted out the contents and lay them on the blanket. A scroll of Vitruvius's *De Architectura* lay atop some papyrus sheets covered with descriptions, drawings, and numbers that were notes from a lecture by Zenon. Many papyrus sheets filled three portfolios. One set had design ideas for gazebos, mausoleums, and other small buildings that might grace a wealthy estate. Garden plans and waterfall designs filled another portfolio. The final one contained drawings of how a villa would appear from different angles and the floorplan and cut-away views that a builder might use during construction.

But nothing revealed why Caelus hadn't come or where he might be.

"Whoever drew these—they're truly talented." Glabrio tapped one of the waterfall plans. "This is something my father would like at our estate."

A quick glance at the drawing inspired the same thought in Volero. Artoria would love it.

He tugged at the trunk lid. "I don't know where a key might be. Caelus took two with matching locks, but he took one key and his man had the other."

Glabrio turned to Sartorus. "Can you open it?"

"With some heavy wire, yes." Sartorus knelt by the trunk and looked up at Glabrio. "Or your cloak pin if you don't mind me bending it."

Glabrio undid the pin and handed it to Sartorus. By the time he folded the cloak and set it on the bed, Sartorus had the trunk lid open and lifted out the toga that lay on top.

Volero leaned over and dug through the contents. He found no letter about where Caelus was.

"Now what?" His shoulders sagged.

"Someone needs to go to Alexandria." Glabrio straightened the pin enough to fasten it again. "If it were possible, I'd go. But as the son of a senatorial family, I would have to get special permission from Hadrian himself to enter the province of Egypt. But even if I was equestrian so I didn't need the emperor's permission, I'd have to request leave from my post from the Urban Prefect in Rome. Saturninus would never give me permission to go."

Sartorus raised one finger. "But I'm not senatorial, and I don't need Saturninus's permission to do anything. I work for Glabrio, not Rome. I'm willing to go to Alexandria to see if I can find out what's happened."

"That's an excellent idea." Glabrio placed his hand on Sartorus's shoulder. "If it was my son, I'd trust Sartorus to find him if anyone could. He's as good an investigator as I am." He squeezed before lowering his hand. "I'll use one of the optios when I need an aide, and Martina knows how to oversee the businesses you normally take care of for us."

A relieved sigh drained Volero's lungs. "I accept your offer. But I'm going to send my best bodyguard with you to keep you safe."

The chuckle that escaped Sartorus made Volero's head draw back.

"Except for an elbow too weak to carry a legion shield on a twenty-mile training march or fend off too many blows in battle, I'm still a military man. I can hold my own in any fight."

"Taurus will go anyway. I'll be giving you a letter of credit to the bank I use there, and you might need to carry enough money to tempt robbers. No one I know has a bodyguard who's better at watching what's going on around them and sensing when something's amiss. Two are safer than one, anyway, and Caelus might need two to help him when you find him. I'd rather send too many than too few. How soon can you leave?"

"Tomorrow?" Sartorus raised his eyebrows at Glabrio and got a nod in return. "Or the next day at the latest. The sooner we start looking, the easier it is to find someone." He gave Volero a confident smile. "And the fewer days you have to worry about whether he's doing well, wherever he is."

"I sent Graptus to the baths so Artoria wouldn't ambush him with questions about where Caelus is. As soon as he returns, I'll have him arrange passage. Since you're living at Glabrio's town house, I'll have him take everything you'll need there. He'll have the letter of credit and directions to the bank I use. I'll be sending Taurus to you as well."

Glabrio tossed the cloak across his shoulders and repinned it. "Then we'll return to headquarters now."

For the first time since Graptus met him at the council, Volero's shoulders relaxed. "Thank you both for helping me find him." He ran his fingers through his hair. "Now I can look for Artoria and tell her what's happened. Missing a boat doesn't always mean something is horribly wrong. I could never calm her down if I wasn't hopeful myself. With you going to find him, I can tell her I am. But I still expect hysterics and accusations."

He swung his hand toward the door. Sartorus walked onto the balcony and headed for the stairs. But when Glabrio passed, he squeezed Volero's shoulder and offered a sympathetic smile.

It was what Volero expected from anyone who knew his wife as well as his niece's husband did.

Then Glabrio whispered in his ear. "Sartorus believes what Martina and I do. He's an excellent investigator, but he'll also be asking God to guide him. That can make all the difference. We'll all be praying for him to find Caelus safe and well."

Volero answered with a solemn nod, and Glabrio followed Sartorus down the stairs.

Back beside the bed, Volero picked up the scroll from the top of the chest. Vitruvius's *De Architectura, Book 1*. Caelus had written that he saved a lot of money by hiring a scribe to make his personal copies of the ten volumes in the Great Library. He opened it, looking for the drawings Caelus had lavished with praise. He found a description of what architects needed to know. As he scanned the list of everything from mathematics to history to medicine to philosophy, his eyebrows rose. He had no idea so much was required.

He opened the portfolio containing the garden buildings. Some were elegantly simple. Others were heavily decorated like Artoria would prefer. All looked like a professional had made them. Some had comments written on them by the famous architect who was training him. Some were drawn by Caelus and others by Lusario, whom Volero had bought to be Caelus's manservant only because he was familiar with Alexandria. Zenon had praised the work of both young men.

He covered his mouth with his hand. Caelus really had been preparing for what could be a profitable addition to the family businesses.

If his son was found safe and well, he would give permission to spend however much time it took to complete his training and pursue his passion in his chosen career. If he started his business in Carthago, he could still take over as paterfamilias and serve on the council when his time came.

Being an architect wasn't a path to great wealth, but Caelus could probably earn a decent profit. He might even earn fame among those wealthy enough to hire him. But one thing was clear. It could make his son happy while he still did all that family and city required.

With the Vitruvius scroll open before him, Volero sat in his tablinum, sipping the best vintage from his local estate. He startled when Artoria burst through the door.

Eyes wide, face pale, Artoria looked as panicked as he'd felt before talking with Glabrio and Sartorus.

"Caelus was supposed to be home today. Why isn't he here?" A tremor he'd never heard before accompanied the breathless words.

"I don't know. His trunks came on the ship he mentioned in his letter, but the captain said he didn't show up at boarding time. They sailed without him."

Trembling hands covered her nose and mouth. "What could have happened to him? Do you think he's hurt?" Her hands dropped away from her face. She blanched. "Or dead?"

He feigned a look of amusement, although there was nothing funny about the situation. "I highly doubt it. It's very easy to get caught up doing something that takes longer than you expect, and before you know it, you're late for an appointment. I think he simply missed the departure time, so they sailed without him."

He rose and took her hand, then led her to the guest chair and guided her into it. "There is no reason to be panicking. I'm not."

"But Caelus was always so reliable…"

"He is, and that's why I spoke with Glabrio about the matter. Sartorus is his business manager and personal aide for Urban Cohort matters. Glabrio says his man is as good as he is at investigating, and Sartorus is going to Alexandria for me to check into the matter. Both of them are confident Sartorus will quickly find out why he didn't come on the *Zefyros*. There is no good reason to expect anything horrible has happened to him."

He settled into his chair and leaned back in it. "We're likely to get a letter from him even before Sartorus and Taurus reach Alexandria. He might even arrive in Carthago on a different ship before they get there."

"You're sending Taurus with him? Is it that dangerous?"

He assumed a patronizing smile. "Going from one of the great cities of the Empire to another? I wouldn't consider that dangerous myself. But I bought Caelus's manservant so he'd have someone with him who knew the city. Two men are always safer than one alone. I've authorized Sartorus to access my funds in Egypt, and I prefer he have a bodyguard if he does that."

"Well, if you're certain Caelus is all right…"

"As certain as I can be without him standing beside me. So, don't be worrying yourself needlessly." He stood. "Caelus did send his baggage, and he had some drawings in the chest that I think you'll want to see."

From a scroll cubicle on the tablinum wall, he took one of Caelus's portfolios. To the collection of waterfall and garden designs, he'd added a few gazebos. It was better that Artoria not see the handsome mausoleums Caelus had drawn for those needing a fitting place for the remains of their dead.

"When he comes home, would you like him to build any of these at our closest estate? Some are quite exceptional." He placed the drawings on the desk.

She stood and started examining them, one by one. After an initial gasp at the beauty of the first drawing, more than a few oohs and aahs accompanied her inspection.

After tidying the stack, she returned them to the portfolio "We have an amazingly talented son. I'm going to show all these to my friends. They're so beautiful that any of them should be delighted to have Caelus build something for them."

"You can pick out a handful to share. A wise businessman shows his best work first to customers whom he knows are ready to buy. He'll want to keep most to only show people who actually plan to build something. Artists don't let others take their ideas and use them for free."

"I hadn't thought of that. But I'll want to show that handful to a few of the council wives with daughters of the right age to marry him."

Volero kept his smile in place. "That's fine. But they might have to wait a few months for Caelus to finish his training before coming home from Alexandria. Perhaps it's better to let him show them himself after he's home."

"Perhaps. But I can start telling them about the beautiful designs I've seen, even if I don't show any to them." She rose. "Caelus will be as sought after as a son-in-law as you were."

After she left the room, Volero's smile faded. Artoria's fear had been doused and having to listen to her constant worrying had been averted for now.

But that didn't mean her fear wasn't justified. It gnawed at him as well.

He turned his eyes back on the Vitruvius scroll, but his mind couldn't focus on it.

His words and manner had convinced Artoria he wasn't worried, even though he was. It took effort not to dwell on the possibility that Caelus was badly hurt or even dead.

Maybe Glabrio and Sartorus were so sure because they thought the Christian god could do something to fix whatever was wrong. Martina would think that, too. He'd heard her say more than once that her god could take anything, no matter how bad, and bring good out of it for those who loved him. Glabrio always agreed, saying he was living proof of that.

But Caelus didn't love their god, and neither did he. So even if the Christian god could do what they claimed for his followers, what did that mean for Caelus?

# Chapter 43

## Leaving for Alexandria

*The Glabrio town house, early morning of Day 23*

The fast ship to Alexandria that Taurus would take to look for young Master Caelus was leaving midmorning. But he knocked on the back door of the Glabrio town house an hour before Master Volero said to be there.

What Martina fed her household was much better than the food Mistress Artoria allowed for the Martinus slaves. She didn't skimp on serving size, and there would be more than enough to feed him, even arriving unexpectedly. Food on a ship wasn't that good, even for the rich passengers. Tasty food and plenty of it before they sailed would partly make up for that, at least for today.

Tomorrow and the days after—bread, cheese, and dried fruit for every meal was most likely since speed mattered. They'd be crossing long stretches of open sea instead of hugging the coast to reach Alexandria in less than two weeks. So, on most days, he'd get no hot stews and fresh-baked bread to satisfy his hunger at a harbor-area taberna. Not until their final port.

When Master Volero told him he'd be going to Alexandria with Sartorus to look for Caelus, he wasn't surprised. Since none of Martinus's other bodyguards were gladiator-trained or as good at knowing when people around them needed close watching, he was by far Martinus's best.

Caelus was an only son. He would inherit all the responsibilities his grandfather and father had borne. Besides, his father loved him. The master would do anything to get his boy home safe.

He knew Sartorus some from their trip back from Martina's Cigisa estate a few months earlier. After his medical discharge from the Urban Cohort, the former optio had married Platana, Martina's lady's maid, so he lived in the town house, too. Even though he was no longer a soldier of Rome, he still served Glabrio as his aide in all the ways he had while under the tribune's command.

Graptus had booked them passage in a cabin. That was a luxury Taurus never had before. He'd escorted the steward to deliver the name of the ship and the letter of credit to Sartorus just before dinner. But he'd spent the last evening before sailing at Martinus's town house with the few he considered friends. It would be at least a month before he'd see them again.

One corner of his mouth rose. He mostly listened because he wasn't one to talk much, but he'd have more than a few stories to tell when he returned.

They would be leaving for the ship from Glabrio's house with one mid-sized trunk between them. He'd packed everything he was bringing in a satchel that he could carry if it didn't fit in the trunk. From what he'd seen of Sartorus, there would probably be room.

The cook's daughter let him in. "We didn't expect you so early. We just finished breakfast." Her smile started slow and grew. "There's some left. Would you like it?"

"I won't say no. Your mother is a good cook."

She led Taurus to the kitchen table before turning aside to fill a bowl with a savory porridge and a plate with fresh rosemary-laced wheat bread, several chunks of cheese, and a heaping handful of dried dates.

"I'll be back in a little while." She waved her hand toward the counter. "Eat as much as you want." After another quick smile, she headed into the peristyle. He sat and devoured what she'd set before him.

But something was odd. In this household of eight people, he would have expected at least two or three in the kitchen this time of morning.

With a chunk of bread in one hand and the satchel hanging from his shoulder, Taurus wandered into the peristyle to find the man he'd be guarding as they searched.

He heard faint voices from the vestibulum, but he couldn't see anyone. They must be around the corner in the part of the first room where visitors were received.

As he got closer, his ears picked up quiet words in Glabrio's voice. Before stepping past the corner into view of the speaker, he paused.

"We give thanks for the many times You've protected us in the past. Please protect Sartorus as he searches for Caelus. Give him wisdom and a discerning mind as he chooses the steps he must take to find him. Grant him success in the hunt, and let him find Caelus alive and well. Please protect Taurus as well as he joins Sartorus in the search. This we ask in the name of Your blessed son, Jesus."

A chorus of voices said, "Amen."

Taurus inched forward to where he could see. Sartorus knelt before Glabrio, who had his hand on his aide's head. Martina, Platana, and the rest of the household surrounded Sartorus, and each had a hand upon him.

He leaned against the wall and crossed his arms. His mouth almost dropped open before he thought to stop it. He'd known for years that Master Volero's step-mother Juliana was a Christian and that Martina was, too. He'd been warned when Volero's father bought him that he was never to tell anyone about their religion, not even the other slaves of the household. The Martinus men were all Stoics who performed Roman rites in public, but in private, they didn't believe in the gods. He'd never heard Juliana or Martina praying to any god, but he'd assumed they did that behind the mistress's locked door. Women often took religion seriously, even when their men didn't.

But seeing that men worthy of admiration like Tribune Glabrio and Sartorus were secret Christians…if someone had told him that was possible, could he have held in the laugh?

Glabrio opened his eyes, and his smile flipped into a frown as his gaze met Taurus's. "We didn't expect you for an hour or so, Taurus."

"I came early so I wouldn't keep you waiting." He held up the bread. "I was in time for some breakfast. But when I was alone in the kitchen for so long… that seemed odd."

The tribune's frown faded and was replaced by a wry smile. "I'd choose eating here over what Artoria serves, too. Perhaps it's a good thing you came in when you did. You may as well know before you leave that Sartorus will be asking God to direct your search."

Glabrio held up one finger. "But you are to tell no one what you just saw. It could mean the death of any of us."

Taurus bristled. "I kept Mistress Juliana's secret for years. Mistress Martina's, too. I know how dangerous it is. You can count on my silence."

Sartorus stood. "Trust between traveling companions always makes a trip better. Everyone here will be praying for our success and our safe return. I'll be hiding my prayers from others, but I'm glad I won't have to hide them from you."

The trunk they'd be taking sat by the front door, and Sartorus waved his hand toward it. "There's room for that satchel. We'll be sharing a cabin, so we might as well share the trunk."

Someone knocked on the door.

Taurus tipped his head toward it. "That would be the cart Master Volero sent to take it to the ship. I'm ready to leave whenever you are."

Sartorus held his hand out to Platana. "I'll be with you in a few moments." Together they entered a chamber off the peristyle and closed the door.

As most of the household headed back to the kitchen, Glabrio came to Taurus's side. "We both know that hunting a missing person can put you in danger." His voice was barely above a whisper. "Find Caelus for his father, but watch over Sartorus as you do. He'll take great risks to do what he thinks is required. I don't want to lose him." He placed his hand on Taurus's upper arm. "You be careful, too. We'll be praying for your safe return as much as for his."

Taurus's head started to draw back, but he stopped it. Rich men considered their bodyguards expendable. They expected protection at all costs, and the best ones sometimes died fulfilling that duty.

What should he say in response?

"I'll make certain we do."

One quick nod and a slap on his arm was Glabrio's answer before he walked away to join his wife, who waited for him by the kitchen door.

Taurus added his satchel to the trunk and opened the door for the men to get it. Then he settled into the shabby wicker chair that sat against the vestibulum wall. He picked at a loose fiber on the arm. Glabrio's father was richer than many kings, and a tribune's yearly salary was more than what many men earned in a lifetime. Mistress Martina had a large estate and two successful businesses.

So, why did they keep using an old, worn-out chair in the most public part of the house? Maybe Sartorus could tell him if he asked.

He leaned back in the chair and stretched out his legs. With the pillows that padded it, he was comfortable enough as he waited while Sartorus said goodbye to his wife.

Sartorus might tell him when they were on the ship, but by then he wouldn't care enough to bother asking.

*On a ship at sea*

The ship was out of sight of land and well on its way to some port in Sicilia. It would be tomorrow before they got there, and that was too long.

Taurus leaned against the rail, watching the wake left by the ship. It was boring, but there was nothing better to do. The worst thing about being on a ship was being forced to do nothing. He'd been born and raised in the local gladiator school, and no one sat around doing nothing in that *ludus*.

Even though it was nine years since Master Volero's father bought him to bodyguard him and his wife, the *lanista* still let him spar with his fighters at least once a week. Brutus had trained Taurus since he turned seventeen, and Taurus fought for him for four years. He still looked on Taurus as one of his fighters, yelling at him if he wasn't working hard enough, showing him how to do something better.

Taurus turned to lean his backside against the rail. Watching Sartorus was more entertaining than the splashes alongside the ship.

Sartorus moved between the different small groups of passengers who stood together talking. Occasionally, he said something, but never too much. Mostly he listened. But his nods and slight smiles made it seem he was glad to be with whoever was there. They seemed to welcome his company, too.

That was not his own idea of entertainment. He didn't like talking to strangers. He didn't even like talking to most of the people he knew. For most of his life, no one much cared to listen to him, so he kept his thoughts to himself.

His mother had been a kitchen slave in the ludus, but she wasn't the mothering kind. She'd been sold before he was four anyway. Several of the women took care of his needs, but that was all. Once he turned six, he was put to work and no longer treated as a child.

Big for his age and not one to let the older children push him around, he wasn't sold like the others when they got old enough to be worth something. They'd all been fathered by a winner on the sand who got time with their mother as the reward for success. From his own red hair, he figured his father was a Dacian, probably sold into slavery after Domitian's legions defeated Decebalus's army at Tapae. But no one ever claimed he was theirs.

It didn't matter anyway. Between death on the sand and being sold to a different owner, long-term friendships weren't expected in a ludus. It was better not to know who his father was than to know it and then have to grieve losing him.

It had been several hours, and the hearty aroma of whatever the cook was preparing in the cabin's galley made Taurus's mouth water. Being a cabin passenger was proving far superior to when he traveled a few times with Master Martinus. He always slept on the deck and ate cold rations he brought himself.

The cook rang a bell and headed toward the canopy behind the cabin with the kettle responsible for the tantalizing smell.

Sartorus and the two men he'd been listening to followed the cook. As he passed, Sartorus summoned him with a curl of his fingers.

When Taurus reached the canopy, Sartorus was already seated with a steaming bowl of stew on a tray that he'd balanced on his thighs. He waved at Taurus, then pointed at the empty chair beside him.

Taurus took the tray the cook offered him and started toward Sartorus. He'd almost reached the chair when a man in an ankle-length, fine-linen tunic stepped in front of him. The embroidered himation wrapped over it and held at the shoulder by a gold-and-silver pin set with amethysts suited a rich man's banquet far better than a ship's meal on a tray.

The wealthy Greek took the seat Sartorus had saved.

With a flick of his fingers, the Greek waved Taurus away. His gaze scanned Taurus from his sturdy leather sandals to his off-white, thigh-length tunic to the plain leather sheath that held an unadorned dagger on his wide leather belt.

His nose twitched. "Slaves should eat with their own kind. Go join them."

Taurus turned and walked back toward the main deck, but he stopped partway along the cabin wall. He lowered himself to sit cross-legged and balanced the tray in his lap.

Rich men usually ignored him when he bodyguarded. It was as if he was part of the furniture as he stood near enough to Martinus to watch over him. To have one order him to leave—that was different.

He inhaled the aroma rising from the bowl. Maybe he wasn't considered good enough to sit with the cabin passengers. But at least he had the same dinner they did, and that was enough for him.

From around the corner, Sartorus's calm words reached him. "I had saved that seat for my traveling companion. There were others you could have taken."

"I don't eat with slaves. No one else wants his sort dining with us." Disdain dripped from the Greek's lips.

"These chairs are for cabin passengers. Taurus has a right to sit with us as part of his cabin passage, paid for by a councilman of Carthago who respects and values him highly."

"What is that to me?" Contempt still coated the Greek's words.

"A lesson, perhaps." Sartorus's voice was as calm as it had been as he chatted with others that afternoon. "A man's worth in the eyes of other men should be determined by the man himself, not his family relations, his wealth, or the importance of his friends. Is he a man of honor and courage, willing to sacrifice himself for the life of others?"

A hint of a challenge colored Sartorus's voice. "Do you see this scar?"

He would be pointing at his elbow now. "I was an optio in the Urban Cohort. I got this saving my commander from an assassin. I almost died, and it ended my career. But I'd do it again in a heartbeat because I value his life as much as my own. A bodyguard like Taurus would do the same for me and more. Can you say you have the courage and honor to do that yourself?"

Chair legs scraped on the deck. Was Sartorus standing up?

"You can expect us both here for breakfast and for all future meals. Until then, I bid you a good evening."

Sartorus came around the corner with his tray. He lowered himself to the deck beside Taurus and slipped a spoonful of stew into his mouth. "Not as good as at home, but not bad for ship's food." He lifted his spoon as if in a toast and resumed eating.

Nothing more was said between them as they finished their meal, but it was the companionable silence between two men who respected each other.

# Chapter 44

## A Request to a Father



*Stephanos's estate, Day 23*

With Jason outside giving Mikro his morning feeding and Lusario on his way to the main house to tutor Stephan, Neferu was arranging what she would use for Jason's lesson on the table.

A tap on the open door announced Menmet's arrival. It was time for tending Caelus's wounds again. Her steps were slow as she approached Caelus's bed.

"So, how are you feeling?" She rested her age-spotted hand on his forehead. "Has the lotus wine doused the pain yet so we can tend your wounds now?"

He opened his eyelids like a man who'd worked too long and only just gone to sleep.

"My leg is throbbing, but your medicine took the edge off, like it did yesterday. But mostly I'm feeling bored." He ran his hand through his slightly damp hair.

Neferu joined Menmet at the bedside, and his gaze shifted from Menmet to her. His tired eyes grew more alert as he smiled at her. "After lunch when Lusario is back, maybe I'll write another story for Jason. Maybe something about dolphins."

"Jason doesn't know what those are." Neferu had heard the word, but she'd never seen one herself.

"I can draw a picture of a ship with dolphins swimming beside it to show him before he reads the story. One of the pleasures of sea travel is watching them play right beside the hull or right ahead of the bow. They swim side by side and jump completely out of the water before diving, then do it again like it's a competition." With his hands, he mimicked what he'd just described.

"I should be able to sit up enough to do that with a tray on my lap. Lusario and I need to start making drawings to replace the ones we lost. Making a dolphin picture for Jason is a good way to figure out how to do that with this leg."

He patted his thigh, and that caused a grimace so small and fleeting she could have missed it. If Menmet's smile hadn't flickered as well, she might have thought she imagined it.

Menmet untied the linen strips holding the bark splints in place. Then she loosened the small sheet of linen she'd wrapped around his leg. "A few more days and I should not need to do this every day. I will wrap your leg with strips then and leave you to heal."

Neferu bit her lip but quickly released it before Caelus could see. Red streaks extended out from the bite marks right next to the hole where the bones came through, and a cloudy fluid oozed from both. Menmet dribbled oil on each wound and wiped it and the pus off. To each break in his skin, she applied honey.

Through it all, Caelus lay with his gaze locked on the ceiling and his jaw clenched.

"Lift his leg a little."

When Neferu did, Menmet pulled the dirty linen out and dropped it on the floor. After slipping a clean piece under his calf, she folded it over the leg from both sides, covering the honey-packed punctures. Then she replaced the bark sections, tying them in place once more with linen strips.

Caelus lay still, eyes closed when they finished.

Menmet patted his thigh. "Rest now."

His eyelids didn't open, but a weak smile accompanied his single nod.

She signaled for Neferu to follow her outside and led her to the olive tree, out of earshot.

"It is not good. His wounds have infected, and he is too hot."

She rubbed her lower lip. "I was glad the bleeding stopped on its own when I had no meat to help it stop. Some bleeding is good. A wound must bleed to clean itself. But not so much it kills a man. With wounds like he has, how much is enough but not too much…it is hard to know."

Menmet's weak smile didn't hide the deep concern in her eyes.

Neferu glanced at the open door. In the shadows, she could see Caelus lying so still…maybe too still.

*God, You stopped him from bleeding to death. Surely You wouldn't have done that only to let infection kill him. I was sure You answered my prayer, but if he's going to die because he didn't bleed enough…I don't understand.*

"What usually happens when an infection like his starts?"

"With a cat bite…the fever often breaks in a few days. With a croc bite… he is the first I have seen that the leg was not mangled so bad that I had to cut it off. I burn the end then to stop the blood. For smaller wounds, that burning can prevent an infection. But what comes after a croc…they usually die."

Menmet wrapped her hand around her throat and squeezed. "But it might be the break, not the bite. With only the bone through the skin…I have seen that before, and more get fever and die than not. But some live."

Caelus raised his hand to his forehead and wiped it. When he stared at his fingers, his mouth turned down.

Did he know what that meant? What it might mean. Menmet had said some live.

*God, let Caelus be one of the ones who live.*

"What can I do to help him get better?"

"He is not too hot yet, but when his friend returns, you could give Lusario a cloth in a bowl of water to cool him. Wetting his face and chest can help."

Jason came around the corner carrying the empty milk bucket. With a wave, he headed toward Menmet's house to rinse off what was left of the milk.

Neferu tipped her head toward the boy. "Let's not tell him what we fear yet. Caelus is good to him, and Jason likes him a lot already. Maybe he'll be fine. Until we know, I don't want Jason to worry that he's losing another person who's been kind to him."

"I will let you tell Lusario what I said when Jason is not listening. He seems a good man who will do what is best for both."

Jason set the bucket on the bench and started their way. When Menmet raised her hand, he returned the wave and headed toward the olive tree.

"Jason is a fine boy. He is lucky to have you." Menmet patted Neferu's arm. "I am glad you both came."

"I am, too." Neferu stepped out of the shade and headed for the open door. Despite all that had happened since Sasobek made her leave home and family, she still thanked God for blessing her with Jason to love and a friend like Menmet who loved him, too.

*Day 26*

Life for Neferu had settled into a routine, but it wasn't likely to last much longer.

Before breakfast, Menmet brought Caelus his cup of lotus-wine. Each time, she felt his forehead and promised to return to treat his wounds after the potion had lessened the pain. Lusario tried to get Caelus to eat more while sharing encouraging words and smiles and proposed plans for what they would do when Caelus could walk on his leg again. But when Caelus closed his eyes and Lusario turned so his friend couldn't see, his fake smile turned into a frown and worry drove the confidence from his eyes.

Before he left for the main house to tutor, his instructions to her carried a joking tone. Don't let Caelus get up and start doing what he usually does. It's too soon for a leg that's not healed yet. Always the "yet" in his words, but his eyes betrayed his fear that "never" was more likely than "soon."

She asked God to heal the poor Roman during her prayers both morning and evening and whenever she first saw him upon entering the house that was now his. But he only seemed to get worse.

During the midmorning break for Jason to feed Mikro, she usually wrote a new story for Jason to read. But he seemed to prefer the ones Lusario had written while keeping Caelus company in the afternoon. His were more exciting with races and chases and wrestling matches. She brought a papyrus sheet to the table and began her tale of the singing frog.

Caelus had drawn the dolphin for Jason three days ago, but it drained his energy enough that he didn't get the story written that day. Nor the next day, nor the day after that. His forehead had gone from warm to hot. Lusario gave no outward sign that he knew what that meant, but Neferu's hope had cooled as Caelus's temperature rose.

Movement on the bed drew her gaze. Caelus was burning up, so how could he be shivering so much she could see his hands and arms moving from across the room?

"Caelus?"

His eyelids parted slowly, and he squinted when he first looked at her. Then with many blinks, he widened them to stare. "Yes?"

"Can I get you something? A blanket, maybe? You were just shivering."

"Something to write on." His gaze focused on his trembling hands. "No. Something you can write on. Even Jason writes better than I can now."

"What did you want me to write?"

"A final letter to my father."

She blinked twice, willing the tears that blurred her vision to not start falling. "Do you think that's necessary?" She stopped herself from adding "yet."

"It can't wait. I might not have much time before I no longer can. What I need to ask him is too important to risk that."

"Jason will be coming in shortly. Can it wait for Lusario to write this afternoon?"

"No. Some of the things I must ask my father—I don't want to tell Lusario because Father might not do what I want."

"I understand." Or did she? If she had been dying instead of her father, could she have asked him to do something for a friend and expected him to do it?

She centered the papyrus sheet in front of her and dipped the pen in the inkwell. "I'm ready."

He cleared his throat, and drew a deep breath. After blowing it out slowly, he began.

*Caelus Publilius Martinus to Volero Publilius Martinus, my dear father, greetings. If you are well, then I am glad. I write to tell you this will be my last letter and to ask you to do one last thing for me when I am gone.*

*If you receive this letter, it will mean I am dead. As I dictate it, I am burning up with fever from an infection of many lacerations and a broken leg. I do not expect to recover.*

"Tell me when you finish each part." His eyes warmed with his wry smile. "Even Lusario has trouble keeping up when taking down my orations."

She stared at him. How could he tell his father so bluntly that he was dying and then smile? Any father's heart would start to bleed when he read his son was dead.

"Ready."

He blew out a slow breath through pursed lips.

*I do not regret coming to Alexandria and learning architecture. These have been the best three years of my life. In the chest from the Zefyros, you can see some of what I have done. I was on the verge of using what I had learned to design and build a villa that combines the best of Roman, Greek, and Egyptian styles. But a hippo attacked and sank our boat. That led to a crocodile attack, so what I had hoped to share with you during my visit home will never happen now.*

*Since I am dying, there are some things I want to ask you to do after I am gone.*

*Please free Lusario. If possible, give him citizenship. Since he is only twenty-six, the best way is to let him become an architect who is your agent over the new design and construction business that he and I were starting. It is what I would have asked of you if I had lived to start the business. He is as skilled as I am and as loyal as any man could ever be. I had planned on us becoming full partners in the business, in practice even if not as defined by Roman law.*

He paused to give her pen a chance to catch up with his words. But even before she wrote the last letters, her mind was racing. Lusario was a slave? What would Zenobia think if she found out? But Akhom treated him like an elite Greek, and if she said nothing, no one needed to know. There was nothing in the way he and Caelus treated each other that would suggest he was a slave to anyone.

"Ready."

*He deserves to have you do this. Twice on this trip he saved me at the risk of his own death. In a knife fight, he killed one of the men trying to kill me.*

He wiped some sweat from his forehead, then waited for her to speak.

Neferu stared at him, then forced her gaze back on the papyrus as she penned his words. Lusario had killed a man to save Caelus? Who would have thought he was anything but a scholar? Jason liked looking at the dagger he wore. No wonder Lusario said it was a tool to be respected, not a toy to play with. She would never look at it the same, knowing it had taken a man's life.

"Ready."

*With only a dagger, he fought and killed a crocodile to keep it from dragging me into the river to become its meal. He did everything possible to save me, but the infection from the bites and my broken leg—no man could save me from that.*

*No man deserves more than he does to be free.*

He turned his head to watch her write.

It was a miracle neither of them had been killed in the river that day. Lusario did deserve whatever Caelus could give him. Surely his father would grant that request.

"Ready."

*If you are willing, I ask one thing more. After you make him a citizen, adopt him. He has become the brother I never had because my twin died right after we were born. He loves me like a brother, too. That is why he risked death to save me. If you do this, you will find him as fine a son as any man ever had. Maybe even better than I have been or could ever be.*

She finished the section, but she wasn't ready to start the next part after what he'd just shared.

"I would never have guessed Lusario is a slave. He acts like a free man."

"That's because I ordered him to act free. I trust you to know, but you are not to tell anyone else. If I'm not alive to confirm that I made him do it, he might be arrested as a runaway. My father bought him from the father of an acquaintance who had spent two years enjoying himself in Alexandria. He'd taken Lusario as payment for a gambling debt just before he returned to Carthago. My father bought him to be my valet because he knew everything a scholar would need to live in Alexandria, but Father had no idea what a treasure he was getting."

He drew his fingers across his sweaty forehead and wiped them on the sheet. "I've never met a person who loves learning more. I had him study with me to be my future partner in the business. He's as smart as I am and at least as good an architect."

She nibbled her lip. Lusario was smart and kind and loyal, and Caelus was, too. They did seem like brothers. "Do you think your father will free him and adopt him?"

"Free him? Yes. Adopt him? Probably not, but there's nothing lost in asking. Father must adopt someone. He needs a male heir to become the next paterfamilias. Lusario's not a Roman now, but Father can make him one. He would be a son that Father could be as proud of as he is of me. We've been like brothers here. Maybe Father will see my logic and do as I'm asking." He rubbed his jaw. "Ready for more?"

She dipped the pen in the ink and waited.

> *Please tell Cousin Martina I have valued her friendship since I first met her. She is as dear to me as any sister could be. Tell her I have no regrets that I came to Alexandria, so do not feel bad about encouraging me in my desire to study here, just like our step-grand-mother Juliana did. It was Grandfather who sent me here, and I would also be thanking him for that if he was still alive.*
>
> *Please tell Mother I love her and goodbye. I know she always loved me and wanted what she thought was best for me, even when we disagreed. Please express my affection and final goodbye to my sisters as well."*

He closed his eyes as he waited for her to finish writing.

Neferu fought to hold in her tears. How many hearts would be broken when this letter was read to them?

God, I thought leaving my family was hard. At least Uncle knows I might return someday. But to get a son's letter, to read the greeting and right away he tells you it's the last one, that he's already dead…

God, please. Won't You keep him from dying so no one must read this letter?

The first tear trickled down her cheek. She wiped it away before Caelus opened his eyes to see it.

"Ready."

> *Please do not grieve for me too deeply or too long. Although short, I have had a good life. It has been a great honor to have you as my father. I could not have had a better one. I have always wanted to make you proud of me. I hope I succeeded.*
>
> *I hope all will continue to be well with you. It is conventional to end may the gods guard your safety, but you don't believe they would do that anymore than I do. Instead, I will say that I wish you a long and satisfying life, like Grandfather had. I am sorry I will not be there with you to share it."*

Caelus turned his face toward her. He'd erased all emotion from it. "When you finish that part, please read the whole thing back to me."

She did as he asked. But try as she might, she couldn't keep her voice from quavering, and she swept more than one tear from her cheeks before reading the last word.

"That should do. All it needs is my signature, and I'll need some wax to press with my signet ring to make my requests official."

"I can ask Jason to run to the main house and get some from Akhom."

He nodded, and she went outside.

"Jason."

Mikro was still drinking, but Jason came to the gate.

"Will you please run ask Akhom to give you some sealing wax? Caelus needs some right away. Then you can finish with Mikro."

His eyes narrowed as he stared at her face. "Were you crying?"

She rested her hands on his shoulders and forced a smile. "A little, but it's nothing for you to worry about."

He trotted off toward the main house, and she returned to Caelus.

"I need the letter here on the drawing tray. If you'll load the pen with ink, I can sign."

"I can be your backrest, like Lusario does." She set the loaded tray on his thighs and raised his shoulders to sit behind him. After she dipped the pen in the inkwell, he signed his name.

He handed the pen back to her. "My hand shook some. Even Jason makes his letters better, but Father should still recognize it."

She helped him lie down again and took the tray to the table.

He fingered the heavy silver ring that never left his finger. "If I'm not able to do it when Jason gets back,"—he slid the ring up and down his finger—"take this and do it for me. After you make the seal by my name, roll the sheet and seal three places along it to keep it rolled until he gives it to Father."

"My father was a scribe. He taught me how to do what you're asking."

"Good. Lusario is not to know I've written this letter until after I'm dead. Please put it somewhere that he won't see it. I'll need to be cremated, and he'll be taking my remains back to go into the family mausoleum outside Carthago. He is to take the unopened letter to my father." One corner of his mouth lifted. "It will be his last act of service to me. I'm certain Father will free him as his last gift to a son he loves. What else he will do…" Caelus shrugged.

She wiped the pen with a small rag and set it and the inkwell back on the shelf.

"I'll tell Lusario to take the letter if it comes to that. But Menmet said she's seen worse, and they recovered. Don't give up hope, and don't give up fighting. It will break his heart to lose his best friend. He loves you like a brother, too." She patted his shoulder, as she'd seen Menmet do so many times. "Rest now."

She put the letter on the shelf with the stories she'd written. She would take it to Menmet's house and put it in her chest before Lusario was alone with Caelus again.

"He's the best friend I've ever had. I'm lucky to have known him these past three years. I only wish there could be more." Caelus drew the back of his hand across his forehead, wiping off some sweat before his limp hand dropped onto the bed. "Thank you…for helping me…do this." His voice faded more with each word.

Before she could answer, he closed his eyes and released a deep breath. His chest stopped moving.

Was he gone? Had they done this just in time? Then he inhaled, but she watched his chest until she was certain it continued to rise and fall.

He might be asleep, but the faint smile that lingered was that of a man satisfied that he'd done what he could to ensure the future of the best friend he'd ever had.

*God, please heal him. Don't make Lusario take him home in a box with that letter to break his father's heart.*

# Chapter 45

## How to Do It?

*Day 27*

With a flick of her fingers, Zenobia sent her lady's maid from her bed-chamber. Dressed in the sky-blue tunic that she found especially flat-tering, she'd chosen a pair of lapis lazuli earrings and matching pen-dant to wear today. Nothing too gaudy. They were merely rich adornments that declared her a wealthy woman to a man accustomed to moving in elite circles.

She strolled to the window and scanned the road atop the levee. In the dis-tance, a man strode toward the house. A man who moved like he knew where he was going and what he would do when he got there.

Stephan's new tutor. Even with the pale blood stains from carrying his wealthy Roman friend, his blue-edged linen tunic, of equal quality to those of Horion and Stephanos, declared him a man of substance. Dressed as she was, he would rec-ognize her as a woman of importance, one who commanded the highest respect.

Of course, she would never do anything that showed her unfaithful to Hori-on, but a woman needed to feel admired by men, even when they knew she was out of their reach. It was enough to see it in their eyes, even if they never spoke a word.

He and the Roman were staying in the worker's village where the old woman who took care of the estate's sick and injured lived. But as soon as they didn't need her care anymore, she would tell Akhom that Stephanos would have given such elite men guest rooms in the main house, not a tiny cottage among the workers.

Her nose twitched. Not where that too-beautiful tutor of her brother-in-law's defective son lived.

The pathetic boy who had already wormed his way into Akhom's regard. The one who couldn't be allowed to do the same with his grandfather.

It was time to get rid of Jason, and it needed to look like an accident. But how could she do it?

For most of the ways she'd envisioned, she would need an accomplice. A man who could acquire what he needed and knew how to use it once he had it. But Akhom controlled the money, and without enough money to pay one, how could she find a man willing to take the risk?

But maybe Karpos could do it. He hated Jason, so he should be happy to help stage the accident.

Lusario of Alexandria was close enough now to see her at the window. She stepped back so he wouldn't realize she'd been watching him.

Stephan had thought it good sport to take Jason out on the levees and leave him in the dark, but that was before Lusario started his lessons. Her oldest son had gone from a reluctant student to one eager to learn what his tutor was teaching. At dinner, he'd begun talking about what his tutor called living honorably. Killing his cousin would never fit that description.

She rubbed her jaw. So, what could Karpos do to set up his cousin's accidental death?

*Late evening of Day 28*

Three oil lamps burned on the table, casting Lusario's shadow on the wall behind Caelus's bed. But no matter how many flames lit the room, it was the darkest place Lusario had ever been.

He dropped the rag into the bowl of water. He'd moved the chair that held it beside where he sat on the bed. After it soaked up some water, he wrung out the excess before wiping Caelus's face and chest for the five hundredth time. Menmet had shown him how to do it, and it was supposed to help cool the fever.

It hadn't.

Hours earlier, he'd returned from tutoring Stephan to find Caelus delirious and Neferu struggling to keep him from getting out of bed, even with his broken leg. He'd taken her place holding him down, but it had been several hours now since Caelus gave up and went to sleep.

Except it wasn't normal sleep. Several times his eyes opened and stared at nothing Lusario could see. Sometimes he muttered words that made no sense before closing his eyelids and lying as still as a dead man.

He wasn't dead yet, but was delirium the last phase before he was?

Would his final act of service for his young master who was more like a brother be getting his remains home to his father in Carthago?

Maybe it wouldn't come to that, but what if it did? Egyptians mummified, but Romans cremated. How would he find someone to do that? Maybe Akhom could help find the person to burn the body, but were there special rites that had to be used for Master Volero to think the right thing had been done? Akhom wouldn't know that, and he'd never been to a Roman funeral himself.

Would the one who provided the wood, bier, and box for the ashes know what to do when there were hardly any Romans this far south? Maybe he'd need to go to Heracleopolis and ask Latro's steward. Or an officer in the Roman garrison there.

But as long as Caelus lived, there was still hope. And anything Menmet thought might help was worth doing, no matter how tired he might be.

With the deepest sigh, he dropped the cloth back in the bowl. His shoulders slumped, and he hung his head.

Then he wrung out the cloth and began again.

# Chapter 46



*Evening of Day 29*

With Jason on one side and Menmet on the other, Neferu carried the dinner tray to what had been her house. Jason turned aside to feed Mikro his last meal of the day, and she went inside to deliver the evening meal to Lusario. Only to Lusario because Caelus had been unconscious for hours.

He was sitting beside Caelus, his gaze fixed on his friend. He glanced at them when they entered. "Just put the bowl on the table."

Neferu put the tray on his lap instead. "You have to eat if you want to keep helping your friend."

Menmet pushed a lock of hair back from Caelus's forehead. "With his leg not crushed, I thought he had a chance." With her fingertips, she swept a tear from her cheek and wiped it on her tunic. "It won't be long now."

Lusario closed his eyes and clenched his jaw. When his eyelids opened, the grief Neferu saw there tore at her own heart.

*God, is it really Your will for Caelus to die like this? When You stopped the bleeding, I was sure You would heal him. I don't understand why You saved him then, only to let him die now. He's such a nice man. He's been so good to Jason. Why did You let Jason come to care for him so much, only to see him die, too?*

She blinked hard, trying to stop the tears before they escaped. Letting her own grief show would only make it harder for Jason when his Roman friend died. Caelus didn't believe in Jesus. They wouldn't be reunited someday in heaven. This separation would be final.

Her tears wouldn't matter for Lusario. Nothing could make him hurt more than he already did.

He picked up the spoon and stirred the stew. "Caelus and I are Stoics. We're supposed to welcome death as the natural end of living. In one of Seneca's plays, the chorus sings, 'There is nothing after death; and death is nothing—only the finishing post of life's short race.' But our race had barely begun. His shouldn't be over yet."

Menmet placed her hand on his shoulder and squeezed. "But your life goes on, so eat my stew. He would want you to."

With a sigh and a slow nod, he raised the spoon to his mouth.

Menmet touched Neferu's elbow and tipped her head toward the door. As they passed through, Neferu glanced back to see him set the tray on the table and return to the death watch beside his friend.

Lusario stood at the door, watching as the cloud-free sky turned orange on the western horizon while the blue above it slowly darkened. Soon the sun would slip below the edge of the world, and the blue would darken to black.

He glanced over his shoulder at his dying friend. Their time together had been filled with deep conversations, friendly arguments, shared dreams, and frequent laughter. But he'd never hear Caelus's voice again, and their dreams of a future together doing what they both loved—those had already died.

He turned his back on the dying light, walked to the bedside, and rested his hand on Caelus's shoulder. Caelus wouldn't hear him, but he would say it anyway. "Your friendship has been the best thing that ever happened to me. Thank you for giving me the life of a free man for as long as you could."

He settled into the chair beside Caelus's bed, elbows on his knees, face in his hands. Why hadn't he seen the croc coming behind them? Why hadn't it been him getting out of the river last? Caelus was the stronger swimmer, but he'd stayed beside Lusario to make sure he could make it across. Now his friend had slipped into unconsciousness. Not the deep sleep that restored, but the coma at the doorway to death.

He felt a small hand on his arm and turned his face to find a teary-eyed Jason. "Is he dying now?"

Lusario gritted his teeth. Whether he spoke the words or not, hope had already died.

"Yes."

"When my baby brother was dying, Neferu prayed to God and he saved Menander."

"Who told you that?"

"I saw it, and she told me later what she did."

"You saw it."

"Yes. Mitéra said Menander was perfect, then she died. But the midwife said it was good she died because he was dying. It was better that she didn't know it was all for nothing. He wasn't crying or moving when Neferu asked to hold him. She prayed, and then he cried and moved. He was perfect, like Mitéra said. Patéras said he was perfect, so he wouldn't need me anymore." Jason's eyes brimmed with tears. "That's why we came here. He'd told people I died as a baby." He touched the side of his milky eye. "He sent me away because he only wanted perfect."

"No one is perfect, not even him. Your father is a fool not to see you're better than most."

"That's what Neferu says." He shrugged. "But she says she loves me, like Mitéra, so she only sees what's good. She says God loves me, too."

Lusario fingered his lip. Before her incantation to stop the bleeding, she'd ordered him out of the room if he wanted Caelus to live. Then the heavy bleeding stopped. Coincidence or not? Was there a god with the power to heal?

"What god does she pray to?"

Jason looked behind him. "I'm not supposed to tell anyone without asking her first. It's our secret."

Lusario rubbed his lip. Was there truly a god who could stop death?

"Go find her and bring her here. Maybe she can do the same for Caelus."

It was only a few moments, but it felt like forever before Jason returned, pulling on Neferu's hand.

Lusario stood to face her. "Is it true you kept Jason's brother from dying with a prayer?"

She came to the edge of the bed. Caelus's breathing was shallow and fast. She touched his forehead with her palm, then his cheek with the back of her hand.

Compassion filled the eyes she turned on Lusario. "God did. I only asked Him to do it."

"Can you ask him for Caelus?"

"I have been, but He's not a puppet. Sometimes He heals; sometimes He doesn't."

"There's nothing else I can do." He rested his hand on Caelus's thigh. "He's the best man I've ever known. If your god can save him, please ask."

She nodded, placed her hand on Caelus's forehead, and took Jason's hand. Jason reached toward Lusario and wiggled his fingers.

As soon as Lusario joined the chain, Neferu bowed her head. "God, I lift up Caelus to You. Please take this fever from him. Clear the infection that's causing it. With Your almighty power, please restore him to health."

Her soft voice turned into whispers and words with no sounds as her lips moved. Lusario strained to hear, but what little he caught was no language he knew. She took Caelus's hand when she stopped, but her eyes remained closed and her breathing slow.

Lusario startled when Jason squeezed his hand.

"Jesus, please heal him." The sweet voice of the six-year-old broke the silence. "Thank you."

Lusario stared at Jason, then at Neferu. They'd prayed to the god Timon swore was real, the one he claimed lived in the people who worshiped him.

A shuddering sigh parted Caelus's lips, and when he drew his next breath, it was deep and slow, like a man sleeping.

Neferu tipped back her head and raised her hands. "Thank You, God!" When she lowered her arms and opened her eyes, they glowed as she gave him the broadest smile he'd seen on her yet. "See how he's breathing now? This time God's answer was yes."

"You prayed to the Christian god."

"Yes, but please don't tell anyone." She bit her lip. "No one here knows except Jason, and it's safer for me if it stays that way."

"I'll keep your secret. My friend in Alexandria worships him, too, and I know how careful he and his group of Christians have to be." One corner of his mouth lifted. "But Caelus is going to want to know why he's not dead when he wakes up. I assume I can tell him."

She mirrored his smile. "You can, as long as you tell him it's a secret that only the four of us can know."

"I will, and he'll keep your secret when I explain why."

She rested her hands on Jason's shoulders. "We'll be with Menmet if either of you need anything." She smiled as she watched Caelus's chest rise and fall, slow and rhythmic. "But I don't expect either of you will be needing me until morning."

"Not if he's really healed."

"He is." She flashed him the most beautiful smile he'd ever seen. "I suspect it will be the first night you've slept deeply since you came. He's lucky to have you as a friend."

"No more than I am to have him." He rubbed his eyes. "But you're right about that sleep. It will be good to go to sleep not having to fear what I'll find in the morning."

She turned Jason toward the door. "Goodnight, then."

Jason took her hand but looked over his shoulder as they went out the door. "I'm glad God made him better. I like you both."

Lusario raised his hand in response. If truth were told, he liked Jason and Neferu more than he ever expected, more than any child or woman he'd known well. Any time he came up river past Thmoinepsi, he'd be sure to stop to see them both.

# Chapter 47

## TELLING CAELUS

*Early morning of Day 30*

Caelus awakened at the first light of dawn, feeling better than he had since the croc clamped its jaws on his leg.

Lusario was asleep, lying on his back on the pallet beside the bed. With his mouth open, he was halfway between breathing heavily and snoring lightly.

He should let Lusario sleep, but he couldn't explain why he felt like he did, fully aware of what was going on around him, like he'd been before the fever burned so hot the delirium came. The last thing he remembered was Neferu trying to keep him in the bed until Lusario returned from the main house. How long ago was that?

The pain was even mild enough he might not need Menmet's lotus wine today.

"Lusario." No response to his whisper, so he spoke it louder when the soft snores continued unchanged.

"Lusario."

Lusario awoke with a snort and rolled onto his side. He raised himself on one elbow, like on a dining couch. "How are you feeling?"

"Not bad. Good, actually, which seems very strange. I thought I was dying."

In truth, he would have bet any amount he was dying. That was why he wrote that letter to Father. It had proven unnecessary, but perhaps he should change the opening to something about his near death. How that made him want Father to know what Lusario had done. How he should be rewarded if anything did happen before he could visit and make the request in person. A man couldn't be too careful when the fate of a friend hung in the balance.

"We did, too." Lusario's grin didn't match those words, but seeing an almost-dead person feeling good again should make any friend smile.

"But I didn't die." Caelus shrugged when Lusario rolled his eyes. His first oratory teacher had pounded into him to avoid stating the obvious…except when it helped make your point.

"I should have. Menmet said there was nothing more anyone could do."

He fingered his lip. "Seneca's chorus was wrong. Even if there is nothing after death, death is not nothing. As I felt it approaching, death became everything as it started to swallow up life. A man's death should serve some purpose. Mine didn't."

Without moving his bad leg too much, he rolled onto his side to face Lusario more directly. "But as death got closer, I couldn't keep my thoughts together. They all slipped away near the end. I think you were talking, but your voice faded into silence. When I was too far gone for you to reach me, no matter how hard you tried, I should have passed on into nothingness."

Lusario sat up and turned to sit cross-legged on the pallet. "I thought I would never talk with you again, too. But Jason came in, and he knew what to do."

"Jason?" Caelus's eyes narrowed. "What did he do?"

"He got Neferu. She prayed, and your fever broke. You started breathing like you were asleep, not close to death."

"She prayed?" Caelus raised his eyebrows. A prayer stopping death? Not likely. "Maybe that was just fortunate timing."

"I don't think so. It was the second time."

He stared at Lusario. "Second time?"

"The second time she prayed for you, and something happened. The first time was the day of the attack. I thought you were going to bleed to death as I was carrying you here. Jason had gone to get Menmet, but you were passed out in my arms and leaving a trail of blood down the road. Neferu had me carry you in here, then told me to go outside if I wanted you to live. But I looked in the window a couple of times."

"What was she doing?"

"The first time I looked in, she was touching your shoulder, speaking too softly for me to hear. The next time she stood with hands raised, whispering words I didn't recognize. I thought it was an incantation to some Egyptian god at the time. When I was in Alexandria the first time, before I came back there with you, I read an Egyptian medical papyrus that gave the words of many of those. Then she came out and said you were asking for me. I figured the bleeding stopped naturally then. But not now."

"What changed your mind?"

"When she prayed today. I was keeping a death watch over you when Jason came in. He said she should pray for you. He'd seen her bring his dying baby brother back to perfect health that way. So, I told him to get her."

"What happened when she came?"

Lusario leaned forward, raised one finger, and waved it side to side. "You can't tell anyone else what I'm going to tell you now."

"Why not?"

Soon everyone would know he'd recovered. What could be secret about that?

"It could put her in danger, and maybe worse."

"Then I won't. But what did she do?"

Lusario put his hands on the pallet by his hips and leaned back on them. "She put one hand on you and took Jason's hand. He took mine, and then she started asking her god to heal you. When she stopped speaking aloud, Jason started, and then it happened."

Lusario stopped talking. It was a game they often played. Get a story to the climax, then wait for the question. But the serious expression on his friend's face didn't look like this was a game.

"What happened?"

"He asked Jesus to heal you. Right then, you went from ragged, shallow breaths to slow, deep ones, enough like sleep I half expected you to snore."

Caelus leaned over and tapped Lusario's arm with the back of his fingers. "I do not snore."

Lusario's half-grin triggered Caelus's smile. "How would you know? You're asleep when you do it."

Caelus's smile faded. A man who would die for you could be trusted with any secret. If Lusario ever became his brother, Father would tell him. But brother or not, Cousin Martina would approve of him knowing.

Lusario never lied to him, so what he'd just said…at least he believed it to be true. As unbelievable as it sounded, he knew one person who'd be nodding in agreement if she heard it.

"It's your turn to swear to tell no one what I'm about to say."

"You know I won't."

Caelus opened his mouth, then closed it. He did know, and what he was about to say might change how this conversation ended.

"My step-grandmother Juliana worshiped the Christian god. My cousin Martina still does, but it's a family secret because Grandfather wanted to protect both them and the family reputation. Father and I still keep Martina's secret now Grandfather is dead. Grandfather told me when I turned fifteen, but my mother and sisters still don't know."

The wisdom of that choice drew Lusario's wry smile, and Caelus mirrored it. How could anyone who'd lived at his family estate not share his grandfather's opinion that they were not to be trusted with a secret about anything?

"I know they prayed together often, but I never heard either of them talk about how their prayers could get someone healed, let alone pull them back from the edge of death. Martina still says her god can work anything out for the good of those who love him, but I've never seen convincing evidence of that."

Caelus shifted his gaze to the sunrise beyond the window. If only he had seen her prayers answered.

"Juliana died a few months before Grandfather, and surely Martina would have prayed for both her and Grandfather not to die. So, she didn't have the power to get her god to do anything." He rubbed his chin. "Is Neferu a priestess or something that gives her the power? Does she have some talisman from a temple or know some special incantation?"

"The Christians don't have priestesses or temples. Any of them can do it...or rather they say their god can no matter who asks."

◆

Lusario drew a deep breath. If he told Caelus what he'd been pondering last night, there might be no going back to what was before. Together as Stoics, they agreed that no gods were real, so no gods had power over the affairs of anyone.

But a man of honor was a man of truth. Caelus had said many times he wanted only truth between them. But where would that truth lead?

"I need you to keep the next thing I tell you between us, too."

Caelus snorted. "It seems to be a day for that. Of course I will."

"My friend Timon—he's a Christian. He's prayed for me more than once. But he always says he can ask for something, but he can't guarantee what will happen. He says the same thing Neferu did about their god not being a puppet. So, he might not give exactly what Timon asks for. He claims his god gives what's best for someone, which might be very different from what they want, and it might be a long time before his god decides it's the right time to give it."

"Hmph." Caelus lay back on his pillow. "That's one way to explain the times a prayer fails. It suggests a positive answer is more likely a coincidence than a direct result."

Lusario stood. He dragged the pallet to the side and moved the chair over by the bed to make face-to-face talking easier for Caelus. This was one conversation where he wanted to watch every nuance of Caelus's reaction as well.

"If it were only one time, I'd agree. But it hasn't been only once. The first was when Florus decided to punish me for wanting to go home to Cyrene instead of to Carthago with him. He promised I'd be nothing but a house slave for the rest of my life, and if I wasn't content with that, he'd make sure I was sent to the mines to work to death."

He suppressed a shudder. Even after three years, thinking about Florus could made his jaw clench.

"He would have done it, too. But before we sailed, Timon said his god had told him that going to Carthago with Florus would turn out much better than I had any reason to expect."

Lusario nudged Caelus's arm. "Then your father bought me, and I returned to Alexandria with you to study to become an architect. When Timon saw me the first time after we returned, he said it was his god's doing." He shrugged. "But I saw no reason to think it was anything but a fortunate coincidence that your father needed someone to go to Alexandria with you and was willing to pay what Florus's father asked for me."

Caelus wove his fingers together and placed them behind his head. "Fortunate is too mild a word for you coming with me. I'd call it the best thing that could have happened for both of us. But it didn't take a god to make it happen."

"I can't argue that point. But it was certainly not what I expected. Not what any slave in my position would have expected. It was often said in the servants' quarters that Fortuna smiled upon free men, but never on slaves like us."

Caelus's eyes turned solemn before he looked away. "I never thought about what it costs a man to be a slave before I got to know you well." He cleared his throat. "You said it wasn't only that one time. What else?"

"He came to our room when I was packing the trunks. Achilleus let him come say goodbye before they left for the family estate. Achilleus's grandmother had died, and many from the town house were going to her funeral. He said he would be praying for us to have a chance to return to Alexandria." Lusario glanced around the cabin. "In a way, he prayed for us to be here. He's told me for years that his god works things together for good for those who believe in him. This time he said God sometimes did it for people who didn't believe. He sends rain on the just and the unjust.

"So, I challenged him to ask his god to make someone give us a commission to build something that would convince Master Volero to let us stay in Alexandria. He said he'd ask."

Caelus's eyes narrowed. "So, you think his god had something to do with Fundanus coming to the quay with his uncle just as we were about to board? That his god made Latro willing to give us a chance to bid on building his villa?"

"I don't know what to think. Could the god who kept you from dying also bring a Roman who wants a new villa at just the right time?"

Lusario shrugged, but only to hide his thoughts at the moment. When Timon asked what he'd do if God brought them a commission, he'd deflected the question with a promise to think about it when that happened. Timon's god hadn't delivered a commission, but maybe he had given them a chance to try for one. Now that they couldn't return to Alexandria with plans when they promised— maybe that chance was gone. But maybe it wasn't.

One corner of his mouth lifted. Timon would say only God knew. And maybe there was more truth in that than he was ready to admit.

Caelus closed his eyes and rubbed his forehead. "I think I need to sleep a while longer." He tapped Lusario's arm with the back of his fingers. "Maybe you do, too, since I woke you so early. But maybe this afternoon after you finish teaching, we can talk with Neferu. She can tell us what she thinks happened and what she believes it means. Until then, I'm willing to consider it possible that we've been partly wrong. I still think most of the gods are just stories passed down by someone's ancestors, not living beings themselves." He blew out a breath through pursed lips. "But maybe there is one god who is much more."

# *Chapter 48*

## Ready to Ride

*Late morning of Day 30*

With a light heart, Lusario listened to Stephan read back what he'd just dictated. When he'd left Neferu at their cabin, Caelus was still asleep. But there was no fever, and his breathing remained deep and slow. In fact, he was sleeping as soundly as Lusario had ever seen.

"Very good. Today, I'd like you to think about what you just read, and tomorrow we'll start with you telling me what you think it means. We'll leave it here on the desk so you can reread it two or three times as you do that."

Stephan capped the inkwell and wiped the tip of his pen. "Want to come with me to the stable to see the horse Grandfather bought for me just before he went downriver?"

"I can do that. My friend's fever has broken, so I don't need to hurry back to tend him."

Stephan led him down from the balcony and through the kitchen, where he grabbed a roll and handed another one to Lusario. It was a short walk past the herb and vegetable garden to the corrals.

A fine chestnut gelding stood by the railing, saddled and waiting. At their approach, it turned its elegant head and nickered.

Stephan walked to its side and stroked its neck. "Grandfather said I was big enough to ride a quality horse. Karpos gets to ride my old mount now." He waved his hand at a bay gelding that was munching hay in the corral.

"He's a fine animal." Lusario crossed his arms. Stephan's new horse was one Caelus would consider worth riding. But the one Stephan had passed down to Karpos was good enough to satisfy Caelus, too.

The stableman came over, and Stephan greeted him with a smile. "This is my new tutor, Lusario of Alexandria."

The stableman placed his palm on his chest. "Nikaure. Do you tutor the new grandson, too? Mistress Zenobia sent word that he would be joining the master's other grandsons to start his riding lessons tomorrow."

Lusario raised an eyebrow. Neferu hadn't mentioned that when he left her this morning, but maybe no one had come from the main house to tell her yet.

"No, but I'm staying in the cottage next to Menmet's that was his before I came. So, I see Jason and his tutor every day. What time should she have Jason here?"

"The mistress wants him to ride with her boys, so when you send Stephan is the time."

"When is that usually?"

"Just before lunch."

"Then I'll go get the boy tomorrow when Stephan finishes with me."

"I'll have Karpos's old horse ready for him." Nikaure turned to Stephan. "Mount up. Your brother is late, as usual, but you don't have to wait."

"Watch me ride, Lusario?"

"For a little while. Then I need to help Caelus with something."

The grin his student gave him was worth the short delay in going home. When he told Jason that he'd get to start riding tomorrow, his news should inspire another smile almost as broad as when Jason knew Caelus would get well.

When Lusario entered the cabin, Jason sat on the edge of Caelus's bed, reading a donkey story to his attentive audience.

He tousled the boy's curly hair. "Where's Neferu?"

"She's with Menmet." Jason ran his fingers through his hair to tidy it. "She wanted lunch to be ready when you came back so Caelus wouldn't have to wait any longer to eat."

"I have news for the two of you, but I can tell her later."

Jason set the papyrus on the bed with two others. "What is it?"

"I'll be coming for you tomorrow to take you for your first riding lesson."

"You will?" Jason jumped to his feet. "I know horses are different than donkeys, but maybe not that different. Patéras didn't want me riding his horses, even though I overheard Gaidaros talking with the stableman about how I should have started a year ago."

Caelus patted his thigh. "I'll be glad when this is healed enough for me to ride again. Lusario and I both like horses with a lot of spirit. Nothing beats a fast horse running full speed to make you feel alive."

Seeing Caelus eager for anything—Lusario had given up hope for that until Neferu prayed. He'd lost any hope for his own future as well...until Neferu prayed to Timon's God.

To a god who had real power because he was real himself. But was he every-thing else Timon claimed?

"Stephan wanted me to see the new gelding his grandfather got him. He looked better than anything we rode in Alexandria. Almost as good as what you had me riding in Carthago."

Lusario rested his hand on Jason's shoulder. "But you'll be starting on a calm, steady horse that Karpos has been riding. I expect you'll enjoy your first day very much."

"Could we go meet my horse after lunch?" Jason's hopeful face made denying his request impossible.

"We can. I'm sure Neferu will watch over Caelus and Mikro for a while."

Caelus's chuckle was music in Lusario's ears. "I don't need watching all the time. I feel good enough now to do almost anything, as long as I won't be walking far."

"That's exactly why I want her to watch you. Menmet would have my hide if I let you get up and rebreak your leg after she's worked so hard to get you to this point. So, I don't want you trying anything yet without me beside you."

"I'll behave myself, Mother." One corner of Caelus's mouth lifted. "But what that means to me might be different from what you and Menmet would agree to."

Lusario adjusted the pillows to raise Caelus's head and shoulders. "Right after we eat, I'll take Jason to the stable for that introduction. When he goes to help Setne with the donkeys, we can ask Neferu our questions."

Caelus's smile faded. "What she's going to tell us…it might change things in ways I never expected when we started upriver."

The happy voices of the women drifted through the open doorway. Menmet entered with a plate of bread, followed by Neferu with dried fruit and cheese.

The warmth of Neferu's smiles, the affection in her eyes as she looked at each man in turn always brightened the room when she entered.

The first question he would ask her is whether Menmet knew about her faith. A careless word to someone not in on the secret could lead to the wrong people knowing what she was.

But what should his second question be?

# Chapter 49

## THE BIGGER QUESTION

*Afternoon of Day 30*

When they returned from the stable, Jason continued down the levee, heading for the donkey corrals. But Lusario entered their cabin. It was time to join Caelus in asking Neferu about the prayer that restored him to health.

While Lusario was still in the doorway, Caelus sat up. "It's good you're back. I'm ready to get outside for a while." He pointed at the corner. "Akhom sent a crutch to help me get around."

"There's a bench to the right of the door." Lusario brought the crutch over. "It's shaded, so it's a good place for our talk."

Caelus gripped his knee and slid his leg toward the edge of the bed. When Lusario stepped forward to help, he shook a finger at him. "I need to figure out how to do this myself."

As he raised both hands, Lusario stepped back to give Caelus room to maneuver.

With both hands gripping his leg just below the knee, he started to slide the casted leg off the bed. Started, and then stopped, as he blew a breath out through pursed lips. "Maybe I will need some help with getting up and down for a while."

Lusario leaned the crutch on the bed and guided Caelus's foot gently to the ground. Then he offered his hands to help Caelus stand on his good leg before handing him the crutch.

While Caelus leaned on the crutch and hopped on his good leg, Lusario stood close enough to catch him if he started to fall. But they reached the bench, and Caelus gripped Lusario's arms as he lowered himself onto one end.

He stepped back inside to get one of the chairs and set it down facing the bench. "Neferu was in the garden when I came back from the stables. I'll get her."

As he turned at the corner of the house, he glanced back at Caelus. With his straight lips and serious eyes, was Caelus as nervous as he was about what Neferu might tell them? Not so much what she would say, but what it might mean going forward. So many times, Timon had told him how a man's whole future depended on accepting what he claimed Jesus of Nazareth had done.

It had been easy enough to brush off Timon's claims. His friend had lived his whole life in a Christian household and became one himself as a child. No matter how smart a person was, what he was taught as truth in childhood was often accepted without question when he grew up.

At least for the things Lusario had seen himself, normal events and fortunate circumstances could explain everything his friend claimed his god had done. But there was nothing normal about how Caelus was dying one moment and only sleeping the next.

Neferu was nothing like his mother or sisters or most other women he'd known. She was smart and practical and kept Jason from reading the fantasy tales about Egyptian or Greek gods. So, how had she come to believe the unbelievable and tap into a power no story-world deity could have?

She raised her hand in greeting when he rounded the corner, then swung her hoe at another weed.

"Neferu."

She finished one sweep with the hoe and leaned on the handle to gaze at him. "Yes?"

"Could you come talk with Caelus and me for a while? We both have some questions about what happened last night. I moved a chair for you under the canopy."

"Of course. I thought you might." She came to his side and leaned the hoe against the wall. "I'm so glad Caelus feels up to coming outside today."

Her usual slight smile broadened, and an eagerness he hadn't seen before lit her eyes. Her normal beauty was enough to make any man stop and appreciate the view. Any man who saw the enthusiasm she radiated now would be envious of him as she walked so close beside him.

One corner of his mouth lifted. Envious until they realized it was the coming conversation under the canopy and not his company that fired that enthusiasm. He'd seen the same excitement many times with Timon.

When they reached the canopy, she settled onto the chair, and he joined Caelus on the bench.

"So…" She crossed her arms. "What did you want to ask?"

"Why I'm still alive." Caelus glanced at Lusario and got a nod in return. "Lusario said I stopped dying when you and Jason prayed to Jesus. We want to know why that worked."

She wrapped her hand around her throat. "What do you know about Him?"

"About Jesus?" Her nod invited him to continue. "I know a little about the Christian god, but not much. My cousin is a Christian, but Grandfather told her to keep it secret from all except my father and me. So other than her telling me that her god sometimes gave her what she prayed for, I don't know much."

"I see." Neferu turned her gaze on Lusario and raised her eyebrows.

"I know a fair amount, actually. My good friend in Alexandria is a Christian, and he's been trying for years to convince me to become one myself. But until last night, I'd never seen anything that couldn't be explained as the logical result of the actions of men or a mere coincidence."

He raised one finger. "Before I forget to ask, does Menmet or anyone else here know you and Jason are Christians?"

"No. I've told Jason we have to be very careful about who knows what we believe and to ask me before he tells anyone. When his mother was dying, I promised Corinna to love him like she would, to take care of him as if he were my own. If Stephanos finds out, I'm afraid he would take Jason away from me."

Lusario glanced down the roadway that led to the donkey stables. She was certainly living up to that promise to her friend.

"He did as you told him. When I asked which god you prayed to when he saw his baby brother healed, he said he couldn't say without asking you first. That's when I sent him to fetch you."

Lusario pointed at Caelus and then himself. "We're both Stoics, and neither of us thought any god was more than a story made up by the ancestors. But gods who only live in stories can't stop a baby from dying. When Jason told me that you praying might save Caelus, I was desperate enough to try anything."

After looking to see that Menmet was still at her loom, Neferu leaned back in the chair. "Jason has the trusting faith of a child because he's seen what God can do, but he's too young to understand what Jesus really did and why. To understand how truly wonderful it is, I think we must have seen more of what's wrong with the world and with ourselves. We need to realize there are things that build a barrier between us and God. Those things are called sins." Her eyes saddened. "With all the horrible things his father did to him, he's seen more of what sin is than most his age, but he wouldn't be able to recognize it in himself."

She shrugged. "Maybe it's much easier for a child than for us. They haven't had so many chances to choose what they want for their own selfish reasons over what God wants. I was older when I met Corinna's cousin, Phoebe, and she told us both about God and what Jesus did."

Caelus massaged his thigh. "My cousin became one of you after my uncle and aunt died. Grandfather brought her to Carthago, and his second wife convinced Martina when she was twelve."

"That's not much different from me." She traced the edge of a brick paver with her sandal. "It was almost eight years ago when I was fourteen. Father had died a few months before, so I was an orphan. Uncle Peduhor treated me like one of his children after that, but Father and I had been closer than most fathers and daughters are. We worked together, and I made copies for him like an apprentice."

Her eyes focused on the shadow of a memory and ended in a wistful smile. "He taught me to write both Demotic and Greek as a child, and even when I was little, he said I wrote my letters better than his. He was always so faithful in his worship of Sobek, so I was, too. He'd even named me Neferusobek."

Caelus's brow furrowed.

"It means Beauty of Sobek." Her deep sigh accompanied a shrug.

"He got the beauty part right." Caelus's grin made her look away without smiling.

When she looked at Caelus again, her face showed no sign that he'd complimented her.

"It's the heart of person that matters, not whether we are pretty or ugly or in between. We choose how we think and act. We have no choice in how we look."

"I meant no offense." Caelus offered an embarrassed smile.

"I'm not offended. It's just been a problem far more than you know." She cleared her throat. "Then Mother died birthing my baby brother when I was Jason's age. My baby brother died, too, so Father was all I had. Then he was struck down suddenly, but he died slowly and in horrible pain. Father had been so careful to preserve ma'at in our home. So many times, he told me that his devotion to the gods of Egypt preserved truth, order, harmony, and justice and that I must do the same. But he'd never told a lie that I had seen or done anything to disrupt order or harmony, so where was the justice in him dying that way? What was the truth?"

Lusario's gaze bounced between the handsome Roman and the gorgeous Egyptian. His appearance had never been a problem for Caelus. But beauty could be a terrible burden for a servant or slave. Especially when someone in power over you thought you too attractive. Zenobia was proof of that, but would her husband or his father be far worse?

Neferu was a rare beauty, but what made her beautiful wasn't just the outside. Her kind heart would attract a good man even if she were hopelessly plain.

She pushed a loose strand of hair behind her ear. "Jason's mother and I had been friends for as long as I can remember, even though her parents were among the elite Greeks in the city. Not long after Father died, her cousin Phoebe came from Alexandria with her husband. They were Christians making their way upriver to tell any who would listen about what Jesus had done. Her husband's grandfather had decided to follow Jesus when he heard Markos speak in Alexandria."

Lusario relaxed against the wall behind the bench. Timon worshiped at a church that he said had been founded by Markos. Had he known Neferu's friend?

"Markos?" Caelus rubbed the hinge of his jaw.

"Yes." Neferu's brow furrowed, then relaxed. "I'm glad you asked about him.

Between when Jesus rose from the dead and when He went up to heaven again, He told His followers to spread out and tell the whole world about what He'd done. Markos was with Jesus in Judea, and after Jesus rose, he became one of those who traveled to Asia and Rome and many places in North Africa and Egypt. He told people about the only true God and sin and the salvation Jesus made possible if we only believe in Him. Phoebe had a copy of his writings from when he was in Rome with Apostle Peter. I made another copy for her and one for me."

Her eyes turned toward Menmet's house, and Lusario looked that way as well. Menmet no longer stood at her loom. Had she gone inside?

"Sin?" Caelus's brow furrowed. "What is that?"

"Oh. I thought since your cousin is a Christian, you would know that word." She turned her eyes on Lusario. "Do you know it?"

Did he know it? Lusario barely stopped the roll of his eyes before she saw it. "My friend has explained it more than once, but I don't mind hearing your version."

Her eyes widened at "your version." Her head tipped, and thoughtful eyes replaced startled ones. "Then for Caelus, I'll explain it like Phoebe did for me."

Lusario crossed his arms. She hadn't liked his response. But he'd spent years listening to Timon talk about his Christian faith, trying to convince him using different arguments. He'd considered it an argument more about philosophy than fact. But it was an indisputable fact that her god had answered her prayer.

Or maybe it was Jason's prayer that got a response. It was right after the boy spoke that Caelus's breathing changed.

"First, you need to know something about God, who He is and what's important to Him. It isn't what many people think."

She gripped her throat and stared into the distance. When her straight lips curved into a smile, her gaze refocused on Caelus, not him.

"I suppose it's always best to start at the very beginning. There are many stories about how different gods created the world. That includes all the people who live in it. I lived in Arsinoe all my life, and the creation stories of Greeks and Egyptians were very different. The gods involved, what was done—there was no agreement on how everything came into being. Even among Egyptians, there are different stories about how everything came to be, and not only are the stories different, but the gods who take part aren't all the same."

She spread her hands and shrugged. "But how can that be? If what the priests at any of the temples are telling us is true, wouldn't they all be telling us the same story?"

She knocked on the chair seat. "This chair is real." She waved her hand toward the levee. "The fields, the houses, the levee, the river, Menmet and Jason—we can all see and touch them and know they are real, not just part of a story someone made up to explain them. There's a reason everything is the way it is, and the truth of it wouldn't change just because someone made up a different story. Shouldn't there be a single story that tells us the truth about how the world started and became what we see today?"

"There should." Caelus fingered his lip. "If there are many stories, all but one of them is wrong. Maybe all of them are wrong, and we haven't heard what really took place yet. Maybe there was no god and what we see just…happened."

She tipped her head. "But what made it happen? I've never seen anything that didn't come from something before it. Have you?"

He leaned back against the wall. "Aristotle is perhaps the greatest Greek philosopher, and he taught that everything had a cause. But the universe—that's what we call everything that is—has always been."

Her brow furrowed. "I don't know why a great philosopher would say that. Doesn't it seem odd that every part of something would have a cause but the whole thing together doesn't? Why would he think that?"

Caelus steepled his fingers and rubbed both sides of his nose. "I can't explain that. It does seem odd when you look at it that way."

He turned his gaze on Lusario. "Am I overlooking something?"

"If you are, then I am, too."

Lusario pinched his lower lip. For a young Egyptian woman to ask a philosophical question neither he nor Caelus could answer…that wasn't the conversation he was expecting. She was questioning the teaching of the most famous Greek philosopher, a man that everyone quoted. Did her ignorance of what every educated man assumed to be correct make it possible to spot what scholars failed to see?

But he wasn't interested in Aristotle or philosophical inconsistencies right now. It was time to get back to the bigger question they were asking. A question about who controlled both life and death.

# Chapter 50

## The God Who Heals

Lusario lowered his hands to his thighs and leaned forward. "So, what should we know about the Christian god before you can tell us about the prayer?"

"That is the most important question, and it deserves a good answer." Neferu tipped her head toward Menmet's cottage. "I can at least start to explain, but I'll need to go help Menmet shortly."

The smile that could make a man's heart rate ramp up lit her eyes as well. "But you won't be going anywhere for a while, so we'll have plenty of time later."

As she looked up at the cloudless sky, she stroked her throat. Then she turned that mesmerizing smile on him and then Caelus. "God created everything we can see and all that we can't. He spoke the words, and everything came into being. So, He's the true God over every land and all people, whether they recognize that or not."

She looked toward Menmet's, and Lusario's gaze followed hers. Menmet was back at the loom. Neferu rested her hands in her lap and interwove her fingers.

"Most of us start out worshiping the gods our parents tell us about. But they're only teaching us what they were taught themselves. How often do we look at what we've been taught to believe and ask if it's true? It can take something that upends our world to get us to do it. My father's death did it for me. I started to question, but I couldn't ask my uncle. He supports his family by selling scented oils to the sanctuary of Sobek. After Father died, I lived and worked with his family doing that."

With a flick of her hand, she chased away a fly. "I asked Corinna about the Greek gods, but she only did what her mother did. She didn't know why. Then her cousin Phoebe came to Arsinoe. She knew all about the Greek gods and why they weren't really gods at all. She introduced me and Corinna to the God who created heaven and earth. So much power, yet He still cares about each person, the slaves in her uncle's household as much as the patriarch himself."

A breeze blew a loose strand of hair across her face, and she tucked it behind her ear again.

"I wanted to know that God, the one who might love an orphan like me. So, I asked Phoebe to tell me everything…what she believed, why she and her husband were traveling up the Nile to share what they believed with others. Even as she was telling me, I knew in my head and felt deep in my heart that I was hearing the truth."

She tapped her chest. "God loves me. Jesus came from heaven and sacrificed himself on a cross to pay for my sins so I could be close to God. He rose from the dead and returned to heaven, proving he was God and had the power to save me, just as he claimed." She closed her eyes much longer than a blink, and when they reopened, they shone. "Perhaps best of all, the Holy Spirit comes and lives within us when we believe in Jesus. Jesus told his followers to ask in his name when we pray. I had seen Phoebe pray for a little girl burning up with fever, and the fever broke. So, that's what Jason and I did."

She looked away, then back at them. "I asked in Jesus's name silently so you wouldn't hear. Jason didn't think about whether that was safe or not since I was already praying aloud."

She directed her brightest smile at Caelus. "And when we did, God answered yes. He healed you from the infection that was killing you."

Lusario cleared his throat, and her eyes swiveled to face him. "But he left the broken leg unhealed. Clearly, he had the power to keep Caelus from dying, but why didn't he heal everything?"

"I don't know. But God often does things I don't understand at the time. Sometimes I can see why later, sometimes not. But I know I can trust Him to do whatever is best for me in the long run. Like Theodoros's cruelty sent us here the day after Corinna died, but I think it will end up better for Jason. I can't imagine how his grandfather could be worse than his father has been. God can make all things work together for good for those who love Him."

Lusario stared at her. How many times had he heard Timon say that same thing? How many times had bad turned into good in his own life, even though he didn't worship their god? But every time, Timon said he'd been asking his god to do it.

Caelus tipped his head back and rested it against the wall. "You've told us some about how you came to be a Christian, but you haven't yet told us much about your god and what those who follow him believe." He leaned forward again. "You haven't explained sin and salvation yet. I want to know more."

Movement at Menmet's house caught Lusario's eye. Akhom stood under her canopy, arms crossed. It was too far to hear his words, but Menmet first shook her head, then nodded. She went into her house, and Akhom started toward them.

"We'll have to hear that later. Akhom is coming. But don't worry. Your faith will stay a secret with us."

"I'm not worried. I trust you. So does Jason. Thank you for being so good to him. You both mean a lot to him." She stood. "I'll go see what I can do to help Menmet now."

She was almost halfway between the houses when she met Akhom. A few words of greeting, and they walked past each other.

Lusario covered his mouth with his hand and rubbed his cheek. Neferu hadn't answered their most important questions yet, but why she abandoned the gods of Egypt to follow a religion for which Rome might kill her—it would color how he looked at what she would tell them later.

They wouldn't have private time for that until tomorrow afternoon, so meaningful conversation was over for the day. But there was no hurry. As she'd pointed out, they still had many days to spend together before Caelus could travel. Plenty of time to learn all they wanted before it was time to leave.

Lusario stood when Akhom joined them under the canopy.

The steward's normally serious expression had been replaced by a human-looking smile. "Caelus, I came to see how you are feeling today. I heard from Stephan that your fever had ended. You are looking much better than when I last saw you."

"I'm feeling as good as I look." Caelus patted his thigh. "Menmet's many years of caring for your people have proven most fortunate for me."

"Indeed. A few more weeks, and I expect you will be healed enough to continue your journey." The steward's gaze shifted to Lusario. "I also wanted to commend Stephan's new tutor on getting a lazy student so motivated."

A wry smile appeared. "I was surprised by what I saw before coming here. I found Stephan in the tutoring room reading his morning lesson again so he could talk about it tomorrow."

Lusario's smile ended in a chuckle. "I only half expected him to do that. I'm glad to hear he did. The young often don't see why the wisdom of long-dead men might still apply, but I started by introducing him to a philosopher his own grandfather might have met in Alexandria. That was enough to sweep the dust and cobwebs off other philosophers in his mind."

Caelus tapped Lusario's arm. "I suspect you fighting a croc to save me made you a man he wants to impress. If a man like you had told me diligence in my studies mattered, I would have worked harder, too."

Akhom's snort was close to a laugh. "It impressed me, and I am not a boy of eleven." His lips resumed their subdued smile. "If he keeps his enthusiasm for the rest of your stay, we can discuss a suitable bonus before you leave."

"I'll look forward to that."

The steward took a step back. "I am on my way to check on something, but I wanted you to know what Stephan did." One corner of his mouth lifted. "If you had seen him with his other tutors, you would understand the full wonder of it."

He tipped his head to Caelus, then Lusario, and continued down the levee path.

Lusario joined Caelus on the bench again. "I wonder what he's planning for a bonus. Stephan isn't a difficult student like Akhom implied when he hired me. The two men who left—it would be a safe bet that Zenobia was the problem, not her son."

"Whatever it is, you'll deserve it and probably more." Caelus gripped his right thigh with both hands and massaged it. "But I'm sorry he interrupted our conversation. I never asked Martina how Juliana convinced her to shift her worship from the gods of Rome to Jesus. Her parents both died of the same fever at her mother's estate near Cigisa, and Grandfather sent his carriage for her. She'd never met either of them before. I don't know if she was already questioning the gods, like Neferu did before meeting Phoebe."

"Going upriver with her husband just to tell others about their god." Lusario shook his head. "Not many women would choose a wandering life like that."

"Father wasn't eager for me to travel to Alexandria to finish my education. It was Juliana who helped me convince Grandfather." A shadow of sadness passed across Caelus's face. "The Markos Neferu mentioned traveled thousands of miles. But he'd known Jesus personally. Did I hear right that she had a copy of what Markos wrote about him?"

"She said she did." Lusario rubbed his palm with his thumb. Timon's friend who copied Vitruvius for them also copied Markos scrolls.

"If she has it here, I would like to read that." Caelus nudged Lusario's shoulder. "It should be more interesting than Aesop's Fables or the donkey stories Jason loves to read to me so I won't get too bored."

"You can ask her." Lusario couldn't count the many times Timon had quoted something from Markos's writings. But did he want to read it himself?

Caelus gripped the bark cast and shifted his leg. "Maybe she would let me make a copy of it myself. Martina would almost certainly love to have it. Maybe I'll have time to make two so we can keep a copy in our own library. When will you get paid so we have some money for our own papyrus roll?"

A shrug was Lusario's response. "Maybe I can ask Akhom to give me a roll as an advance on my salary so I wouldn't have to go to Thmoinepsi to buy one."

"He might ask why you want it, but I suppose we can say we're going to be replacing the drawings, as best as we can remember them. Then we won't risk exposing Neferu."

Lusario turned his gaze on Menmet's house. The last thing he would ever want to do was put Neferu in danger. "And it is true. We will be redrawing what we can. Now that you can sit up for a while without much difficulty, we should get started."

"If she'll let me, I can work on making the copy while you're tutoring. We can work together on replacing the drawings in the afternoons." Caelus patted his thigh. "Thanks to those prayers, I'll soon be walking again, and we'll be needing them when we get back to Alexandria."

Lusario's answer was a silent nod. Thanks to those prayers, he still had a future as Caelus's partner doing what they both loved. But what else did that mean going forward?

# Chapter 51

## A Runaway



*Late morning of Day 31*

"It's time to ride." Karpos stood in the doorway of the tutoring room. "Let's go."

Lusario glanced at him, then focused once more on the tablet Stephan had just finished writing. "You've done a fine job on this." Stephan's grin was what he expected now. "Think about it, and you can tell me what else you learned from it tomorrow." He closed the tablet with a snap and set it back on the desk for Stephan to look at later. "You can go ride now. Tell Nikaure I've gone to fetch Jason and will bring him shortly."

Karpos walked to the desk and picked up the tablet. "Mother said Jason knows nothing about riding, even though he's six. I started when I was five." He dropped the tablet back on the desktop.

"Some people are natural riders because they understand how horses think. With his skill with donkeys, I expect Jason to be a very quick learner. Like he is with everything else he does." Lusario crossed his arms. "I've tutored many boys, and I've never seen one who learns as fast as he does at so young an age. In a few years when you begin your studies, you can try to do as well."

Karpos bristled, and Stephan choked back a laugh.

Lusario tipped his head toward the door. "Go. Don't keep Nikaure waiting when he has other things to do."

The brat led the way onto the balcony, but Stephan looked back with a grin before he disappeared through the doorway.

After one final look around the room to make certain all was ready for the next session, Lusario headed for Neferu's cottage. Jason had been almost bouncing at breakfast in anticipation of his first day in the saddle. Could even Neferu have kept a small boy focused on his studies when the prospect of a horse beneath him lay before him?

When Lusario and Jason arrived at the stable, Stephan and Karpos were already mounted. Standing beside a mounting block, a gray gelding turned his head to watch their approach.

Nikaure summoned them with a curve of his fingers. Jason scurried to his side.

"Jason, I am Nikaure. Master Stephanos's horses are in my care. Today, I will start teaching you to ride like a grandson of Stephanos should." He raised his eyebrows. "Are you ready?"

"Oh, yes. Gaidaros and Koshari let me ride the donkeys. But these are so much bigger."

Nikaure pursed his lips to stop the smile. "Their size is not the only difference. A good horse is a noble animal, and your grandfather only keeps good horses."

Jason lowered his chin. "Patéras had good horses, too. He didn't let me ride his." He glanced at Nikaure without raising his head.

"You shouldn't ride my horse now." Karpos glared at Jason and then at Lusario.

"Stephan's old horse is your horse now. This horse is Jason's." Nikaure rested his hand on Jason's shoulder. "I will show you how to mount and how to use the reins to direct where he goes. That will be enough for today, and you will stay here by the stable where I can watch."

Jason's vigorous nod drew Nikaure's smile. "Climb up on the mounting block, swing your leg over his back, and straighten in the saddle."

When he was seated, Jason leaned forward and patted the gelding's neck. "What's his name?"

"Basileos."

"King?" Jason's eyes widened. "Grandfather does have noble horses."

A fleeting smile curved Nikaure's lips. "Stephan named him when he started riding. But Basileos is worthy of a noble name."

As soon as Jason was well seated, Nikaure knotted the ends of the reins together and handed them to him.

He placed his fingertips under Jason's chin and lifted. "Keep your chin up and your shoulders square. Sit proud with your shoulders straight up from your hips."

Jason adjusted his posture to look like an elite Greek, not a shy boy, and received Nikaure's approving nod.

"Take one rein in each hand. Pretend you're holding two baby birds. You don't want to hold the reins too tight or you'll squash them. But not so loose they could fly away."

"Like this?" Jason's eager eyes sought Nikaure's approval.

"Yes. To turn, look where you want to go. Then, pull sideways to turn his head that way. He'll go where his head points."

"I do that with the donkeys." Jason's smile was more confident.

"That's good, but a fine horse likes a more subtle hand. To get him to slow down or stop, pull back on the reins until he does. But don't keep pulling on them after that. Move your hands forward a little to relax the reins. If you pull too hard, it can hurt his mouth, and he could stop listening to what you're telling him with the reins."

Solemn eyes and total focus accompanied Jason's slow nod.

"To get him to walk, squeeze his sides with your legs until he moves forward. You don't have to kick him for him to obey you. He carried both Stephan and Karpos at your age, so he knows what a small boy's squeezes mean."

Nikaure stepped back. "Now practice."

As the horse took its first step, Jason grinned at Lusario. "I'm riding."

"You certainly are." Lusario's grin was almost as big.

Nikaure watched with crossed arms as Jason guided the horse around the stable area. Then he turned to Lusario. "Koshari told me the boy was better with donkeys than anyone he had ever seen. I expect he will learn quicker than most."

"Lusario." Stephan's voice behind him turned both Lusario and Nikaure to see what the youth wanted. "Jason's going to like Basileos. He's a good horse." He leaned over to pat his horse's neck. "This one has better breeding and more spirit, but Basileos has heart."

The scream of a child joined the scream of a horse. Thundering hooves made both men spin around.

Jason was bent over the horse's neck, hanging onto the breast strap close to where it attached to the saddle on both sides. The horse streaked across the adjacent field, running as hard as a chariot horse nearing the finish line.

In six strides, Lusario reached Karpos and yanked him off his horse. He hurled himself onto its back and drove his heels into its flanks to chase the bolting horse. Basileos had angled across the field, and now a waist-high mudbrick wall stood between the boy's horse and Lusario.

He nudged his horse into a canter, and its responsiveness when he flexed his calves was exactly what he hoped for. As he rode it straight toward the wall, he gauged its stride to choose the launching point for the jump. A quick squeeze with his thighs, and the horse gathered itself on powerful haunches. As he leaned close over the horse's neck, it launched them both over the wall. After its sure-footed landing, Lusario began the race of his life.

Time stood still as he urged his horse to its fastest gallop, hoping against hope that Jason could stay mounted until he caught up. When he came alongside, he reached over and wrapped his arm around Jason's waist.

"Let go!"

Jason obeyed his shouted command. He scooped the boy off the panicked animal and set him on his own horse's withers, fenced in by his arms. Then he reined in.

When the horse came to a stop, Lusario blew out a breath between pursed lips.

"Are you all right?"

Jason nodded. "I wasn't ready for him to do that, so it was scary. But I grabbed the straps from the breast band and held on." He turned to smile up at Lusario. "But going that fast—I never thought I would do that."

"Since you're not hurt, we'll go get him and lead him back to the stable."

"Can I ride him back? I don't want to go that fast yet, but someday I will."

"You can, but we'll walk the horses, and you'll stay right beside me."

A vigorous nod was Jason's answer.

Lusario lowered Jason to the ground. Then he dismounted, lifted Jason into the saddle, and handed him the reins. After remounting behind the boy, he nudged his horse into a walk.

Jason tried to hand him the reins.

"You keep the reins."

Jason bit his lip. "I'm not sure what to do to keep him from taking off like Basileos."

"I'll watch and correct anything you could do better. You'll do fine."

Jason focused on every word as Lusario coached him and did exactly as told. When they caught up to Basileos, he was munching on some long grass. Lusario helped Jason mount the now-calm beast, and they headed back at a walk.

"I can't wait to tell Neferu how fast I went." Jason grinned at him as if staying on a bolting horse was a normal part of a day's ride.

"Why don't you just tell her that I taught you today and that I think you'll be a natural rider. Hearing what happened could make her worry every time you come to the stable."

"I don't want her to worry. It can be our secret like how you killed Scaly Zenobia."

Lusario reached over and tapped Jason's arm with the back of his fingers. "Our secret until I say we can tell others."

As they approached the corral, Karpos was nowhere to be seen, but Stephan met them at the gate.

"Where did you learn to jump a wall like that? Will you teach me?" The boy was bouncing like an eager puppy.

"Caelus taught me. He likes to ride fast across open country, and he doesn't want to let gates limit where he can go."

He pointed at Nikaure, and Jason rode past to be helped from his horse.

Lusario dismounted and tapped Stephan's chest. "Your mother would want to kill me if I taught you how to do that. A man can fall and break his neck if his horse misses the jump. So, no jumping or running your horse at full speed until your grandfather gives you his permission."

Stephan turned what started as a giggle into a chuckle. "She doesn't like it when Grandfather lets me do things she thinks I'm not ready for. Karpos isn't ready, but I am. I'm sure Grandfather will agree." He stroked the horse's neck before patting it. "But what if you leave before he comes back?"

"Then you'll have to wait for someone else who can teach you. I won't do it without your grandfather telling me I can."

As Lusario led Karpos's horse back to the corral, Nikaure joined him with Basileos.

"I do not understand why this horse took off like that. Both Stephan and Karpos rode him as their first mount. Nothing ever spooked him." Nikaure ran his free hand through his hair. "At least the boy stayed on. Coming off at that speed, he would likely have broken his neck."

"That's what I was afraid of." Lusario glanced over his shoulder at Karpos's gelding. "It's why I didn't use the gate."

"I had not seen him jump before. Your riding—most impressive. I have not seen anything like it. Were you in the cavalry?"

A city slave like him as a cavalryman? Lusario laughed at the prospect. "No, but I learned to ride with someone who likes racing the wind and jumping walls better than using gates. Stephan's old horse looked as good as the ones I rode that could clear a wall that height, but you never know until you try the jump."

"I can saddle a fourth horse if you would like to ride with the boys. One that Master Stephanos or Horion ride. They could use the exercise."

Lusario's eyes sought Jason and found him by the corral of a chestnut stallion even Caelus would call splendid. "I'd like that. Between the two of us, we'll soon get Jason riding as if he'd started when elite Greek boys usually do. And if Basileos tries something like that again, I'll be there to stop him."

They reached the corral, and Nikaure tied Basileos to the railing before holding out his hand for Lusario's reins. "We can, and Master Stephanos will be pleased to see it."

"Until tomorrow, then." He started toward the worker's village. "Jason!"

His small friend trotted over to join him, and they headed for home.

Zenobia stood at her loom in the women's room, but her mind wasn't on the linen tunic she was weaving. The success of Karpos's errand was uppermost in her mind, and someone should come to report at any moment.

She startled when her younger son appeared at her side. He should have been smiling. He frowned instead.

She turned to her lady's maid, who worked at the loom beside hers. "Go tell the cook to prepare a platter of rolls, fruit, and sheep cheese. I want it at the table under the garden trellis. Stay there while he prepares it and come fetch me when everything is set out and ready."

"Yes, Mistress." Her maid dipped her head and left the room.

She rested her fists on her hips and matched her son's frown. "Well?"

"Jason came for his riding lesson. Nikaure put him on Basileos. He bolted, like you said he would."

Karpos opened his mouth as if to speak, then focused on his feet and said nothing.

"And then?"

Karpos raised his chin, and his eyes threw daggers, but not at her. "That tutor of Stephan's —he ruined everything."

"What did he do?"

"He took my horse. He grabbed me and pulled me off so he could mount him. Then he almost rode him into a wall, but they jumped it at the last moment. Jason was still on Basileos when he caught up and picked him off before he fell."

"So, Jason's not hurt at all?"

"No!"

"Did anyone see what you did?"

"No. I was careful, like you said."

"Good. Remember, you are not to mention what you did to anyone, especially not to your brother. He might say something to Lusario."

"Stephan wouldn't come back here with me. He wanted to stay and ask Lusario to teach him to ride like that." His frown deepened into a scowl. "He'd rather be with that tutor than do things with me."

Zenobia reached for him to give a quick hug.

He shoved her hand away. "I hate him even more than Jason."

A strand of hair hung down on his forehead, and she pushed it back. "Akhom only hired him for two months to give us time to find a better tutor for Stephan. When we get a real tutor, he'll be leaving. When he's gone, I'm sure Stephan will be eager to do things with you again."

She held her finger to her lips. "Remember, what I asked you to do today is our secret."

Karpos tightened his lips. "I'm not stupid. I won't tell anyone."

"I know, dear. You can go eat what you want from the trellis table. I'll be down shortly."

He spun on his heel and marched out.

The smile she'd worn for Karpos faded.

She needed an accomplice more capable than an eight-year-old boy if she was going to get rid of Jason before Stephanos returned. Time was of the essence since she had no idea when that would be.

But who could that be? She didn't know of anyone who would help her simply because she asked.

As she massaged her temples, she closed her eyes.

She had to ask Akhom for any money she spent, and he'd never give her money to hire a killer. He might give her money to buy some clothes or jewelry, but she'd have to show Stephanos what she bought and explain why she needed it when he returned.

Besides, she'd have to make a trip to Thmoinepsi to get anything herself, and Akhom always sent her lady's maid and a couple of men as guards to watch over her.

So, she would need to force someone to help her, and it would have to be someone who worked on the estate. Maybe someone she could threaten to accuse of stealing, like she had the shepherd. But the penalty for murder was much greater than that for theft, so maybe it would take a threat of claiming he attacked her. That would make Stephanos and Horion demand that he be killed.

But how best to kill the boy? It should still look like an accident, and there were several obvious possibilities. But who could she trust to do what was required for Jason's death without fail?

She squared her shoulders and assumed her usual elegant air. Karpos would be eating with her in the garden. She didn't like to keep her favorite son waiting too long, so she descended the balcony stairs.

With some careful thought, the best way to get rid of Jason would become clear.

# *Chapter 52*

## PLANNING THE NEXT STEP

*Early morning of Day 32*

While Jason gave Mikro his morning milk in the garden, Neferu entered their house to prepare for his lessons.

Caelus sat on the edge of his bed, scraping the last of Menmet's porridge from his bowl.

"How are you feeling today?" She picked up the three latest story sheets and set them on the table.

He handed the empty bowl to Lusario.

"Ready to do more than lie here staring at the ceiling. I want something more mentally engaging."

"More engaging than Lusario's stories of political intrigues, shifting loyalties, and fierce battles that determine the fate of ant empires?"

Her teasing smile drew Caelus's chuckle and Lusario's snort.

Lusario stacked the bowl with his own. "You told me you wanted animal stories. You never said what kind. Jason likes them. I have a few more to write before he'll know whether the Formicans or Mirminkians end up ruling the hillside."

She half-sat on the edge of the table. "What little boy wouldn't like them?" She flashed a smile at Lusario, then Caelus. "Or what adventurous man like the two of you? But I'm also wondering whether your Roman ants will defeat the Greek ones, or whether the events of human history will be reversed."

"We were wondering"—Caelus glanced at Lusario—"if you have your copy of the writings of Markos here. If so, would you mind if I make a copy for my cousin Martina? Lusario is going to ask Akhom for a papyrus roll as an advance on his salary so we can start replacing the drawings we lost. But we could use it for copying Markos's writings as well."

Her breath caught. Caelus wanted to make a copy, just as she had done several times for Phoebe? Would he feel the excitement she did the first time she read Phoebe's copy?

287

"I do. Did you want to know a little about him and how he came to write it before you make the copy?"

Caelus looked at Lusario and raised one eyebrow. A barely visible shrug was Lusario's answer to whatever the silent question was. She'd never seen two men before who spoke to each other so much without words. More like twin brothers than the master and slave they legally were.

"We would." She expected Caelus to speak, but it was Lusario who answered.

"Phoebe said he was born near Cyrene, but his family had a house in Jerusalem, so he was in Judea when Jesus was teaching and healing. He knew Apostle Peter and the other disciples who stayed with Jesus from the start. Ten years or so later, he was in Rome with Peter. He wrote down Peter's teachings while he was there and came to Alexandria in the third year of Claudius's reign. He went other places, but later he came back to Egypt to stay. He started the Alexandrian church where Phoebe worshiped."

"I was born in Cyrene." Lusario's quiet words drew her gaze to his eyes. Caution lurked in them, but why would that be?

"My friend Timon worships in that church. He told me about Markos's death at the hands of a mob during Nero's last year."

"Being a child of God is wonderful beyond all words, but it's not without risk, especially for those who are bold in telling others about Jesus." She nibbled her lip. Had it proven fatal for Phoebe and her husband?

"Your friend must really trust you to have shared like he did. He must care about you a great deal."

"He's a good friend." He glanced at Caelus. "One of the two best I've ever had."

She gave both of them an encouraging smile. "Anyone who had either of you as a friend would be truly blessed."

"You can always count us among your friends." Caelus lifted his thigh with his hands and shifted it on the bed. "We both owe you our lives. If we can ever help with anything, just let us know."

Lusario's slow nod confirmed that promise for him as well.

"Well, it's almost time for both of us to start tutoring, so I'm going to fetch the codex from my trunk now. You might want to read some while I'm teaching. We can discuss any of it this afternoon when I'm free for a couple of hours."

She looked back at them as she headed out the door. She had wondered what it would be like to live like Phoebe, sharing the truths about life and death and eternal life with God with others. Others who might never hear the truth except from her. Who would have thought that a sinking boat and a hungry crocodile would make that possible?

◆

Lusario stood. "You said you wanted to sit outside for a while after you move around some, but it's safer to read forbidden things where no one can wander by and see it." When Caelus gripped his offered forearms, he pulled his friend to his feet; then he brought over the crutch. "While I'm teaching, do you want to start copying her codex?"

"I think I'll read it first. I don't think it will be so long I can't do that before you get back from tutoring Stephan and riding with Jason." Caelus took his first step and grimaced. "I'm surprised they use a horse that bolts so easily as the first ride for a small boy. You could have struck a gong by the ear of mine, and he would have just turned and stared at you."

"Nikaure said the horse had never bolted before with Stephan or Karpos. I'll keep a close eye on him. Maybe we'll ride over so you can see Basileos." Lusario couldn't stop the grin. "I'm sure Jason will want to show him off to you. Nikaure is letting me ride all the stallions so they get more exercise while their master is away. When you see the chestnut I'll have today, you'll be wishing you were Jason's riding instructor just to get to ride him. I haven't seen as fine an animal since we left Carthago."

"You have a mean streak, did you know that? Dangling a splendid horse in front of a man who can only hobble around with a crutch." Caelus wrinkled his nose. "But maybe I'll get to try him before we leave. You can tell Akhom that's part of the bonus you want for teaching two of the three grandsons."

That earned Lusario's chuckle. "Stephan and Jason are a pleasure to teach. Karpos…I'd rather clean the triclinium alone after a banquet than spend a day teaching that one."

"You'll never have to do either." Caelus tapped Lusario's upper arm with the back of his fingers. "I'll make sure of that."

Lusario stayed beside Caelus as he hobbled toward the doorway.

"After you take the horses back, we can start recreating the drawings. I think we'll remember enough to win over Tranquilla. I'm not sure if we should go downriver to talk with Latro and sell our ideas to his wife as soon as I can travel or go on to the estate to select a good location or two for the villa first.

"Your leg won't be strong enough to do anything much for a couple of months, so maybe going downriver first is a better idea. We need to speak to Latro anyway before he decides to hire the local builder."

"You're probably right." Caelus bounced his eyebrows at Lusario. "And between now and when we leave, we can learn more about the god who healed me."

Lusario nodded because that was what Caelus expected. But could what they learned change the future that he didn't want changed?

# Chapter 53

## First Questions

*Early afternoon of Day 32*

Lusario's smile broadened as he rode Horion's chestnut stallion toward their cottage. It was a magnificent animal, better than any he'd seen at the Martinus estate.

He had taken all three boys out riding, and even Karpos had been in a good mood for most of the ride. Until he noticed Jason and Basileos were already forming a bond, that is. That irritated Karpos, but hardly anything about Jason didn't irritate that spoiled son of a mother who encouraged the worst in him.

Neferu was working in the garden when they rode up. When she looked up, her eyes widened and she inhaled sharply. First, she stared at her small boy on the big horse, then she turned worried eyes on Lusario.

His smile and slight nod were meant to calm her fears, and maybe they worked. At least she didn't say anything.

Jason rode up to the garden wall. "This is Basileos. Nikaure said he's mine now, and I'll be riding him almost every day. He's really fast."

His mouth opened, and he looked at Lusario before he closed it. Then he bit his lip over almost letting their secret out.

"But I didn't ride him fast today. Stephan wanted to race Lusario, but he said they didn't have a good place to do it without risking one of the horses getting hurt. The racetracks are finished with smooth sand so they won't."

"Hmph." Karpos wrinkled his nose. "It was my horse that Lusario made jump the wall and run so fast yesterday, so I could do it, too."

Lusario raised one finger. "Your horse is good enough, but you only just moved up from Basileos. You're not ready for either the speed or the jump."

Stephan moved up alongside Karpos. "I can ride a fast gallop for a good race, but I couldn't jump the wall the way Lusario did. If I can't, you sure can't. I'm a much better rider than you."

"You are not! I'll show you." Karpos started turning his horse toward the low wall between Menmet's cottage and the next one over.

Lusario moved the stallion in front of Karpos's horse and gripped the halter. "If I see you try it and you survive the jump with no broken bones, you'll be walking back to the main house. I'll be taking this horse back to Nikaure and telling your mother you're not ready for any horse until your grandfather gets back and has a talk with you about how smart men don't deliberately do stupid things with their mounts that can break their horse's leg or their own neck."

Karpos sputtered, then dropped the reins on the horse's neck and crossed his arms. "She wouldn't listen to you." His lip curled into a sneer.

"I think she loves you more than anything, and she'd be endlessly grateful to me for keeping you safe for her."

Karpos opened his mouth, then closed it without a word. But he picked up the reins and only glared when Stephan snickered.

Then his gaze settled on Mikro. A feral smile appeared but was quickly erased.

Menmet shoved her hands onto her hips. "Don't you be thinking you're coming back here for the donkey, Karpos. There are plenty of us watching, and Akhom himself said the tiny thing should be here with us until it gets big enough to feed itself. You don't want to have to tell your grandfather how you hurt one of his donkeys. He might think you're not to be trusted with a horse either."

He rolled his eyes and moved his gelding on the far side of Stephan's. Then he stared off to the right away from everyone.

"I'm going to take everyone back to the stable, and Jason and I will be back soon."

Caelus lounged on the bench in the shade where he could watch Neferu and Mikro. He laced his fingers atop his head and leaned back against the wall. "I'd have to say you're right about the stallion. A finer piece of horseflesh would be hard to find. I envy you sitting in that saddle, but I don't envy what you're doing to earn it."

Lusario shrugged. "For a mount like this, it's worth it."

He reined away from the garden wall. "Let's go, boys. Nikaure has more important things to do than wait for us so he can tend these horses after our ride."

Stephan and Karpos nudged their horses into a fast trot and were heading toward a canter. But the path between the village and the main house wasn't meant for racing.

"Rein them in!" His shout drew an instant response from Stephan, who settled back into a walk. But Karpos trotted ahead of them, pretending he didn't hear or maybe flaunting that he didn't care.

Stephan reined in and waited for them to catch up. Then he fell in beside Lusario.

"Grandfather won't like how he's riding. I bet Mother will be angry when Grandfather makes him stop."

Lusario offered him an encouraging smile. "Perhaps by the time your grandfather gets home, he'll be both older and smarter about what he does."

Stephan's snort accompanied a shaking head.

Lusario watched the willful boy urge the horse to a canter. If he were a betting man, that's one bet he'd never take.

When Lusario returned to the house with Jason, the boy trotted over to say goodbye to Neferu. She'd just fed Mikro, and he scratched under the tiny beast's chin before heading down the path to go help Setne.

Neferu finished washing the last of the milk from the feeding bucket and strolled over to join him and Caelus, who sat on the bench by the door.

Lusario brought out the chair for her and settled in beside his friend.

She gripped the top of the chair. "What shall we talk about?"

"Markos, of course." Caelus shifted on the pillow she'd brought over to soften the seat for him. "I read the entire thing through once, and I want to ask about parts of it section by section. But we can wait until tomorrow since Lusario hasn't had a chance to read any of it."

Lusario crossed his arms. "I know a fair amount about what must be there. For three years, Timon has tried to persuade me to become a Christian."

Caelus raised his eyebrows at Lusario. "I never knew about that."

Lusario shrugged. "I looked on it as a friendly philosophical discussion. We discussed many other things from the lectures we heard. I wasn't looking for a change from the Stoic principles we both follow."

"I wasn't either, but that was before I almost died." Caelus fingered his lip. "Now I want to know more about the god who seems to have answered prayers to keep me alive. Not once, but twice."

"I'll be happy to explain anything I can, but I hope Lusario will feel free to ask questions even though he hasn't read it yet." Neferu gave him an ambiguous smile. "I hope you'll share some of what your friend told you about the different questions you both might have."

"I will." Lusario flexed his jaw.

As ignorant of the teachings of the Greek philosophers as she was, would she and a scholar like Timon share the same view of their god and what he supposedly did?

Caelus slapped the top of his thighs. "Then let's start. I have a question about the first sentence. The 'beginning of the good news about Jesus Christós son of God.' Christós—is it his last name? I wouldn't expect a Greek last name for a Jew from Galilee who became a famous religious teacher. Was he part Greek?"

"No. Markos doesn't write about his ancestry, but on his mother's side, he was from David. That was the second king of the Jews."

"Was his father's line royal as well?"

"His step-father Joseph descended from David, too, but he's not one of Jesus's ancestors. Mary became with child without lying with a man. God Himself overshadowed her, and she gave birth to Jesus. I don't know exactly how that happened, but we know he's God's son because a messenger from God, an angel, told her that's what would happen before it did. God Himself also declared Jesus was His son when Jesus was baptized. You read about that already."

"A virgin woman gave birth to him?" Lusario's head drew back. "How can that be?"

Neferu's chuckle raised his eyebrow. "It is certainly not what we would expect, and it's not like the stories of the Greek gods fathering demigods by lying with women. But the God who can make the sky, the earth, and everything on it, including us, would have no problem forming one little baby in a virgin woman's womb."

When Caelus looked at him, Lusario shrugged his response. It was impossible in the normal way of things, but for a god who could create everything and even stop death when a little boy asked… He couldn't argue it was beyond reason.

Caelus turned his gaze back onto Neferu. "That last name Christós—is it why his followers are called Christians by Tacitus?"

"It is why we're called that, but it's not his last name. It's what he is—God's anointed one. A king of Israel was called God's anointed one, and the Jews were hoping for a new king to drive out the Romans."

"So that's why Pontius Pilatus asked him if he was the king of the Jews during the trial. Why he crucified him as a rebel against Rome." Caelus stroked the underside of his jaw.

"Yes, but Jesus didn't come to lead an army to free the Jews from Rome's rule. He was here for a much greater purpose." She drew a deep breath, as if she were about to tell them something important. "He came to free all of us from the sins that separate us from God."

"There's that word 'sin' again. Which leads into my next question." Caelus rubbed behind his ear. "It doesn't start out talking about what Jesus was doing. It quotes some prophet about a messenger preparing the way and then talks about someone called Joannes baptizing in a river not too far from Jerusalem. He said it was a baptism of repentance for the forgiveness of sins. I have several questions about what he means by that."

"I'll try to answer them as well as I can. I only have the gospel Markos wrote to share with you, but three other men wrote about what Jesus said and did. Some of what I'll tell you came from them. Two of the gospel writers were among the twelve apostles who traveled with Jesus from the beginning of his teaching and healing. Matthaios was a tax collector at Capernaum on the Sea of Galilee. Joannes and Peter worked as fishermen there. The fourth writer was Lukas. He was a physician who traveled with Apostle Paul for several years and talked with many eyewitnesses of what had happened before he wrote his gospel. Phoebe read all their writings back in Alexandria, and she taught me what they said. But I've only read what Markos wrote. His was what Peter taught."

Caelus chuckled. "A tax collector and two fishermen. I'd bet there was conflict between those three."

"Maybe at the start, but it wouldn't have lasted long. When we follow Jesus, we become brothers and sisters, and past differences don't matter anymore. Paul wrote in one of his letters to some churches he started in Galatia that in Christ there is no Jew nor Greek, male nor female, slave nor free. We're all one in Christ Jesus."

Lusario's mouth twitched. No Jew nor Greek. Many thousands of each had died in what the Romans called the Jewish Uprising thirteen years ago. Many Greeks he'd known had been killed in Cyrene. Rome had purged Egypt of its Jews after it put down the revolt. But Timon told him about the Roman from his church who braved the Greek mobs ridding Alexandria of its Jewish population to save two Jewish women who worshiped with them. He'd been too late, and Timon still grieved their deaths.

"Shall we talk about sin now?" Her eyes softened when she turned them on Lusario. "If there are things about sin that your friend Timon told you that you want to share with us, please do."

He felt his ears heat. Had he known this conversation was coming, he would have paid closer attention. "I will."

Caelus tapped Lusario's arm with the back of his fingers. "I've seen you two arguing from a distance. Sparring with words like they were swords but both smiling when you finished so I couldn't tell who won. Was this one of those arguments?"

"No. You can't decide a disagreement about religion with facts and logic."

Her head tilted. "I never trained in the logic of the philosophers that the Greek boys start to study when they're Stephan's age. But it seems to me that a disagreement about a God who is real could be decided using facts and common sense." She pushed a strand of hair behind her ear. "That's the kind of logic most of us use."

His lips curved into a smile even though he didn't intend them to. "If the subject of the disagreement is, in fact, real, then facts and logic are useful weapons."

"Good, because facts and common sense are what I have on my side." The smile she flashed him broadened his own.

"We'll be talking about sin and repentance and forgiveness. We'll talk about what it takes to pay for our sins so God can allow us into His presence." Her smile faded, and the eyes she fixed on him looked deadly serious. "We'll start with sin because that's the source of all the problems in the world. It's also something we all do, no matter how hard we try not to."

Lusario leaned back against the wall and crossed his arms. "So, what is sin?"

Timon had told him many times. But no matter how smart she might be, would a rural Egyptian woman with no philosophical training have the same explanation?

"First, I need to tell you something about God because sin isn't just about the things we do or don't do. It's about our relationship with Him." Her eyes warmed. "And there is nothing in this world more important than how we respond to His love for us."

"His *agape*?" Caelus's eyes narrowed. "What do you mean by that?"

"It's a different kind of love than what we usually see. It's a decision, not an emotion, and it's unconditional. You can't earn it by the things you do or lose it by doing the things you shouldn't. It's when I want what's best for another person, even if that costs me something. It's doing whatever I can to help when someone needs it, even if I'd rather not."

Lusario drew a sharp breath. That was the kind of love that Timon had told him about. In fact, what she said was almost exactly what Timon said. But if the woman who taught her and Timon had been part of the same Christian group, perhaps he should expect that Phoebe would tell Neferu the same thing Timon told him.

Neferu raised her eyebrows at him. When he didn't speak, she continued. "More than a thousand years ago, God gave His prophet Moses instructions on how He wanted His people to live. Moses included them as part of his writings about God freeing the people we call the Jews. He took them from slavery in Egypt and gave them the lands we call Judaea and Galilee. Moses was the man who led them back to the land God had promised Abraham."

"I've seen one of those scrolls. Timon was reading one in the Great Library. The Greek translation of one, anyway. He said the second Ptolemy paid to have the Hebrew scrolls translated when he was trying to add a copy of everything that had ever been written to his library collection."

"I would love to see those. To read God's own words that He spoke to Moses… But I don't expect I'll ever go to Alexandria." She scanned the area around them. "At least for now, my life is here with Jason."

Lusario's gaze followed the road to where it ended at the main house. Her life was with Jason now, but what would happen when he outgrew her? It was five more years, at most, before the boy moved on to a tutor who would teach him the formal logic of the Greeks and Romans, not the common sense she valued. He'd need to learn the philosophy she said made no sense and know the stories of the Greek gods, even if he didn't believe them.

Zenobia was jealous of her. She would delight in turning Neferu out into a world that didn't value a smart woman or one who followed a forbidden God. All it would see was her beauty, and beauty was a curse if a woman had no one to protect her.

When that time came, what future could there be for the kindest person he'd ever known?

# Chapter 54

## What God Commands

Neferu cleared her throat. "As I was saying, there were many detailed commands in those for how His people should live, but Jesus summarized them all as being part of the two greatest ones."

She focused on Caelus. "Remember where the one teacher of the law asked him what the greatest commandment was?"

"I do, but tell Lusario." He tapped Lusario's arm again. "You can watch for that when you're reading."

"After a group of Jewish leaders tried to trap him with a question about widows and marriage, Jesus answered so wisely that one of the teachers of the law truly wanted to know what Jesus thought was God's greatest commandment. Jesus said, 'The first of all the commandments is: "Hear, O Israel, the Lord our God, the Lord is one. And you shall love the Lord your God with all your heart, with all your soul, with all your mind, and with all your strength." This is the first commandment. And the second, like it, is this: "You shall love your neighbor as yourself." There is no other commandment greater than these.'"

She leaned forward. "So, if we haven't loved God with our heart, soul, mind, and full strength, then we've sinned against God. And if we haven't cared about other people as much as we care about ourselves, we've sinned against Him again."

Caelus covered his mouth with his palm and blew out a slow breath. "I read that, but who can possibly do it? There are a few people I care about a great deal, maybe as much as you're describing. But if I'm honest, it's probably fewer than I should. Most of us care about ourselves most of all. We all love ourselves more than any other person, even the person we might love most in this life." He fixed his gaze on Lusario. "But I do know one person who cared about my life more than his own."

Lusario returned his gaze with a shrug. "Saving you was saving me, too. And I owed you for diving into the sea."

Neferu's brow furrowed. "Diving into the sea?"

"I was knocked overboard, and Caelus jumped in to keep me from drowning."

Caelus's wry smile accompanied his shrug. "But I knew the dolphins wouldn't try to eat me."

He laced his fingers and rested them atop his head. "Grandfather, Father, me, Lusario…we've all been Stoics who don't recognize any god as real, so the question of loving a god never came up. I also know people who truly want to honor their gods, who will make do with less so they can give larger offerings of money and food and wine. Such people might believe their god is more worthy of worship than the next man's god."

He gripped his thigh and repositioned his leg. "But I wouldn't use the word love to describe how they feel toward their own god. And I've never seen any evidence that their love for their god is of the magnitude you describe. I think deep down, most people realize their god isn't deserving of what your god commands."

Caelus raised one finger. "But Markos writes that the whole Judean countryside and all the people of Jerusalem were coming to Joannes to confess their sins and be baptized. 'The whole countryside' and 'all the people'—that's probably exaggeration, but there must have been a lot of them. So, there was something about how they were worshiping that wasn't satisfying them. What did they think was wrong?"

Neferu's eyes widened as she stared at Caelus. Then her eyes closed, and when they reopened, they were as calm as ever.

"I don't know everything they did, but maybe it wasn't that they were doing anything wrong. Maybe it was because they knew what they were doing wasn't enough to bring them as close to God as they wanted. He wants us to know Him, and you don't get that just performing some rite. Father and I used to do that with Sobek, but it didn't help me know my father's god. No one ever told me I could, and there was nothing about Sobek that even made me want to know him."

A gentle smile curved her lips. "But God has always wanted people to come to Him, to know Him as the One who made and loves us. He's not some god our ancestors made up who doesn't care about us. He called His chosen ones His children. He wants us to love Him like He loves us."

Her eyes shifted between the two of them. "But He's holy and perfect, and by His very nature, He cannot abide sin in His presence. Sin can be many things, some horrendous, some that might seem insignificant to us but not to God. It can be something we do that we shouldn't. Or something we don't do when we know we should. And it might be something we only think, not something we actually do. God knows our every thought as if we were speaking it aloud."

A fleeting grimace crossed Caelus's face, and he squeezed his right thigh. "Serving a god where you have to watch your every thought and deed…that's quite a burden for anyone to bear. Why would someone choose that god?"

"Why would anyone choose a difficult truth over a comfortable lie? Truth matters. I'd rather serve God who's real than something made by human hands that's not a god at all. Jesus himself said, 'You shall know the truth, and the truth will set you free.' I've known what it's like to believe in a lie. But now that I follow Jesus, I truly am free."

She clasped her hands and rested them in her lap. "So, out of His love for us, He gave Moses instructions for making sacrifices that could cover their sins so they could approach Him. The sacrifice of an animal that was free of any blemish was what He required. They were always to give God their best, not something of little value. But He didn't tell them to sacrifice because He needed what they gave Him. It told them how serious their sins were in God's eyes. To cover those sins, to be forgiven by God is why they shed the blood of the best."

Caelus blew out a slow breath. "So, when Joannes said to come be baptized to get forgiveness when they confessed their sins, I can see why so many would seize the opportunity."

He raised one finger. "But, why did Jesus come to be baptized? If he was the son of this god, why would he need it?"

"Markos didn't write it down, but Matthaios did. Joannes asked him that question because he knew who Jesus was. After all, God himself said Jesus was His Son, and a son can always be with his father. Jesus said that he did it to fulfill all righteousness. It was an example for those who did need it."

Caelus tightened his lips. "So, why they came makes sense, but the voice saying Jesus was his son and the Holy Spirit landing on Jesus…that's three things, and when Jesus spoke the two commandments, he said 'The Lord our God, the Lord is one.' Are there three gods or one god for Christians?"

She closed her eyes and froze. Through pursed lips, she released a breath. "I wish Phoebe and her husband were here. They might be able to explain better than me. But they're only people like me, so maybe they couldn't explain it either. None of us have the mind of God. Many things are beyond my own understanding. But I can tell you how I think about it."

Hoofbeats behind her made her turn.

Stephan dismounted and tied his horse to the gate post before sauntering toward them. "I volunteered to bring the invitation to dine at the main house tonight. I told Mother that you were getting around now, so she wants both of you to join us for family dinner. Jason is supposed to come, too."

Caelus rested his hand on his thigh. "It's all I can do today to get this far from my bed, so I can't handle a dinner invitation yet. But I would be delighted to join your mother as soon as I'm getting around better."

"I'll tell her." He wiped his hands on the sides of his tunic. "She also told me you're both welcome to read anything in Father's library. And she wants Lusario to come even if he's the only one."

"I'll bring Jason up and be pleased to stay."

Stephan scrunched his nose. "She also told me to make sure Jason washes off the donkey stench before he comes. Dinner will be served in about an hour."

"He's helping Setne right now, but I'll go get him so he'll be smelling fresh enough to please your mother." One corner of Lusario's mouth lifted. "I'll bathe as well. I probably smell like horse."

A grin was Stephan's first answer. "Me, too, but I don't think that's a bad smell. See you at dinner." He mounted and trotted away.

Lusario stood. "Looks like it will be tomorrow before you can tell us more."

The relief in Neferu's eyes was as great as Lusario expected. Caelus's questions had become difficult ones.

"Perhaps you'll have time to read a little when you get home from dinner." She stood as well. "I need to tell Menmet it will only be three of us tonight, and then I need to feed Mikro. But I look forward to answering as many of your questions as I can." She flashed a smile at Caelus. "Menmet and I will do our best to take care of you until your friend returns."

As she walked away, Caelus tapped Lusario's arm. "I found many places in Markos's work that I have questions about. I expect you will, too, after you read it. She's not a scholar like we're used to, but I think we'll learn all we'll need as we question her."

"I expect we will." Lusario's gaze rested on Menmet's doorway where Neferu had disappeared. A man was responsible for acting in accord with what he knew. What if Caelus came to believe things that were too dangerous to know?

What if they both did?

◆

Neferu waited until she was through Menmet's doorway and out of the men's sight before she steepled her fingers and covered her mouth.

Caelus was questioning every little thing, and even though Lusario hadn't read Markos yet, he was, too. She'd expected some questions since Caelus was hearing it all for the first time, but Lusario's friend Timon had been telling him about Jesus for more than three years.

Trying to tell him, but had Lusario let himself listen, really listen, with an open mind? While Caelus's questions seemed to come from open-minded curiosity, skepticism coated Lusario's comments.

She'd told them she welcomed every question, but what if they asked things she couldn't answer and that made them stop asking? So many things about God were beyond what she knew, many things that she hadn't yet figured out and maybe never would.

But what she did know was that the Holy Spirit came when she confessed her own sins and declared her faith in Jesus. God had forgiven them all as if they had never happened. She felt God's presence whenever she prayed, and she never felt alone. She'd seen God's love for her in so many ways, and she'd seen His power to change anything. When she prayed for Baby Menander and then for Caelus, they were both dying, and God stopped their death.

*God, give me the words these men need to hear. Open their minds to see Your truth, then open their hearts to commit themselves to it. As Phoebe did for me, please use me as the one to pull back the curtain so they can enter into the joy of belonging to You.*

# Chapter 55

## WHO'S AFTER JASON?



*Evening of Day 32*

Lusario stood, arms crossed, contemplating his blood-stained fine-linen tunic. He only had that and the plain tunic he was wearing that Menmet had borrowed from someone so she could wash the other.

Through pursed lips, he blew out a slow breath. "Which do you think I should wear to the main house?" He plucked the chest of his tunic. "This one looks clean enough, but she's picky about odor. That one"—he pointed at the blue-edged linen one—"smells better but looks like I've just come from a knife fight."

A knock on the doorframe drew both their gazes.

The youth who usually opened the door at the main house stood with something made of fabric in his hand. "Mistress Zenobia sent this. She said you were to wear it to dinner."

He entered, placed it on the bed beside Caelus, and left.

It unfolded when Lusario picked it up, and he caught the smaller item that tumbled free before it hit the ground. One hand held a clean fine-linen tunic that almost reached his knees. The other held a matching tunic in Jason's size.

Laughter exploded from Caelus's lips. "Looks like Zenobia wants only clean-smelling, well-dressed dinner companions tonight."

A frown was Lusario's reply. There was nothing funny about what it might mean.

"But should I wear it? For a woman I barely know to give me clothing to wear while she entertains me…is she sending a message I don't want to receive? When a mistress does such a thing…"

A roll of Caelus's eyes was his first answer. "As far as she knows, you're a Greek scholar of some means. She's a married Greek woman with an overseer who watches over her for his master. She wouldn't be stupid enough to risk her husband or father-in-law suspecting she's done anything she shouldn't while they were gone. Besides, she invited me, too, so I don't think she particularly wants you except for conversation."

Caelus picked up the good tunic and tossed it to him. "My mother enjoys the compliments from the men my father entertains, but she would never do anything to betray Father. I expect Zenobia is the same. You should wear the tunic."

With tightened lips, Lusario shrugged. Then he donned the expensive clothes.

Caelus and his father were men of integrity, and Volero's wife would never deliberately disgrace herself. But in both Cyrene and Alexandria, what Master Volero and Artoria would never do was considered fine in some elite households as long as no one outside learned of it. Zenobia had dressed and bejeweled herself fit for a banquet when she was only meeting her son's tutor. He'd seen her watching for him more than once as he walked over to teach her son.

What a lonely Greek woman left behind while her husband enjoyed himself in the capital city might want of him—it wasn't a discussion of the teachings of Plato or a discourse on landscape design.

Pleasant but uninterested was the message he'd send her tonight. That should be enough to take care of a problem on the horizon long before it reached him.

But until Caelus was recovered enough to travel, he couldn't afford to offend her. A woman who felt rejected might demand that they leave the estate right away, no matter what his deal with Akhom might be.

If Lusario had been allowed to pick his seat at Zenobia's table, it would not have been the one she gave him. With a table that seated three on each side and two on the ends, he'd expected her to choose the head of the table. Instead, she seated herself in the middle seat with her sons on each side. Jason was seated across from Karpos while she placed him directly opposite her.

He'd kept his feet tucked beneath his seat with his ankles wrapped around the chair legs after he felt something brush against his sandal. Jason did the same, but that was to avoid the kicks that Karpos delivered every time he noticed his small cousin had let his legs get within range.

Zenobia said nothing to stop it, even though she must have noticed Jason's small jerk each time a kick connected.

She'd asked too many questions about his life, but he'd deflected most of them with descriptions of locations, not activities, and turned the conversation to Alexandria whenever he could. As Caelus had ordered, he played the free man he wasn't by emphasizing the educated man that he was. The main course was over, and the dessert now sat before him. Soon he'd be able to excuse himself to take Jason home and listen to Caelus laugh about how he'd managed to keep her from learning more than she should.

Stephan popped a fruit-filled pastry into his mouth. "Where are we going to ride tomorrow? I sure like you riding with us instead of Nikaure. He always took us on the same route and not as far. But when are you going to teach me to jump?"

Lusario wiped his mouth with the green-dyed linen napkin that matched Zenobia's tunic. "I told you that won't happen until your grandfather tells me personally that he wants me to do it. But you wouldn't have time to learn much before I'll be leaving, anyway."

Stephan turned his gaze onto his mother and rubbed his palms together. "Please persuade him to stay. I like learning the way he teaches things."

Zenobia placed her elbow on the table and leaned her chin on her hand. She looked at him sideways. Then her fingers drummed on her cheek like he'd seen tavern women do to attract wealthy patrons.

"What can we offer you to get you to stay?"

He stiffened, then forced himself to relax. He picked up his goblet and leaned back in the chair: "I tutored in the past, but Caelus and I are architects now. I don't plan on being a full-time tutor again. I only offered to teach Stephan for the two months that we're waiting for Caelus's leg to heal. Then we'll be going back to Alexandria."

She straightened, and her mouth curved down before she forced it back into a smile. "I don't know what Stephanos and Horion find to do in Alexandria for so long when they go there."

Lusario offered a social smile, copying what he'd seen on Caelus so many times. "Anything you'd want to see or do can be experienced there. It rivals Rome itself for all things good and has much less of the things that are bad."

"Perhaps I should have Akhom watch some of your lessons so he will know what to look for in the next tutor." She opened her mouth before wiping first one, then the other corner with her napkin.

She licked her lips before they relaxed into a seductive smile. "Perhaps Stephanos can hire you to build something. Then you could stay on longer to tutor Stephan half days and build with your Roman friend the other half. If that takes long enough, you can be Karpos's first tutor."

She directed a doting smile at her younger son. "He's so clever, even more so than Stephan, and Stephan is certainly the smartest boy in the neighborhood."

Stephan was just taking a sip of his watered wine, and he almost spit it out trying not to laugh. "The only thing Karpos is good at is complaining about everything."

He sobered when his mother turned narrowed eyes on him.

Lusario cleared his throat. "If we're still here when Stephanos returns, we could certainly discuss him hiring us to build. But design work and turning those designs into buildings take enormous amounts of time, so I highly doubt I would have spare time for tutoring."

He glanced at Karpos and got a glare in return. "A student like I expect Karpos to be would do better with a more traditional tutoring style than I employ."

He lifted his goblet to Stephan, whose eyebrows rose. "Your older son has been an exceptional student for me, and I expect he will continue to excel with his next tutor and when he goes to Alexandria to complete his studies." He gave Stephan his broadest smile. "When you're studying there, you'll have to come see me occasionally."

Stephan's mouth curved into his biggest smile, and Karpos's formed as big a frown.

Zenobia leaned in again. "It's a credit to your understanding of young boys that you see how truly exceptional my sons are. Their grandfather is extremely proud of them. If only Theodoros could have a son as smart and handsome and truly exceptional as my own boys, but…well…not every child is as blessed by the gods as mine have been. Some men simply have to make do with lesser things."

Jason seemed to shrink as Zenobia focused her contemptuous gaze upon him. He acted like a different boy than he did when she wasn't there. How he probably acted at the Arsinoe estate when his father was so cruel.

Lusario fought the urge to order her to stop it.

"It is too soon to tell what the baby boy will become, but I would agree that Stephanos can praise the intelligence and diligence in study of both Stephan and Jason to all his friends. He could hold either up as an example for their own sons to follow."

Zenobia's jaw twitched when he spoke Jason's name alongside Stephan's, but Lusario had no regrets that he'd irritated her with his words. Jason straightened his spine and squared his shoulders and gave him a grateful half-smile.

But Jason's smile turned full when Stephan raised his goblet. "To Jason, the cousin I didn't know existed but I'm glad he does."

Lusario glanced over the rim of his goblet as he drank the toast.

Zenobia was staring at Jason with hate-filled eyes. Then they veiled, but if she'd had a tail, it would have been swishing like a cat's as it prepared to pounce.

What would Jason's life be like after his grandfather and uncle returned? Would they be like his aunt, whose wrinkled nose proclaimed her nephew a disgusting intruder, or like him and Caelus, who saw a smart, sweet boy who should make any father proud?

*Morning of Day 33*

Lusario rolled the scroll and set it in its cubicle. "That's enough for today. You can go to the stable. I'll fetch Jason and be there shortly."

Stephan tidied the stack of tablets on the desk and placed his stylus next to them. "If we go to the western wheat field, there's a stretch of sand where we could have a short race."

"But Jason and Karpos will be with us. Jason would be content to watch us, but your brother wouldn't be able to resist trying to race us. He's far from ready for that." Lusario turned from the cabinet of scrolls. "A man should consider how what he does might affect others, and tempting Karpos to do something he shouldn't is not a good idea."

"I suppose you're right. Meet you at the stable." Stephan started out the door, then paused. "I've been wondering…does a horse always run fast if something pricks its rump?"

Lusario narrowed his eyes. "A cavalry horse that trained for battle might not, but most others will. Why do you ask?"

Stephan leaned over the balcony railing and scanned the courtyard before turning back to Lusario. "Right after he dismounted, I saw Karpos drop something and sweep dirt over it when you were chasing Jason."

A frown joined Lusario's narrowed eyes. "Did you see what that was?"

The youth moved back to the doorway and lowered his voice. "Not then, but I looked later. It was a pin like women use to hold their hair."

Lusario's stomach knotted. Basileos had never bolted before that day.

"Do you know whose it was?"

Stephan shrugged. "Most of the kitchen women use them. It gets hot in there. I suppose it's cooler to put your hair up."

Lusario tousled Stephan's hair. "Don't go pricking your horse's rump or anyone else's to find out."

The boy grinned in return. "I won't. Like you say, a man thinks about what might happen before he acts. Which philosopher said that?"

"Lusario of Alexandria, but there might have been others. It's common sense, and that can be more valuable than what any philosopher says."

One corner of his mouth lifted. Neferu would agree that common sense had much greater value than formal logic when they gave different answers. Behind those beautiful eyes and charming smile was a mind far wiser than that of any woman he'd met and smarter than many men.

He rested his hand on Stephan's shoulder and guided them both onto the balcony. They descended the stairs together.

He gave Stephan a gentle shove toward the kitchen. "I'm going for Jason. I'll be with you shortly."

As Stephan disappeared into the kitchen, Lusario was left rubbing his jaw. Did Karpos plan to make Jason's horse bolt the first time he was in the saddle? Was it of his own accord, or did someone else put him up to it? If someone else, then who?

If he were a betting man, there was only one suspect that he'd wager money on.

Zenobia. Was anything more dangerous than a mother defending her young?

Jason was no threat to Stephan. The youth was a grandson any man could be proud of. Even the horse Stephan rode declared his grandfather's favor toward the firstborn of his oldest son. But no one could fail to see that Jason, even with his one good eye, was far superior to his brat of a cousin.

She made no secret of her disdain for Jason. She'd probably told Karpos how to get Basileos to bolt. But what else might she do to get rid of a nephew before his grandfather could see the contrast and favor the better boy?

During the riding session, Lusario kept his eye on Karpos. He mostly kept his horse between the two boys. Jason's enemy would get no chance to make Basileos rear or run before he could talk with Caelus and Neferu about what he'd learned.

He bided his time while Jason fed Mikro and waited until the boy headed down the path to help Setne. When and how much to tell Jason about his attempted murder—that was not something to decide on his own.

Caelus was making his way to the bench overlooking the garden, and Neferu had just returned from taking their dishes back to Menmet when he fell in beside her.

"I learned something from Stephan this morning that you and Caelus need to know."

The friendly smile she always gave him when he first spoke to her vanished. "You look like it's something serious."

"It is, and I want to discuss what we should do about it with the two of you."

She stayed at his side until they reached Caelus.

"You look like you had a bad morning." Caelus settled onto the bench, crossed his arms, and leaned back against the wall.

"Not as bad as I'm afraid it could get."

Caelus's head drew back. "What happened?"

"Stephan told me he found a hair pin where Karpos had dropped it and brushed dirt over it with his foot. It was too near where Basileos was standing when he bolted. I think Karpos pricked the horse to make it run so Jason could fall off and maybe die." He stared at the main house before turning back to the two people who cared for the boy at least as much as he did.

Neferu's eyes saucered, and she covered her mouth with both hands. "Oh, God! No!" Still crossed, she lowered her hands to her chest. "Karpos has been cruel to Jason since the first time they met, but do you really think he would try to kill Jason?

"We should ask Akhom what he thinks." Caelus leaned forward. "He's known

Karpos since he was born. He can probably tell us whether Karpos did it as a mean prank without thinking about what could happen." His brow furrowed. "Do we really think a spoiled eight-year-old boy had lethal intent?"

"Karpos is meaner than a hyena, but he's not very bright. I doubt he came up with the idea." Lusario drew a deep breath. "I think Zenobia might be behind it, and if she tried to kill Jason once, she'll probably try again."

Caelus's head drew back. "Why do you say that?"

"At dinner last night, I saw how much Karpos hates his cousin, so it might have just been the boy. But when Zenobia didn't realize I was watching the way she looked at Jason, I saw a cold hatred that equals Karpos's hot anger. I think she's afraid their grandfather is going to prefer Jason over Karpos, and she doesn't want to risk that."

"I think he would want to, but Akhom can't help us right now." Neferu rubbed her upper arms, as if she were cold. "Menmet mentioned that he left this morning to tour several of Stephanos's farms that are some distance from the main estate. He's going to be away at least a week, maybe more. I don't know who he left in charge while he's gone, let alone whether they can be trusted with our concerns. Most are afraid to get Zenobia mad at them, so they might warn her of our suspicions to gain her favor."

Her head tilted. "But would any woman actually kill her nephew to keep her father-in-law from loving another grandson?"

Caelus snorted. "Have you read enough Roman history to know what women with imperial ambitions for their sons do?"

She shook her head.

"Agrippina was the fourth wife of Claudius, but he wasn't her first husband. She brought a son from an earlier marriage with her. Historians claim she murdered the emperor to make that son his replacement. The whole empire paid for it by Nero ruling Rome, but so did she. He had her murdered."

Neferu gasped. "But that was for control of an empire. Men have done much worse things than women for the sake of power."

"It might only be a few small estates in the balance here, not an empire, but I think Zenobia might kill Jason to benefit her sons if she thought she could get away with it."

Caelus's breath caught, and he massaged his thigh before releasing it. "But we won't let her. I can't go far with this leg yet, but Neferu and I can watch over Jason when he's here at the cottage. You take him riding, so that's covered. So, he's most at risk when he goes to the donkey stable. He could stop doing that until Akhom returns."

Neferu closed her eyes and tipped her head back. "He gave Koshari his word that he'd look after the donkeys. He won't stop without us telling him why." She bit her lip, and sadness filled her eyes. "I don't want him to know someone here hates him enough to kill him if we don't absolutely have to tell him. He knows his father has always wished he would die. He's only just getting over being hated that way. So…" She turned to Lusario with a shrug and a smile. "Until Akhom comes back or Jason's grandfather comes home, you or I will need to go everywhere with him."

"I agree. I'll go watch him with the donkeys now, but I won't let him know why. If you want, you can go ahead with answering Caelus's questions this afternoon without me."

"We'll wait for you." Her lips twitched, then curved into her most appealing smile. "Your questions are as important as Caelus's are…to me and to God."

As he strode down the levee path that led to the donkey stables, Lusario fought a smile. She was as eager to explain her god to him as Timon had ever been. For Timon, it was out of deepest friendship. But why was it so important for her?

# Chapter 56

## Beginning the Hunt

*Alexandria, Day 34*

Taurus leaned on the railing as the rowboats pulled their ship backward into the quay in Eunostos Harbor. Had someone told him a month ago that he would go to Egypt by way of Sicilia, the isle of Kauros south of Crete, and the shortest route across the open sea that cut two days from the time most ships took to reach Alexandria, he would have thought it impossible. But two days could be the difference between a living Caelus and a dead one, so speed, not expense decided their route.

Sartorus joined him. "I'd heard Alexandria was the jewel of the Empire. That lighthouse, the public buildings fronting the Great Harbor—Carthago can't match them."

He wrinkled his nose as he rubbed his jaw. "But Roman Egypt has many strange rules. We have to exchange all our money for Egyptian coins before we leave the harbor, but as soon as we get that done, we'll hire a cart for the trunk. Then we'll visit the garrison for directions to the address we have for Caelus."

"Won't the ones renting carts know where it is?" Taurus's eyes narrowed. Surely that was the same in Carthago and Egypt.

"They should, but I'll get honest directions from a soldier. I patrolled the warehouse district in Rome, and some who rented carts went the wrong way first to increase the fee."

He pointed toward the stone-and-concrete buildings to the east. "Volero let me read Caelus's letters describing places he went in the city. We're heading for a town house less than a mile past those. We should be walking past the Great Library and the lecture halls where Caelus spent most of his time."

"Did he leave the city much?"

"Some, but I think that was mostly to look at ancient buildings." Sartorus shrugged. "He wrote to Martina, too, and what he seemed most excited about were the things he was studying."

Taurus's mouth curved into a frown. For a younger Caelus, when something exciting came in the door, caution went out the window. Had he grown out of that in the past three years?

The rowboats finished their work and cast off from the ship. A wide gangplank was lowered to connect deck and dock.

Sartorus shoved back from the rail. "You and I can manage the trunk ourselves. We'll be off the ship and at the money exchange before the rest of our companions on this trip get help with their baggage."

Taurus answered with a nod and followed Sartorus toward the cabin. One corner of his mouth lifted. The rich Greek Sartorus had lectured the first day about honor and courage and the worth of a man would be glad he didn't have to dine with a slave anymore. Probably glad he didn't have to dine with Sartorus. But so far, it had been the best trip Taurus had ever taken.

Protecting whoever his master said, whatever the cost, was his job. But there were men who deserved protection, whether Volero said to or not. Beyond any doubt, Sartorus was one of them.

A walk down the main street of Alexandria took Taurus and Sartorus past a set of buildings that surrounded a tree-shaded garden with many benches. Sitting on them were well-dressed Greeks and Romans in togas. Others stood around talking, with some moving their arms like Master Volero did when making a speech to the council. To the north stood a temple with two tall, pointed stone columns and a theater.

Obviously a place that important men gathered, but many young men were mixed in among them. It didn't look at all like the Forum in Carthago where Taurus had sometimes gone with Masters Gaius and Volero.

"What are those?" He swept his hand to encompass all the buildings.

Sartorus scanned the area. "I'd say the Mouseion, the Great Library, and many lecture halls. Caelus would have spent a lot of time here. We might be coming back to speak with people he knows."

He pointed up the street. "We should be almost to the Latinus town house. I have a letter from Volero saying that I'm the agent for the father of Caelus Publilius Martinus. It authorizes me to use anything his son has, including his lodging. So, our trunk can stay there while we look for Caelus. If he's there, we might be booking passage right away to take back Caelus's explanation of why he wasn't on the ship. Volero expects him to come home with us or book passage on a ship to return to Carthago as soon as possible after we leave. If he isn't there, then we'll be staying at the town house while we look into where he might be."

He tapped Taurus's shoulder as he smiled. "I've been praying for us to be on a ship home within three days. Platana is much better company than you, although you aren't too bad." His smile faded. "The last time I hunted for a man who'd been missing this long, we found what was left of him in a field at the estate of a man who was supposed to be his friend."

He closed his eyes and blew out a deep breath before opening them again. "But missing is sometimes only missing, not dead. If I were a betting man, I'd bet that we'll find him alive. I don't get the sense that Caelus is gone. If he had died in Alexandria, surely someone he knows here would have let Volero know."

Taurus furrowed his brow. "What if he was not in Alexandria?"

Sartorus sucked air between his teeth. "Now that's a different story. I think we'll find where he went, but…" A shrug was followed by silence.

They kept walking, but Taurus stole a quick glance at the former optio that Master Volero was counting on. There were a lot of ways a man could die, especially if no bodyguard was watching over him. Gods weren't real, so prayers did nothing. Sensing and feeling were not as good as seeing and knowing.

If something truly bad had happened to Caelus, trying to find him could prove fatal. It was good Master Volero had sent him along to make sure at least Sartorus came home.

*Latinus town house*

The cart man took no unnecessary detours, and Taurus soon raised his fist to knock on the town house door.

First it opened halfway. Then the doorkeeper stuck his head around its edge.

Sartorus stepped forward. "We're here to see Caelus Martinus."

"Martinus isn't here."

"Then I want to speak with the house steward. I've come from Martinus's father."

A quick nod, and the doorkeeper stepped back against the wall, pulling the door open as he did. When they passed through, he closed and bolted it.

"Wait here, please. I'll tell him you're waiting."

While they stood in the vestibulum, Sartorus took Volero's letter from the small satchel that hung at his side.

It was only moments before a man of about fifty came from the rear of the house.

"I'm Nicandrus, steward of the Latinus town house. Canis tells me you've come from Caelus Martinus's father. How may I help you?"

"Caelus Martinus was expected in Carthago on the *Zefyros* twelve days ago. His trunks arrived. He did not. I've been commissioned by his father, Volero Publilius Martinus, to find out why."

He handed the letter to Nicandrus, who scanned it and handed it back.

"Ah. Martinus mentioned something about writing his father to inform him of his delay. He and his manservant went upriver, and Caelus said to expect him back in about three weeks. That would be two days ago. But I wouldn't say they're late. It's not unusual to stay longer than planned when people go upriver. I expect them any day now."

"Where exactly were they going?"

"I believe he said somewhere near Heracleopolis Magna, but neither said exactly where. Fundanus might know more. He's Martinus's best friend here. He went with them to the docks on the lake where the boats bound for the Nile leave the city."

He waved his hand toward the stairway. "Allow me to show you where you can stay while you're here. Follow me." He snapped his fingers, and the doorkeeper came over.

Taurus grabbed the handle on one end of the trunk and pointed at the other. When the doorkeeper gripped it, they followed Sartorus and the steward up the stairs.

Nicandrus led them into a room with a view of the harbor through the window and the view of a fountain through the door.

Sartorus looked out the window, then scanned the room. "Two beds?"

"The menservants here mostly sleep in their master's room. The smaller is Lusario's."

"Then we'll both stay here."

"Very good. I'll see if Fundanus is in and send him to you if he is. Do you need anything else at the moment?"

"Thank you, but I don't think so."

With a tip of his head, the steward left.

Sartorus sat on the smaller bed and bounced a couple of times. "This is softer than I ever had in the Urban Cohort. I'll take this one. I don't think you'd fit in it anyway."

Taurus's mouth twitched as he stopped the smile. Cabin service on the ship, the best bed here—traveling with Sartorus had many benefits.

"Before Fundanus comes, there's something I need you to do."

Taurus fixed his gaze on Sartorus and waited for his orders.

"I want you to listen carefully to every conversation with anyone about what Caelus has been doing and where he might be. If we're questioning someone and you think there is something we need to know that I didn't ask about, you are to ask that question before we end the conversation. That's how I work as Glabrio's aide, and I want you to fulfill that role while we're in Egypt."

Taurus's eyebrows shot up before he could stop them. So, the respect Sartorus had insisted he be shown on the ship would carry over to what they did in Alexandria?

Sartorus's mouth curved into an amused smile. "You look surprised by that."

"I didn't expect you to use me for more than a bodyguard."

The smile turned into a chuckle. "I'd be a fool if I didn't use your eyes and ears as we gather information. Every military man knows the newest recruit might notice something the twenty-year veteran missed. The wise officer listens to every report because any might prove vital to success. Volero said you're the best he's seen at watching what's going on around them and sensing when something's amiss. Since Caelus isn't here, we'll be hunting for him. I'm going to need all the help I can get."

Taurus blanked his face, but it was hard not to show how much he appreciated being valued for more than his muscles and skill with weapons. What Master Volero had said—he could have said that about himself, if anyone ever bothered to ask. Sartorus planned to use all he could do, and he'd make sure the optio wasn't disappointed.

A knock on the door frame turned their heads to find a man about Caelus's age.

"Nicandrus said you wanted to speak with me about Caelus Martinus." His eyes narrowed. "Why?"

Sartorus stepped forward. "I'm Gaius Flavius Sartorus. When Caelus Martinus's trunks arrived in Carthago on a ship he never boarded, his father asked me to come find out why."

"He was about to board when a conversation with my uncle changed his plans. Lusario wrote a letter explaining that for the captain to deliver to whoever picked up their baggage. I gather the captain failed to deliver it?"

"He claimed they brought their trunks to the ship and then never showed up to board. No message came as to why. Then he had to give up his berth at the quay, so he sailed without them."

"Lusario delivered a letter to the ship. Whenever he says he's done something, then he has. But however it came to be lost, I can tell you where Caelus went. Or rather, where he planned to go and when he planned to return."

"Where do you think he is?"

"He and Lusario went upriver to my uncle's estate near Heraclepolis Magna to see about designing a villa for my aunt."

"Did he say how long that would take?"

"It's usually five days by boat both there and back, but they'd planned to look at some ancient temples and tombs on the way. Then a week for figuring out a possible building site or two and making drawings of what they might build. They're both excellent architects, so that should have been more than enough time. So, three weeks or less. They could have been back as soon as five days ago. But since they weren't, I figured it took longer to do the work than Caelus expected."

He nudged one of three large trunks with his foot. "Lusario packed these in case they weren't allowed to come back to Alexandria. I was to arrange to ship them to Carthago if they couldn't." He fingered his well-trimmed beard. "Frankly, I'm surprised they aren't here. Caelus wanted to return quickly and be ready to show their proposals to my aunt and uncle the day they got back from Ephesus. He didn't want to risk Uncle Latro deciding on another builder before he could try for the commission. If he had a commission in hand, he figured his father would let him return."

One corner of his mouth lifted. "Uncle Latro is back now, and I told him Caelus had gone upriver to draw up plans. Aunt Tranquilla is very eager to see how they propose to blend the best of Roman, Greek, and Egyptian to greatest effect. They'll wait to see what the two of them design before making any decision."

Sartorus rubbed behind his ear. "Have you heard from Caelus since he left?"

"No, but I only half expected to. They should have been home only a week after any letter could make it down river. They were supposed to be back to present their plans in the Alexandrian town house as soon as my uncle returned so he would hear their proposal first. They'd planned on drawing preliminary sketches at the estate and making more formal drawings on the boat back and while they waited here for Uncle to return."

Sartorus wiped his mouth with the back of his hand before turning his gaze on Taurus. "We need to go upriver to find them."

"I can help you get started. I sent them off at the river dock. I can tell you how to find the boatman my uncle told them to use." Fundanus tilted his head as his eyes narrowed. "Do either of you speak Egyptian?"

"I never expected I'd come to Egypt, so it's only Greek and Latin for both of us."

Sartorus raised his eyebrows to confirm that, and Taurus gave him a nod. The Dacian and Germanic words he'd learned in the ludus were not useful in polite conversations.

Fundanus pursed his lips and blew out a slow breath. "As far as you'll be going and as many people as you might need to ask something, you need a translator."

"Where do you suggest we find one?"

With one finger raised, Fundanus paused before speaking. "I might know the perfect man to take…if his master will lend him while you need him. Timon is Lusario's best friend. He belongs to Achilleus, an Alexandrian student Caelus and I both know."

He went to the desk and took a wax tablet from the drawer. "I'll draw you a map to his father's house here in the city. If he's in town, I think it very likely that Achilleus will be willing to help you find Caelus and Lusario. He wasn't a friend of Lusario's first master, but he offered to lend Diokles the money he needed to pay back a friend so he could take Lusario home to Cyrene. He's the sort who likes to help people whenever he can."

Sartorus summoned Taurus with a curve of his fingers, and they both watched Fundanus draw his map.

"If you can't have Timon, let me know, and I'll try to find someone else for you. Caelus is one of my best friends, and I count Lusario as a friend as well. I hope to hear that you find nothing wrong with either of them." With a snap, Fundanus closed the tablet and handed it to Sartorus. "But if there is, I'll want to know that, too."

*The Achilleus town house*

Taurus's knock made a small window in the door open. "Who seeks entry?"

"Gaius Flavius Sartorus to see Achilleus. He's come about Caelus Martinus and Lusario."

The window closed, and the door opened into a large room. The doorkeeper swept his hand toward some chairs on the wall. "Please be seated. I'll see if Master Achilleus is available."

Taurus scanned the room they entered and the peristyle garden beyond it. Furniture, statues on pedestals in the pool, walls painted with garden scenes—all declared Achilleus's father a wealthy man. By the pool, a woman trimmed fading flowers from one of several shrubs whose sweet fragrance drifted toward them.

The doorman entered a room off the garden, and a young Greek came out and strode toward them.

"I'm Achilleus. I understand you came about Martinus and Lusario. Why?"

"Fundanus sent us to you. They were supposed to arrive in Carthago almost two weeks ago to visit Martinus's father. Their trunks arrived, but they never boarded the ship. It appears they went up the Nile instead. They haven't returned when expected, and we intend to look for them. Fundanus said we'll need a translator."

Achilleus stood, arms crossed, nodding as Sartorus explained their visit.

"He thought you might consider renting Timon to us. His knowledge of Lusario and also of Caelus might prove helpful when we're faced with choices about what the two of them might have done."

With a final nod, Achilleus turned to the woman. "If Timon is home, send him to me."

She tipped her head and disappeared into the private area past the peristyle.

When Achilleus turned back to them, his eyes and mouth bespoke caution. "Timon has always served in our household. I value him highly, and we're not in the habit of renting our slaves or servants to anyone."

So, Fundanus was wrong about Achilleus's helpfulness. Taurus assumed his bodyguard pose, legs spread, arms crossed. Too bad. What Lusario's friend knew about the men they were hunting could have made the difference between finding them and not. The subtle shift in how Sartorus stood declared his acceptance and regret.

"We're from Carthago and don't know this city. So, can you recommend somewhere that we can hire a translator?"

A short, slender Greek with a slight limp came through the doorway where the woman had gone.

Achilleus turned and summoned him with a curl of his fingers. "Timon. Caelus Martinus and Lusario appear to have gone missing. These men have come from Caelus's father looking for him. Neither of them speak Egyptian, so they need a translator. Would you like to help them search?"

Timon's eyes widened. "Missing?" He gripped the back of his neck. "I would very much like to help."

A slight smile accompanied Achilleus nod to his manservant. Then he turned to face Sartorus. "I won't rent Timon to you, but he can go with you to help however he thinks appropriate. You'll need to take the canal across to the Nile at Hermopolis Parva and then go up the river. We have estates near Naucratis, so we own some small riverboats. They ferry passengers between Alexandria and Hermopolis when we aren't using them ourselves. I can lend you one since you might need to stop where the commercial boats don't land. It's small, but it's sound for Nile travel. With only the three of you, I think a four-rower boat would suit. Timon can take care of those arrangements for you."

"How much will that cost?"

The tension in Sartorus's shoulders relaxed, and Taurus suppressed a smile. No wonder with both translator and transportation now provided.

"Nothing. I know Martinus, and I want to help." He rested his hand on Timon's shoulder. "Are you ready to go with them now?"

"The sooner the better." Timon pulled a deep breath and released a sigh.

"Then get what you'll need and take them to get started today."

Timon nodded and returned to the private area.

When Timon was out of earshot, Achilleus raised his index finger. "Timon is important to us. Make sure nothing happens to him. That's why I'm lending you one of our boats. You can trust our crew completely. Going upriver with strangers might not be safe, especially if you're looking for someone who's gone missing." His gaze settled on the daggers on their belts, and a wry smile appeared. "But you don't look like men who are unaware of dangers or ill-prepared to deal with them. Timon and Lusario have been close for years. He would take foolish risks to help his friend. Don't let him."

Sartorus raised his chin and squared his shoulders. "Taurus is the best bodyguard Volero Martinus has, and I've been a soldier. We'll take good care of Timon and your boat's crew."

With a satchel slung over his shoulder, Timon rejoined them. Achilleus placed his hand on Timon's shoulder. "May the god with real power protect you and grant success in your search."

Timon's answer was a slow blink and a quick nod.

A satisfied sigh came from Sartorus. "From what Fundanus told us, I expect we'll have him back to you within two weeks. Thank you, Achilleus."

Achilleus tipped his head. "It's my pleasure to help. I'll look forward to hearing of your success. *Vale.*"

Palm up, Achilleus swung his hand toward the front door, then returned to the room from which he'd come.

Timon shifted the strap on his shoulder. "Where are you staying?"

"In Caelus's room."

"Then I'll leave this there. I can probably get everything arranged for us to leave early tomorrow."

As Timon led them into the street, Taurus shook his head. How had they managed to get both a translator and the boat they would need so easily? But Sartorus had closed his eyes like he did when he was talking with his god before they knocked on Achilleus's door. And the way Achilleus put his hand on Timon…it was a lot like what Glabrio had done to Sartorus before they left. He knew which god Glabrio asked to grant them success. But who would a rich Greek think was the god with real power to do that?

# Chapter 57

## Catching the Scent

*The canal to Hermopolis, Day 35*

Taurus leaned against the post holding up the canopy. The few clouds had still been tinged with pink when they left the dock in Alexandria and headed across a lake to reach the canal that would take them to the Nile. For long stretches of time, the rowers kept up a steady rhythm until the pilot called for a brief rest. With no breeze strong enough to fill the sail, it stayed furled on the wooden boom closest to the deck while the two top spars that joined at the mast lay atop the boom. That was opposite the sails on the *corbita* that carried them from Carthago, where the sail hung from the top spar and was furled by ropes pulling it up.

But whether a sail went up or down to catch the wind, it moved a boat faster than a few men with oars. The canopy would seat two comfortably, and Sartorus and Timon had offered to let him sit while one of them stood. But he was tall enough to feel cramped when he sat under it, so he chose to stand, even though there was not enough room between helmsman and rower benches for more than four strides to stretch his legs. When he tired of standing, he sat for a while on the trunk in front of the canopy where they'd stowed their satchels and two canvas-wrapped scabbards and swords. He was more than ready to reach Hermopolis and get off the boat.

When they reached the docks where canal boat passengers switched to riverboats, the rowers maneuvered the boat against the dock. Dareios tapped one of the rowers on the shoulder as he passed. The man stowed his oar and moved to the pilot's post.

Dareios jumped from boat to dock. "I'll take you to the Latro booth. Their agent has seen me around, as I've seen him. He might be cautious about answering the questions of strangers, but being with someone he recognizes might make him more willing. If he sends you somewhere, I can also help you find it."

"A good plan." Sartorus stepped over onto the dock. "Lead the way."

After a short walk up the wharf, the four of them stood at a booth labeled "Latro riverboats."

Sartorus moved forward to stand by the counter. When the agent didn't turn around from his desk, he cleared his throat. "I'm Gaius Flavius Sartorus. I've been sent to you by Vibius Fundanus, the nephew of Vibius Latro. He said Latro told his friend Caelus Martinus to come to you to rent a boat to go upriver to Heracleopolis Magna. That was twenty-four days ago, and Martinus has since disappeared. We're trying to find out where he went."

The agent clasped his hands on the counter. "Martinus—early twenties, dressed equestrian and traveling with a Greek about his age and a single trunk. I remember him. He wanted to rent a small boat for just the pair of them to go to Master Latro's estate near Heracleopolis. We only have one that size, and it had just gone upriver. He said they couldn't wait eight days for its return. I recommended one of Constans's small boats,"—he pointed at a booth about twenty feet away—"but he couldn't even wait four days for it."

"So, what did they do?"

"They rented a six-rower boat from a pilot that I've often seen taking passengers from this set of docks." His mouth turned down. "But I haven't seen the boat they rented come back, which is surprising, given what that boat would cost them to rent per day."

Sartorus sucked breath between his teeth. "That doesn't sound good. Can you tell me who owns that boat? They might know if something happened to them."

"Whoever owns it, they don't have a booth of their own. I see the pilot talking with people when they arrive from Alexandria to get passengers. But I can at least tell you where they spent the night here before they went upriver."

"Where is that?" Sartorus's frown that had deepened as the agent spoke faded.

"It's an inn I often recommend to travelers." He reached under the counter and pulled out a papyrus sheet. "I get the question enough I decided to make this for explaining it."

As he began explaining with his map, Dareios nodded. "I know that inn. It is a good one. I can take you there before I rejoin my crew."

Sartorus reached into his purse and took out a few coins. As he shifted them in his hand, his mouth turned down.

Timon touched a coin in his palm. "Let me."

He picked up an obol and gave it to the agent. "As a thank you for all the help you've given us."

The agent smiled, and turned back to his desk.

"This way." Dareios started up a street leading away from the dock.

Sartorus smiled down at the short, slender man next to him. "I'm not used to Egyptian coins. Thank you, Timon."

"Everyone used to Roman money has problems when they first come here.

The obol was the right amount for a thank you. The tetradrachma is roughly your denarius. So, the drachma is like your sestertius, and six obols make one of those."

Dareios slowed to walk beside Sartorus. "It's less than a couple of hours to Naucratis, so it would be possible to get there for the night after we talk with the innkeeper."

"Let's do that. We don't want to take longer anyplace than we have to. If they're not at the estate, the sooner we find where they really are, the better."

Dareios turned and walked through the inn's courtyard gate. He led them up to a middle-aged man relaxing under an olive tree. "Good day to you, Gaios. We've just come from Latro's rental agent, and he said he sent a young Roman and his Greek companion here about three weeks ago. Caelus Martinus and Lusario. They were going upriver, and we're hoping you know where they went next after here."

The innkeeper rose. "I remember them, Dareios. Pleasant young men. The Greek asked me to recommend an inn in Naucratis. I don't know if they stayed there, but I always send my wealthier guests to the Inn of Chnoúbis. Hermos takes good care of people, as I do. He sends his guests to me as well." He scanned their party. "Will you need two rooms or more tonight?"

"We're in a great hurry this time, so we need to spend tonight in Naucratis. But perhaps coming back."

Gaios raised his hand in a leisurely wave. "Give my regards to Hermos."

"I will."

Dareios led them from the courtyard and headed toward the docks. "We'll get you to the inn at Naucratis in time for dinner. I'll prepay the toll before we beach the boat for the night so we can leave quickly tomorrow."

Sartorus slapped his arm. "Today could not have gone much smoother. Thank you for your help making it so."

Dareios looked over his shoulder at Timon. "We're glad to do it. Any friend of Timon's is worth what it takes to find him."

Taurus followed the others, always watching the people around them. It was second nature for him. After so many years as bodyguard, he had to try not to do it.

The search so far couldn't have gone much smoother. Most people weren't quick to answer the questions of strangers. Those that were often gave answers that were only partly true or even completely lies.

Sartorus had been an optio in the Urban Cohort. He would have been centurion if his arm hadn't been too damaged by a murderer's dagger. His job had been to catch criminals for whom dishonesty in word and deed was second nature. A healthy suspicion of everyone was normal in that job.

But he was taking what strangers said at face value and acting on it. So far, that had proven wise. Was he just unusually skilled at telling the truth from a lie, and he knew it? Or did those fleeting moments of silence when he was probably asking his god to guide him have something to do with it?

He shrugged. It didn't really matter how he did it. All that really mattered was whether he found Caelus and brought him safely home.

*The inn in Naucratis, evening of Day 35*

Taurus stood behind Sartorus and Timon, arms crossed. Timon knew where the Inn of Chnoúbis was, so Dareios left them on the dock with a promise to get them in the morning. He'd taken the boat wherever his crew would spend the night with the bow resting on the sandy shore.

Now the innkeeper Hermos stood before them, happy to answer Sartorus's questions about the men they hunted.

"I remember Caelus and Lusario well. I don't know which inns they will use upriver, but Caelus did name the cities where they planned to spend the night. Terenuthis, Babylon and Memphis.

Hermos looked past Taurus to a door behind him, turned his gaze back on Sartorus, and stroked his jaw. "They asked me for a room where I could see the door from the office counter. They wanted to keep what was in their trunk safe while they looked around." He tightened his lips. "They're young enough that perhaps they didn't know, but a wealthy man takes a bodyguard when he travels upriver. They both wore daggers, but I doubt they knew how to use them. But whether you know how or not, if you need to use one, it's often too late anyway."

Taurus stopped himself before he snorted. Caelus had never traveled alone before, and a Cyrenian valet wouldn't be any more protection than a housemaid. But a bodyguard who was any good saw trouble before it arrived and was ready.

"Lusario did." Timon's quiet voice turned both men toward him. "He trained with a bodyguard when they first came to Alexandria and went to the gymnasium to work out and practice once a week."

Hermos's eyebrows rose. "Really? He didn't look like most bodyguards, so I never would have guessed. Robbers probably wouldn't think he was either. Anyway, I decided to offer the advice I would give my own son if he were traveling unguarded like they are. They welcomed it."

Sartorus's eyes closed, and when he opened them, his gaze locked on Hermos. "What did you tell them?"

"I told them they should hire a guard to watch over the trunk whenever they left it. Most innkeepers wouldn't watch their room for them, and some even let themselves in to steal. So, I told them to ask at the harbor garrison about where to hire a guard and what would be a reputable inn for their stay." He smiled, like he appreciated them respecting his advice. "They thanked me and said they would do that for the rest of their trip. They said they would stay here on their way home and give me names of inns I could recommend in the future…or warn people about." A wry smile accompanied laughing eyes. "They're as likely to find bad ones as good ones."

Sartorus tightened his lips and nodded his appreciation. "Then we'll ask at the garrisons as we proceed upriver. If we find the guard, we'll know the inn. Anything more?"

"Not that I know of now, but if I think of something else, I'll tell you before you leave tomorrow."

Hermos tipped his head toward a Roman couple with a bodyguard who had just entered the courtyard. "If you'll excuse me."

Sartorus's smile and nod sent the innkeeper to his new customers.

"A helpful man. It's good they stayed here." Sartorus pointed toward the dining room. "Ready to eat?"

"Absolutely." Timon tipped back his head and sniffed. "It would be worth staying here for the food alone."

They settled in at a table in the back corner of the dining room. Taurus rubbed his hands together as he watched the serving girl carrying dinner to a table of well-dressed Greeks. A man could get used to having food as good as a master would get at every meal.

The serving girl had just placed the bowls of hearty stew and a plate of rolls before them when Sartorus paused before his first bite. He'd done that since the first time they ate together on the boat. It looked too much like the silent prayers of Mistress Juliana and Martina to be anything else.

But Taurus raised an eyebrow when Timon traced a curve on the tabletop and tapped it with his finger. Sartorus straightened, drew a curve that was the mirror image, touching on one end and crossing Timon's line a short way up from the other. Timon's nod and smile received the same back from Sartorus, and the mood at the table became suddenly lighter.

They ate mostly without speaking, as he and Sartorus had on the ship. But when they finished and climbed the stairs to the room they were sharing, Sartorus closed and bolted the door.

"So, we serve the same master." Sartorus's words were statement, not question, as if he already knew the answer.

"As does the boat crew." Timon's eyes warmed.

What started as a slight curve of Sartorus's lips turned into a broad smile. "Good. I'll be asking God to guide the choices we have to make as we go upriver, and I welcome all their prayers that I make the right ones."

Taurus's gaze bounced between the two of them as his eyes narrowed. "So, you're both Christians?" He spoke in a whisper.

Timon's whole body tensed before his eyes asked Sartorus if it was safe to say.

Sartorus's single nod relaxed Timon's narrowed eyes. "You can tell him. He knows several of us, some for many years. He keeps secrets well."

"We are."

Traveling in the company of so many Christians—not what Taurus had expected when he watched Glabrio pray in Carthago. He caught himself frowning without realizing he'd started. Had Master Volero known what Glabrio and Sartorus were? Either way, did it matter?

"What about Caelus's manservant?"

"The last time we spoke, he wasn't, but only God knows what he is now."

Taurus replied with a silent nod. The Martinus men were Stoics, not Christians, and they hid the forbidden religion of their women lest anyone find out they lived with one. It was best for a slave to be whatever his master was if he wanted to get along well.

But if Timon and the boat crew were all Christians, what was Achilleus? He'd sent Timon off asking the god with real power to grant protection and success. That was too much like what he'd seen in Glabrio's house for the Greek to be anything else.

And maybe that explained him giving them a boat and crew so his manservant could hunt for a friend.

# Chapter 58

## Protecting Jason



*Stephanos's estate, midday of Day 35*

When Lusario came to get Jason for the riding lesson, the boy hadn't finished feeding Mikro yet. But Caelus sat on the bench under the tree, so Lusario stood beside him while Jason tended his charge.

Caelus lifted his chin to look at Lusario's face. "Does anyone know when Akhom will be back?"

Lusario joined his friend on the bench. "I asked Stephan if anyone had heard, and he said no."

"I wish he'd get back." Caelus tipped his head back to rest it against the wall. "Until he does, we can't stop worrying about whether Jason is safe."

Lusario sucked a short breath through his teeth. "Maybe we can't stop even then. He's safe as long as we're here, but what will happen when we leave? Will his grandfather see what an extraordinary boy he is, or will he only see that bad eye like Jason's father did?"

"I've wondered about that, too. He's been reading your tales of the ant wars to me, and he does so well for his age. He reminds me of Father's favorite dog when I was a boy. Always eager to please, content simply to sit beside him and get an occasional ruffling of his fur. The slightest praise brings out that grin." Caelus massaged his thigh. "I remember how my own grandfather and father were always proud of what I did well and told their friends about it." He gripped just below his knee and lifted his leg as he shifted on the bench. "I'd find it a pleasure to do that if Jason were my own son." He pointed at his crutch.

"So would I." Lusario handed it to him.

To be a father...was that a pleasure he would ever know? If Master Volero would only agree to it, someday he would be free. Then he could look for a smart, kind woman to marry and raise a family with her. Nothing would make him happier than having a boy like Jason and a wife like Neferu. He stopped the sigh before Caelus heard it. It could be years before that happened, if it happened at all. But if he were free now, he wouldn't be wanting someone like Neferu. He'd want her. And if Jason was truly an orphan instead of a rejected son who still belonged to his father and grandfather, he'd want Jason.

They'd gone a dozen steps when Caelus stopped to rest. "Jason is beyond fortunate that his mother's best friend would be willing to come with him to his grandfather's estate when he was exiled here."

Neferu walked up behind them. "I had no choice in the matter, although I would have chosen to come if I had a choice. To save myself from having nowhere to go and no way to support myself, I made myself a bondservant to Corinna to be nanny and tutor to Jason. She was afraid her husband had no intention of doing anything to educate him like an elite Greek boy should be. She had no money to hire me, so I suggested I work for room and board and belong to her, not Theodoros. We could simply agree to end the contract early if we wanted since I didn't receive any money that I had to pay back. Everything I owed was already paid by whatever work I'd already performed."

With her right hand, she rubbed her upper arm. "My father was a marketplace scribe, and I'd made copies of that kind of contract for him. So, I thought I knew everything that should be in it." She rested her hand on her stomach. "But I failed to include a provision that her death would free me. It's never in the contracts where bondslaves get paid money when they sign. Neither of us expected her to die while I served her. But she'd written a will leaving everything she owned to Jason. That included my contract. So, for the next four years, I belong to him."

Caelus shifted his full weight to his good leg. "It's a very good thing for Jason, but how did you come to be in such a desperate situation that you would make yourself a slave?"

A smile curved her lips, but Lusario saw the shadow of sadness in her eyes. "My uncle took me in when Father died. With no warning, I had to leave home to save Uncle Peduhor and his family. We made scented oils, and most of our business was with the sanctuary of Sobek in Arsinoe." She looked away. "Sasobek is the wab priest who bought our oils. He wanted me for his second wife, but when he learned I was a Christian, he demanded I deny Jesus and return to the worship of Sobek and the other Egyptian gods."

When she turned back to them, she glanced at Lusario before her gaze settled on Caelus. "When I refused, he said I had to reject my Lord or be cast out before he would buy anything from Uncle again. I asked God what I should do, and I thought He told me to go to Corinna, even though I hadn't seen her for years, not since her marriage."

The shadow had vanished, replaced by the warmth he'd seen so often when she watched Jason. The warmth he found so pleasing when she seemed to focus her gaze on him alone.

"I thought God guided me to her for my own safety, but now I wonder if it was actually for Corinna and Jason. She finally decided to believe Jesus saved her as she was dying. My promise to love Jason like she would calmed her fears for him before she died. Only God knew what Theodoros would have done with me if that will hadn't made me come with Jason when he was banished. And I don't have to worry about Sasobek seeing me here and doing...I don't know what. So, God protected both of us."

Lusario massaged his palm. Did her god really guide her anywhere, whether for herself, her friend, or Jason? So many times, Timon had claimed his god directed his actions, but he'd always thought that was just Timon's way of looking at reasonable choices and random events, not what really happened.

She turned her warmest smile on Lusario, and it felt like the sun rising in the winter. "I think God has used you to protect Jason, too. You were there to rescue him from Karpos's attempt to kill him." Her gaze and smile shifted to Caelus. "You're both protecting him until Akhom returns."

Caelus placed his hand over his heart. "If we're still here when Stephanos returns, I'll do what I can to convince him he has a treasure in that boy, whatever he might look like."

They turned at the sound of a cart behind them. One of the gardeners led the donkey that pulled it. "Mistress Zenobia sent this for Caelus Martinus so he could also join her for dinner." He took a folded tunic from the cart and held it out. "She said anyone who smells like a stable should bathe before coming."

Lusario rolled his eyes at Caelus, and Caelus's mouth twitched as he stopped a laugh.

Caelus took the tunic and draped it across his shoulder. "Tell your mistress I accept her invitation. Just leave the cart here. We'll come when we've all cleaned up."

When the man was out of earshot, Caelus rubbed his jaw. "It's always good to study the enemy whenever you can. When that's combined with a good meal and the fun of seeing you deflect her nosey questions, only a fool would turn down the offer." He tipped his head toward their house. "Time to dress for dinner... and my first chance to gauge how dangerous a worried mother might be. My mother was always jealous of my grandfather preferring Martina to my sisters." He nudged Lusario. "I prefer Martina to my sisters, too. Any sane man would. But Mother would never have tried to kill her to end the competition."

Lusario straightened. "I think Zenobia has already. Only me being there prevented it."

"You might be right, and if you are, it's up to us to make certain that she doesn't try again."

A solemn nod was Lusario's first response. "And if she does, that she doesn't succeed."

*Evening of Day 35*

The sun had dropped below the horizon when Jason and the two men returned from dinner. Neferu and Menmet sat outside, waiting for them.

When Neferu could see the donkey cart approaching in the fading light, Menmet rose. "I'll put Jason to bed. You three need to talk about what to do to protect Jason until Akhom or Stephanos returns, and he shouldn't hear you."

Neferu tipped her head back against the wall. "Thank you. I'm hoping Caelus will have some ideas. It's good that he feels well enough to be up and around now."

As Lusario helped Caelus from the cart, Neferu gave Jason a hug before Menmet took him inside for the night.

With Caelus settled on the bench by their door and Lusario leaning against the wall beside him, Neferu strolled over to stand before them.

"What do you think? Is Zenobia going to try to kill him?"

Caelus fingered his lip. "I'm not an expert on how women think, mothers or otherwise. I've never understood mine. But I saw the same thing Lusario did. Mostly she acted like I'd expect from a lonely elite woman. She dressed for a banquet, and her manners toward us were what I'd expect from Mother at my father's banquets."

He tapped Lusario's crossed arm with the back of his fingers. "She had a hard time deciding whether she should flirt more with this handsome Greek scholar or the first wealthy Roman she's entertained, but she only wanted some compliments on her food and appearance. I suspect her husband doesn't show his appreciation for her as much as she'd like nor as much as he should. Father would have found it amusing to watch, but I feel sorry for her. Her Horion probably isn't as bad as Theodoros, but treating someone like they don't matter can hurt as much as cruel words. So, she's made Karpos the focus of all her affection."

"But do you think she would kill Jason to protect her son's interest?"

With the back of his hand, he rubbed his mouth. "If Stephanos was here, probably not. She wouldn't risk being sent away and having to leave Karpos. But if she thought she could do it without him knowing…maybe. So, we need to keep our guard up even after Akhom gets home."

Caelus glanced at Menmet's house before turning his gaze on her. "With one of you on bodyguard duty whenever Jason leaves here, there's been no time for you to explain more about your god. When Zenobia's summons to dinner interrupted our conversation three days ago, you were about to tell us how you have one god who is also three gods. We have time for that now."

She laughed. "You would ask me the hardest question, one that Phoebe said even the leaders of her church couldn't explain. I asked that question, too. I don't have the mind of God. No one does, not even the most brilliant men in Alexandria." Caelus grinned at her tease, and Lusario at least smiled. "So, I don't know if this is exactly right, but I can tell you what I've seen and heard and felt. Maybe that will help."

Caelus raised his eyebrows at Lusario. "Will it?"

◆

Lusario's head drew back. How would he know? But Jason had called on Jesus to heal, and whoever she worshiped, whether one or three, had done it.

"We won't know until we hear what she has to say, but maybe." Her face turned solemn, so he gave her an encouraging smile. "She's the smartest woman I've ever met, so I expect it will."

She rolled her eyes, and he stifled a chuckle.

"Maybe you haven't met enough women. I'm not that smart, but I'll try not to disappoint you."

Her eyelids closed, and her jaw clenched. When her eyes opened, she looked as relaxed as he'd ever seen her.

"Remember how God overshadowed Jesus's mother when she was a virgin and she became with child? The angel told her that her baby would be God's son. When Jesus was baptized, God spoke from heaven, and some of the people heard Him say Jesus was His son. So, Jesus was both the son of a woman and the son of God. He lived in this world like any man, but he did it without ever sinning, without doing something that would separate him from God the Father. That's why he was the one who could pay for the sins of us all. All we have to do is accept that he did that for us and believe in him."

She looked at Caelus. "Remember how the Spirit of God, the Holy Spirit, came to be with Jesus when he was baptized?"

Caelus blew out a deep breath. "Yes, but I didn't understand that part about the heavens opening and it descending on him like a dove."

"Jesus told his disciples that he and the Father were one, that the Father was in him and he was in the Father. He said he and the Father would send the Holy Spirit to be with them, to live within them, after he returned to the Father in heaven. He also said that *he* would be with them always, but it's the Holy Spirit who actually lives in us."

She stood facing them, but her gaze wasn't focused on them. "I don't know exactly how it all works, but I know the Holy Spirit came when I confessed my own sins and declared my faith in Jesus. I feel God's presence whenever I pray, and I never feel alone. I've seen God's love for me in so many ways, and I've seen His power to change things when I ask in Jesus's name, like he said we should. I watched God save a dying baby, and I saw Him save you."

She offered them a subdued smile. "So, I'm no great scholar or leader of the church, but I know God is real, and He's here with me right now."

When Lusario realized he was frowning, he relaxed his mouth to a slight smile. If Timon were standing beside him, he'd be nodding and smiling like when he made the winning move in tabula. His best friend might even elbow his ribs at her last statement. He'd been saying the same for years.

She pushed a loose strand of hair behind her ear. Her gaze was locked on him, and he felt his ears heat. Then it shifted to Caelus.

"Maybe trying to explain God is like when you described an elephant to Jason. You even drew him a picture. But I think he won't really *know* what an elephant is like until he sees one with his own eyes. God invites us to come and see, and Jesus made that possible. He came and walked among us as a man, and he made it possible for our sins to be forgiven so we can be with God forever. That starts in this life and never ends because he gives us true life after death. Most Egyptians mummify their dead so they'll have an afterlife, but they won't really have one. Only faith in Jesus can do that."

A movement near Menmet's house drew all their eyes. When the elderly woman got close enough, she summoned Neferu with a curve of her fingers.

"Jason wants you to come say goodnight. Did you figure out anything?"

Lusario walked over to her at Neferu's side. "We agree that Zenobia hates Jason. Whether she'll try to hurt him…there's no way to know for certain. So, we'll keep watching him like we have until his grandfather returns. Caelus and I plan to talk with Stephanos before we leave to make certain he knows what's happened and will take steps to keep it from happening again."

Menmet patted his arm. "It's so good you're here. He's a dear boy. It would break all our hearts if something happened to him."

"We'll do our best to make certain it doesn't."

Menmet slipped her arm in Neferu's, and they strolled toward her cottage.

His jaw clenched. He would do his best, but would it be enough?

# Chapter 59

## Some Questions Answered

*Stephanos's estate, Day 36*

While Lusario straightened the bed sheets, Caelus sat at the table and scraped the last bit of porridge from his bowl.

"Take a look at what's laying on top of your ant stories." Caelus waved toward the shelf where they kept their drawings.

Lusario picked up the top sheet. "A donkey. Not quite up to your usual standards, but not bad."

Caelus laced his fingers and rested them atop his head. "I've been showing Jason how to draw. He has a natural eye for it." He leaned forward to rest both forearms on the table. "I'm really going to miss him when we leave. No matter what it is, even the smallest thing I do for him makes him so happy and grateful. It reminds me of how Grandfather encouraged me to try new things that caught my interest. I understand now why he enjoyed doing that so much."

Lusario set the donkey back on the shelf. As a slave himself, his own father wasn't the one who set the limits on what his son could do. But he had encouraged Lusario to do whatever he could to make him a widely respected tutor. That was within the few possibilities a slave like him had.

"I'll miss him, too. I never thought creating stories for children would be one of my special skills. I might keep writing new chapters of my ant saga and send them to him."

"You should make a copy and give it to one of the librarians for the Great Library." Caelus pointed at his crutch.

Lusario handed it to him. "I don't think you want the sought-after architect, Lusario of Alexandria, to be well known for writing children's stories. It's not something to inspire confidence in my engineering skills."

He would miss Jason, but he would miss Jason's tutor even more. If he were a free man, he could consider asking her to become his wife. She was a wonderful mother to Jason, and she treated Menmet better than some women treated their own mothers. If he could propose a marriage, would she consider accepting him?

He stacked his bowl with Caelus's and set them by the door.

But everything depended on them getting Master Volero to decide they could start a business. Then, if he would agree to Caelus's request that he be freed to be Caelus's partner...

He suppressed the sigh so Caelus wouldn't ask what was wrong. It wouldn't be the end of a bright future for his friend, even if they didn't get the career of their dreams. Caelus would have other good choices, but the door to the two things he wanted most would remain forever closed.

*Evening of Day 36*

The clatter of the cart brought Neferu to the road to greet the returning diners.

"I hope you had a good dinner."

"I liked the sauce." Jason wrinkled his nose. "But she put me across from Karpos again. He always kicks me."

Her eyes narrowed as she turned her gaze on the men before returning it to Jason. "Maybe he just swings his feet under the table and doesn't mean to."

"No. He slides down in his chair so he can reach me. Sometimes she tells him to sit up straight, but only after he's kicked a few times. But Stephan is nice to me now. He even talks to me like he wants to."

She placed her hands on his shoulders and bent down to his level. "Well, that's a nice change. I didn't expect it to take long for him to start liking you." She drew him closer for a quick hug. "Run in to Menmet. It's time for bed." She straightened. "I want to talk with Caelus and Lusario a little before I come in."

She waited until Jason was out of earshot. "What happened tonight?"

Lusario glanced at the main house. "It's the same every night. But this time she seated herself across from Caelus instead of at the head of the table. Stephan was across from me, and she put Karpos where he could be mean to Jason. That was worse tonight. Stephan likes his little cousin and talks to him. Karpos looked mad enough to spit over that. But Zenobia is always gracious toward us."

He nudged Caelus. "Especially her rich Roman guest." He got an eye-roll in return.

"She spoke with you at least as much as with me. She mostly ignores Jason, but there are times when the way she looks at him..."

Caelus blew out a slow breath. "It's only for a moment before she masks what she's thinking. Taurus is my father's best bodyguard, and he'd be moving close behind Father and placing his hand on his dagger if anyone looked at Father that way."

"I'm so glad you're watching over him." She hugged herself. "I keep praying that Stephanos will get home soon and that he'll make sure that stops."

Palm up, she swung her hand toward the bench. "Menmet is putting Jason to bed again, so we have a while for your questions. Shall we?"

Caelus took a step. "Definitely. I have many questions about sin and salvation and repentance."

After Lusario brought out a chair for her and the men were seated, she cleared her throat. "So, what do you want me to tell you about first?"

Caelus drummed his fingers on his injured leg. "You said sins were anything that your god said we shouldn't do and things we should do that we don't. But that's so vague. So, what are some examples, and who decided those were sins?"

"God Himself gave us guidance on that. When Moses was leading the Jewish people out from slavery in Egypt, God told him many things about how to live to please Him, and some of the most important were written down on stone tablets."

"Written down?" Caelus's eyes narrowed. "By whom?"

◆

Lusario crossed his arms. Timon had told him this story. A pillar of smoke and fire leading a group of escaped slaves, a god covering a mountaintop in clouds and fire, a man coming back from within the cloud with tablets that the god himself had engraved—it made for a dramatic story, but it hardly seemed likely.

"By God Himself. The ten most important He engraved on stone tablets. The others Moses wrote down. Those include many about how to live every day and what could allow them to approach God even though their sins had separated them from Him. I'll talk about that later. Tonight, I'll tell you about those ten and about what Jesus said were the two most important. They summarize what were in the ten. What was in all of them, actually. They sound simple, but they can be a huge challenge to obey. Impossible for a person to do in their own strength. That's why Jesus came."

She stroked her chin. "I think I'll start with Jesus's summary."

Her gaze rested on him for only a moment, and her smile dimmed. He relaxed the frown he didn't intend for her to see into a smile and nodded. Then she focused on Caelus again.

"Jesus said the first of all the commandments is 'Hear, O Israel, the Lord our God, the Lord is one. And you shall love the Lord your God with all your heart, with all your soul, with all your mind, and with all your strength.' This is God's most important commandment. Jesus said the second one is this: 'You shall love your neighbor as yourself.' He said there is no other commandment greater than

333

these two, and that everything in the Law and the writings of the prophets hangs on them."

Her gaze shifted between the two of them. "So, you can see why it's so important for us to love God with our heart, soul, mind, and strength. If we don't, then we've sinned against Him. Since God also told us to care about other people as much as we care about ourselves, we've sinned against Him when we don't."

Caelus scratched behind his ear. "You used *agape* for love again. A decision, not an emotion. That makes sense, but to decide something and act upon it, we have to know the details of that decision. Maybe when you tell us the ten, that will help."

Lusario rested his hands on his thighs to keep from crossing his arms again. He'd been through this with Timon. Except for the first four about God, a good Stoic would follow them all.

Neferu leaned forward. "The first four are about how we show our love for God. Foremost, we can have no other god but Him. No saying Fortuna smiles when it's God who blesses. The second says we can't worship anything made by human hands. No idols. The third tells us to not take God's name in vain. No cursing, no oaths using His name, like I've heard people say 'By Zeus' and 'By Jupiter.'"

Caelus cast a sheepish smile toward Lusario. "We're both guilty of giving Fortuna credit, but it was only a figure of speech for Stoics like us. And I've said 'By Jupiter' more times than I can count, even though I know he's not real."

"But at least you didn't know you shouldn't before tonight. The fourth is a gift as much as a commandment—remember and keep the Sabbath holy. God set aside one day a week when we should gather with other believers and worship Him. Since Phoebe and her husband left, I've never had anyone to do that with. But someday I might." Her gaze shifted between them. "I'd love to do that with you."

Lusario shifted on the bench. Her eyes bored into him, and he looked away without speaking.

"I think most would like that day of rest, whether they use it to worship your god or not." Caelus leaned back against the wall. "What are the other six?"

"They have to do with how we treat other people. If we love others like we love ourselves, we won't murder or steal or lie to get someone in trouble or begrudge the good things someone else has, wishing we could make them our own. We should also honor our father and mother."

She twisted the brass filigree ring she usually wore. "Wishing what others have was mine instead—that's one even small children break. This was my mother's. I've always loved it, but when we were young, I envied the silver ring with a cameo that Corinna had."

"I wouldn't argue with any of those." Caelus grabbed his knee and adjusted the position of his leg. "I don't know anyone carefully living by Stoic philosophy who would. I think my father abides by them. At least I've never seen him do any of them. Since becoming a man, I've done the same."

He looked at Lusario and raised his eyebrows.

Lusario wanted to nod, but was Caelus asking for confirmation that both he and Master Volero were good Stoics or questioning whether Lusario had been as well?

He rubbed his jaw. He'd killed in self-defense, so that wasn't murder. His owners had always fed him enough, clothed, and housed him. So, he hadn't had to steal to survive. He'd deceived Florus to get his trunk of notes to Carthago, but he'd never lied to get another into trouble.

But he had begrudged the things others had. What slave hadn't? Not just things, but freedom itself.

Her gaze remained on him, as if waiting for him to answer. He didn't want to, so he needed a diversion.

"From what I've seen, I can't picture you ever willfully breaking one of those commands. You'd make a good Stoic, too. A Stoic's sense of honor should keep him from deliberately breaking them as well."

"Hmmm." Her eyes narrowed, then the smile that curved her lips was too much like Timon's when he'd just scored a point in an argument.

"But is being honorable in how you treat other people enough to keep you from being separated from God? Didn't you say most Stoics don't think any gods are real? So, aren't they breaking the first great commandment and the first four of the ten?"

Her finger traced her eyebrow, and the smile vanished. "Does Stoic philosophy tell you that you have to forgive others for whatever they do to you?"

"No." Caelus's voice drew her gaze from Lusario, and he was glad of it.

"Seneca said that to forgive all is as inhuman as to forgive none. He said that the wise man should not pardon that which should be punished, but exceptions might be made for those too young to know what they should do or those who do what is wrong out of ignorance."

"But Jesus said we must forgive others. He even said we can forfeit the forgiveness of our sins that God would give us if we refuse to forgive those who sin against us."

Lusario leaned forward, resting his elbows on his knees. "That's demanding too much. It's not humanly possible to do that. During the Jewish Uprising under Trajan, thousands were killed, and the public buildings of Cyrene were destroyed. I was among those who got out of the city just before that happened." His jaw clenched. "But many I knew weren't as lucky. Trajan had to bring in colonists because so many farmworkers were killed. He had to rebuild the city and repair the roads that had been torn up. I could never forgive the ones who did that."

Caelus turned wide eyes on him. "I didn't know you were caught up in that."

Lusario shrugged. "Father tutored for a rich Cyrenian businessman, and he took the two of us with him when he boarded one of his ships and fled ahead of the mobs."

Sympathy filled her eyes as she met his gaze. "I'm so sorry. I can only imagine what it's like to lose so many in war." She bit her lip. "You won't like what else Jesus said."

"What's that?" Lusario raised his chin. He'd listened his whole life to things he hadn't liked and had to live with them without complaining.

"He said we should love our enemies, bless those who curse us, do good to those who hate us, and pray for those who abuse us and persecute us."

"Whew!" Caelus's head drew back. "That goes way beyond anything a Stoic philosopher would say. No one would do that. Who could?"

Her eyes warmed with her gentle smile. "Jesus did. After the Roman soldiers had beaten and scourged and mocked him, as they were crucifying him, he said, 'Father, forgive them for they don't know what they're doing.'"

Lusario and Caelus stared at her. Without a sound and with a strange serenity, she looked back.

Caelus finally broke the silence. "Carthago is the provincial capital. I've ridden past the execution field. I've seen what the soldiers do, and no man dying there could say that."

"But Jesus did, so when he told us we have to forgive to be forgiven, he truly meant it. He had forgiven the unforgivable himself."

She clasped her hands in her lap and stared at the ground. When she raised her head, she focused on the wall between them.

"Many of God's commands are easy for me to obey, but I struggle against not forgiving."

"Is it Sasobek? Because he took your family from you?"

That was a pain Lusario knew too well. He'd lost his home and family because of Diokles's gambling and Florus's hatred for Achilleus. Even though the future he lost had been replaced by a better one, he would never forgive those two for what they did.

Her gaze rested on Menmet's house before she turned back to them. "No. Forgiving him has been easy. What he did was natural for most men. He does try to serve Sobek well, and he believed what he said about me disrupting ma'at." She bit her lip. "And his pride had been hurt when I wasn't interested in marrying him before he learned I was a Christian. It's a problem...being too pleasing to men's eyes."

Lusario rubbed his lip to hide a smile. That a widower would want her was no surprise. She would mother his children well, and who wouldn't want a beauty like her as his wife? She would attract even happily married men. Zenobia was right to fear what Horion would think of her.

"It's Theodoros. All the cruel things he's done and said to Jason for something the dear boy can't help. How he kept pressuring Corinna to give him another son. He didn't care at all about the grief she bore each time a baby died. Then when she was carrying Menander, he ignored her again." Her fingers wiped the corner of one eye. "Before they married, she dreamed of a good husband and a large family. She didn't get either."

Dreams that turned to ashes—Lusario knew those too well. His had risen like a phoenix only because Volero Martinus bought him to serve Caelus. "Do you blame him for her death?"

"No." She gave him a weak smile. "She would have died no matter how loving her husband was. But it broke her heart to watch him try to crush Jason's spirit, to tell the boy he wished he'd been left for the dogs when he was born instead of loving him like a father should. Like my father had and even my uncle did. Then for Jason to learn his father had let people here think he'd died as a baby. I'm afraid of what it will do to Jason if he finds out someone here wants him dead, too."

She sighed. "Apostle Paul wrote to the Romans that we should never avenge ourselves, but leave it to the wrath of God, for it is written, 'Vengeance is mine, I will repay, says the Lord.' I confess that I asked God to do it quickly to Theodoros, and I shouldn't have. That wasn't loving my enemy, like Jesus commanded. I asked Him to forgive me for asking."

The door of Menmet's cottage opened, and a small figure filled the doorway and waved.

"We can talk more tomorrow." She stood and returned the wave. "He loves Menmet now, but he has a hard time getting to sleep without me tucking him in."

Lusario stood as well. "What will you be telling us next?"

"We've talked about sin, but not salvation. About what God did that we could never do ourselves."

Caelus pointed at the crutch, and Lusario helped him to his feet. "We'll look forward to it. What I read of Markos, what you've told us...I still have more questions, but I'm enjoying these conversations."

"I'll do my best to give you God's answers. Goodnight."

Her brightest smile was a fitting ending of their evening as far as Lusario was concerned.

As she walked away, Lusario couldn't take his eyes off her. So far, he found no contradictions between what she said and Timon's explanations. He'd treated those conversations in Alexandria as philosophical discussions, disagreements between two friends who had different views of life.

But she would agree with Timon's words that he had so easily discounted. Maybe this wasn't just philosophy. What he decided to believe about their god and about Jesus might control his future after death, just like Timon claimed.

He glanced at Caelus. But one thing was certain. What the man beside him decided and how his father responded would control both their futures while they all lived.

# Chapter 60

## A Liar and a Thief

*Terenuthis, Day 36*

Taurus walked last as the party left the dock and headed toward the port garrison in Terenuthis. He had no trouble both scanning what was around them and carrying one end of the trunk holding their satchels and both his and Sartorus's *gladii*. But this time, Timon had beaten him to the first handle. For a short, scrawny man, the trunk wasn't light. But he'd let Timon take a turn because he wanted to, and the rower on the other end was fit enough to handle more than half when they went up or down steps. Their pilot had chosen to stay with the boat, and the rower would take the name of their inn back to him.

Sartorus entered the garrison and came out with the name of the place where Caelus could hire an honest guard. Everywhere Caelus and his manservant had spent the night, the leader of their search planned to find the guard Caelus hired and then hire him to take them to the same inn. A few well-chosen questions should tell whether any problems that might make Caelus vanish were developing as the pair went upriver.

This time, finding the right man proved easy. As the guard led them to the inn, Sartorus walked beside him.

"What can you tell me about Martinus and his companion?"

"Not much. It wasn't Martinus who hired me. His Greek friend did. I only saw the Roman for a few moments at the inn. They left me to watch their door from the courtyard while they visited a couple of temples and the Roman baths.

"As long as they were gone, I sat and watched." The guard shrugged. "No one tried to enter. I left when they returned for dinner. The dining room there is open to the garden. The second-floor doors are visible, so they could watch themselves."

One corner of Taurus's mouth lifted. He'd spent many hours himself standing around watching men where there was never any danger and the only thing he had to fight was boredom.

"From what you saw of them, did there seem to be anything worrying them?"

The guard chuckled. "They were talking about drawing what they'd just seen when they came back. Happy like a child with a new toy. One said something about Babylon the next day."

The guard swept his hand toward an archway leading into a courtyard with flowers blooming around a fountain. "Here's where I brought them."

Sartorus reached into his purse and took out an obol. "Many thanks for your help. May you have a more interesting time than Martinus and Lusario paid you for."

With a nod and a smile, the guard took it and left.

Timon and the rower set the trunk down while Sartorus paid for a second-story room, and Taurus beat Timon to the handle when the rower gripped his again.

"Thanks for carrying it this far. I can take it upstairs now."

With a smile of relief, Timon stepped back. "Good. It was heavier than I thought. I don't think I could do my half getting it upstairs."

Taurus stared at him. Maybe it was something weaker men did, but no gladiator would ever admit he couldn't do something until he'd tried and failed. He was only a bodyguard now, but that hadn't changed. He lifted his end, and he and the rower began the climb.

When they returned to the courtyard, Sartorus took some coins from his purse and turned to Timon. "Enough for six at the baths?"

Timon divided them into two groups and tapped the smaller one. Sartorus gave them to the rower. "For any who want to go."

The rower grinned as he closed his hand around the coins. "We'll go in shifts to watch the boat. I'll be back for you early." With a wave, he headed out the archway to the street.

After slipping the remaining coins into his purse, Sartorus tipped his head toward the exit. "Let's go as well. It might be a while before we have the chance for a Roman bath again."

Timon pointed toward their second-story room. "I can stay and watch the trunk. Hermos said it was better to have a guard."

Sartorus snorted, then rested his hand atop Timon's shoulder. "I'll trust Someone else to watch over it while we all go." He wrinkled his nose. "You'll be sitting beside me tomorrow. I'd rather you bathe."

The two shared a chuckle, and Taurus felt a frown growing until he stopped it. He and Timon were slaves. What the boat crew was…only they knew. Sartorus wasn't rich by Martinus standards, but he made very good money as Glabrio's aide and Martina's business manager. But you wouldn't know it the way he treated them all as his equals, and Achilleus's people didn't seem surprised at all that he did. Achilleus had even let Timon decide if he would go with them.

Maybe it was just something Christians did. It wasn't that way with Master

Volero and his friends. But he had to admit, it felt good to be in the company of men who acted as if they only saw another man when they looked at him, not whether he was slave or free.

*Memphis, Day 37*

As their boat passed by Babylon, Taurus had more time than he wanted to look at the two huge square-based pyramids and a third about half their size on the west side of the river. On the east side stood a legion fortress.

Close to it, a canal flowed into the river from the east, and boats big enough to be called small ships entered the river there. Dareios called it the Canal of the Pharaohs and said it connected to the Red Sea. Timon had heard someone talk about it as Trajan's Canal in a lecture hall by the library. He said Trajan moved where it entered the Nile some distance south to where it was now, so of course it now bore the emperor's name.

Whatever its name, Rome collected tolls where canal and river met, and waiting their turn to pay could sorely test the patience of any man in a hurry.

Almost any man. He'd mastered waiting with nothing to do while the one he was guarding did whatever they wanted.

Sartorus strolled forward to stand by the pilot. "Caelus planned to stay here, but it's a short distance to Memphis. I think we can skip this stop and move on to track their movements there without missing anything important."

"I agree." Dareios pointed at the boat ahead of them. "One more and it will be our turn to pay. Then we can raise the sail and reach Memphis in less than an hour."

Taurus leaned against the canopy pole and turned his eyes back on the pyramids. The lighthouse in Alexandria and these were called two of the great wonders of the world. Of the two, the lighthouse deserved the name more. It did something more useful than hold the bones of a ruler who'd been dead for more than two thousand years.

At least that's what Timon said about it, and he ought to know. His master had studied in the same lecture halls and library as Caelus, and Timon went to every lecture his master did. Timon wasn't much to look at, but he was at least as smart as the rich Romans like Master Volero who ran Carthago. Probably smarter.

When the toll was paid, up went the sail, and they left the Great Pyramid behind. But off to the west, they passed many more smaller ones. Egyptians had made the west side of the river the land of their dead, and their important men built their tombs as if they'd be homes in the afterlife.

But he'd heard Master Volero quoting some Stoic philosopher. There is nothing after death, and death is nothing—only the finishing post of life's short race. He'd seen enough men die when he fought on the sand to believe it. He expected nothing more when his own time to die came.

When they reached Memphis, Dareios guided their boat to the docks, and Taurus took his usual trunk handle as Sartorus led them to the garrison. When he came out, a burly Greek walked beside him.

Palm up, Sartorus swung his hand toward the man. "Lusario hired Demetrios to guard Caelus's trunk at an inn their pilot chose. He'll take us there now."

As they continued up the street in the direction of the inn, Sartorus cleared his throat. "From what you saw of Martinus and Lusario, did there seem to be anything worrying them?"

A snort was Demetrios's first answer. "Maybe not worrying them, but something wasn't right."

Sartorus shortened his stride, and their whole party slowed. "Why do you say that?"

"The pilot taking him to the inn kept saying things, like he was trying to get your Roman mad at him."

"What sort of things?"

"About him only wanting to rent a fine stallion, about paying double for some service when he didn't have to. It wasn't the words as much as how he said them. Mocking. Resentful." He rubbed under his jaw. "And how he looked at him." He pointed at a doorway about fifty feet ahead. "There's the inn."

Sartorus stopped and turned to face Demetrios. "What happened then?"

"The Greek didn't like it. He watched the pilot like I would watch someone who might be dangerous. When the Egyptian left with the two men carrying the trunk, he said, 'Enjoy your old buildings, young Roman. They may be your last. Most do not find much to see between here and Thmoinepsi.'"

"Do you think he meant more than the ancients hadn't built much along the next stretch of the Nile?"

"Maybe, because there are a lot of tombs with small temples between here and there."

"Was that all?"

"No. I went into the inn with them and watched the pilot until he went back to his boat. As they were leaving, he spoke Egyptian to one of the others."

Sartorus's eyebrows dipped. "What did he say?"

"I might be willing. Let's talk."

"Willing to do what?"

"I don't know, but the Greek tensed up like it was a threat."

"Do you know the pilot's name?"

"One of the men who left with him called him Temhotep as they went out the door."

"What else did you see?"

"Nothing that Temhotep did. I watched the room while they went out for a while. I left after they ate, and I came back to guard the next day. They'd rented mules and were gone most of the day. But when they came back, I heard something."

Sartorus's massaged his palm with his thumb. "What?"

"The Roman was complaining about a lying son of a snake charging for tolls that didn't exist and doubling the landing fees. The Greek pointed out it was only a few drachmas, and a wise man didn't accuse another of being a liar and a thief when he still needed him to get where he wanted to go."

Sartorus drew his head back. "Did that calm Martinus down?"

"It did, but he said he'd hold his words back only until they got to Thmoinepsi. After that, he might not."

Sartorus blew out a long, slow breath. "What then?"

"They took the satchel the Greek carried up to their room. When they came back down, they went to dinner. The Greek gave me a drachma when they finished eating with his thanks for doing a good job. I left and never saw any of them again."

Sartorus fished a drachma from his purse and held it out, and Demetrios placed his hand under it. "Thank you for all your help."

When the coin landed in his palm, Demetrios grinned. "Any time. A drachma for what I'd already said for free…it's been a pleasure."

As the guard walked away, Taurus took several deep breaths and willed his heart rate to slow. Caelus Martinus was as honest as his father. Master Volero would have been furious to be cheated like that, and he might not have let it pass. But he always had Taurus along when he traveled, and angry words can be spoken safely with a gladiator there to protect you.

Had Caelus been wise enough to heed Lusario's warning about saying nothing until he didn't need that boat crew anymore?

Or had he spoken his mind and was now missing because of it?

Sartorus locked gazes with Taurus. With tightened lips, Taurus shook his head. When Sartorus tightened his lips and nodded, no words were needed.

They walked the final few feet to the inn's doorway. After they passed through it, Sartorus stepped back by the rower. "Don't leave until I've talked with the innkeeper."

Taurus stood by the trunk, arms crossed, as Sartorus paid for a second-floor room and asked his usual questions. It was a good thing Demetrios told them so much. The answers the innkeeper gave to those questions revealed less than they'd learned from the guard.

The tension between Caelus and the pilot had been obvious, but not beyond what the innkeeper had seen before. His inn was known for hosting the elite, both Roman and Greek, and poorer men who served them sometimes took offense and saw arrogance where there was merely different manners and more formal ways of speaking. From what he saw, Martinus and Lusario seemed like pleasant young men excited about their first trip up the river. He liked the ancient buildings himself, so he'd enjoyed hearing what they'd found most to their liking during their visit. They'd planned on staying with him on their return trip, but when they didn't show up as expected, he figured they'd said it but not meant it.

When the innkeeper led Sartorus up to show him their chamber, Taurus gripped his trunk handle and followed the rower to the balcony. With a sweep of his hand, the innkeeper invited them all into the room.

Sartorus drew a finger along his lower lip as he took the offered key. "We're in some hurry to get to Heracleopolis. Can we get there in two days?"

The innkeeper leaned against the railing. "Aphroditopolis is too far for most to make it in a day, so probably your young men stopped somewhere in between. Peme maybe. But there's not much there to interest most Romans. Probably no guards to rent. Only a few tombs and temples and nothing spectacular. Most travelers don't bother with them, but they might have since they spent so much time looking at wall carvings. But Aphroditopolis is the nome capital, so there are public buildings and the necropolis for the cows of Hathor. They could have spent some time there."

Sartorus stared at nothing as he massaged his palm. "Could we make it in a day if we start just after dawn?"

"I know some who have done it. Aphroditopolis to Heracleopolis in a day— that should be easy enough, so I think you can reach the other capital with two full days travel."

"Then that's what we'll try. We'll want to eat very early."

"I'll have my cook prepare bread, cheese, and fruit tonight so you can eat by first light or take it with you."

Voices below them in the courtyard made him glance over the balcony edge. "New customers. If you'll excuse me." He'd taken three steps away before Sartorus could respond.

Sartorus turned worried eyes on Taurus. "No guards to rent poses a problem. It's the guards who get us to the inns. "Do you expect we'll miss anything we shouldn't if we skip their next stop and go on to the capital?"

Taurus raised one eyebrow. It still felt odd when the leader of the hunt listened so much to his opinion. "Probably not. Demetrios saw a lot, like I would, but others didn't. Maybe there was nothing to see, but maybe they missed it. If we can't find anyone who saw them in Aphroditopolis, we can backtrack." He scrunched his nose "We don't know where they stopped between here and there, anyway."

Sartorus glanced at Timon, and he was nodding. "Lusario isn't one to imagine things. If he was worried by what he was seeing, something was wrong. God will guide us to the right person in Aphroditopolis, so we'll know what to do next."

The rower squeezed the back of his neck. "I'll go back to the boat now." He lowered his voice to a near-whisper. "We'll be praying about this."

"I know." Sartorus closed his eyes and tipped his head back. "Father, please let Caelus and Lusario be safe somewhere. Guide us to them quickly. In Jesus's name we ask this. Amen." He spoke even quieter, and the echoed amens were whispers.

Taurus's gaze darted from the optio to the manservant to the rower. Silence filled the room, and no one moved. All eyes were closed, but it felt like someone was watching him. He froze, like a man trying not to be spotted by the perimeter watchmen.

After the silence, Sartorus's face relaxed and he opened his eyes. "We're going to try for Aphroditopolis tomorrow. Please tell Dareios we'll be ready to leave at the crack of dawn."

The rower's slight smile vanished. "I'll be back then, and he'll have the boat ready when we reach the docks."

As the rower headed for the exit, Taurus's gaze followed him. Scholars trained for skirmishes of words, not weapons. If a pilot with a crew of seven decided to move against Caelus and Lusario…being at the mercy of a man who hated you was risky at best and could turn deadly.

But if it had, how were they going to find what remained of an only son to take home to a father who hadn't wanted him in Egypt in the first place?

# Chapter 61

## ON THE VERGE

*Stephanos's estate, Day 37*

The riding lesson was over, and Lusario sat at the table with Caelus, working on their drawings.

With a broom in one hand and a plate of raisins and cheese in the other, Neferu entered.

"Menmet sent these in case you get hungry." She placed the plate on the table. "Jason will be helping Menmet in her garden for a while longer before he goes to help Setne. Leaning over to grab the weeds that need to be pulled by hand is getting hard for her. He's doing a fine job with it."

Broom in hand, she walked toward the corner farthest from the door, but she glanced at the table and slowed as she passed.

Lusario set aside a drawing of a row of columns where each had a different decoration at the top.

She came over and stood by his elbow. "That's pretty…"

"That's pretty, but…" Lusario looked up at her. "You can tell us what you think is wrong."

"Well…they don't match."

Caelus's chuckle furrowed her brow. "They aren't meant to. We studied the columns in the temples we visited, and these are some of the different designs we saw at the top that would be easy to duplicate in a house. I was surprised by how many styles of papyrus plants have been used as the capitals atop the columns. Others are variations on what you would see in a Greek or Roman house. We're going to give Tranquilla some choices. We can use her favorite for the whole villa or use a mix of different ones that she likes."

He wiped his pen tip and set it down. "Do you have time to answer more questions now? Zenobia has invited us for dinner again. The messenger said she had something special for tonight, so we might be getting back too late."

"I have time." She leaned the broom against the counter and joined them by the table. "At least until Jason finishes helping Menmet weed."

"You said we'd talk about sin and salvation when we started, but I don't remember seeing the word 'salvation' in what I read." Arms crossed, Caelus leaned back in his chair.

"Maybe not that word, but its meaning is there. Being saved from what we deserve because of the sins we've committed. Maybe I should start with what people had to do to cover their sins so they could approach God before Jesus came."

"Is that what wasn't satisfying all the ones who came to Joannes for his baptism?"

"Yes, but it is what God told Moses to tell the people of Israel to do. So, it's what had to be done if anyone wanted God to allow them in His presence. Once a year, the high priest would make a special sacrifice to atone for the sins of all the people during the last year. The sacrifice had to be a male without blemish and from the best of the flock. Its blood covered the people's sins and allowed them to approach God for a while. But every year that sacrifice had to be repeated. It wasn't that God needed what they sacrificed. Killing one of their best animals was a way for them to understand how serious any sin was because a holy God can't abide it in His presence."

Caelus picked up the pen and rolled it between his fingers. "Animal sacrifice is part of Roman rites, too. But it's used to show gratitude for some way a god helped us or to gain the gods' favor so they'll help us in the future. Sometimes it's to appease a god who might be angry before he does something to us. Or maybe someone makes a vow and the sacrifice is part of fulfilling it." He wiped the tip with scrap of cloth. "I get the feeling the sacrifice you're talking about is different."

"It is. People aren't separated from God because He's angry with us. It's because He's righteous and holy and pure, and He can't abide what's unrighteous in His presence. Anything short of perfection is not enough, and not one of us is perfect. We all do things that are sins, like we talked about before. Things that build a barrier between us and God, and we can never tear down that barrier ourselves."

Her finger traced a stain on the table. "But He loves us so much that He opened a way for us to be able to be with Him, even though we aren't fit to be in His presence. What He told Moses was a temporary fix with the blood of the animal that died in our place. The second was the permanent solution when Jesus took on all our sins and paid for them with his death so we wouldn't have to."

Caelus sealed his ink bottle with its wax plug. "I noticed that Markos described three times when Jesus predicted what would happen, how he was going to be a sacrifice. The third was as he was leading his disciples to Jerusalem that last time. He even knew it would be the Romans who would kill him." His lips formed a grim line. "For a person who wasn't a Roman citizen, that could mean crucifixion. I don't know how he was able to ride into Jerusalem, knowing he might be on a cross before he left again."

"It was his love for us. Agape love is unconditional, sacrificial. By his suffering and death, Jesus opened the way to God for us. All we have to do is confess our sins and believe in Jesus as our savior who removes the sins that made us unfit to be with God."

Caelus pointed at the shelf. "Would you get me her codex?"

Lusario took the linen-wrapped gospel from the high shelf where they kept it when Caelus wasn't reading it. Each time he got it down, it felt like a box with something living inside. But when it was opened, would there be a friendly puppy eager to lick him or a coiled snake ready to strike? Caelus had gone from intellectual curiosity to fascination with what he was reading there.

But if he'd been the one who was dying when they prayed, would he do anything different?

"Was Passover the day the high priest made the annual sacrifice? Markos wrote that he was arrested on the day when they sacrificed the Passover lamb." Caelus's finger traced the two lines that made a stylized fish on the cover.

"That would seem a likely choice, but he chose that day for another reason. The first Passover was when God freed the people from slavery in Egypt. When Jesus died, he freed anyone who believes in him from their slavery to sin."

Palm up, Lusario invited her to sit. She shook her head and remained standing, so he sat again.

"On the first Passover, Moses led the people of Israel out from slavery in Egypt. God told Moses to go to the pharaoh and tell him to let God's people go sacrifice to Him in the desert. Of course, the pharaoh refused, so God sent several plagues on Egypt that harmed the Egyptians but not the Israelites. The pharaoh told Moses he would let them go if Moses's god would stop the plague. But each time when it stopped, the pharaoh broke his word and wouldn't let them go. That happened nine times. The tenth time was the death of Egypt's firstborn."

Neferu slowly shook her head. "The pharaoh's stubborn pride cost his people so much. But God gave those who believed in Him a way to be saved. He told Moses to have the Israelites paint their doorposts with the blood of a freshly sacrificed lamb before sunset and then stay inside until morning. During the night, God would travel through Egypt, killing the firstborn male of both people and livestock. When He saw the blood on the door, He would pass over that house, and the firstborns inside would live. After the pharaoh lost his own oldest son, he ordered the Israelites to leave Egypt."

Her eyes warmed. "Those Passover lambs died to save those who believed God's word to Moses. God told them to sacrifice an unblemished lamb every year in remembrance of Him freeing them."

Lusario had his gaze fixed on an old stain on the table when Caelus nudged him. "You said Timon showed you some of the writings of Moses in the library. We should get him to show us where this story is when we return. We should read Moses's complete writings."

"I'm sure he'll be glad to help." Lusario couldn't stop the wry smile. How many times had Timon tried to get him to do just that?

She straightened their pile of drawings. "Jewish men were supposed to go to Jerusalem for the Passover celebration every year. Jesus knew he was going to die when he entered Jerusalem for that Passover. He planned from the beginning to be the perfect sacrifice that would not just cover sin but remove it from any who believe he died to save them and rose from the dead afterwards."

Caelus opened the codex to a place near the back. He tapped the page to draw Lusario's attention. "Right here, Jesus is celebrating the Passover with his closest disciples. I didn't understand what he was doing. But if the Passover celebrates when the blood of a sacrificed lamb on a doorpost turned judgement and death away from the believers inside, what Jesus said makes sense. 'This is my blood of the new covenant, which is poured out for many.' He was declaring himself the sacrifice that would remove sins, but who are the many? What was the old covenant?"

"Between God and the people of Israel. The new covenant would be for all people, including you and me. I wish I had the gospels of Matthaios and Lukas to share with you. Phoebe had them memorized and shared them with me, so I know what they say, even if I don't have a copy for you to read. Jesus said his blood of the New Covenant was for the sins of many *for the forgiveness of sins*. The sacrifices under the old covenant could never be perfect because an animal's blood can't completely erase the sins a person commits. But Jesus's sacrifice was perfect because he had never sinned. It would never have to be repeated. All we have to do is confess our sins, believe Jesus's sacrifice paid for them, and follow him as Lord. Our sins are forgiven completely, and we can approach God through Jesus."

"Hmmm." Caelus fingered his lip. "All we have to do. That makes it sound easy. But what does it mean to follow him as Lord?"

Soft footsteps drew all eyes to the doorway. Jason entered and gave Neferu a hug.

"I've finished pulling weeds. I'm ready to go help Setne."

She moved the broom to the corner. "I'll walk with you today. It's been too long since I got away from the cottages, and watching you with the donkeys is always fun."

Her broadest smile lit her eyes when she turned them back on Lusario and Caelus. "We can talk about that tomorrow. We'll be back in time for cleaning up before dinner."

When they were outside, Jason took her hand and swung it as they headed for the levee path.

"I'm glad she took Jason today." Caelus laid his hand on the codex. "You can read Markos while they're gone. It's not very long."

He squeezed the back of his neck. "I could feel the truth of it as I read. It's hard to explain why, but you'll probably feel it yourself when you read it."

"I can do that." Lusario could do it, but did he want to? A man was responsible for what he knew. Maybe that was why he had avoided reading what Timon urged upon him for years.

Caelus stared out the open doorway. "I've been thinking a lot the last few days. Between what I've read and what Neferu has told us, I might be on the verge of deciding to be a Christian like my cousin Martina."

Lusario nodded because that was the response Caelus wanted, but he wanted to ask if he knew what that could mean. Both his grandfather and father had hidden what the women of the family were. How upset would Master Volero be if his only son embraced an illegal religion that could keep him from ever being a leader of Carthago, like his ancestors had been for generations? One that put him on the wrong side of Roman law.

Would Volero's anger at what his son had done be directed at him for not keeping Caelus from doing it? And if it was, what would his master decide to do?

# Chapter 62

## Growing Hostility

*Aphroditopolis, Day 38*

The sun cast long shadows when Taurus set his end of the trunk down outside the harbor garrison. The rowers had spent time on the oars to take them upriver faster than the wind alone, so Dareios had taken trunk duty to spare his tired men.

A frown had replaced Sartorus's usual smile when he came back out. "The optio remembered Lusario. He told him there were no guards to rent. When I asked if he recommended an inn to them, he said no, but he saw they were with three Egyptians. Two carried a trunk, and the other one made a snide remark about having to guard it themselves. They probably went to an inn the pilot suggested."

"So, where do we go now?" Timon bit the corner of his lip.

"I described the inns they had been staying at in the other towns. Then I asked where he would send them if they wanted the same kind here. He gave me three names."

He spoke their names, then turned to Timon. "Which do you think is the right one?"

Timon closed his eyes. A deep breath, slowly released, relaxed his shoulders. A long moment of silence passed before he pointed toward a street leading away from the docks. "Three blocks that way."

Timon took his place beside Sartorus, and they started up the street.

Taurus erased the frown he didn't want anyone to ask about. Sometimes Sartorus decided what they should do. Sometimes he asked Timon to do it. But no matter who chose their next step, there were always closed eyes, a silent prayer, and then a decision that turned out to be the right one. It was almost enough to make a man wonder...

From behind a counter, the innkeeper greeted them with a smile. "You are in luck today. I still have a room with four beds."

"We might be needing three of them." Sartorus greeted smile with smile.

"We're looking for two young men, one Roman with equestrian stripes, the other Greek. They might have stayed here three to four weeks ago. They would have had a single trunk with bright brass fittings.

"Martinus and Lusario." The innkeeper beamed.

Taurus looked at Timon and raised one eyebrow. A smile and shrug were Timon's response.

"Yes. Martinus's father sent us to find him, and we've been tracking him upriver. Did there seem to be anything unusual when they stayed here?"

"Now that you ask…Three Egyptians came with them. Two carried their trunk, and the other seemed in charge. That one acted like he didn't like the young Roman." He snorted. "The two you're seeking talked about him after he left. The Roman said he didn't know if he could stand even one more day of the pilot, and his Greek friend told him a man could put up with anything if saying something could get the wrong man mad at you."

"Did you see them with the pilot again? Or hear what their plans were after staying here?"

"It's less than a day to Heracleopolis. The canal to it leaves the Nile at Thmoinepsi, and Lusario asked about the canal boats there. Martinus asked about the garrison where the boats land. They went to the Roman baths but were only gone a little while. Then they stayed in their room except for a short time when dinner was served. I had many guests that night who kept me busy. So, I didn't get a chance for much conversation with your friends. In the morning, only the other two came to take their trunk back to the boat."

He reached into a drawer and took out a key. "Will you be wanting the room?"

Sartorus held out his hand. "Yes. Lodging for three." He raised his eyebrows at Dareios, who nodded. "And dinner for four."

Sartorus tossed Taurus the key, and they carried the trunk upstairs. As they walked along the balcony, he looked over the edge. When Sartorus approached the stairs, he said something to Timon too soft to hear, and the smiled vanished from both their lips.

It might be only one more day until they reached the estate. Caelus should be there, preparing to build like he'd wanted for years. But what would they do if he wasn't?

*Stephanos's estate, evening of Day 38*

As the man led the donkey cart away, Lusario watched Neferu stroll over to join them on the levee path. The smile she gave him when first meeting always brightened whatever he was doing.

She hugged Jason, then turned him toward Menmet's cottage. "You're a little later tonight. Hurry in and get ready for bed."

He flashed a smile and trotted off.

She hugged herself, then crossed her arms. "So, what happened tonight?"

"Some things were different." Caelus waved his hand toward their usual bench and started their stroll toward it.

"Good things or bad?" She walked beside Lusario instead of guarding the opposite side of Caelus as she had before.

He liked the change.

"Maybe both. She planned for Karpos to sit across from Jason so he could kick him, but Stephan switched places without her permission. It would have been too obvious what she was up to if she had insisted he sit where she wanted, so Jason didn't have to avoid the under-table kicks tonight."

"Well, that's an improvement."

Lusario drew a breath between his teeth. "Maybe not. Karpos was furious that Stephan protected his cousin."

"What did Zenobia say?"

"Nothing, but when she thought we weren't watching too closely, the way she looked at him…" He shook his head. "It's been seven days since the first attempt on Jason's life, five days since we've known about the danger. The way her hostility is growing, the level of hatred I see makes me suspect she isn't through yet, that something else is coming. She's not likely to stop until she succeeds or gets caught trying."

She bit her lip. "I've been praying for Akhom to get back or Stephanos to come home. I don't want Jason alone until we've talked with them."

They reached the bench, and Caelus lowered himself onto it. "It's another three weeks before I can go downriver. Surely one of them will be back sooner than that. Until then, we'll just keep watch like we have been."

He handed Lusario the crutch. "Do we have time for a couple of questions now?"

Lusario had seen those worry wrinkles on her brow too often since Stephan revealed the first attack. But as soon as Caelus asked, they relaxed. "Of course."

"I was looking at the last pages again where Jesus was talking with his eleven closest disciples after he rose. He told them to go into all the world and preach the gospel to the whole creation. 'Whoever believes and is baptized will be saved, but whoever does not believe will be condemned.' He left no doubt that there are only two possible choices."

When her eyes turned on Lusario, he looked away. Too often he got the feeling that she read his mind, even when he tried to hide his thoughts from her.

"You're right, and I hope you both make the decision I have."

"We're definitely thinking about it."

When Caelus spoke those words, Lusario's stomach knotted. Caelus wasn't just thinking about it. If Lusario were a betting man, he'd bet almost any amount that his friend was about to take that leap without counting the full cost.

"I find the list of signs that will accompany their preaching interesting. Laying hands on the sick and they get well. You've definitely done that. Driving out demons, speaking new languages, picking up snakes and drinking poison without being harmed—have you done any of those?"

Her laughter was musical. "Sometimes I speak another language when I pray. Phoebe did, too. But I'm not going to test God by drinking poison or playing with snakes. I'm not one of the apostles Jesus was commissioning there. I'm just a believer who knows the Holy Spirit can do anything, and I'm not afraid to ask."

She placed her hand over her heart. "Remember I told you that I can't tell God what to do. He wants us to ask, but He'll always do what's best in the long run, even if it's not what I might want right now."

Caelus shifted on the bench to face her. "When you've seen a miracle yourself, when you've been the one healed, it's obvious the one who prayed was asking a real god with real power. Without your prayers, I might have bled to death. The fever wouldn't have broken, and the infection would have killed me. I can understand why the ones Jesus or his disciples restored to health would want to follow him."

"Neferu." Jason's small voice reached them as he waved before heading toward Mikro for a final check before dark. Then he joined them.

"I came to say good night." He slipped his hand into Neferu's. "Tonight, will you put me to bed instead of Menmet? I miss the prayer of blessing you say before I go to sleep."

She bent over and kissed the top of his head. "Of course. We were just about to say goodnight anyway."

They headed toward Menmet's cottage, hands clasped and swinging.

Caelus blew out a long, slow breath. "The more I learn, the more I'm inclined to think Cousin Martina and Juliana were right to become Christians. I haven't quite decided yet, but I'm considering doing it myself."

Lusario's heart rate ramped up. He'd seen it coming, but hearing Caelus speak it still triggered waves of worry. Before they sailed three years ago, Volero Martinus had told him to keep Caelus away from dangerous situations and people who could get him into trouble. Who would have thought the best and kindest woman would be the one to make him fail? And there was nothing he could have done to stop it.

"Father is planning on me following in his footsteps as a councilman of Carthago, becoming duumvir like Grandfather did and like Father will before long. It's not like living in Rome, where the senators all go through the motions of worshiping the Roman gods, whether they believe in them or not. Worshiping other gods is fine as long as you take part in the Roman rites."

He squeezed the back of his neck. "But from what Jesus said is the most important commandment and what Neferu said about the first of the ten laws God gave to Moses, being a Christian wouldn't let me pretend like Father does. Grandfather never let anyone know what Juliana and Martina believed. I expect Father continued hiding Martina's faith. But she married the son of a consul of Rome who's the tribune of the Urban Cohort there, and I don't know if she's hiding her faith from her husband or not. So, maybe it's not as big a problem for Father as I suspect it might be."

He shrugged. "But whatever I decide, I want to get you freed before I risk getting Father angry with me for choosing Jesus."

Caelus slapped his arm. "I have to take care of my fellow architect. It would be too hard to do what I want without you."

"Getting your father angry before he approves of us starting the business wouldn't be wise either."

"True." Caelus's leaned his head back against the wall. "It's been a long day. Zenobia's dinners are delicious, but spending time with her is exhausting. I'd rather have a bowl of porridge here. So, let's go to bed."

As Lusario held the door for Caelus to enter, he couldn't stop the sinking feeling in his stomach. How angry would Volero be when he learned his only son had become a Christian? It might be years before his owner was ready to free him. Would he punish Caelus by refusing when Caelus asked? Would he let them start their business or refuse to let Caelus pursue his dream out of spite? Lusario swallowed hard. Would Volero sell him to strip Caelus of someone who was important to him?

He helped Caelus out of Zenobia's fine tunic and into a roughly made one for sleeping. Just when things seemed to be going Lusario's way, he faced another un-known future. His friend might think he hadn't decided yet, but he had. Timon told him many times that once an honest man recognized the truth about Jesus, he never turned back.

So, maybe all he could do was ask Neferu to pray to her god that Master Volero wouldn't reject his son over his new-found faith.

He'd always believed the only wise choice for a slave was to follow the religion of his master. After all, none of the gods were real, so it didn't matter which one you pretended to worship. But if Caelus became a Christian while Volero was ashamed to admit there were Christians in his family, what would that mean for him? If no god was real, he could stay Stoic with the father or adopt the religion of the son.

But a man of integrity had only one choice—admit the truth, no matter the cost. Still, before he bet his life on it, how could he be absolutely certain what he'd learned was the truth?

# Chapter 63

## Not Where They Should Be

*Thmoinepsi, Day 39*

Taurus boarded last, and the boat moved away from the dock. They might as well not have stopped.

It had been three weeks since Caelus and Lusario would have asked for directions, but the optio at the port garrison claimed he'd never seen them. Maybe he wasn't on duty that day, so he couldn't swear whether or not two young men, one Roman, asked where to rent a guard or wanted to report a pilot for demanding money for tolls that didn't exist. Maybe only Lusario came in, and the optio saw hundreds of Greeks in three weeks. Maybe it was so unimportant to him he simply forgot.

But it was less than half a day to Heracleopolis, so most passengers unloaded at the riverboat dock and bought passage right away on a canal boat to the nome capital. Maybe they did, too.

When Sartorus went to the bow to tell Dareios what they'd learned, Taurus rested his hand near the top of the canopy post. "So, what does your god tell you we should do next?"

Timon shifted on the seat to look up at him. "I haven't asked Him yet. We're most likely to find Caelus and Lusario at the estate, working on their building plans. I expect we'll go to the estate as soon as we reach Heracleopolis. Our search could be over by dinnertime. It's too bad Caelus's father has had to worry so much because Lusario's letter didn't reach him."

Over by dinnertime? Maybe…but after what the last innkeeper said, maybe not.

"Sartorus sent Master Volero a letter reporting Caelus was well when he went upriver and that we're following. He'll have it in two weeks. But that won't help much."

"Why wouldn't it let him stop worrying? Going up the Nile isn't like crossing the frontier into the wild lands outside the empire."

Taurus bent to put his head inside the canopy. Then he lowered his voice. "He shouldn't stop until we see Caelus standing before us. Robbers can kill you just as easily in the best part of the most civilized city as on a lonely desert road. Caelus's grandfather bought me out of the arena to guard him because he knew that. We know they were traveling with a thief. What else the pilot is…" He shrugged, and his lips twitched as he tried not to laugh as first shock, then worry took Timon's smile away.

*Heracleopolis, early afternoon of Day 39*

Taurus stood, arms crossed, beside Timon and Dareios while Sartorus rented three mules from the stable recommended by the garrison optio.

"How long do you think you'll be gone?" Dareios looked over his shoulder toward the harbor.

"It's three miles to the Latro estate. So, there and back could be less than an hour at a trot, more like two hours at a walk. Why?"

"I'll land the boat and come back here to wait for someone to tell me what we're doing next."

"Then about an hour. I'll come back and tell you even if Sartorus is staying longer because Caelus is there."

Timon's brow furrowed. "Trot?" He blew out a breath between pursed lips. "I've never ridden before."

Taurus placed a hand on the small man's shoulder. "We all have a first time. I'll teach you how to ride it. As smart as you are, I expect you'll catch on quicker than most."

At a wave from Sartorus, they walked over to mount and ride to their final destination. Final, assuming they found Caelus. But if they didn't…

They were halfway to the estate when Sartorus slowed from a trot to a walk to rest the mules. Timon pulled back on his reins and smiled at Taurus. "You were right that this isn't too hard as long as someone teaches you how to do it. Thanks."

Taurus answered with a nod and a quick smile. Normally, he would have stopped with that. But there was something about Timon that made talking with him more comfortable than most.

"Be glad it's only three miles instead of twenty and more than half at a trot. That was my first ride with Caelus's grandfather. I ride a lot bodyguarding Master Volero. Horses, not mules, but it's about the same."

Timon leaned forward and patted his mule's neck. "I'm glad Master Caelus didn't report his pilot to the optio. He might have forced him to refund what he'd cheated Caelus out of. Demetrios heard Lusario say it was only a few drachmas.

For so little, making him give it back is probably all the optio would do, but with soldiers, you never know. And thieves can turn vicious after you corner them. Being in the right is no protection against an angry man with a knife. As Apostle Paul said, if possible, as far as it depends on us, we should live at peace with others, and that sometimes means letting some things pass."

Taurus stared at him. "That's something your god commands? But there's no justice in that."

"Perhaps not." Timon twisted in his saddle to face Taurus straight on. "But God shows us mercy instead of enforcing justice. He tells us to do the same. In fact, if I want to be forgiven for all that I've done wrong, all the things that separate me from God, I need to forgive others who have wronged me."

"Sartorus."

At Taurus's call, Sartorus turned in his saddle and rested his hand on his mule's rump. "What?"

"Did you just hear that?"

"I did."

"Do you agree with it?"

He reined in his mule to drop back beside Taurus and Timon. "I do, and I'll be glad to explain why when we have time." He tipped his head toward the estate buildings rising ahead of them. "Time and privacy. We'll have plenty of that on the boat back."

Taurus's gaze shifted to Timon, whose usual slight smile turned into a broad one, and back to Sartorus. Did he want that explanation of what Christians believed? Or might it lead to something he didn't want to think about?

"It can wait."

Taurus held the reins of Sartorus's mule as their leader talked with the steward of Latro's estate. He didn't need to hear the words to know what Sartorus heard. Caelus wasn't there, and he never had been.

A grim-faced Sartorus strode back and mounted. "They never made it here. So, we'll go back to Thmoinepsi and see if we can find a canal boat that brought them to Heracleopolis. If not, we'll go back downriver, asking if anyone's seen them along the way."

He swung his mule toward the town and kicked it into a trot. In silence, Taurus and Timon rode behind.

Back in Thmoinepsi, they divided the canal boats into three groups. Timon served as interpreter for Taurus and Sartorus as they asked one group while Dareios and the helmsman took care of the other two.

When they came back together, one thing was clear. None of the boatmen had seen the missing men.

"What now?" Dareios's mouth drooped, and Taurus stared at him. The tone of voice, the sad eyes—the pilot had never met either man, wasn't even close to someone who had. Why did he look like the failure to find them mattered to him?

Sartorus closed his eyes and blew out a breath through pursed lips. Timon and Dareios closed theirs, too. That could only mean one thing. Taurus's mouth twitched. They were praying to their god.

"So,"—Sartorus ran his fingers through his hair—"we'll spend the night here. In the morning we'll start back down river. We know they disappeared somewhere between here and Aphroditopolis. We'll stop at every estate on the river and ask if they saw them or heard from anyone who did. We need to find someone who saw something that will help us find the pair. Someone willing to tell us what they saw."

Dareios pointed north. "I've landed the boat up there. Come as soon as you're ready in the morning, and we can start."

Sartorus reached into his purse and took out a handful of coins. "Get enough for all of us to eat for a couple of days. We'll check the inns here to be certain they didn't stay at one, then join you after dawn to start the search."

Taurus fell in beside Timon as Sartorus led them toward the first inn. "I'm sorry."

Timon's brow furrowed. "For what?"

"For losing your friend."

"We don't know that I have yet. When we pray, I don't sense that Lusario is gone. We still might find them somewhere downriver. God can work all things for good. Maybe He's doing just that, but we can't see how yet."

Taurus almost snorted, but he didn't. He liked Timon more than any man he'd ever met. After less than a week, if Timon called him a friend, he'd be honored. No one he knew was smarter than the short, scrawny Greek, and he didn't want Timon to realize he thought him a fool to expect a god to turn bad into good. If he were rich and a betting man, he'd be willing to bet almost any amount Caelus Martinus was long dead and Lusario was either killed with his master or had run away so they never would find him.

# Chapter 64

## Too Soon to Decide

*Stephanos's estate, Day 39*

With a tray of bread, cheese, and dates, Neferu had just come from Menmet's house with the men's lunch when she saw Lusario bringing Jason home from his riding lesson. They were still some distance away, and Jason was talking with the smiling man, almost bouncing as he walked beside him. When they reached her, Jason flashed her a smile before going to feed Mikro. But Lusario stopped beside her.

She hugged herself and rubbed her arms. "How is he doing?"

Lusario tipped his head toward her boy. "The way he is with donkeys, I expected he'd take quickly to riding. He's already a better rider than Karpos."

"I suppose Karpos hates that."

"He does, but Stephan thinks it's funny. He keeps teasing Karpos even though I've talked with him about that." He rolled his eyes. "Brothers."

He took the tray from her and earned her smile.

"I'm so glad to have you and Caelus here. Not that I'm glad Caelus was hurt so badly that he couldn't travel, but I am glad to have you both in Jason's life. To have two men he thinks the world of treat him like he's something special—after his father, he needed that so badly."

Lusario balanced the tray on one arm and popped some cheese into his mouth.

"I'm glad, too. We didn't get to the estate to see the building site. But if we had, I couldn't have stopped Basileos bolting, and Jason could have been killed." His eyes grew serious. "And I would never have met the most extraordinary woman of my acquaintance."

Since she left childhood, she'd been told she was beautiful. The way hungry eyes followed her when she passed by had made her uncomfortably aware of the effect she had on men. Over time, it had grown easier to ignore them. But when Lusario said that, her cheeks heated before she looked away.

"I'm not anything special. But it has been wonderful getting to know you and Caelus. Especially sharing with you about Jesus."

He offered her the tray. She shook her head.

"I've enjoyed all our conversations. Sometimes you make me think, like after a lecture when I talk with Caelus or Timon. Caelus would have been bored past enduring if you hadn't kept him entertained. The best part of this trip has been getting to know you…and Jason."

◆

Lusario fixed his gaze on the most beautiful woman he'd ever seen, but she was so much more than a beauty. So loving to Jason, so kind to everyone, the smartest woman he'd ever met.

"And I'm sorry I'm going to be leaving so soon. It's three weeks since the croc broke Caelus's leg. I figure after six weeks, he'll be healed enough that he can go back downriver to see if we can get the commission." With his foot, he drew a circle in the dirt. "We haven't talked about it, but maybe he could go alone. We both care about Jason, so maybe he'll let me stay longer." His gaze returned to her enchanting eyes. "Stephanos needs to be back before we can know whether Jason will be safe here. Whether you'll have a future here."

"I have a four-year contract. His future and mine are joined until then."

Did her shrug speak regret or relief about those four years?

He broke eye contact and massaged his palm. What he said next might change what she thought of him. Maybe it was too soon to say it, but if a man waited too long, it could become too late. He'd always been a man who didn't set his heart on the impossible. But if a man wouldn't take a risk for his heart's desire, he'd never get it.

"I wish there could be a future…for us. But there's something I haven't told anyone here." He looked over at the loom where Menmet was working. "What I'm about to tell you—you can't tell anyone." He cleared his throat. "I'm not what you think. Caelus ordered me to act like a free man, but I belong to his father. He bought me to be Caelus's valet because I knew Alexandria from living there before. But as soon as Caelus realized I could learn what it took to be an engineer alongside him, he decided to ask his father to free me when we became architects."

He fixed his gaze on her face. Whatever she spoke would be kind. It always was, but her eyes should reveal her true thoughts.

"So, as much as I wish there could be a future for us, I'm only a slave, and I can't ask anyone to be my wife as long as I am."

Her lips, her eyes, the way she stood—there wasn't even a flicker of surprise. Did she know already, or simply not care about him enough for it to matter?

"Caelus plans to ask his father to free me as soon as we get the business going. Maybe Master Volero will even be willing to do it before then since I kept the pilot and helmsman from killing us and saved him from the croc. If you want me to, I can ask Jason to cancel or sell your contract so you could marry me when I'm free."

Her eyes widened at "marry," then they warmed like when she looked at Jason. It wasn't that she didn't care. She liked him for himself, regardless of what he was. He almost reached out to take her hand, but stopped before she would see it. She hadn't said anything. Maybe that smile only meant friendship, not the affection between woman and man.

"I'm not free to do what I want either. I have almost four more years on my contract with Jason. If I asked him to free me, it would make him feel that I didn't love him, and I'm not sure I could bear being parted from him now, anyway. I promised Corinna I would love him like she did, and God has already put a love for him in my heart that's more than I ever thought possible."

She leaned to look past him toward Jason. "Until I know his grandfather will love and protect him, I can't leave him. Being so young, there's so much more he still needs to learn about God and following Jesus as Lord. I can't leave him in a household where everyone would be telling him to believe in the Greek gods with no one helping him to grow in his own faith in Jesus."

"I understand. But what about after the contract expires?"

◆

A proposal of marriage was the last thing Neferu expected. What should she say?

They'd known each other for only three weeks, but that was enough to know he was willing to die to save a friend. Enough to see him show a one-eyed boy the affection a father should. Bravery, loyalty, kindness, intelligence. He embodied all of them. She did like him, more than any man she'd ever known. It would be easy to grow to love him. But as much as she liked him, she couldn't tell him she'd marry him when neither one was free.

But even if he were free, he didn't believe in Jesus. She wanted a marriage like Phoebe and her husband had, with God at the center.

"As long as you aren't free, as long as neither of us are, there's no point in us talking about this." The smile she offered him dimmed. "The way you are with Jason, I know you'll be a wonderful father. Some woman will be so fortunate to become your wife after you're free."

"I don't expect my freedom before you become free again." The intensity of his gaze deepened, and her heart rate rose.

"I don't want just some woman. Even if Master Volero frees me now, I'm willing to wait for you to be free."

"But I can't ask you to wait for me. What you feel today might not be how you feel after you leave here. It would be wrong for either of us to expect nothing would change in those waiting years when we aren't even together. It wouldn't be fair to make you promise to wait."

His shoulders sagged, then straightened. "Are you more worried that my feelings will change or yours? If I were free to ask and make that promise, would you want it?"

Her heart longed to tell him yes. But he didn't believe in Jesus yet, and he still might not in four years. He might not want a wife who would place Jesus above all others, even if that meant dying for her faith. Any children they had she would raise to know God and follow Jesus, even if he didn't. Would he want that?

"I haven't asked God what I should do when Jason no longer needs me. What I want might not be His will."

His eyebrows dipped as his smile turned into a frown. "Are you saying your faith is what might keep us apart?"

She dropped her gaze to the ground, then raised her head to look into his eyes. "It might. You might not want a Christian woman, and I want a man who loves the Lord."

His jaw dropped. Then his mouth curved into a smile that was both wry and sad. "Timon has told me for years that my life after death depended on whether I believed in his god. Now you tell me that our future depends on me making that same choice. Do you care for me at all?"

"Oh, yes. Why do you think I've wanted so much to share with you? With Caelus, too. You've both become dear friends, and I care more than you can imagine about what both of you decide."

He snorted. "Is that all I am to you? A dear friend?"

"No. If I let myself, I could love you as a man. Any woman could. But I'm not free to make that choice now. Please don't ask me to. Only God knows what lies ahead for both of us. What I want more than anything might not be what's best for me or for you."

"Very well." His teeth clenched, but he flexed his jaw to relax it. "We'll be here at least three more weeks. You and I don't have to decide anything yet. You can keep telling Caelus and me more about your god." One corner of his mouth lifted. "Timon has been trying to make me a Christian for years. Maybe you'll succeed where he hasn't."

He waved his hand toward the bench where Caelus waited for them. "Shall we?"

She answered with a smile and a silent nod.

*God, please make Caelus's father free him soon. But please let him see he'll only be truly free when he gives his heart to You.*

# Chapter 65



## Found!

*Thmoinepsi, morning of Day 40*

Taurus stood back from the group, arms crossed. Sartorus, Timon, and the crew had gathered once more for a quick prayer before shoving the boat into the river and heading south.

Sartorus closed his eyes and lifted his chin. "God, please guide us to the ones who know what we need to find Caelus and Lusario. Please let them be alive and well when we find them. We ask this…"

The time between "this" and the spoken "amen" was just long enough for a silent "in Jesus's name." Taurus heard it in his mind, even though none of their lips spoke the words that ended every prayer where no one might hear.

They boarded and joined the boats heading down the canal to the river.

From the pilot's post in the bow, Dareios looked back. "East bank or west?"

Several pairs of eyes closed, and for a moment the only sound was the splash of one pair of oars. Then Sartorus's eyelids opened. "We should search the west bank."

Timon and the crew members nodded in agreement. But was that just because Sartorus was leading the party or because they got the same message somehow?

Since Naucratis, Taurus had been watching Sartorus and Timon pray as they worked their way upriver. As they approached each town where Caelus might have stopped, they asked their god to guide them to the person with the information they needed and the wisdom to know what to do with it.

And each time, they found the right person to get them to the next place where the young men stayed. Each time, the innkeeper knew something about what came next.

But that could have been coincidence. When faced with choices, the one Sartorus made was always a reasonable one. One he might have made himself without any god's help. But this time Sartorus asked for something beyond what coincidence should do.

What were the odds of finding even one person along that stretch of river who knew what had happened to a Roman stranger and was willing to tell? It might just take the help of a god with real power to find out.

As for the two men being alive and well… They'd vanished more than three weeks ago between Aphroditopolis and Latro's estate. After so long with no word from either of them, Caelus Martinus was probably neither.

And Lusario…even if he was alive, he'd be a fool to let them find him. A slave could be executed for the death of his master even if he had nothing to do with it. And a master dying so far from anyone who cared could set any slave free. His lips tightened. A ruthless slave might decide to help death along and then disappear to gain that freedom.

So even if they did find where Caelus had gone, would they bring a son back to Master Volero or only a box of ashes for the family mausoleum?

*West bank of the Nile south of Thmoinepsi, afternoon of Day 40*

For the thirteenth time, the boat pulled into a landing that served an estate or a village. Each time, Taurus left the boat with Sartorus and Timon and walked to the nearest cluster of buildings. Each time, Timon asked the people there if any had seen a young Roman man with red stripes on his tunic and his Greek servant. They might have had a single trunk with bright brass fittings and a leather satchel or have come ashore from a six-rower boat.

Twelve times the answer had been no. If Taurus was a betting man, he'd wager that twelve was about to become thirteen.

No sooner had the three of them jumped down to the shore than a one-man fishing boat pulled in beside them.

Timon greeted him in Egyptian and Greek and got a Greek reply.

Sartorus stepped forward. "Do you know if anyone near here has seen a young Roman, maybe in a red-striped tunic, and a Greek about the same age with him?"

The fisherman hung a mesh bag filled with fish from his shoulder. "There's a young Roman here who got attacked by a croc and a Greek about the same age who's been tutoring Master Stephanos's oldest grandson and riding with him and the two younger ones."

The biggest grin split Timon's face, and Sartorus's smile wasn't much smaller. "Those sound like them. Could you take us to them?"

"I can. They're staying next to our healer's cottage in the worker's village. Follow me."

They climbed up some steep steps to reach a grassy track atop the levee. Just ahead, the levee broadened to hold a cluster of cottages, each with short mud-brick walls surrounding a small garden and an olive tree or two.

Timon's arm shot out as he pointed. "There's Lusario." He cupped his hands around his mouth. "Lusario!"

The man with dark curly hair spun from his conversation with a pretty Egyptian. He raised a hand, then strode toward them. Timon broke into a trot until he reached him. They hugged with several slaps to the back, then stepped apart.

The fisherman shifted his bag of fish. "Looks like you found them."

Sartorus took a chalkon from his purse and held it out. "Thank you."

After taking it, the man flipped it in the air and caught it. "My pleasure. These fish are needed at the main house now." He tipped his chin toward Lusario. "He'll be eating one tonight."

With long strides, he walked away.

From a bench under an olive tree, the young man Taurus no longer expected to see alive rose with the help of the woman and placed a crutch under his arm.

"Is that Caelus Martinus?" Sartorus asked the question, but his broad smile said he already knew the answer.

"It is."

Sartorus closed his eyes, tipped his head back, and whispered, "Thank You, God!"

As they continued their walk toward the cottage, Taurus cast repeated glances at Sartorus. To search the correct side, to have a man who knew exactly where Caelus was land his fishing boat just as they landed themselves…were these mere coincidences or was something else involved? Had the god Timon and Sartorus believed in actually helped them find Caelus and the slave he treated like a friend?

Now that the search was over, was it even possible to tell the difference?

◆

"I'm glad to see you, but why are you here?" With fists on his hips, Lusario stared past Timon at the two men striding toward him. "Why is Volero Martinus's bodyguard here and who is that with him?"

"Sartorus used to be an optio for the tribune in charge of the Urban Cohort, so he's hunted missing men before. Tribune Glabrio is Caelus's cousin's husband. When your trunks arrived in Carthago and the captain said you never got on the ship, Caelus's father was afraid something horrible had happened to him. So, he asked Glabrio for help."

"But I wrote and delivered a letter for the captain to give to whoever picked up the trunks. It told Caelus's father we were about to get a commission to build a villa, and he would be coming home later."

"The captain claimed he never got anything. Sartorus works for Glabrio now. He volunteered to come find you, and your father sent Taurus to bodyguard him as he searched."

"So, why are you with them?"

"When Fundanus told them you'd gone upriver and were late returning, Sartorus wanted someone who spoke Egyptian to go with them to look for you. He sent them to Achilleus to ask for me, and we came here on one of his father's boats."

Sartorus tipped his head to Lusario in passing, but he didn't stop until he reached Caelus.

With Timon at his side, Lusario followed.

"Caelus Martinus? I'm Gaius Flavius Sartorus. When your trunks arrived without you, your father sent us to find you."

Caelus balanced on his good leg and spread his arms. "Here I am. I must say, I'm amazed that you found us. The pilot and helmsman of the boat we rented tried to kill us. We swam the river when a hippo made the boat sink, and a croc almost finished the job before I could get out of the water. Lusario rescued me, and we've been waiting for my leg to heal." One corner of his mouth turned up. "But that sounds like a fanciful story, so I wouldn't expect someone looking for me to be checking river estates for a man with a broken leg."

Sartorus paused, then rubbed his lip. But his straight lips relaxed into a slight smile.

"Your cousin Martina knows a God who can direct the paths of men. Timon and I asked Him to guide our search, and He did. Your father sent us to bring you safely home. Even with your bad leg, we can get you back to Alexandria now."

Lusario's brow furrowed. If they left now before Stephanos returned, who would protect Jason?

His gaze lingered on the extraordinary woman standing beside Caelus. Who would protect her?

Caelus caught Lusario's eye before shaking his head. "We can't leave yet. Until the estate steward gets home or Stephanos returns from Alexandria, a young boy is in danger." He pointed toward Jason, who was tending Mikro. "His tutor might be as well."

Palm up, he waved his hand toward Neferu.

"You say Fundanus told you we were late returning. Did he mention whether that meant his uncle hired the other builder?"

Sartorus's brow furrowed. "Other builder?"

"I can answer that." Timon stepped forward. "He said something about his aunt wanting to see what you proposed before any decision is made."

Caelus raised his eyebrows at Lusario, and they exchanged fist pumps. "I want to visit the Latro estate to select a building site before I go back. Then we can prepare some complete designs for her to consider."

As Sartorus crossed his arms, his smile faded. "How soon can you finish doing that?" He scratched behind his ear. "I could delay returning by a few days, but not as much as a week. We do need to send a letter to Volero immediately to let him know we found you injured but recovering. You can tell him what you plan to do before we all return."

"But I'm not going with you. I need to talk to Stephanos, and we have work to do for the new villa."

With his eyes mostly on the group of strange men, Jason took the milk pail to Menmet's house and rinsed it. Then he came to Neferu's side and stood close behind her, hiding his bad eye.

Neferu drew him out and placed both hands on his shoulders. "This is Jason, grandson of Stephanos. His grandfather has been in Alexandria since we came, so he hasn't had the pleasure of meeting Jason yet." She leaned over Jason to smile at him. "Jason is an expert on taking care of donkeys, and he's supposed to check on the ones with babies every day until the regular donkey handler returns. So, we'll go do that now."

She held out her hand, and Jason took it.

"I am so glad someone will be setting his father's heart at rest over his missing son. I can imagine how hard it's been not knowing whether Caelus was well or not. I'd worry terribly if Jason was missing."

As they walked away, Caelus turned to Lusario. "Would you let Zenobia know that searchers have come from my father, so we won't be joining her for dinner tonight?"

"I'll be right back." As Lusario started toward the main house, he glanced over his shoulder.

How would Volero react when he got Caelus's message? Would relief that his son was alive and well override anger at his refusal to come home with the searchers? Would Volero's anger include him when Caelus stayed in Egypt?

Once Caelus set his mind on something, he wasn't likely to change it. But a good Roman son did what his father told him. How would his friend balance his future as a man with his duty as a son? And what did that mean for his own?

# Chapter 66

## UNEXPECTED INVITATIONS

When Lusario was out of earshot, Caelus turned to Sartorus. "I won't be going back with you, but I will want you to take something to Father that I want hand-delivered to make certain he gets it."

He settled onto the bench with a grunt. "What I'm sending—it's for your ears only." He pointed toward the garden. "Timon, Taurus, leave us for a while. There's another bench back there."

He waited a few moments. "Are they around the corner now?"

"They are. What is it?" Sartorus stepped closer so even a whisper could be heard.

"A letter. I wrote it when I was dying from an infection from the croc bite. Actually, I was too shaky to write it myself, so I dictated it to Neferu. She was to give it to Lusario to take back to Father with my remains. But since I didn't die, I want you to take it with you when you return to Carthago. Except for the part about me dying, everything I wrote remains true."

"I can do that." Sartorus spread his legs and stood like the sentries at the garrisons. "Is there anything in it that I should know?"

"Do you know my father well?"

"I do. I married your cousin's handmaid, and we live in the same town house. Volero often joins us for a meal."

"Good. It's a request for Father to free Lusario. Not just to free him, but to make him a citizen by making him an agent for a new family enterprise where he'll be the chief architect and oversee building construction. When I thought Father wasn't going to have a son any more, I asked him to consider adopting Lusario once he was a citizen. I still think that's a good idea since there's no finer man and I look on him as my brother, but Father might not want another son since I'm not dead."

He squeezed his neck and tipped his head back to loosen his muscles. "Father might not want one of his slaves to become his son, even if Lusario is one of the smartest men I know and certainly one of the most loyal friends a man could ever have. He wrestled a crocodile to keep me from being dragged into the river and eaten. He killed it with a dagger while he did that."

He looked toward the main house, then back at Sartorus.

"Neferu attacked the croc with a hoe so he could get on its back to kill it. So, I owe her my life as well. I can't leave before I know she and Jason will be safe here after we go. It's a matter of both honor and friendship for me to protect them."

"Hmph." Sartorus turned his eyes toward the main house as well. "I think your father respects my opinion. If I tell him I think Lusario is a man worthy of what you're asking, I expect he'll request early citizenship. But adoption… he's proud of his Roman bloodline. Even prouder of being a Publilius Martinus whose ancestors helped start Carthago and have served it for generations. Still, there's nothing lost in asking."

"Thank you." Caelus lifted his knee with both hands and adjusted his splinted leg. "Since you and Timon both asked Martina's god to guide your search, can I assume you're Christians?"

"You can."

"And her husband, is he as well?"

"The whole household is."

"Taurus wasn't when I left, but is he now?"

"No."

Caelus drew a breath between his teeth. Much might depend on the answer to his next question.

"Is my father?"

A wry smile tugged at the corner of Sartorus's mouth. "Not yet, but Martina and Glabrio haven't given up on him."

"She can be quite persuasive, but Father isn't easy to persuade." Caelus fingered the corners of his mouth. "Neferu is. Jason, too. They prayed when I was almost dead." He tapped his chest. "And here I am. I asked her how that was possible, and she's been telling Lusario and me about Jesus and why she's a Christian. She has a copy of Markos's writings, and she let me read it. I plan to make us a copy before we leave."

In the distance, Lusario strode along the levee path.

"Timon's been talking to Lusario for four years, but he's still skeptical. As for me…I'm almost ready to join you."

For the first time, Sartorus's smile broadened to a grin. "Martina will be glad to hear that. It's been in her prayers since I've known her."

"Lusario's almost back. We can talk more later."

"I'll tell Timon and Taurus they can go wherever they want now."

"While I'm thinking of it…" Caelus stroked his throat. "We lost our trunk and almost all our money when the boat sank, so Lusario has been tutoring to earn enough for return passage. Do you have some I could have? Father will pay you back when you get home."

"Of course, and I can pay the estate steward for what it costs for the three of us and our boat crew to stay here a few days. I can also give you enough to replace much of what you lost before we go."

Sartorus headed around the cottage to the garden to tell the men.

Caelus released a contented sigh and felt a smile grow. Tranquilla would get them their first commission. Sartorus would take his request to a grateful father who should be eager to grant freedom to Lusario for saving him.

Then his smile faded. But what could he do to ensure Jason and Neferu had a good future as well?

◆

Lusario returned from the main house to find Timon sitting on the bench beside Caelus. Sartorus and Taurus had brought out the chairs. An aura of companionable silence surrounded the group.

Tonignt, he would have preferred a bowl of Menmet's stew while talking with Timon to what lay ahead of him. But he was never the one making the choice.

"Zenobia extends her welcome. She'll be sending someone to the landing to tell your men where they can eat and spend the night. But she wants the visiting Roman to join us at the main house for dinner. The cart will be here at the usual time. We'll go as soon as Jason cleans up." He scrunched his nose. "She prefers we all smell recently bathed as well."

He directed a teasing smile at Timon. "She expects Menmet to feed you and Taurus, but our neighbor makes a tasty stew and good bread. The food at Zenobia's table is excellent, but I'd rather dine with you."

Sartorus raised an eyebrow. "What did you tell her about us that she wants me at her table?"

"Just that Caelus's father sent you to look for us when we didn't arrive in Carthago. Her husband went to Alexandria on business with his father a few weeks ago, and she's desperate for anything to break the monotony until they come home. Caelus said to let her think I'm educated Greek elite, so she treats me like him. She's lonely and bored, so find something interesting to tell her about. Then she'll invite you again. It's almost worth it for the food."

Lusario waved his hand toward the other cottages. "Follow me, and I'll take you to where you can bathe. Then I'll help Caelus get ready."

Caelus put his hands behind his neck and arched his back. "She has two sons who will dine with us. Jason will be there, too. I'll want to know what you think of her and the younger one after you've seen them with him."

Sartorus picked up his chair and set it back inside. "Is there some reason for concern?"

"Her youngest already tried to kill Jason once with a bolting horse."

"I'd say that's a reason." Sartorus took a step to follow Lusario, then paused. "I'll be watching."

*The main house, evening of Day 40*

Caelus sat in his usual place, but he was the only one. Zenobia had chosen the head of the table so she could seat the two Romans opposite each other and next to her.

Perhaps she'd said something to Stephan about protecting Jason. He sat across from Lusario and started out more subdued than usual. That left Jason sitting across from his tormentor, but he slid his chair back a little so Karpos's kicks missed more often than hit.

For the first time since she'd invited him, the meal started with a salad course, like she'd ordered a Roman style meal with two Roman guests.

With a chiton of fine blue linen and silver armbands that matched her necklace and earrings, she was as elegant as he'd seen her yet.

As two housemaids removed their plates, she dabbed at her lips with a napkin that matched what she wore.

"I understand there are two others in your party." She lifted her goblet to her lips, but stopped before sipping. "Who are they?"

Lusario raised his goblet as well. "Timon is a fellow scholar from Alexandria. I've known him for several years. A brilliant man. I think you'd enjoy conversing with him."

"Hmmm." She took the sip. "And the other?"

Caelus glanced at Lusario. He found his friend's gaze focused on his plate, but he caught the single twitch that revealed silent laughter. "Taurus Martinus frequently travels with my father. He came with Sartorus to help find me. A man traveling alone to somewhere he's never been is not wise, and two heads are better than one when searching. I believe you would find both an entertaining addition to our conversations."

She rested her hand over her heart. "Then by all means, invite them to come tomorrow."

"I shall."

He swirled the wine in his goblet. The ex-gladiator had spent more hours in elite Roman banquet halls than he had. Grandfather and Father both praised him as exceptional at seeing what hid behind social masks. Perhaps no one was better equipped to size up the danger Zenobia posed.

And if he was there when something started, no one was more likely to stop it in time.

*Chapter 67*

JUDGING THE RISK

*Early afternoon of Day 41*

Lusario and Caelus were finishing lunch after the riding lessons when Timon and the two men from Carthago entered the cottage.

Caelus leaned back in his chair. "I wondered where you were this morning. You missed Jason reading the latest chapter of Lusario's heroic saga of the war between the Formicans and Mirminkians for control of their empire. Mark my words, it will rival the *Iliad* itself when he writes the final chapter."

Taurus furrowed his brow. "Aren't those two words for ants?"

Caelus nodded and shifted his gaze to Timon. "I'd wager you never knew he was so gifted at writing children's stories."

Timon choked back a laugh. "I'm not surprised. He's been good at everything he put his hand to."

Sartorus half-sat on the edge of the counter. "After dining with Zenobia last night, I wanted to look around and have a casual talk with the stableman about that bolting horse. So, we all took a walk. Except for the boat crew. They were going to Thmoinepsi to see if they could get hired to take people to Heracleopolis or Aphroditopolis. Since we won't be leaving for a few days, Dareios thought they might as well do something useful that made Achilleus's father some money, like they would in Alexandria. They'll be back every evening to check on our plans."

"What did you learn?" Caelus pushed the remaining cheese toward them.

"He's glad Lusario took over riding with Karpos. That boy is trouble." Sartorus took a slice. "His mother lets him do whatever he wants, and the workers are afraid to cross him. I saw that last night when she put him across from Jason. You're wise to watch carefully until the grandfather gets home."

A woman's soft humming announced Neferu's arrival before she stepped through the door. She picked up the nearly empty plate and offered it to each of the three visitors in turn. When she reached Taurus, she shook the plate a little. "Big men need more food. Please, take the rest."

373

With a crooked smile, he scooped up the remaining four pieces.

"Jason is almost ready to go tend the donkeys. Shall I take him today?"

Lusario rose and stepped close to her. "I'll do it."

"And I'll go with him." Timon pushed off from his place beside Sartorus.

She flashed a smile of thanks. "With so many here to keep Caelus company, I'll go help Menmet." She looked back over her shoulder as she passed through the doorway. "Don't let him do anything I wouldn't."

Sartorus crossed his arms when she was gone. "What would that be?"

"I have no idea." Caelus shrugged.

"We'll be back in plenty of time to clean up." When Lusario stepped outside, his first glance went toward Menmet's cottage. A smile grew when he found the finest woman he'd ever met watching for him so she could wave before stepping inside.

Timon cleared his throat and tightened his lips so his smile didn't become a too-teasing grin. "She likes you."

"I like her, too."

"And…?"

"And nothing. She has four more years of bondservant contract with Jason, and I'm not free. It doesn't matter what either of us want."

"I wouldn't be so sure. God can work all things for good for those who love Him."

"She loves him, but I don't."

"Not yet, but anything can change."

Timon's comment deserved Lusario's eye-roll. "Enough on that topic."

They finished their walk to the donkey stable without speaking. When Jason began his inspection of the three foals and their mothers, they lounged against the stable wall.

Lusario finally broke the silence. "I'm glad you'll be joining us for dinner tonight. I told Zenobia you're an Alexandrian scholar, like me."

"I am a little nervous." Timon squeezed his neck. "I don't want to say something I shouldn't."

Lusario kicked a small rock to the side. "You'll fit in fine. When she asked what I did the first time I ate with her, I told her about places I've been. You can do the same."

"But I haven't been anywhere."

"Then talk about something we've learned. Probably not philosophy. She's not a deep thinker, but history would be good." He nudged Timon's shoulder. "Or maybe the latest women's fashions in Alexandria. I'm sure that would fascinate her."

Timon nearly choked. "I know even less about that than you do, but I can try."

Lusario covered his mouth before rubbing his cheek. "I'm not sure what Taurus can talk about. I did meet him in Carthago, but we never spoke. He guarded Caelus's grandfather then. The one time I ate with the town house slaves before I came back here, he listened the whole time instead of talking. But Caelus made sure he was invited tonight. I can't imagine what a Greek woman would have in common with a gladiator bodyguard."

"Caelus wanted him to watch Zenobia. Apparently, he's very good at reading what people think, not just what they say. Sartorus asked his opinion often on our trip upriver."

"You treat him like he's been a friend for a long time. He seems to like you a lot." Lusario nudged Timon. "But there's no accounting for taste."

"I like him, too. Sartorus trusts him completely. So does Volero Martinus. Taurus has known the family secret about Caelus's grandmother and cousin since he was bought out of the arena. He thought they only took Jesus seriously because they were women." Timon chuckled. "His face the first time Sartorus and I asked God for guidance and got it—it was like he'd seen a two-headed goat. Now when he sees God show us the right next step—it's like he expects it. I think he'll be asking why we believe on the trip back downriver. He might be one of us before we reach Alexandria again."

Lusario rubbed behind his ear. "I don't know about that. You've tried to explain it well enough to convince me for a long time. I'm not there yet."

Timon's smile slowly broadened into a grin. "But that was before you saw God's power to heal." He tapped Lusario's arm. "And before a certain woman spent time answering all of Caelus's questions…and some of yours."

"It's wisest for any slave to follow the religion of his master." Lusario gave Timon the shrug he deserved. Any slave as smart as his friend should know that was true.

"It might be the safest, but that doesn't mean it's wise." Timon turned serious eyes on him. "What should a slave do when one of his masters accepts Jesus as Lord before the other one does? Truth matters, even for a slave. Even when accepting it carries a cost."

Timon picked up a pebble and threw it. "You both have seen how God answered Neferu's prayers. I think Caelus is on the verge of becoming a Christian."

Lusario sucked in a breath. "I hope not. Caelus says his father doesn't believe any god is real. But serving Rome means he pretends he does. How is he going to react when he learns his son won't even pretend to follow Roman religion so he can take part in the rites like a councilman or duumvir must?"

His mouth curved down. "My Cyrenian master charged me with keeping his son from questionable activities with unsavory people in dangerous places. Any Roman father would want the same. Three years ago, when Volero told me to look after his son in Alexandria, I assumed that same responsibility for Caelus."

"Hmph." Timon faked indignation. "So, you think Christians are unsavory people doing questionable things in dangerous places? You think Martinus will blame you for what Caelus decides?" He wrinkled his nose and shook his head. "From what Sartorus has said about the husband of Caelus's cousin, I think Martinus knows even the smartest men who faithfully serve Rome can decide Jesus is the Son of God, and he counts one of them among his best friends."

A deep sigh was Lusario's response. "Maybe you're right. I certainly hope so. Or at least I hope I've been freed before Volero decides to blame me for anything."

When Jason finished checking the babies, he joined them.

Lusario ruffled his hair. "You don't smell too much like donkey today, but your aunt will still want you to bathe before dinner."

Jason sniffed and grinned up at him. "But you smell a little like horse."

Lusario placed his hands on Jason's shoulders and turned him toward the path home. "Then we better go take care of that now. Timon and Taurus are joining us for dinner, too, so your aunt won't like it if we're late."

Jason's shoulders drooped. "I hope I sit across from Stephan tonight."

"The earlier we get there, the more likely that is."

"Then let's run." Jason took off up the path.

Lusario and Timon exchanged shrugs and trotted after him.

*Evening of Day 41*

On the way back from dinner, Lusario walked on one side of the donkey with a lantern hanging from a pole. Taurus carried a torch on the other side. Both kept their eyes scanning the pathway ahead of them. After Zenobia mentioned more than once that one of the gardeners had seen a viper nearby, Taurus had asked for torches. He wouldn't let the group leave until he could light the way.

Lusario saw the same things he'd seen at every dinner. Sartorus let Caelus, Timon, and him carry the conversation while he watched and listened.

Taurus sat three seats down and across from Stephan, listening to every word, watching every expression on the woman at the head of the table. That was made harder by Stephan peppering him with questions after he let the boy look at his dagger. But when Zenobia thanked him for entertaining her son so well and asked him to join her again tomorrow, the bodyguard's slight smile and slow nod, first to her, then to Sartorus, conveyed extra meaning when he said that he'd also found time with her family worthwhile.

When they reached the path that branched off at the far end of the worker's village, Taurus traded the brighter torch for the lantern. After an exchange of goodnights, he led Sartorus and Timon into the alleyway that went to the cottage they'd been assigned.

Zenobia's man who led the donkey prevented any discussion of what each had observed. The three who turned off would undoubtedly discuss what it all meant, but Lusario would have to wait until they came to Caelus and him tomorrow to learn what that was.

At their cottage, Lusario held the torch high while the donkey man turned the cart around. After he gave the man the torch, he helped Caelus out of the cart and handed him his crutch.

They didn't speak until the creak of the wheels and the thuds of donkey feet on dirt faded to silence.

Caelus leaned heavily on the crutch. "I thought that dinner was never going to end." He chuckled. "If I didn't have two sisters and a mother who loves to entertain, I would never have thought a woman could talk for so long answering a simple question by a stranger. And then Timon would ask another, and she'd talk on and on about that one. Where did he learn to do that?"

"I don't know. I've never seen him do it before."

"Well, wherever he did, it certainly got her to let her guard down with us. I can't wait to hear what Sartorus and Taurus thought of her."

As they approached their cottage, Neferu rose from the seat by the door.

Caelus tapped Lusario's arm. "Looks like someone is eager for a conversation."

He stopped the smile before Caelus saw it. She'd been waiting for him.

"We don't have anything to tell her."

"Yes, you do." He almost whispered that. When they were close enough for Neferu to hear… "I want to copy a little more of the codex before I retire. I particularly want to finish one section. Why don't you keep Neferu company out here for a while?"

Neferu pushed the door open for him. "I wouldn't mind."

As Caelus passed through the doorway, he turned his face so only Lusario would see the wink.

Lusario cleared his throat. "Would you like to go for a stroll?"

A musical laugh was her answer. "When it's this dark? It's too hard to see the vipers that come out in the evening to hunt. You were wise to use torches coming home."

"It was Taurus who insisted."

"I'm glad. I wouldn't want you—any of you—to be bitten. We can just sit here or under the tree and chat for a while."

"The tree."

If Caelus heard their words, he'd be teased about it tomorrow. He led them to the bench.

She gazed at the faint glow of the dying sunset. "What did Sartorus and Taurus think about Zenobia?"

Well, maybe she hadn't been waiting for him. She'd been waiting for information that either he or Caelus could give her.

"We'll find out in the morning. We couldn't talk about it with the man Zenobia sent with the cart listening."

In the growing darkness, her sigh was deep. "I've been praying for Akhom to come back early. He should be back any day, but what if you have to leave before he comes? Or before Stephanos comes. I can't watch over Jason when he goes to the stable for riding or when Zenobia wants him at the family dinner."

"We aren't leaving when Sartorus does. Timon said Tranquilla wants to see our designs before she decides anything, so we'll be going to the Heracleopolis estate when the splints come off. It's not very far, and he'll want to come visit you and Jason as much as I do."

"He is very fond of Jason. You both are."

He was fond of Jason, but fond wasn't the word he'd use for her.

A man only won if he persevered. He'd lost too many people in his life already. She wouldn't be one of them if he could help it. But how could he convince her?

"I already told you what I feel for you. Caelus thinks we'll be coming back with a commission to build. From what Timon said, I think so, too. When Volero hears about me saving Caelus, maybe he'll be freeing me soon. You know what I want after that. If you want it, too, I'll figure out how to make it happen."

"Ifs and maybes…it's too soon to make final plans. I can't for another four years. But I care about you, too. You're very special. To me and to Jason."

Her hands rested in her lap. Palm up, he reached over and left his open hand there. She placed her own in his and he interlaced their fingers. They sat in silence until the pale orange glow faded to gray. Then she rose.

"Good night, Lusario. Rest in God's peace."

"You, too." He watched her until she disappeared into Menmet's cottage.

God's peace. Could a man have that before he decided to follow her Jesus? Did it always come after he did?

Caelus was ready to find out. But was he?

# Chapter 68

No Greater Love

*Early morning of Day 42*

The morning sky had barely changed from gray to blue when Taurus followed Sartorus and Timon to Caelus's house. Before Jason and Neferu came, they would share their observations about Zenobia.

She had focused her attention on her new guests, and she had found Timon especially entertaining. Lusario would likely tease him about that today. But she hadn't spoken to Jason or about him. It was as if he wasn't there.

Caelus sat at the table, and the others gathered around. "You all got a chance to see Zenobia and her sons last night. Your thoughts?"

Taurus fingered the handle of the dagger he always carried. "The three of you who ate with her the night before, you saw a veiled hostility toward the boy. Lusario described her as a cat swishing its tail before pouncing."

The snort that image triggered was almost a chuckle. Then he sobered. "But last night, I saw nothing of that cat. Only a few fleeting glances at her nephew, and each time she seemed surprisingly satisfied to have him there."

He tipped his head back and rubbed under his chin. "During my days on the sand, the one who was paired against you might be friendlier than usual before a bout. I've done it myself. It's to make your opponent like you enough that he doesn't want to kill you. But with even the slightest hesitation, the advantage shifts to the man who cares least whether his opponent lives or dies."

He crossed his arms. "Has anything happened that should make her like Jason more? Or something to make her think him less of a threat to her boy?"

Caelus leaned forward to rest his arms on the table. "Neferu has been praying since they first came here that Zenobia would accept Jason into the family. If she were here, she might say those prayers are beginning to be answered."

Sartorus gripped the back of the empty chair. "Sometimes God does answer our prayers by changing another person's heart. I've seen it myself. But it's not

379

wise to assume that's happening from one day's change. I'd advise staying cautious until you can talk with the grandfather."

"We will." Caelus's lips tightened. "And we'll have a few more dinners for you to watch for things Lusario and I might miss. We don't know for certain that it wasn't Karpos's idea to make the horse bolt. It's clear he hates Jason. So even if Zenobia is reconciling herself to her nephew being here, Jason might still be in danger."

The approach of a young boy's voice, answered by a woman's, ended their conversation.

Taurus forced his frown to relax as Jason came through the door, smiling at all of them. Experience warned that it was never safe to assume you knew another's mind. For as long as they stayed, he'd keep watching.

*The main house, early evening of Day 42*

Jason stood near Timon, waiting for his aunt to tell everyone where to sit. But he already knew it would be better than last night.

While they were riding that morning, Stephan told him that Karpos had fussed and fussed at breakfast about not having the best seat across from the man who knew all about daggers and swords and spears and hunting wild boars. And Aunt Zenobia always gave Karpos what he wanted.

But tonight, that made Jason smile. Taurus would sit beside him and Stephan opposite. No one would poke him or kick him during this dinner.

He watched the men who'd come looking for Caelus and Lusario. The Roman, Sartorus, smiled at him some, but he mostly ignored him.

Taurus was scary looking. He never said much, and he frowned a lot. But when he sharpened his dagger that morning, he told Jason to bring a piece of wood. Then he carved a rough version of a small donkey and promised to show him how to do it tomorrow. His lips didn't smile often. But his eyes did when he looked at Jason, and that was good enough. He even let Jason feel of his red hair that came from his Dacian father, or so he thought. His father had ignored him, too, like Patéras had.

But when he opened the trunk with the stable Gaidaros made and showed them Voskos's animals, it was Timon who sat on Lusario's bed and played with them like he did himself.

He would miss them all when they were gone.

When they left, would Lusario and Caelus go, too? He wiped the corner of each eye, then sniffed.

Karpos sidled over and poked his side. "Hey, donkey boy. See that box on the bench? It came for you from Koshari today. It's something for Mikro. Maybe you'll know what to do with it. Maybe not."

"From Koshari?"

Karpos shrugged. "That's what the delivery man said."

Jason strolled over to the bench, and his nasty cousin followed close behind.

His mouth twitched. Zenobia's spoiled son wanted to know what his friend had sent him. He probably wanted to break it. But whatever it was, he wouldn't let Karpos too close.

He picked up the box. It was made of rough wood and held shut by a hasp. He shook it, and maybe something moved inside.

He pulled the V-shaped pin out of the loop and lifted the slotted plate. As he tipped the lid back, he froze.

◆

A soft whimper turned Timon's head toward the small boy. Then the rustle of scale rubbing scale drew his gaze to the box in Jason's hands.

Jason stood as still as a statue, eyes locked on what lay inside. Then a scaly brown head with beady black eyes rose from within the box.

"Don't move." Timon inched toward the pair, slowly raising his hand so he could slam the lid shut and take the box from Jason.

But before he reached him, Jason tossed the box. It landed only inches from Karpos's sandals and only three feet from Timon. The viper stayed in the box and coiled. The rustling grew louder, and its head drew back as its neck made an S-curve.

It was ready to strike.

With the lid on the side closest to him, could he flip it closed fast enough to trap the viper inside?

"Don't move, Karpos. Don't make a sound." Ever-so-slowly, he bent over, his arm hanging down, his hand ready to flip the lid.

Almost there. The snake's gaze stayed fixed on the wild-eyed boy.

Then a blood-curdling scream burst out of the boy's mouth.

Timon stepped close enough to grab Karpos at his armpits and tossed him aside. The snake struck…and missed.

But it stayed in the box.

He stepped back and reached down to flip the lid closed. That should be safe with the snake facing away from him, still focused on Karpos.

But as he reached, it twisted and struck upward, piercing his hand. As it coiled to strike again, he flipped the lid closed and kicked the box away from Jason. Then he backed away, grabbing Jason's hand and dragging him with him.

The box hit the bench leg…and tipped sideways.

The viper wriggled free.

It headed for Karpos, who had stayed where Timon tossed him. The boy backed up and froze against the wall.

The viper coiled to strike.

◆

Screaming like a Germanic warrior, Zenobia flew past Timon and stepped on the snake, pinning it so it couldn't reach her son. She lifted him and hurled him four feet away.

But she'd stepped too far back from the head, and the snake drove its fangs into her calf. She stumbled back, but her boy was still too close. When it started toward him again, she grabbed its tail.

It sank its fangs into her arm. But before it let loose, her free hand grabbed it not far from the head. It twisted and thrashed, but as long as she held tight, the fangs couldn't reach her a third time.

Taurus charged past the others, slid his hand up her arm, and grabbed the snake right behind its skull. With dagger drawn, he dropped on one knee, pinned it against the stone floor, and cut off the head.

While the decapitated body writhed, he put the head in the box, dropped the slotted plate over the loop, and replaced the pin.

Caelus grabbed one of the dinner servers. "Send someone for Menmet. Have them take the cart and get her and Neferu back here as quickly as possible. Tell them a viper bit someone."

The servant ran from the room.

Zenobia stared at the blood on her arm, oozing freely from two fang marks. Her calf already throbbed with intense, spreading pain.

She'd traded jewels worth three year's wages for that carpet viper. It was supposed to kill with a single bite. But nothing had gone right since Theodoros's brat had come.

At least Karpos was safe…but she would die.

◆

Taurus rose to find Timon, ashen-faced, holding his wrist while he looked at his hand. Two rivulets of blood oozed out of the fang marks.

Tears streamed down Jason's cheeks. "Please, God, don't let him die."

Taurus went down on one knee and drew the boy into his arms. As the small boy shook with gasping sobs, he placed the hand that had ended the threat on the back of Jason's head. "Shhh. Everyone is safe now. I killed it."

His jaw clenched. He longed to tell Jason Timon would be all right. But he probably wouldn't be.

When Caelus started toward them, Jason pulled free and ran to him. "It's all my fault."

Caelus tipped Jason's chin up to look into his eye. "No, it isn't. It's whoever put the snake in the box so it would bite you."

"It got me." Timon clamped his jaw and closed his eyes. "What was it?"

"A viper. It got her twice." Taurus stood, took Timon's upper arm and guided him to a chair. "Maybe the old healer knows what to do."

Timon laid his oozing hand in his lap. "I should have read the part about snakebites in Celsus's *De Medicina*. But I never expected a viper would bite anyone I knew." He blew out a long, slow breath. "I do know Cleopatra killed herself with the bite of one."

He closed his eyes. His breathing turned slow and deep.

Taurus would bet anything his friend was asking his god to do something. Would that god listen and help if he asked as well? He hadn't prayed to any god for anything…ever, but if nothing else could save Timon…

*God of Timon, if you're real like he says you are, don't let him die.*

◆

Lusario joined the group standing around Timon. "Did it bite you?"

Timon offered a shaky smile. "It did." He held out his hand, and two thin streams of blood were oozing from a pair of fang marks. "I guess I won't get to see any of your designs become real buildings."

With one hand over his mouth, Lusario stared at the wound. Had Timon coming to find him killed his best friend?

"Why did you do that? Karpos is nothing to you."

"But he's precious in the eyes of God. I'm called to *agape*. Remember what Jesus said? There's no greater love than to die for another."

Lusario felt a lump grow in his throat. He'd almost lost Caelus, but Neferu had prayed. He couldn't lose Timon like this. Not when she had that kind of power.

He gripped Timon's upper arm. "But you're not going to die from this. I only studied the part of Celsus about climate, air, and water supply for picking a healthy building site. That's all Vitruvius said we'd need." He rested his hand on Timon's shoulder. "But I saw Jason and Neferu ask your god to stop Caelus dying. Maybe they can do that again. She should be here soon."

Sartorus placed his hand on Timon's other shoulder. "We don't have to wait for them. Any of us who believe can ask. It's the Holy Spirit who heals. I'm alive because He does. So, let's pray."

Caelus led Jason over and placed him in front of him with his hands on Jason's shoulders. "I want to join you, too. I just read where Jesus sent his apostles out to tell the world the good news about what he'd done, and he told them that poison and snake bites wouldn't hurt them while they did their job. Prayers in the name of Jesus saved me twice. I believe he's the Son of God, like he claimed, and I want to ask God to save Timon the same way."

He curled his fingers. "Taurus, come join us."

The ex-gladiator stood like a statue, shoulders squared, arms crossed. Then his shoulders relaxed, and he stepped forward to join the cluster of Christians around Timon.

Sartorus bowed his head. "God, we come before you to pray for the healing of our dear brother Timon. Undo any harm the venom has done. Stop it from doing any more. Send Your Holy Spirit upon him to heal him completely. In Jesus's name we pray."

The small boy's voice blended with those of the men as they all said "amen."

Lusario stepped back. He'd seen Caelus come back from the edge of death twice. If Timon survived a deadly viper's bite, that would make three times that God stopped death when His people prayed.

Caelus had made his decision, and he'd chosen Jesus as lord. Maybe it was time for him to do the same.

# Chapter 69

## Not Over Yet

Zenobia limped to the table and collapsed into her chair. Holding her bitten arm tight against her chest, she pulled up her tunic to look at the bite on her calf. Each bite already hurt more than anything she'd ever felt before, not just at the place where the fangs went in, but spreading out from it.

The venom was already doing to her what it should be doing to Jason.

Her handmaid scurried in and came to her side. "They said you were snakebit, Mistress. Someone has gone for Menmet. She'll know what to do."

Zenobia's snort was delicate, as her mother had taught her. The healer would know what to do for a snakebite, but the viper she bought was one of the most lethal. Whatever the old woman did, it wasn't likely to help.

She tipped her head back and closed her eyes. By all the gods of Greece and Egypt, let a curse be on that scrawny Greek who came looking for Lusario. If not for him, the fangs would have pierced Theodoros's brat, and he'd be the one screaming in pain before he died.

But at least the red-haired one killed the viper before it bit Karpos.

"It's all my fault." Jason's wail drew her gaze as he clung to Caelus.

It was.

She clenched her teeth, partly from pain, partly from bitter disappointment.

But when Karpos ran to her, she forced a weak smile and pushed the tunic off her lap to cover the fast-spreading purple around the bite marks.

Eyes wide with fear, he stared at her arm. "Are you going to be all right, Mother?"

She rested her unbitten hand on his cheek. "Menmet is coming. She's very good at healing people."

He slipped his arms around her and gave her a hug. What delighted her each morning was torture now. The pressure shot lightning bolts of pain through her injured arm, but she still drew him close with the other one.

Stephan had walked up behind him. "Can I do anything, Mother?"

She shook her head.

Eyes closed, she rested her cheek on Karpos's head. "I love you, precious. Never forget that."

His reply was muffled against her chest. "I know. I love you, too. I'm sorry I didn't do it just like you said. I'll do better next time."

Stephan's eyes saucered. He stared first at his brother, then at her. "You plan—"

"Silence. Don't you say anything to anyone." Venom coated her words as she glared at her older son.

He took a step back and said nothing.

His silence was disturbing. He should have said, "Yes, Mother," like he always did when she gave him an order. Her eyes shot arrows at that Greek tutor who'd started Stephan talking about honorable choices and speaking the truth.

A commotion in the courtyard was followed by Menmet entering the room with Jason's too-pretty tutor carrying a basket behind her.

"Go find two men to take Mistress Zenobia up to her chamber. Take some water to her room right away, and bring up some hot water as soon as you heat it."

"What is *she* doing here?" Zenobia's hiss stopped the tutor mid-stride. "Keep her away from me. Get her out of my house!"

"But I might be able to help with—"

Zenobia picked up her napkin and hurled it at the brat's tutor.

"Get her out of my sight!"

Menmet took the basket. "She won't come up with us. I can do this alone."

The door keeper and one of the gardeners appeared at the door.

"Let's get Mistress Zenobia up to her room so I can tend her." Menmet stepped back to give them room.

Zenobia scrunched her nose, then spat at Neferu. "I told you not to come here before. This hasn't changed anything."

As the men carried her out, she looked back at her boys. Karpos's shoulders drooped, and his chest jumped with each sob. Tears ran down his cheeks, and he didn't even try to flick them away.

Stephan stood behind him, his arms wrapped around his little brother, holding him close as she had done so many times. His gaze was fixed on the top of Karpos's head, and a single teardrop trickled down his cheek.

But when he raised his gaze to her, his mouth straightened, his chin rose. Then his lips tightened, and he slowly shook his head.

◆

Lusario spun at the feral cry behind him.

With the knife from a serving tray in his hand, Karpos charged toward Jason. He raised it to strike…

Taurus grabbed his arm and snatched the knife away.

"It's all your fault that Mother's hurt!" The hysterical cry of the heart-broken boy ended in tears. "If she dies, I'm going to kill you!"

Karpos ran from the room and up the stairs.

A fresh set of tears flowed down Jason's cheeks. "I didn't know there was a snake in there. I never meant to hurt her."

Stephan came over and squatted before Jason. "It's not your fault. Whoever put that snake in there tried to kill you. Mother wasn't expecting to get bit." He looked at Timon, then turned sad eyes on Lusario. "And she wasn't planning to hurt your friend." One teardrop started down his face, but he flicked it away. "She did it to herself. I'll help my brother see that, but it will take time. And when Father and Grandfather get home, I'll tell them why she died."

Lusario rested his hand on the boy's shoulder and squeezed. It wasn't time for words. "We can talk tomorrow."

Stephan gave him a tearful smile and followed his brother from the room. Lusario watched through the doorway as the grief-stricken youth slowly climbed the stairs and headed toward his mother's room for a final goodbye.

Caelus came to stand beside him. "He'll grow into a fine man, thanks to you. No one could have done better." Then he turned to Timon. "How are you feeling?"

With one finger, Timon pressed where the fangs went in. No swelling, no bruising, just two small holes that would close over soon. "If I didn't know I'd been snakebit, I'd never guess it. I wonder if I'll have a scar to show for it. That would impress the people back home." He looked up at Lusario and bounced his eyebrows. "When God wants to heal, He really heals."

Lusario rolled his eyes. "Go ahead, say it. You told me so. You think you finally won the argument. But you didn't. I'm the real winner." One corner of his mouth twitched. "And when a man finally admits the truth, it's time to act upon it."

He turned to face Caelus. "I'll join you in believing. What we've learned here has convinced us both. Where that will lead…" He shrugged. "But, as Timon has told me for years, God can work anything for good for those who love Him."

His eyes sought Neferu, who stood a few feet away with Jason wrapped in her arms. With eyes that glowed and a smile that lit up her whole face, she whispered amen.

*Early morning of Day 43*

Caelus lounged in the chair outside their cottage, holding a now-empty porridge bowl. Neferu had made breakfast for everyone and stayed to eat with them because Jason was there. Taurus and Sartorus had carried over the bench from under the tree so all could sit together.

Jason sat between Taurus and Timon. He normally scraped every last morsel from his breakfast bowl, but today more than half was left. He stirred it, loaded the spoon, and dumped it back into the bowl.

He chewed his lip. "What's Karpos going to do if Aunt Zenobia dies?"

Taurus slipped an arm around him. "Nothing with us here to protect you."

Jason leaned back to look up at the man who seemed like a giant beside him. "But you won't be here forever. What then?"

Taurus's jaw twitched, but the sound of cart wheels spared him from answering. Menmet was back, and that could only mean one thing.

"It's over." Menmet handed the basket of medicines to Sartorus when he helped her out of the cart. "It's never an easy end when a snake bites. You hurt all over, not just at the bite. With those two bites, she hurt worse than I've seen before. Then what she saw got blurry. At the end, her head hurt so bad she said she wanted to die. Before I could even mix up something to help, her eyes rolled back, and she was gone."

She wiped away a tear. "She wasn't always like you saw her. When she first married Horion and came here, she was a sweet young thing who didn't know how men could be. He was no worse than most until Karpos was born. With two healthy sons, he didn't need her anymore. She knew she meant nothing to him, so Karpos became everything to her." Another tear leaked out and dribbled down her cheek. "Theodoros was always the worst one. Horion at least loves his sons, but he didn't do right by her."

She sniffed and patted Timon's shoulder. "I'm so glad I didn't have to watch you go through that, too."

"Let me get you some porridge." Neferu took the basket from Sartorus and turned toward the cottage they shared.

Menmet shook her head. "I'm too tired to eat right now. I'll make myself something when I wake up." She took the basket back and headed for her cottage.

She'd taken three steps when she turned back. "I almost forgot. A message came from Akhom that Stephanos and Horion should be home today. It's a terrible thing to come home to." After a deep sigh, she walked away.

Caelus covered his mouth and squeezed his cheeks. Jason was right. They could keep him safe until they had to leave, but what then? Would Horion be as unhappy as Zenobia over a new grandson at the estate? How could Stephanos not like Jason more than Karpos? Any sane man should, but if he was like Theodoros, ashamed to claim a less-than-perfect heir, he might not.

And if neither one cared about Jason, would they try to stop Karpos from getting his revenge?

"Jason, would you like to stay with Lusario and me?"

Jason perked up. A smile started to form, then froze. His eyes narrowed. "Could Neferu stay with you, too?"

"Of course. She goes wherever you go." A glance at Neferu caught her nodding vigorously before she turned her eyes on Lusario. His friend's gaze locked with hers, and they shared a smile that revealed more than friendship. Then Lusario's ears turned red as he refocused on Caelus. A quick tip of his head approved the proposal.

"There's nothing I would like more." Jason's biggest grin faded. "But will Grandfather let me go with you?"

"I expect I can convince him it's the best possible choice for all involved."

Jason scooped up some porridge and slipped the spoon into his mouth. The bowl would soon be empty, as usual.

It was the perfect solution, if he could convince Stephanos to go along with it. He'd often watched his own father try to sway stubborn men to his way of thinking in the council chamber. Sometimes he lost, but most times he won. Father was a master of persuasion. It was a skill he would need himself someday.

But something more important than the running of a city depended on his success right now.

Jason's future hung in the balance. This was one time he couldn't afford to lose.

# Chapter 70

## A Future for Jason



*Main house, morning of Day 43*

Stephanos sat in the courtyard, eyes scrunched, rubbing his forehead. When he and Horion left for Alexandria a month and a half ago, he never expected to come home to find his daughter-in-law dead, a surprise grandson who'd been hidden from him for six years, and his eight-year-old grandson standing in front of him demanding that he be allowed to kill his new cousin for murdering his mother.

Akhom was supposed to take care of everything in his absence. He'd seen his trustworthy steward two days ago at his northernmost farm near Aphroditopolis. Everything had been fine when Akhom started his tour of the outlying farms ten days ago. A wealthy young Roman and his Greek friend were his unexpected guests while the Roman's broken leg healed. But Akhom considered them fine men, and the Greek had turned Stephan into an eager student. That was a wonder in itself. Akhom wasn't one to give praise too freely, but he spoke well of Jason, too.

Karpos stamped his foot. "I don't know why you're not doing something. Jason turned the viper loose, and it killed Mother. I told him I'd kill him if she died. It's only fair."

The boy's normal voice was irritating enough, but this yelling and whining… Stephanos glared at Horion, who sat beside him. His son only shrugged.

"Grandfather." Stephan stood on the balcony by the study room. "May I say something about this?"

Stephanos summoned him with a curl of his fingers. "Come speak."

When the youth stood before him, he cleared his throat. "Jason didn't kill Mother. She tried to kill him. She put the viper in the box, Karpos gave it to him, and he opened it. But a friend who came looking for Lusario and Caelus knocked the box out of Jason's hands. Then the snake went for Karpos, and

Mother sacrificed herself to save him." He glanced at his father. "You could say Mother accidentally killed herself."

Karpos slugged his brother, but Stephan only winced and stepped away from him. "There's nothing wrong with Jason except a milky eye. You'll like him when you get to know him. I do, and none of what happened is his fault."

"That's all I want to hear about this for now. I'll decide what's appropriate." Stephanos pointed his finger at Karpos. "And don't you dare try to kill your cousin until I say you can do it." He flicked his hand. "Now go, both of you."

Karpos smirked at Stephan before tromping into the kitchen.

Stephan's gaze followed his brother. "Yes, Grandfather." Then he tipped his head and went back upstairs.

Stephanos stood. Stephan's version was probably the true one. He couldn't let Karpos kill Jason even if it wasn't. Maybe he should just send the boy back to Theodoros. But if his son had lied for six years about Jason's existence, was that the best thing to do?

"I'll deal with this later. Let's go for a ride."

*Midmorning of Day 43*

Caelus sat on the bench, watching Jason with Mikro. On the day Jason's aunt died, it might seem disrespectful to do everything as usual, so Neferu wasn't tutoring today. Lusario hadn't gone to teach Stephan either.

But Caelus did send Taurus to the main house with his request for an audience with Stephanos. He would start by offering condolences, then move to the real purpose of his visit.

But why was it taking Taurus so long to return?

The creak of cart wheels was his answer. Stephanos had agreed and even sent the cart for him.

When they reached the main house, Taurus helped him out of the cart and walked beside him. The doorkeeper took them into the reception room, which was across the courtyard from the room where the viper had delivered its death sentence to Zenobia. Stephanos was alone at his desk, looking over estate records.

Caelus placed his hand over his heart. "*Salve.*" Nervousness brought out his Latin. He switched into Greek. "I'm Caelus Publilius Martinus. First, I want to offer my condolences on the death of your daughter-in-law."

Stephanos nodded his acceptance. "Thank you. A most unpleasant way to die. She will be missed by many."

The lack of feeling in Stephanos's words would have raised Caelus's eyebrows if he hadn't already donned a mask to conceal his thoughts.

"I also want to thank you for the gracious hospitality your steward has shown my partner, Lusario of Alexandria, and me. We have been here for three weeks while my leg heals."

Stephanos nodded toward Taurus. "Is this the man who fought a crocodile for you? No wonder he won."

Caelus chuckled, and it made one corner of Stephanos's mouth turn up. "No. That was Lusario. He'll be here tomorrow morning to tutor Stephan. He doesn't look at all like a croc fighter. Taurus is one of our family bodyguards. He came with my father's friend to look for us when we didn't return to Carthago as expected."

Stephanos leaned back in his chair. "Akhom spoke of Lusario's excellence as a tutor. You're both most welcome to stay until your leg is healed." He clasped his hands on his desk. "So, why did you want to speak with me today? Your man made it sound like a matter of some urgency."

"It might be." Caelus shifted his weight onto the crutch, then back to his good leg, but Stephanos didn't invite him to sit. "Your grandson Jason is very concerned that his cousin has sworn to kill him for killing his mother. I'm sure you don't approve of that, but as long as Jason remains here, it's impossible to be sure it won't happen anyway."

Caelus glanced away, then trained his gaze on Stephanos again. "Of course, Jason wasn't responsible. But grief and hatred can make grown men do things they know they shouldn't. With the irrational hatred Karpos bears for Jason…" He tightened his lips and shook his head. "With a child, I would expect desire to become deed. I don't want to see that. I'm sure you don't either."

Stephanos picked up a stylus and drummed on the desktop. "Stephan told us what really happened. I've ordered Karpos not to kill his cousin."

"But even the greatest respect for an honored grandfather or father might not stop a grieving child. And what if you aren't here to control him?"

Stephanos leaned back in his chair, his eyes unreadable.

"Karpos gave Jason the box that held the snake. Did you know that wasn't the first time he tried to kill his cousin?"

Stephanos straightened, and his eyes narrowed. "What did he do before?"

"Jason has only started riding here because his father wouldn't let him. Karpos tried to kill Jason by making his horse bolt the first time he rode. Only Lusario's superb horsemanship and quick action saved him."

"I hadn't heard of that."

"Stephan can tell you about it. He's planning to ask you to let Lusario teach him to jump walls and ride a horse running full out."

"He'll get a no from me." A wry smile curved Stephanos's mouth.

"As would my son if I had one. Death can take us too easily." He shrugged. "I never thought a boat pilot would try to murder me or a croc would grab my leg to make me a meal. But none of us knows when our lives will end. If something happens to you before Jason is grown, what will happen to him?"

Stephanos leaned back in his chair. But he said nothing, so Caelus forged ahead.

"I'm sure Horion knows Jason wasn't at fault. Like you, he knows Zenobia's hatred for the boy made her get the viper that caused her own death. But might he blame Jason for making her do it to protect Karpos's place as your heir? Might he share her concern?"

"He doesn't need to. My sons will inherit equally."

"But Theodoros's sons won't. He sent Jason to you when Menander was born because he doesn't want him. He'd even let you think he died as a baby. You didn't even know Jason existed until you got the letter from Akhom, so no one expects you to be fond of him yet. But I'm sure you don't want his cousin lying in wait to kill him, especially if he succeeds. The scandal that would cause…your imagination is as good as mine for how that would go."

Stephanos's jaw clenched.

It was time to switch from describing the problem to offering the solution.

"But I can keep that from ever happening. I'll gladly take Jason with me to train him to be an architect like we are. He owns Neferu's bondservant contract, so she'll keep caring for him and educating him. Lusario tutored elite Greek youths before we studied together in Alexandria. You can see from Stephan what a fine job he does. We'll make certain Jason receives a superior education, like I did as a youth and young man, and we'll train him in a skill with which he can make his own living when the time comes."

He shifted his weight to the crutch, then back to his good leg. Taurus took a step toward him but stopped when Caelus raised his hand. His own father would never have made an injured man stand so long. But whatever it took, he'd do it for Jason.

"He's already showing unusual talent as an artist, and with our training, he'll become highly sought after."

Stephanos fingered the corners of his mouth. "What would people think if they learned I let strangers take away one of my grandsons? Theodoros's wife did trick me into naming him so he couldn't be exposed. Disposing of a defective baby is normal, but it would be a disgrace to cast off a boy of his age that way."

Caelus raised one finger, like his father did in council to focus his audience. "But you wouldn't be casting him off. You would be letting him come with us as an apprentice to learn a valuable trade that is well respected. For a good architect, there's much honor associated with it. For the most successful, even fame. The day might come when people speak the praises of Jason of Alexandria, grandson of Stephanos of Thmoinepsi, as one of the finest architects in Egypt and Africa Proconsularis."

The tilt of Stephanos's head declared him almost ready to agree. Fame and respect of the elite were important to him, even if Jason's happiness might not be.

"He'll be spending time in Carthago as well, where my father is on the city council and will soon be duumvir, as my grandfather and great-grandfather were before him. One of our ancestors was even governor of the province."

"Hmm."

Stephanos's nod gave him hope. Success was now within reach.

"Normally you would pay us for taking him, but due to his youth and our fondness for the boy, we'll train him as an artist for free and provide room, board, and living expenses for him and his tutor. When he's old enough, we'll train him as an architect as well."

Stephanos's eyes narrowed. "Others would wonder why I'm not paying you, as is customary."

Caelus kept his surprise from showing. Most wanted something for free when they could get it. "You may pay me, if you wish, and I'll set it aside for Jason's use when he's older. But given his father's hostility toward him, the contract should assign him completely to our custody, not his father or uncle, in the event of your death."

Caelus moved to the edge of the desk and offered his arm. "Are we agreed?"

Stephanos hesitated, then gripped his forearm. "Agreed."

"Lusario will go with Sartorus to Thmoinepsi and get the proper paperwork prepared. After we both sign it, they will file it to make it official."

He stepped back, and Taurus moved up beside him. "Until later."

Stephanos nodded and turned his eyes back on his accounts.

When they were in the courtyard and out of Stephanos's sight, Caelus punched Taurus's arm. "We did it. Jason is ours."

Taurus's grin was almost as big as his own.

*Neferu's cottage, Day 45*

Caelus sat at the table, working on his copy of Neferu's codex. Since she would be coming with them, he'd always have access to the original. But he still wanted his own.

Lusario appeared in the doorway, but only half of him. Then he stepped inside.

"Ta-da!"

Their dioptra, as shiny as it had been when they packed it in Alexandria, rested in his hands.

"You got the trunk back." A grin split Caelus's face as he slapped the tabletop with both hands.

"You should have seen us." Lusario's grin was a big as his own. "Dareios hired several small boats that lowered nets around where Temhotep's boat sank to keep a croc from approaching underwater. He had someone drop a couple of carcasses a little downstream to draw all the crocs away. Then while someone stood on each boat with a spear to make sure no stragglers came over, someone slipped into the water, dove, and hooked onto the trunk handles. After he was back aboard, they just pulled the trunk up."

He looked back over his shoulder. "We have the trunk out here. Sartorus said it's too wet and slimy to come inside."

After placing the dioptra on the table, he got Caelus's crutch. "Come see what we recovered."

Outside, Taurus knelt by the trunk and held up the first treasure.

Lusario raised it over his head as if it were a trophy. "The wax tablet from Latro telling his steward to host us and give us everything we need."

Next came the portfolio of their drawings. Lusario took one out and handed it to Caelus. "I'm surprised the ink stayed in place as well as it did. We'll be able to redraw most of them."

Taurus tossed him a leather sack.

"Coins don't mind a soaking at all."

He handed it back to Taurus. "The only thing we lost was the rope. After soaking so long, it won't be calibrated anymore. But we can get another in Heracleopolis."

A satisfied sigh summed up all Caelus was feeling. "So, we can go on to the Latro estate as soon as I can travel."

Sartorus rubbed his lip. "We can stay a few more days and help you get there. Dareios's boat is full with just the three of us, but we'll hire a boat in Thmoinepsi for the four of you. After we get you settled at the Latro estate, we'll go back downriver, then home to your father with any messages you want to send."

"The four of us and Mikro." Lusario waved his hands above his head like two donkey ears. "Jason would never agree to leave him behind."

Caelus rubbed behind his ear. When the boat sank, he had thought the trunk and its contents were lost forever. But with a little cleaning and some time to dry, it might be useful again. Or at least the brass parts could be used to make another. The plate with Grandfather's name was as bright as ever, and Father would be pleased if he kept using it.

"First, I need to write a message for Fundanus to pass on to his aunt and uncle. We should be able to go downriver in three weeks or so with all the drawings Tranquilla will want to see. Then she can make her choices of what we'll build."

"I can take anything you want to him and send back anything you might need." Timon straightened from where he leaned against the wall. He touched the two marks on his hand. "I'll have quite a story to share when I get home." He patted the scar on his leg. "Two more marks that prove I serve a God of miracles."

Caelus's gaze moved from Sartorus to Taurus to Timon. "I thank you all for coming upriver to find me. And I thank God for everything that's happened that led me to Him."

Lusario moved over beside Timon. "That led us both to Him." He placed his hand on Timon's shoulder. "As my wisest friend often says, God can work all things for good for those who love Him."

# Chapter 71

EPILOGUE

*The Latro estate near Heracleopolis, three months later.*

Lusario sat at the table outside the cottage where Neferu and Jason lived. He and Caelus had rooms in the main house, but Jason wanted to be close to Mikro. The wee donkey wasn't so small anymore. Jason had started weaning him, but it would be a few more weeks before he no longer gave the foal any milk. Latro's steward already had him helping the estate's donkey wrangler, and the boy was loving it.

Neferu had lunch ready inside, and Caelus was late. A man got hungry when he was working, and directing the construction site for the villa kept them both busy. But Neferu insisted it was only polite to wait until Caelus arrived to eat.

"Lusario." Caelus's voice came from behind him.

When he turned, his head drew back. Standing beside Caelus was Taurus, and they both had a strange smile.

"Taurus brought me some letters from Carthago." From a satchel slung on Taurus's shoulder, Caelus lifted out a bundle of papyri.

He began sorting them. "One from Father, two from Mother, one from Martina, and another from Sartorus. Father sent me a gift as well."

He peered at the next in the stack. "This one doesn't seem to be for me."

He handed it to Lusario.

It was sealed with wax that bore Volero's seal. He slid his finger under the flap and lifted. The wax broke in two, and he opened the sheet.

> *This is to inform all concerned that Lusario of Alexandria, slave of Volero Publilius Martinus, aged twenty-six years, has been manumitted in Carthago, Africa Proconsularis. As he will be my agent operating the Martinus Architecture and Construction firm, the special exception has been made to grant citizenship to a man under thirty years of age.*

*Henceforth, he will be known as Volero Publilius Lusario.*

Below those words, Volero had signed and marked more wax with his signet ring.

Lusario froze and stared at it. Free and a citizen. Caelus had said it would happen someday. But to have this document in his hand—he tipped his head back and looked up to heaven.

*Thank You, God.*

As soon as he told Neferu, he could ask Jason to cancel her contract, making her a free woman again. Then they could marry and raise Jason together. It wouldn't be official until Stephanos died, but Jason would be their son in every way that mattered, even though he still belonged to Stephanos under Egyptian law.

Caelus slapped his arm. "It's official, partner. We're going to do great things together."

"We will." Lusario fought to control the grin, but it broke free anyway. "It's good to see you, Taurus. How long can you stay?"

"I told you Taurus brought a gift from Father." Palm up, Caelus held his hand out toward their friend. "He asked Taurus if he would like to join us here for good, and he said he couldn't think of anything better to do. Father thought being an architect was much more dangerous than any of us anticipated. You and I might be getting into trouble again, and Taurus would be the perfect man to get us out of it."

"Is that Caelus I hear?" Neferu stepped through the doorway. "Taurus! What a delightful surprise."

"Lusario has an even better surprise for you." Caelus poked Lusario in the side. "Why don't you two go for a walk so he can tell you? We can serve ourselves. We might even leave enough for you, but Taurus is a big man. So, I won't guarantee that."

Lusario offered one hand to her, still holding the letter in the other. "Let's go around back. I have something to show you, and they don't need to be watching."

She placed her hand in his, and they strolled behind the house.

He handed her the letter, and she started to read. With each line, her smile grew bigger. She bounced on her toes as she finished, then folded it carefully and clutched it to her chest.

"This is wonderful. It's all you ever wanted."

"Not quite all." He moved a loose strand of hair behind her ear. "Neferu of Arsinoe, now that I'm free to ask, will you become my wife?"

"Oh, yes." She stroked his cheek with her thumb. "There's nothing on this earth that I want more. For now and for eternity, we'll be together. We've been so blessed by God."

He drew her into his arms, and the letter fluttered to the ground as she wrapped hers around him. His lips lowered to hers, and the promise of love in a future together was sealed by their first kiss.

Blessed by God. There was no better way to describe what he was.

For years he'd resisted, but God had been patient. Timon never gave up trying to convince him, and Neferu had explained so much more. But after seeing God's power as He answered their prayers…how could he not believe?

He'd experienced the love of God, received forgiveness through Jesus, and felt the power of the Holy Spirit.

Any man of honor, whether slave or free, must yield to the truth once he saw it. He had seen the truth, and the truth had set him free.

# Finis

### I'D LOVE TO HEAR FROM YOU!

If you enjoyed this book, it would be a real gift to me if you would post a review at the retailer you purchased it from. A good review is like a jewel set in gold for an author. Other great places to share reviews are Goodreads and BookBub. If you've read others in the series, it would be great if you post a review of those, too.

I'd also love to hear from you at carol-ashby.com
or directly at carolashbyauthor@gmail.com.

If you're wondering how Lusario and Caelus came to be such good friends, you'll love their backstory in my novella, *Crushed Hopes and Hopeful Beginnings*. It takes place three years before *River of Life*, and it's available in ebook, paperback, and hardcover at Amazon and many other online book sellers.

**Want to hear about what I'm working on next,
upcoming releases in the Light in the Empire series,
and free gifts only for newsletter subscribers?**

For free gifts and other special offers, advance notices of upcoming releases, and info about my latest writing adventures, please sign up for my newsletter at https://carol-ashby.com/newsletter/

# Light *in the* Empire Series

***Dangerous times, difficult friendships,
lives transformed by forgiveness and love.***

*River of Life* is the fourteenth volume in the Light in the Empire series, which follows the interconnected lives of several Roman families during the reigns of Trajan and Hadrian. Each can be read stand-alone. The novels of the series will take you around the Empire, from Germania and Britannia to Thracia, Dacia, North Africa, Egypt, Judaea, and, of course, to Rome itself.

Although each can be read stand-alone, here are some groupings based on the appearance of some characters in more than one story.

Drusus family: *The Legacy, True Freedom, Second Chances, Forgiven*

Lentulus family: *Blind Ambition, Faithful*

Crassus family: *Blind Ambition, Faithful, Honor Bound*

Sabinus family: *The Legacy, Honor Bound, More Than Honor, What Matters Most*

Glabrio family: *What Matters Most, Truth and Honor, River of Life*

Martinus family: *Truth and Honor, Crushed Hopes and Hopeful Beginnings, River of Life*

Titianus family: *True Freedom, More Than Honor, What Matters Most, Truth and Honor*

Brutus family: *Faithful, True Freedom, Honor Bound*

The Dacians: *Hope Unchained, Hope's Reward, True Freedom*

For more relationships based on time, location, and the people involved, visit https://carolashby.com/novel-relationships/

### Coming in in 2025: Please Help Me Choose!
### Who would you like to see in a future story?

I grew to love several of the characters in *River of Life* while I was writing. That usually happens, and sometimes a future story takes shape in my head even before I finish. But more often the next hero or heroine is chosen because readers tell me who needs to come back as a story lead.

Readers who loved Galen as a teen in *Blind Ambition* wanted to see him as a grown man, so he became the hero in *Faithful*. People who asked for Brutus and Africanus to have their own story found out what happened to them in *Honor Bound*.

Since people kept asking what happened to Leander's beloved but long-lost sister in *True Freedom*, it was clear Ariana would need her own story in *Hope Unchained*. People who met Ursus in *Hope Unchained* asked what happened to him, so he returned with his childhood name of Matti in his quest to know God better in *Hope's Reward*.

In *What Matters Most*, Septimus, who was rather like a Great Dane puppy in *Honor Bound*, comes back four years older, and Tribune Titianus from *More Than Honor* and *True Freedom* faces the most dangerous assignment of his life. I'm SO glad people asked for still more of them after the earlier books.

For those of you who asked for more of the Martinus family, I hope you've enjoyed their story in this book.

But there are many more characters in the books of the series that I would like to spend more time with, and I hope there are some for you, too. Who would you most like to see in a future story? What was it about them that made you want more of them? I'd love to hear what you think. It will guide what I write next.

Some possibilities:

Aulus of *True Freedom?*

Septimus or Manius of *Honor Bound, More Than Honor,* and *What Matters Most?*

Someone else I haven't mentioned? (I can't wait to see who shows up here!)

Please tell me who you'd love to see again as a comment at carol-ashby.com or directly at carolashbyauthor@gmail.com!

I'm thinking about writing a short story or novella about someone from Sextus's or Calvia's households in *Honor Bound* or Gracchus's household in *Hope Unchained* and *Hope's Reward* to give to newsletter subscribers. Which would you rather have?

Please go to my website, carol-ashby.com, and share your thoughts in the comment box. Sign up for the newsletter, and you'll get the story when I finish it. Looking forward to hearing from you!

## SOCIAL CLASSES IN ROMAN EGYPT

The social class of persons living under Roman rule determined so many aspects of their lives. The Roman citizen (*civis*) was at the top, but there were different orders within that group. Senators and equestrians made up the noble orders, and they were treated differently under Roman law than ordinary citizens. If convicted of a crime, their punishment was usually milder. Special restrictions applied as well, such as forbidding a senator's daughter to marry someone not of the noble orders.

The free noncitizens were called peregrines. Even if a peregrine (*peregrinus*) was extremely wealthy, they still didn't have the legal protections and privileges conferred by citizenship, even when the citizen was poor. The importance of this was especially clear in criminal cases. Whereas a peregrine might be crucified, a citizen would be beheaded.

Slaves were legally classified as living thing (*res mortales*) and treated as mere property. But if a male slave who was at least thirty was freed by a Roman citizen who was at least twenty, the freedman became a citizen with limited political rights. That freedman's son had full rights and might even become emperor, like Pertinax did in AD 193.

While the class structure in most of the Roman world was fairly constant regardless of the province, Egypt was a different matter.

In 30 BC, Octavian (soon to be made Augustus by the Roman Senate) defeated Mark Anthony and Cleopatra VII (the last Ptolemy who was pharaoh). When he took possession of Egypt, he didn't make it a regular Roman province. Many of the policies and the political organization of the Ptolemies were left in place but modified as Augustus saw fit. The changes did not improve life for the non-Roman people of a county whose final ruler had caused so much trouble for their new emperor.

Because Egypt provided a third of the grain that fed Rome, Augustus made Egypt the personal property of the emperor. To keep any political rival with imperial ambitions from gaining control over Egyptian wheat, no senator could enter the province without asking and receiving permission from the emperor. Equestrians who were important public figures needed the same permission. Whereas other Roman provinces had members of the senatorial order as their governors (proconsuls), the governor of Egypt was always an equestrian who was chosen by the emperor. He served only as long as the emperor wanted him there, and he was only a prefect, not a proconsul.

The *praefectus Aegypti* usually served one to three years, occasionally as long as four or five. He and the other main Roman officials lived and worked in Alexandria. Each year, he traveled the province with some of his officials for four or five months. He would travel to one town in the Delta and another farther up the Nile to hold court and review local administration and finances. Egyptians viewed the Prefect of Egypt as a viceroy representing their pharaoh, the emperor who lived in Rome.

The Roman military presence included two legions made up of citizens and a mix of auxiliary units of noncitizens with Roman officers, with a total force up to 18,000 men. Garrisons of infantry and calvary were spread through the province, and a fleet based in Alexandria provided escort for the grain ships, patrolled the coast, and policed the Nile. Legionaries served for twenty-five years, and many chose to remain in Egypt upon retirement.

Most Roman citizens in Egypt were retired military and their descendants. Legionaries were well paid, and they often invested in businesses or lent money at interest while serving. The hefty retirement bonus allowed most to become well-to-do and buy land upon retiring. The local Egyptians did not always view retired military men as welcome additions to their communities, partly because they were exempt from many of the taxes and unpaid civic service required of Egyptians. But part of it was the attitude of superiority that being a Roman citizen encouraged.

Visiting Egypt as a tourist was popular among wealthy Romans. Like today, wealthy tourists might be welcomed for the money they spend while being thought arrogant in their treatment of the locals. The Pharos lighthouse in Alexandria and the Great Pyramids near present-day Giza were considered two of the Seven Wonders of the World, and Roman tourists visited them often during the Late Republic and Empire.

To understand the class structure under Roman rule, it is helpful to consider what it replaced. The Ptolemies were the dynasty of Greek pharaohs who ruled for three hundred years after Alexander the Great of Macedon conquered the Persian rulers. When Rome took over, some of the old ways were left in place, but others changed.

Before becoming a Roman colony, Egypt had been ruled by Macedonian Greeks. The first Greek pharaoh was Ptolemy I Soter, one of Alexander's four top generals who divided his empire after his death. The Ptolemies considered themselves Greeks, not Egyptians, and having Greek ancestry brought advantages that were not given to native Egyptians, even the wealthy ones.

The citizens of three great cities (*poleis*) had special privileges. Each *polis* retained the social and political structure of a Greek city-state even into Roman times.

Naucratis was a Greek trading city built on the Canopic branch of the Nile in the 7th century BC. An older Egyptian town became a military post for Greek mercenaries who fought for Pharaoh Psamtik. The pharaoh gave them land there as a reward, and it was the most important and only official Greek trading city in Ancient Egypt. Alexandria was built by Alexander to be his new capital of all Egypt after defeating the Persians who ruled it. The third was Ptolemais, built by Ptolemy I, the first Macedonian Pharaoh. Emperor Hadrian added a fourth (Antinoopolis) in AD 130.

Greek citizens of these cities were the Urban Greeks. Rome gave them special privileges such as exemption from mandatory unpaid civic service and some taxes. Many owned land far from their city. A citizen of one of these cities could join a Roman legion, becoming a Roman citizen as soon as he enlisted. Other Egyptian Greeks could only join an auxiliary and only became Roman citizens after serving their twenty-five years.

Egypt under the Ptolemies was divided into thirty nomes, each with a capital city (*metropolis*). These were the country towns with up to a few ten thousand people. Greeks in these cities were metropolites. They were proud of their Greek ancestry, considering themselves above their neighbors of Egyptian descent, and they modeled their society, both social and political, on that of a *polis*. Ptolemaic nome governors (*strategoi*) had both military and administrative duties, but Rome stripped them of any military roles. Each was appointed by the Roman prefect.

The biggest change that came with Roman rule was the demotion of the Greek population outside of the four major cities to the status of "Egyptians." But among themselves, they continued to stress their Greek heritage and to look down upon ethnic Egyptians.

The final distinct social class was the Jews. Records of Jews living in Egypt date back to the 6th century BC. Under the Persian Pharaohs, a Jewish military unit guarded the southern border of Egypt at the First Cataract of the Nile near present-day Aswan. On a nearby island at Elephantine, there was a temple to Yahweh.

The Ptolemies allowed the Jews, who had spread throughout Egypt, to practice their religion unhindered. Many Jews settled in Alexandria, and one of the five city districts was entirely Jewish. The Jews supported Augustus, and he continued the favorable policies of the Ptolemies, even allowing them to have a council of elders while refusing to let the Alexandrian Greeks have a city council. Hostility between Jews and Greeks in Alexandria led to bloody confrontations in AD 38 and appeals to the emperor. Caligula ordered them to peacefully accept the status quo.

Even though the Egyptian Jews remained loyal to Rome during the First Jewish War, when the temple in Jerusalem was destroyed, the Jewish temple in Elephantine was stripped and demolished so it wouldn't replace the destroyed one. The old temple tax that supported the Jerusalem temple was quadrupled and dedicated to the Roman god Jupiter. But the Jews were allowed to keep following their religion's laws.

The tolerance of Rome ended during the Jewish Uprising of AD 115-117, where several hundred thousand Greeks and Romans were killed by Jewish mobs in Cyrene, Cyprus, and Egypt. The population of Jews in Alexandria was killed or fled. From the Delta to Thebes, battles of Roman auxiliaries and legions with Jewish guerillas raged until AD 117. All Jewish property was seized and became the property of the state, and surviving Jews were exiled. What had been the Jewish Quarter in Alexandria was no more.

The Roman government combined all people who weren't Roman citizens, citizens of the four Greek cities, or a Jew in to the category "Egyptian." Many former distinctions between Greeks and ethnic Egyptians were maintained by the local populations, but to Rome, they were all only "Egyptians."

River of Life takes place twelve years after the Uprising, and the Roman-style town house where Caelus Martinus and Lusario live is in the area east of the Great Library that used to be the Jewish Quarter of Alexandria. In the Faiyum region upriver from Alexandria, the wealthy Greek Stephanos and his sons worship Greek gods and consider themselves superior to the ethnic Egyptians who live around them. The ethnic Egyptian Neferu, who once worshiped the Egyptian gods, has become a Christian after learning about Jesus from a Greek woman and her husband who are spreading the gospel along the Nile.

If you'd like to learn more about what it was like to live in the Roman Empire, please visit my Roman history website, Life in the Roman Empire: Historical Fact and Fiction at https://carolashby.com. There are lots of articles there about different topics, including some specifically about living as a Christian under Roman rule.

1) As a child, Neferu followed her father's lead and worshiped the Egyptian gods. Why was she ready to leave her childhood faith when Phoebe told her about Jesus? Why do you think she gave up everything to stay faithful? How did her choice affect others? Do you know someone who had to choose between a safe life and their faith? What did they decide?

2) It was common for Greeks and Romans at the time of this story to abandon babies with physical defects. Why wasn't that Jason's fate? What strengthened him against the cruelty of his father? How did Neferu help him after his greatest loss? Why did he care what she believed? Have you had the opportunity to help someone through a terrible loss?

3) Caelus Martinus is the only son of a wealthy Roman who helps run Carthago, and Caelus is expected to follow in his father's footsteps. Lusario is his father's slave, bought to be Caelus's valet while he studies in Alexandria. In the intensely class-conscious Roman society, how did they come to be such close friends? Have you ever had a close friendship with someone from a very different background? What made that possible?

4) When they started their trip up the Nile, Caelus and Lusario both agreed with the philosopher Seneca that thinking any god was real was foolishness. Have you known someone like them? How did they react to you if they knew you were a Christian? Did they ever ask you a question about your faith? What happened?

5) Timon had tried to share his faith with Lusario many times, and he'd been uninterested. Why? What made him listen to what Neferu told him? What struggles did he face as he considered what he had believed versus what Timon and Neferu believed? Have you or someone you know faced the same struggles?

6) Temhotep started out content to earn the passage money taking two young men upriver. What started him disliking Caelus? What made it worse? Why did he let his ruthless helmsman convince him to act on that animosity? Have you ever had to deal with a person who wanted to harm you? What did you do?

7) Taurus started out thinking genuine belief in a god was for women, not strong, successful men like Volero Martinus and his father. What happened after he

learned some of the people he liked and admired were also Christians? How have the beliefs of the people you admire affected your own beliefs? How have you affected others?

8) Timon had explained agape love to Lusario more than once. What choice did it lead Timon to make? What effect did it have on Lusario? On Taurus?

9) Zenobia didn't want Jason or Neferu at the estate. Why? How would you describe her relationship with her sons? Did you expect that to lead where it did? Have you known someone like her? How did you deal with them?

10) At the end, Caelus expected his father to grant his requests about staying in Egypt and about Lusario. But he waited to tell his father about his new faith so his father would do what he asked. What did he think might happen when his father found out? Was he right to wait or should he have told his father right away? Have you ever been in a situation where what you believed was the right choice threatened relationships with family and closest friends? How did you handle that?

11) *River of Life* is a story of unlikely friendships, of friendship opening the door for sharing one's faith, of reluctance to consider what would threaten a person's chosen path, and of courage to accept the truth and whatever that brings. What touched you most? What made you think about what your own choices would be?

I'd love to hear your thoughts about *River of Life*. Please go to Contact Carol at carol-ashby.com (my author website) and share your thoughts in the comment box. Or email me directly at carolashbyauthor@gmail.com. While you're there, please sign up for my newsletter to hear more about what I'm writing and what I'm learning with my research and to hear about new releases and special offers. Thanks!

# Glossary

*agape*: unconditional love, the love that's a decision, not an emotion

andron: room reserved only for men, used for business and entertaining, the formal dining room

bondslave: indentured servant who serves as a slave for a fixed time defined in a contract

chiton: a floor-length tunic style worn by Greek women

*corbita*: merchant ship, typical size 90 feet long, 25 feet wide with one large sail midship and a second small angled sail in the bow

*decempeda*: a 10-foot measuring rod used in building construction

Demotic script: a phonetic alphabetic script used to write Egyptian words

*dioptra*: a classical astronomical and surveying instrument

*domina*: female head of a Roman household

*familia*: the Roman family unit consisting of the paterfamilias, his married and unmarried children regardless of age, his son's children, and his slaves

fuller: person or business doing laundry

*gladius*: pl. *gladii*; the standard Roman military short sword.

*hesyu*: people pulled into the river by a crocodile, "the blessed drowned ones"

hip-bath: a tub sized for sitting while an attendant poured water over the bather

himation: rectangular cloak that passed under the left arm and secured at the right shoulder

*idu*: Egyptian for boy

Iliad: Homer's epic poem about the Trojan war

*lanista*: the head trainer of a gladiator school

*ludus*: training school for gladiators

*ma'at*: the ethical and moral principle that required all Egyptian citizens to act with truth and honor in all aspects of their lives. Cosmic harmony was achieved by correct public and ritual life. Anything that disturbed cosmic harmony could lead to harm of both the individual and the state. Egyptians were to seek truth, balance, order, harmony, law, morality, and justice. The opposite of ma'at was chaos.

metropolis: class of city in Egypt, capitals of the nomes

metropolite: Greek-ancestry residents of an Egyptian metropolis

*mitéra*: Greek for mother or mama

mortuary temple: place for worship of deceased pharaoh where priests made daily food offerings to the dead; usually adjacent to pyramid or rock-cut tomb necropolis: a large, designed cemetery with elaborate tomb monuments like pyramids and mortuary temples

nome: administrative division of Egypt, 22 in Upper Egypt, 20 in Lower Egypt

*patéras*: Greek for father

*paterfamilias*: Oldest living male of an extended Roman family, the patriarch who owns everything

peristyle: a space within a building, such as a court or internal garden, surrounded by a row of columns

*Salve*: hello, the standard greeting in Latin

*taberna*: tavern or shop selling prepared food

*tablinum*: reception room and main office for the master of a Roman house

*tholos*: the round room of a Greek-style public bath with hip-baths along its walls

*triclinium*: dining room with couches for reclining while eating

*Vale*: Goodbye, standard Latin farewell

*wab* priest: priest who maintained the cult temple and only performed rituals outside the inner sanctuary

# *References from Scripture and Ancient Literature*

**A comment about capitalization of the words used for God**

Some Bible translations capitalize all the pronouns referring to God, with pronouns for God the Father, Jesus as God the Son, and the Holy Spirit all being capitalized. Other Bible translations don't capitalize any of the pronouns referring to God.

I usually capitalize when it's a believer speaking or thinking and don't capitalize when it's someone who doesn't believe in God. I did that in this story. But I also found that some of the conversations between Neferu and the two men became too confusing about whether their words and thoughts referred to God the Father or Jesus.

So, to avoid that, I decided for this story to capitalize the pronouns for God the Father while making them lower case for Jesus, the Son of God. This does NOT mean that I think Father God is worthy of those special capitals while Jesus isn't. As Jesus told his disciples, "I and the Father are One."—John 10:30 (ESV)

**Some history of Mark the Evangelist and his gospel**

Mark had a leading role in spreading the gospel in Egypt and North Africa. According to Coptic historical tradition, he had joined Peter in his missionary work during the early 40s and returned to Libya and Egypt during the reign of Claudius to start the church there. He mostly remained in Alexandria as the head of the church until his martyrdom. Coptic chronology has him mostly in Africa (the area of Cyrene in present-day Libya and Alexandria in Egypt) from AD 43 until his death in 68.

In his *Ecclesiastical History*, Eusebius wrote that early Christian traditions place Mark in Africa from as early as the first years of Claudius (41-44) to as late as the reign of Nero (54-68). He provides a specific date for Mark's arrival in Alexandria as the third year of the reign of Emperor Claudius, which was AD 43. It is believed that Mark heard the sermons of Peter in Rome in AD 42-43 and wrote them down. He left for Alexandria in AD 43 and passed through Cyrene, where his family originated and where he might have been born before his family moved to the Jerusalem area. He was the leader of the Alexandrian church until he was martyred there in AD 68.

**A Note from the Author**

Jesus's words to Andrew: "Come and see." John 1:39

Peter's response to Jesus's question at Caesarea Phillipi, "You are the Christ, the Son of the living God." Matthew 16:16

Fruits of the Spirit: Galatians 5:22

Peter's command to believers: "…but in your hearts honor Christ the Lord as holy, always being prepared to make a defense to anyone who asks you for a reason for the hope that is in you; yet do it with gentleness and respect…" 1 Peter 3:15 (ESV)

**Chapter 22**

Neferu and Jason talking about God for the first time

Jesus and little children: Mark 10:12-16

**Chapter 49**

Neferu talking with Caelus and Lusario about the greatest commandment.

The sincere question: Mark 12:28-34

The hostile question: Matthew 22:34-40 and Luke 25:28. In Luke, this leads into the parable of the good Samaritan (Mark 12:28-34)

The Gospel of Mark is what Neferu has read and copied. Caelus reads it and asks her many questions.

**Chapter 53_**

God as the God of all people, with all believers being one in Christ Jesus: Galatians 3: 23

God giving instructions through Moses on how His people should live: Mark 12:24-26

Questions about the baptism of Jesus by John and the Holy Spirit: Mark 1:2-11

God the Father, Jesus, and the Holy Spirit: John 10:30

**Chapter 54**

"And you will know the truth, and the truth will set you free." John 8:32 (ESV)

**Chapter 59**

Discussion of revenge and forgiveness is from what Phoebe taught Neferu if it's not in Mark.

"If possible, as far as it depends on you, live at peace with everyone." Romans 12:18 (CSB)

Vengeance belongs to God: Matthew 5:38-42, Romans 12:19, Deuteronomy 32:35

"If I want to be forgiven for all that I've done wrong, I need to forgive others who have wronged me." — Neferu. (Matthew 6:14-15)

Love your enemies: Matthew 5:43-48

Israel is to obey God's commands to worship only Him and be blessed: Deuteronomy 11:13-17

But God sends rain on the just and unjust: Matthew 5:45

**CHAPTER 61**
Jesus predicts his death
1st time: Mark 8:31-33 after Peter's confession in Caesarea Philippi
2nd time: Mark 9:30-32 after the transfiguration as they were passing through Galilee on the way to Capernaum. Jesus was trying to avoid anyone knowing where he was so he could teach his disciples.
3rd time: Mark 10:32-34 when they were on their way to Jerusalem for the Passover feast and disciples were astonished and those who followed were afraid
Jesus's sacrifice at the Passover, not the Day of Atonement
The Day of Atonement and the sacrifices for sin: Leviticus 16:1-34
The final plague: Exodus 11:1-10
The Passover: Exodus 12:1-32
Israel's annual celebration of the Passover: Leviticus 23:5-8, Numbers 28:16-25

**CHAPTER 62**
Jesus's commission of the Eleven: Mark 16:15-16
Signs that will accompany them: Mark 15:17-18

**CHAPTER 68**
"Greater love has no one than this, that someone lay down his life for his friends." John 15:13 (ESV)

**WHAT PEOPLE KNEW BEFORE THE STORY STARTED**
Neferu owned a copy of the gospel of Mark (Markos), but her friend Phoebe had come from Alexandria and was familiar with Matthew, Luke, John, and some epistles. These she shared orally with Neferu and Corinna. Neferu was very familiar with Markos's gospel because she made copies of it for Phoebe to take upriver.

Lusario came into the discussions with Neferu and Caelus with some knowledge of the Christian teaching after many discussions with his friend Timon in *Crushed Hopes and Hopeful Beginnings*. Here's a summary of Timon's message to Lusario.

> "God's *agape* love is so great that He came to earth Himself as a man, as Jesus. He chose to die as the perfect sacrifice, not just to cover sin but to tear down the barriers between us and God. All we must do is believe." (John 3:16)

> "The essence of us, our soul, lives on past our body's death. After we die, we either spend eternity with God or go to a place of outer darkness." (Matthew 8:10-13)

> "We make the choice ourselves by accepting the forgiveness of God that Jesus made possible or by rejecting it." (John 3:18)

**WORKS BY ANCIENT AUTHORS**
The paraphrases of what was written by ancient authors are based on my

interpretation of the original sources as translated in the Delphi Ancient Classics ebook series.

The direct quotations of the philosopher Seneca are from the following:

Seneca, Lucius Annaeus. Delphi Complete Works of Seneca the Younger (Illustrated) (Delphi Ancient Classics Book 27). Delphi Classics. Kindle Edition.

# *Acknowledgements*

Most of all, I thank God for the opportunity to tell this story of faith and true friendship, of soaring hopes and deep disappointments, and how God truly can bring good out of anything even before someone loves Him.

No one can write the best book possible without the help of many others. Here are a few who helped me more than I can fully express.

I'm especially thankful for Lisa Garcia, my dear friend of many years. She's also my treasured alpha beta reader, and she's helped me with every book in the series. When I'm stuck on a scene, I ask for her prayers, especially while I'm writing the spiritual scenes. It never fails to start things flowing again. When it comes to spotting typos, she's as good as a copy editor. I'm blessed by her friendship and prayers both in my writing and in my life.

I want to thank Carlene Havel for volunteering to alpha-beta read River of Life. It's a first for us, and her insights and skill as a wonderful writer of Biblical fiction herself have been a blessing. So were her prayers as I worked on this longest and slowest of my projects.

Christine Dillon, the inspiring author of the contemporary Grace series and now of the Light of the Nations series of Biblical novels, has been a wonderful beta reader for my books. With an author's eye and the spiritual insight of a missionary, her help in getting things just right has been a blessing. I'm so glad to have her as my writing buddy.

I want to thank Sherril Odom and Andi Tubbs for beta-reading some of the beginning chapters and for praying for me as I was writing. It would be impossible to write these stories without people praying for me.

Terry Shoebotham is my kindred spirit, local writing buddy, and prayer partner for so much of life. Every author should have a Terry to share about books and life in general., especially over a plate of Chinese or Indian food or a cup of coffee from her kitchen.

I also want to thank Katie Powner, my long-time critique partner, for her prayers and wise editorial comments. She is a Christy-award-winning author herself whose four novels are among those I can't say enough good things about. You can't beat any of them for a wonderful contemporary read.

Thanks also to Mesu Andrews for praying with me for inspiration and greater efficiency as I tried to create this story with much less writing time than I used to have. As a leading writer of Biblical fiction, she truly understands how we rely on God's inspiration to get things right. She also shared her author insights on some challenging spiritual scenes. It's so fun to have a friend who delights in archeological discoveries from Old Testament and Roman times, like I do.

Many thanks to my author friends who prayed for me when I was struggling with something and asked for the best help anyone can give. I especially thank Ronda Wells for sharing her medical knowledge so I got the injury and illness scenes right. Anne Perreault, an equestrian who has taught horses and riders and done show jumping herself, was an invaluable advisor for the horse scenes. Other authors who prayed for me whenever I asked and sometimes let me bounce things off them include Tessa Afshar, Dana McNeely, and Jessica Marie Holt. Many thanks to all!

And to all you readers who prayed for me as I wrote River of Life: thank you SO much! I couldn't do it without all your prayers.

I want to thank Andrew Budek-Schmeisser for being my prayer partner and good friend as I've written so many of these books. It wouldn't be possible to write the spiritual conversations without prayer, and the prayers I need for anything are only an e-mail to Andrew away. With his expertise with horses and combat and with an artistic background as a painter, I can ask him for advice on action scenes and whether a cover is both artistically stunning and appealing to men. Despite serious health problems, he's always willing to help.

My line editor, Wendy Chorot, has once more brought her editorial skill and her deep spiritual insight to bear to make the many spiritual scenes feel like real people asking the deepest questions about life. She's been my editor since the first volume, Forgiven, and I'm looking forward to her doing it again with the next volume in the series. Working with her is always a delight.

Roseanna White has designed yet another fantastic cover that captures the location of the story and the friendship between the leading men. She planted a surprise that you might not notice until you hit a certain place in the story. I can't count how many times someone has said this cover is gorgeous, and they're right! I especially appreciate her prayers when I'm working on a hard part, too.

I also thank my family (son Paul, daughter Lydia, her husband Paul, and granddaughter Payton) for the joy they bring to my life. They didn't have to be cover models for this one, but they would have if we'd needed them. I'm so blessed by my kids.

But after God, my greatest thanks to go my amazing husband, Jim. This time he did more than listen for the nth time to small variations on a scene. He stood outside in a tunic in windy 30-degree weather so I could photograph him with the lighting just right. He provided the body for Lusario, and now I can tell people I'm married to a cover model. He's also the model for the best of my heroes with his kindness, patience, and humor. I'm so blessed to be his wife.

# About the Author

Carol Ashby has been a professional writer for most of her life, but her articles and books were about lasers and compound semiconductors (the electronics that make cell phones, laser pointers, and LED displays work). She still writes about light, but her Light in the Empire series tells stories of difficult friendships and life-changing decisions in dangerous times, where forgiveness and love open hearts to discover their own faith in Christ. Her fascination with the Roman Empire was born during her first middle-school Latin class. A research career in New Mexico inspires her to get every historical detail right so she can spin stories that make her readers feel like they're living under the Caesars themselves.

Read her articles about many facets of life in the Roman Empire at ca-rolashby.com, or join her at her author website and blog, The Beauty of Truth, at carol-ashby.com.

# LIGHT *in the* EMPIRE SERIES
*Dangerous times, difficult friendships,*
*lives transformed by forgiveness and love.*

The Light in the Empire Series follows the interconnected lives of several Roman families during the reigns of Trajan and Hadrian. Join them as they travel the Empire, from Germania and Britannia to Thracia, Dacia, North Africa, Egypt, Judaea and, of course, to Rome itself.

Although each can be read stand-alone, here are some groupings based on the appearance of some characters in more than one story.

Drusus family: *The Legacy, True Freedom, Second Chances, Forgiven*
Lentulus family: *Blind Ambition, Faithful*
Crassus family: *Blind Ambition, Faithful, Honor Bound*
Sabinus family: *The Legacy, Honor Bound, More Than Honor, What Matters Most*
Glabrio family: *What Matters Most, Truth and Honor, River of Life*
Martinus family: *Truth and Honor, Crushed Hopes and Hopeful Beginnings, River of Life*
Titianus family: *True Freedom, More Than Honor, What Matters Most, Truth and Honor*
Brutus family: *Faithful, True Freedom, Honor Bound*
The Dacians: *Hope Unchained, Hope's Reward, True Freedom*

For more relationships based on time, location, and the people involved, visit
https://carolashby.com/novel-relationships/

Available in paperback and hardcover editions at Amazon, Barnes & Noble, and many other online booksellers. All ebooks are available at Amazon with some in Kindle Unlimited. Some are available at Kobo and for Nook ereaders.

**The Drusus Family Stories**

### *Forgiven*
*Are some wounds too deep to forgive?*

With a ruthless father who murdered for the family inheritance, Marcus Drusus plans to do the same. In AD 122, Marcus follows his brother Lucius to Judaea and plots to frame a zealot for his older brother's death. But the plan goes awry, and Lucius is rescued by a Messianic Jewish woman. Her oldest brother is a zealot and a Roman soldier killed her twin, but Rachel still persuades her father Joseph to put his love for Jesus above his anger with Rome and hide Lucius until he heals.

Rachel cares for the enemy, and more than broken bones heal as duty turns to love. Lucius embraces Joseph's faith in Jesus, but sharing a faith doesn't heal all wounds. Even before revealed secrets slice open old scars, Joseph wants no Roman son-in-law. With Rachel's zealot brother suspecting he's a Roman officer and his own brother planning to kill him when he returns, can Lucius survive long enough to change Joseph's mind?

If you're wondering what made the Drusus brothers become what they are, you can find out in *The Legacy*, set eight years earlier, and *True Freedom*, set four years earlier.

### *The Legacy*
*When Rome has taken everything, what's left for a man to give?*

Betrayed by a ruthless son who'll do anything for power and wealth, Publius Drusus faces death with an unanswered prayer—that his treasured daughter, Claudia, and honorable son, Titus, will someday share his faith. But who will lead them to the truth once he's gone?

Claudia's oldest brother Lucius arranged their father's execution to inherit everything, and now he's forcing her to marry a cruel Roman power broker.  If only she could get to Titus—a thousand miles away in Thracia. Then the man who secretly told her father about Jesus arranges for his son Philip to sneak her out of Rome and take her to the brother she can trust.

A childhood accident scarred Philip's face. A woman's rejection scarred his heart. Claudia's gratitude grows into love, but what can Philip do when the first woman who returns his love hates the God he loves even more?

Titus and Claudia hunger for revenge on their brother and the Christians they blame for their father's deadly conversion. When Titus buys Miriam, a secret Christian, to serve his sister, he starts them all down a path of conflicting loyalties and dangerous decisions. His father's final letter commands the forgiveness Titus refuses to give. What will it take to free him from the hatred poisoning his own heart?

Join the people you met in *Second Chances* eight years earlier in this tale of betrayal, hatred, love, and forgiveness, where even bad things can work together for good.

### <u>*Second Chances*</u>
*Must the shadows of the past destroy the hope of the future?*

In AD 122, Cornelia Scipia, proud daughter of one of Rome's noblest families, learns her adulterous husband plans to betroth their daughter to the vicious son of his best friend. Over her dead body! Cornelia divorces him, reclaims her enormous dowry, and kidnaps her own daughter. She plans to start over with Drusilla a thousand miles away. No more husbands for her. But she didn't count on meeting Hector, the widowed Greek captain of the ship carrying her to her new life.

Devastated by the loss of his wife and daughter, Hector's heart begins to heal as he befriends Drusilla. Cornelia's sacrificial love for Drusilla and her courage and humor in the face of the unknown earn his admiration…as a friend. Is he ready for more?

Marriage to the kind, honest sea captain would give Drusilla the father she deserves…and Cornelia the faithful husband she's always longed for. But while her ex-husband hunts them to drag Drusilla back to Rome, secrets in Hector's past and the chasm between their social classes and different faiths erect complicated barriers to any future together. Will God give two lonely hearts a second chance at happiness?

Join the people you met in *The Legacy* eight years later in this tale of healing and new beginnings. Surprising things happen when God opens the door.

### The Crassus, Lentulus, and Brutus Families Stories

### <u>*Blind Ambition*</u>
*Sometimes you have to almost die to discover how you want to live.*

It's AD 114 in the Roman province of Germania Superior, and being a Christian carries a death sentence. Tribune Decimus Lentulus is on the fast track for a stellar political career back in Rome. When he's robbed, blinded, and left for dead, a young

German woman who follows the Way finds him. Valeria knows it's his duty to have her and her family killed, but she chooses to obey Jesus's command to love her enemy and takes him home to care for him.

It's not his miraculous recovery that shakes Decimus to his core. It's the way they love him like family and their unconcealed love for Jesus. In spite of himself, he falls in love with the Christian woman Rome wants him to kill. Can Valeria hide her faith to follow him into the circles of Roman power? Or should he abandon his ambition to help rule the Empire and choose to follow a different way?

Discover what happened to the people of *Blind Ambition* eight years later in *Faithful*.

### *Faithful*
*Is the price of true friendship ever too high?*

In AD 122, Adela, the fiery daughter of a Germanic chieftain, is kidnapped and taken across the Roman frontier to be sold as a slave. When horse-trader Otto wins her while gambling with her kidnappers, he entrusts her to his friend and trading partner, Galen. Then Otto is kidnapped by the same men, and Galen must track them half way across the Empire before his best friend loses a fight to the death in a Roman arena.

Adela joins Galen in the chase, hungry for vengeance. As the perilous journey deepens their friendship, will the kind, faithful man open her eyes to a life she never dreamed she'd want?

A trip to the heart of the Empire poses mortal danger to a man who follows Jesus, especially when he must seek the help of an enemy of the faith for Otto to survive. Tiberius hunted Christians when he governed Germania Superior and banished his own son when he became one.

When Tiberius learns sparing Galen offers a chance at reconciliation, he joins the trio on their journey home. Can his animosity toward the followers of Jesus survive a trip with the Christian man whose courage and faithfulness demand his respect?

Follow the continuing saga of the people you met in *Blind Ambition* from the frontier of Germany to the heart of the Empire in *Faithful*.

### *Honor Bound*
*Honor had forced him to protect her. Time would tell if he'd regret it.*

Marcus Brutus owns estates, ships, and gladiator schools that increase his fortune daily, but his greatest treasures are his honor and his wife. When she reveals her faith in Jesus before dying after the birth of their son, he's consumed by hatred for the unnamed Christian woman who led his beloved to abandon the Roman gods, making him lose her in this life and the next.

For fifteen years, Licinia's father hid her Christian faith. But now her father is dead, and a ruthless political enemy is hunting for anything to destroy her brother. When she becomes the target, her brother sends her to their estate in Germania. But is that far enough to protect her from an evil man who will stop at nothing?

When a carriage accident leaves Brutus injured and his best friend near death after rescuing Brutus's son, Licinia welcomes and cares for them. But her strange habits and his friend's unexpected recovery make Brutus suspect she's the Christian who corrupted his wife. When her brother's enemies come for her, does honor require him to protect her or turn her over as an enemy of Rome? And when Licinia's heart is drawn toward the pagan man who makes money off death, can she reconcile her growing affection with her love for Christ?

If you read *True Freedom* and wondered what happened to Africanus and Brutus, you can find out in *Honor Bound*.

Find out what happens to Ariana's brother Diegis from *Hope Unchained* twelve years later in this tale of hope and a future never imagined until God opens the door.

### The Dacian Stories

*Hope Unchained*
*Can the deepest loss bring the greatest gain?*

Rome's conquering army took Ariana's family and freedom, but nothing can take her faith in Jesus. When she rescues a tribune's wife from certain death, her reward is freedom and a chance to free her brother and sister. But first she must catch up with the slave caravan before they vanish forever, and tracking them from Dacia to the coast seems impossible for one woman alone.

Discharged from the legion with a hand crippled by a Dacian knife, Donatus faces a future without hope. When the tribune asks him to escort Ariana on her quest, it's the only work he can find. It means four weeks with a Dacian woman and a gladiator bodyguard, but it takes money to eat. A man without options must take what he can get.

But a lot can happen in four weeks. Even battle-hardened men can be touched by love and forgiveness, and it's easier to face an enemy with a sword than to face the truth. When his moment of truth comes, what will Donatus choose, and what will that mean for both of them?

If you read *True Freedom* and wondered what happened to Leander's beloved sister Ariana, you can find out in *Hope Unchained*. If you wonder what happened to Ursus from *Hope Unchained*, he's the hero in *Hope's Reward*.

### *Hope's Reward*
*Must the secrets we hide destroy our hope for a future?*

For a gladiator slave, each time you step on the sand, it's kill or die. When Ursus decides to follow Jesus, he must choose to die the next time he's ordered to fight…or run away. He runs, taking again his childhood name, Matti. But he isn't just trying to escape. He's running to Thessalonica, where he hopes to find other Christians like the woman who led him to faith.

When Felicia's new husband, Falco, almost kills her in a fit of rage, her uncle won't help her end the marriage with his business partner. He will send her to her sister in Thessalonica, but only if she tells no one she plans to divorce Falco and demand her dowry back before she gets there. When Matti interrupts a robbery too late to save Felicia's money for traveling by sea, he offers to bodyguard and escort her overland to their mutual destination.

After Matti risks everything to save her from Falco's assassins, Felicia fears taking the danger to her sister's family. When his Christian friends take them in, she discovers the deepest desires of her heart. But will the secrets of Matti's past make a future together impossible?

If you wonder what happened to Ursus in *Hope Unchained*, he's the hero in *Hope's Reward.*

### *True Freedom*
*The chains we cannot see can be the hardest ones to break.*

When Aulus runs up a gambling debt to his father's political enemy, he's desperate to pay it off before his father returns to Rome. His best friend Marcus suggests they fake the kidnapping of Aulus's sister Julia and use the ransom money. But when the man they hired kidnaps her for real, Aulus is catapulted into a desperate search to find her.

Torn from his childhood home by Rome's conquering armies and sold as a farm slave to labor until he dies, Dacius's faith gives him strength to bear what he must and serve without complaining. After a deadly accident makes him one of Julia's litter bearers, he overhears Marcus advising her brother to kidnap her. When Dacius almost dies thwarting the kidnapping, a Christian couple pretend Julia and Dacius are their children to keep her brother from finding them before her father returns.

But pretending to be free again makes returning to slavery more than Dacius can bear, while acting like a common woman opens Julia's eyes to dreams and destinies she never knew existed. With her brother closing in and her father almost home, can she find a way around Roman law and custom to free them both for the future they long for?

## Tribunes of the Urban Cohort: Titianus and Glabrio

### *More Than Honor*
*Duty and honor had anchored his life, but only truth could set him free.*

Devotion to duty and dogged determination make Tribune Titianus the most feared investigator of the Urban Cohort. Honor drives him to hunt down anyone who breaks Roman law, but it becomes personal when Lenaeus, his old tutor, is murdered in his own classroom. Why kill a respected teacher of the noble sons of Rome, a man who has nothing worth stealing and no known enemies? Had he learned something too dangerous to let him live?

Pompeia was only a girl when Titianus studied with Father before her family became Christians. She and her brother Kaeso can't move their school from the house where their father was killed. But what if the one who killed Father comes to kill again? Kaeso's friend Septimus insists they spend nights at his father's well-guarded home. But danger lurks there as well. As Titianus hunts for the murderer, will he discover their secret faith and arrest them as enemies of the Empire?

When Titianus gets too close to finding the killer, the hunter becomes the hunted. While he recovers at his cousin Septimus's house, Pompeia becomes the first woman to touch his heart. But a tribune's loyalty is sworn to Rome, no matter how he feels. When her faith is revealed, will truth and love mean more to him than honor? Does honor require more than devotion to Rome?

If you're curious about what happened with Manius's family, Kaeso's family, and Titianus a year before *What Matters Most*, you can find that story in *More Than Honor*.

### *What Matters Most*
*When faced with impossible choices, how do you decide what matters most?*

For ten years, the incorruptible Tribune Titianus enforced Rome's laws. He's four days from leaving the Urban Cohort to teach at his brother-in-law Kaeso's school when Emperor Hadrian and the Praetorian Prefect draft him to secretly investigate and thwart an assassination plot...one that might involve his own commander. He can't refuse, but if Hadrian's enemies discover his Christian faith, will it mean death for everyone he loves?

Titianus's cousin Sabina returns as a widow to her father's house after six years of misery in a marriage that sealed a political alliance. She's dreading the next marriage Grandfather will arrange with someone seeking his support. When her brother's best friend Kaeso offers the encouragement and friendship she's longed for, can she escape the chains of society's expectations to gain what her heart desires?

The new tribune Glabrio wants two things as Titianus trains him: to discover for their commander who Titianus is investigating and to gain the support of Titianus's powerful relatives. Marrying Sabina would secure the backing of her grandfather, but because of the teacher, she's making choices no noblewoman should. As he gets closer to both his goals, will he realize in time what matters most?

If you're curious about what happens to Glabrio in his next assignment, you can find that story in *Truth and Honor*.

<u>*Truth and Honor*</u><br>*Is truth worth the price if it costs you everything?*

For Tribune Glabrio, descended from three consuls of Rome and determined to be the fourth, commanding the troops policing Carthago appears ideal for hastening his political rise. Arriving from Rome with the secretly Christian Sartorus as his aide, Glabrio discovers the man he was to replace has vanished without a trace. Was the missing tribune too close to finding the counterfeiters Glabrio is now hunting? But no matter the cost, duty and honor require him to enforce Roman law.

Orphaned as a child and taken to live with her pagan grandfather, Martina met Jesus through her step-grandmother. Their faith was a well-kept secret, even from most of their family. With both grandparents now dead, her uncle helps Martina hide the faith he doesn't share. But after a single dinner at her uncle's, the new tribune is determined to get to know her. No matter what she does to discourage Glabrio, he won't leave her alone. But if he discovers her faith, will it mean her death?

When Martina rescues Glabrio from the counterfeiter's schemes, he learns the people who risked everything to save him share the faith that got his grandfather executed. Embracing that faith could cost him the future he planned on. As an officer of the empire, it's his duty to reject it…but what if it's true?

If you're curious about what happened between Glabrio, Titianus, Kaeso, and their families almost a year before *Truth and Honor*, you can find that story in *What Matters Most*.

**The Martinus Family Stories**

### *Crushed Hopes and Hopeful Beginnings*
*Can God work all things for good if you don't even think he's real?*

When Martina rescues Glabrio from the counterfeiter's schemes, he learns the people who risked everything to save him share the faith that got his grandfather executed. Embracing that faith could cost him the future he planned on. As an officer of the empire, it's his duty to reject it…but what if it's true?

Lusario was content in Cyrene as part of the Philandros household. After he returns from serving the youngest son, Diokles, while he studies in Alexandria, Lusario expects to become a paid tutor for his master, earning the money to buy his freedom. But when Diokles uses him to pay a gambling debt, he must go to Carthago as the slave of a man who hates him. His once-bright future is gone forever. So why does his Christian friend Timon insist things will turn out so much better than he expects?

But Carthago brings new people, like Caelus Martinus, and new possibilities into Lusario's hopeless world. Could Timon be right? When Lusario sees a chance to escape his fate, will going for it give him a future again, or only hasten his death?

*Crushed Hopes and Hopeful Beginnings* is a short novel about the turbulent lives of Lusario and his friends three years before Carol Ashby's next full-length novel, *River of Life*, when two of them embark on a journey up the Nile that changes everything.

### *River of Life*
*When the future you dreamed of looks impossible, maybe God has a better one planned.*

Driven from home because of her Christian faith, Neferu lands a position tutoring Jason, her childhood friend's young son. Jason's father despises him and banishes both the boy and Neferu to his ancestral estate, where Jason becomes the target of a family member who wants Jason's inheritance for her own boys. How can a mere servant thwart her mistress before her young charge is killed? Knowing what she does, is her life at risk as well?

When Lusario's new master, Caelus Martinus, decided they would train together to work as architects, Lusario's once-bleak future seemed bright. But if they don't get a commission within a month to design a building, both will lose the future they long for.

During their trip up the Nile to compete for a building contract, disaster strikes, forcing Neferu to rescue Lusario and Caelus from certain death. As the threat to Neferu and Jason grows, both men would do anything to protect her and the boy. Might death await them all if they fail?

The Light in the Empire novels are available in paperback and hardcover editions at Amazon, Barnes & Noble, and many other online booksellers. All ebooks are available at Amazon with some in Kindle Unlimited. Some are available at Kobo and for Nook ereaders.

**I'd Love to Hear from You!**

If you enjoyed this book, it would be a real gift to me if you would post a review at the retailer you purchased it from. A good review is like a jewel set in gold for an author. Other great places to share reviews are Goodreads and BookBub. If you've read others in the series, it would be great if you post a review of those, too.

I'd also love to hear from you at carol-ashby.com
or directly at carolashbyauthor@gmail.com.

**Want to hear about upcoming releases in the Light in the Empire series
and free gifts only for newsletter subscribers?**

For free gifts and other special offers, advance notices of upcoming releases, and info about my latest writing adventures, I hope you'll sign up for my newsletter at https://carol-ashby.com/newsletter